Fanning the Flames

A GOING DOWN IN FLAMES NOVEL

Fanning the Flames

A GOING DOWN IN FLAMES NOVEL

Chris Cannon

Entangled Publishing, LLC
2614 South Timberline Road
Suite 109
Fort Collins, CO 80525
Visit our website at www.entangledpublishing.com.

Entangled Teen is an imprint of Entangled Publishing, LLC.

Edited by Erin Molta
Cover design by Cora Graphics
Cover art from Depositphotos

Manufactured in the United States of America

First Edition April 2017

This book is dedicated to my family for all of their love and support and to everyone who believes in dragons.

Chapter One

Bryn waited outside the Directorate's offices on the top floor of the library at the Institute for Excellence, aka, shape-shifting dragon school, on what had to be the world's most uncomfortable couch. The black leather antique looked like it would be comfortable, but the seat angled back and the cushions jutted forward, throwing her off balance. Given the Directorate's controlling nature, they'd probably had the couch custom made for this very purpose. *Asshats*. She worked at keeping her temper and her fire under control. Red dragons, like her father, were known for having bad tempers. Controlling her fire when she was angry wasn't always easy. You'd think her mother's Blue dragon genes would've evened out her temper, but that didn't seem to be the case. Sure, she could breathe ice, but fire was her dominant element. Now that both her parents were dead, her maternal grandparents had taken her in, and they expected her to act more like a Blue.

Valmont, her knight and secret boyfriend, sat next to her, shifting around and frowning. "There is something fundamentally wrong with this piece of furniture. I feel like it's mocking me."

Jaxon huffed out a breath. "It's meant to make you uncomfortable, in order to give whoever is waiting to interview you the upper hand. The longer they make you wait out here, the more uncomfortable you become and the less likely you are to have all your faculties when they finally agree to see you."

Suspicion confirmed. "Asshats," Bryn muttered. Despite the fact that the Directorate was the ruling body of shape-shifting dragon society, they seemed to have a twisted sense of humor.

Jaxon snorted but didn't respond. He paced back and forth in the ten-foot waiting room they'd been stuck in for the last thirty minutes. Back and forth. Back and forth. Back and forth.

Bryn reached out and grabbed his forearm. "Can you stop pacing? You're just making the situation worse."

Frost shot from his nostrils. A Blue dragon losing control of his breath element meant he was just as annoyed by this situation as she was. Good to know.

"I can either pace, or I can rip someone's head off. Which would you prefer?"

"Can we choose whose head you rip off?" Valmont asked. "Because that might affect our preference."

Bored, Bryn focused on her fingernails and turned them a deep plum color. She was skilled at manipulating Quintessence, her life force, to change her coloring. She used it in place of makeup and nail polish and even used it to color her hair. Medics channeled Quintessence to heal people, and that's what Bryn wanted to do with her life.

The door to the office popped open. A Directorate member gave a smug smile. "Sorry to keep you waiting."

Right.

"Come this way."

Bryn entered the conference room, followed by Valmont. Jaxon came in last.

Jaxon's father, Ferrin, was the Speaker for the Directorate. Bryn liked to think of him as "the Asshat Extraordinaire." He sat at a long mahogany table flanked by other Directorate members. Bryn's grandfather sat to the right of Ferrin. He acknowledged Bryn with a nod. She nodded back and waited to see why she'd been dragged out of bed at six in the freaking morning on a Saturday.

Ferrin gave a condescending smile. "Thank you for joining us at this early hour."

As if we had a choice.

"After some discussion, the Directorate has decided to appoint Jaxon Westgate and Bryn McKenna as Student Body Directorate Liaisons. Other students can come to you with concerns. If you feel those concerns deserve our attention, you may contact one of us to address the matter."

Holy crap. She didn't think the Directorate would ever allow a female, her in particular, to hold a position of authority, no matter how slight.

"Jaxon, I know you won't bother us with petty concerns," Ferrin stated in his holier-than-thou voice, "but we've drawn up these documents for you to go over with Bryn, since she's more than likely uneducated in the important matters we deal with."

"He just couldn't play nice, could he?" Bryn said to her grandfather.

The corners of her grandfather's mouth turned up for a fraction of a second before they slammed back down again. "Bryn, it is true you are less familiar with the Directorate, but I trust you will read through the manual and follow the Accords set out by the Speaker for the Directorate."

"Of course I will," Bryn said in a mock serious tone.

Jaxon leveled a glare at her. *Right. Like that look works on me.*

"As I was saying, I trust Jaxon will make appropriate choices and guide Bryn to do the same." Ferrin set the two-inch thick manual on the table and pushed it toward Bryn.

Valmont put a hand on Bryn's arm. "Allow me." He retrieved the manual and rolled it up like he planned to swat a fly. Ferrin was a pest. She doubted whacking him with a rolled-up manual would do any good, but it might be fun to watch.

"There is also some confidential information we'd like to share." Bryn's grandfather pushed to his feet. "We believe there are other hidden doors in the vaults below the library, similar to the one Bryn and Valmont discovered using Blood Magic and their dragon-knight bond. We've spoken to the authorities in Dragon's Bluff, and they've given us a short list of townspeople who would volunteer to become a dragon's knight in order to facilitate finding these doors."

The population of Dragon's Bluff was comprised of humans descended from knights who had vowed to fight side by side with dragons, if the need arose. They carried latent magic in their blood. If any adult human stepped in to perform an act of chivalry protecting a dragon, the spell activated, creating a magical bond between the knight and the dragon. This was not something to be taken lightly.

"Who volunteered?" Jaxon asked.

"Those who lost loved ones in the attack on Dragon's Bluff." Bryn's grandfather cleared his throat. "We have informed them that they might be putting their lives at risk, and they still want to help. Given the personal nature of the bond, we thought it best for the volunteers to meet dragons they'd be suited to work with. So, it's your task to find students who are willing to participate in the project. We'd start with the select few you vouch for."

"Are you only using student volunteers?" Bryn asked. "Or will adults be volunteering, too?" It didn't seem right that students would be the ones taking all the risks.

"We're starting with students," her grandfather said, "and we will insist on pairing females with females and males with males to avoid any awkward situations."

And now it felt like everyone was staring at her like she was involved in some sort of sordid relationship. She turned to Valmont. "I didn't think we were that awkward."

"Perhaps they're referring to your landings," Jaxon said from her other side.

She turned to him and smiled sweetly. "I tend to concentrate on speed while I'm in the air, rather than sticking the landing."

"You're free to go now," Ferrin stated.

Valmont grabbed Bryn's hand and pulled her toward the door. "Let's run away while we have the chance."

Good idea. They dashed from the room to the stairwell and down three flights of stairs. When they reached the ground floor, they bolted for the exit. Without discussing it, Bryn shifted to her dragon form. She didn't even have to think about shifting anymore. It was innate.

She moved her tail around so Valmont could climb onto her back. Once he was settled between her shoulder blades, she pushed off into the sky, basking in the sensation of the air flowing over her body like cool water.

The one benefit to being up psycho early on a Saturday was a wide-open sky with no air traffic. Flying with Valmont made her feel at peace. Like all was right in her world.

And given how screwed up the world had become lately, it was a nice reprieve. After the attack at the Valentine's Day dance, everyone seemed to be jumpy, and rightfully so. The hybrids that had kidnapped Rhianna, and forced Zane to become her knight so they could locate a hidden door in the vaults of the library, were still at large. Seeing Zane murdered right in front of them had affected them all. Thank goodness Rhianna had released him from the dragon-knight bond before he'd died.

Still, it had taken more than a month for Rhianna to start smiling again. During this time, Jaxon had been surprisingly supportive and patient with his girlfriend.

"It's like we have the entire school to ourselves," Valmont said, interrupting Bryn's thoughts.

"It's nice." Now that it was April, the dogwood trees on the school grounds were in full bloom. Green shoots were poking through the flowerbeds. "I bet the flowers will be beautiful in a few weeks."

"It's funny. No matter what type of turmoil is going on, the Directorate still makes sure to keep the grounds immaculate."

"It's all about appearances around here." There was no better example of this than Rhianna being declared unfit to marry Jaxon, due to the limp she'd developed after one of the attacks on campus. Even though the injury wasn't genetic and couldn't be passed on to their future offspring, Jaxon's father had insisted on voiding the arrangement. And that had led to the nightmare of a situation she currently found herself in. A lineage check had determined that she and Jaxon were compatible. Bryn's grandfather had submitted a petition for Bryn and Jaxon to marry. If the Directorate approved the union, Bryn would have to marry Jaxon after graduation. No matter how many times her grandmother explained that marriage was a business contract which produced children and love had nothing to do with it, Bryn couldn't get on board with the plan.

"You're too quiet," Valmont said. "What are you thinking about?"

She didn't want to burden Valmont with thoughts of her possible arranged marriage. They'd hashed it out and decided they could still be together, even if she married Jaxon, because Jaxon planned to continue his relationship with Rhianna. They'd buy a ginormous house where she and Valmont could shack up in one wing while Jaxon and Rhianna lived in another part of the house. Still, they'd have to pretend to be married whenever they went out in public. And that would totally suck.

"I was thinking it's time for breakfast." *No harm in a white lie. Right?*

"Didn't you grab a bagel before we went to the meeting?" Valmont knew that wasn't enough food for her. He was teasing.

Trying to lighten the mood, she played along. "Haven't you ever heard of second breakfasts?"

"I thought that only applied to Hobbits."

"Nope. It works for shape-shifting dragons, too."

They descended and landed outside the dining hall. Bryn dug her talons into the grass in an attempt to smooth out her landing. This resulted in hunks of sod being ripped out of the ground as she stumbled forward.

"Dang it." Why couldn't she figure out this landing thing?

Valmont chuckled but didn't comment.

After he climbed down, she shifted to human form, and together they stomped the hunks of sod back into the ground.

Inside the dining hall, Bryn wasn't surprised to find the tables mostly empty. Maybe she could scarf something down and then go back to sleep.

Valmont yawned and stretched. "I vote for carry-out and a nap."

"You read my mind."

"Bryn, I'm so glad I ran into you." Garret walked toward her with his left arm hanging limp in a sling. He'd also been injured during one of the attacks on campus when giant hailstones had ripped through his wing. Since his injury had been beyond what the medics were able to heal, he was no longer able to fly.

"Good morning, Garret. What's up?" She hoped it was something quick so she could put her nap plan into action.

"Why don't we eat breakfast while we talk?" Garret suggested, as he moved toward the buffet and picked up a plate.

Well, crap. There went her plans for a mid-morning siesta.

"Sure." Bryn loaded her plate with a little bit of everything and then followed Garret to the table where he normally sat with his Green dragon clan. It seemed odd to eat at a different table with a different view. For the entire time she'd been at school, she'd always sat in the same place with her best friends, Black dragons Clint and Ivy.

Garret stirred cream into his coffee. "Thanks to your grandfather's generous donation, I've been working on the prototype for the prosthetic wing, and I think we're ready to test it."

"That's wonderful."

"I'm glad you think so, since I hoped you'd help us test it out."

"Sure. What can I do for you?"

Garret pulled a folded up piece of paper from his shirt pocket and passed it to Bryn. She opened it and saw what appeared to be half of a hang glider.

"That's a rough sketch of the prototype for a dragon who still has one functional wing, like me. I'd strap it around my flank like a saddle, sliding my injured wing inside the two layers of fabric. It's more like hang gliding than true flying, but it's a start."

"I think it's a wonderful idea."

"I'm configuring a pulley mechanism which would allow the wearer to flap the wing, but it's still a work in progress. If you'd spot me during the trial runs, I'd feel better than going solo. With your speed, if anything goes wrong, I figure you have the best chance of assisting me."

"If you attached the wing to an actual saddle, it would give me something to grab onto if you needed help."

"A handle is a good idea." Garrett scribbled away on his piece of paper, jotting down notes and drawing plans.

Valmont shoveled in his scrambled eggs and bacon and gave her puppy dog eyes. She inhaled her omelet in record time and stood. "Let me know when you need me."

"Aren't you going to eat?" Garret looked at her plate and then blinked. "That was like some sort of magic trick. One second the food was there and then, in the blink of an eye, it was gone."

"It's my special skill," Bryn said. "I make food disappear."

Garret went back to scribbling on his paper. "I think we'll be ready to run trials by the end of the week."

Bryn backed away from the table and gestured for Valmont to follow. "Sounds good. Talk to you later."

Valmont grabbed her hand. As they exited the dining hall and descended the front steps, he laced his warm fingers through hers.

"Don't you want to fly back to my room?" Given a choice she'd choose flying over any mode of transportation.

"No," Valmont said. "It's a beautiful morning, and I'd like to enjoy a leisurely stroll. Walking seems more peaceful."

"Oh, okay." Strange. She'd fly everywhere if she could, but he preferred to walk. If he were a dragon, he'd choose flying. Walking was the best alternative humans had. *Whack!* That thought was like a smack to the back of her head. She froze.

"What?" Valmont drew his sword and turned in a circle like he was searching for the enemy.

Bryn shook her head. "Sorry. I had a weird thought."

"About?"

Telling him that for the first time she'd thought of herself as a dragon, not a human, seemed odd and trivial. She was a dragon, but she'd always thought of herself as a person. Thinking of herself as a dragon and Valmont as human was strange.

"Nothing important." She moved forward, tugging him along. "I need to go back to sleep. My brain isn't working properly."

"A nap would do us both good."

They walked in silence through the front door of the Blue dorm. A few dozen Blues were up and about, reading on the couches or eating at the restaurant in the back of the main floor. Bryn nodded at the Blues who acknowledged her and ignored the ones who pretended she was invisible. The good news was, about forty percent of her fellow Blue dragons now begrudgingly accepted her.

When she reached her room, Bryn found an envelope shoved partway under the door.

She heard Valmont groan.

"It's probably just a note." When she'd first come to the school, she'd received many threatening notes and letters, but that seemed like a lifetime ago.

"Allow me." Valmont retrieved the envelope while Bryn unlocked the door. They crossed the room and sat on the couch together. Valmont held the envelope up to the light like he was trying to see the contents. "Doesn't look evil."

"Go ahead and open it." Bryn yawned. "I don't think evildoers are up at this ungodly hour on a Saturday morning."

"You're probably right. Bad guys do prefer to skulk around at night." He pulled open the flap and extricated a piece of notebook paper.

Can we meet for lunch? And I'm sending a note so Jaxon won't hear me call you and insist on accompanying me. You're welcome, Rhianna

"She must have dropped this off while he was in the

meeting with us." Bryn walked over to the phone but paused before picking it up. "What are the odds Jaxon is with her right now?"

"Ninety to one hundred percent. Pretend you're calling about something else. That way if he overhears, he won't know what's going on, because I've had more than my fill of his delightful personality for one day."

"Agreed." And she knew just what to say. Rhianna answered on the third ring. "Hello, it's Bryn. I thought maybe we'd get together later today and go to Suzette's for lunch. Jaxon is welcome to come along, of course."

Rhianna laughed. "That's a wonderful idea. I'll ask him."

Through the phone Bryn heard Jaxon protesting he had far too much homework and needed to study for a test. Then there was the sound of a door slamming.

"That worked like a charm," Rhianna said.

Suzette's was a teahouse in Dragon's Bluff where female dragons dragged their sons and made them sit in an ultra-feminine environment surrounded by flowers and lace while they discussed china patterns. This resulted in their sons never willingly going to Suzette's later in life. The floral nightmare main room was actually a front for a tearoom in back where women could get away from the men in their lives without fear of being tracked down and interrupted. It was pure genius.

"Good. Come to my room at eleven and we can go to lunch." Bryn hung up the phone. "I declare it's nap time."

Valmont glanced around like he was looking for something.

Bryn walked over and sat on the couch. "What are you doing?"

"So far this morning, every time we've talked about taking a nap, someone has interrupted our plans."

Bryn patted the spot on the couch next to her. "True. So get over here before it happens again."

He joined her on the couch, stretching his arms above his head and bringing them down so one was around her shoulders.

Bryn laughed. "Was that you being smooth?"

"Yes," he said. "It's from the *How to be a Smooth Boyfriend Manual*." He grinned. "So how'd I do?"

"I barely noticed it at all." She rolled her eyes.

He puffed out his chest like he was proud.

"Guys are weird," Bryn informed him.

"And yet you still love me." He leaned over toward her slowly.

"I do, but aren't you supposed to say that *you* love *me*?" Bryn asked when his lips were a fraction of an inch from hers.

"That's the boring way to do things."

She poked him in the ribs. "Don't tease the dragon."

He laughed. "Fine. I love you, Bryn McKenna."

Happy warmth blossomed in her chest, and it had nothing to do with her fire.

At eleven on the dot, a knock sounded on Bryn's door. She didn't bother looking through the peephole to see who was there. Finding Jaxon on her doorstep made her regret that maneuver.

"Jaxon? What are you doing here?"

"Hello to you, too." Jaxon walked past her into the room and turned in a circle. "Where's Rhianna?"

Bryn shut the door. "She's not here yet."

Jaxon frowned. "That's not like her."

Another knock sounded on the door.

"I've got this one." Valmont crossed the room and opened the door.

Rhianna stood in the hallway with a smile on her face.

When she saw Jaxon standing in Bryn's living room, her eyebrows shot up. "Jaxon, did you decide to join us for lunch at Suzette's?"

"Absolutely not."

Rhianna stepped inside, and Valmont closed the door.

"Then why are you here?" Bryn asked.

"I just received a message from my father. Tomorrow, the Directorate would like us to meet some of the people from Dragon's Bluff who volunteered to become knights," Jaxon said. "My father wants Rhianna and me to volunteer so he doesn't doubt the loyalty of the Blue dragons who are searching for secret doors, or whatever it is they want to find."

"And that's a problem because…" *Where is he going with this?*

"Last night, when we discussed this, Jaxon didn't want me to participate in the experiment." Rhianna crossed her arms over her chest. "After a heated discussion, I agreed not to do it if he volunteered in my place."

"Which I agreed to do." Jaxon rammed his hand through his hair. "Now after this mandate from my father it seems that what I want is irrelevant."

"Welcome to my world." Bryn threw her arms out wide. "It sort of sucks, but you get used to it."

Valmont cleared his throat and glared at her.

"I didn't mean you." Bryn laughed. "You're one of the best parts of this messed-up situation."

Valmont grinned, and a single dimple appeared on his left cheek. "Of course I am. I'm fabulous."

Jaxon reached up to pinch the bridge of his nose. "If I'm paired up with someone like your waiter—"

"You should be so lucky," Bryn shot back. Her stomach growled. "I declare this conversation over. Anyone wishing to eat lunch can join us at Suzette's."

"Good-bye." Jaxon was out the door in five seconds flat.

Rhianna chuckled. "Looks like this is the day where I get what I want for a change. Strange that it's due to Ferrin."

"I'm sure he's working some sort of angle to use this situation to his advantage." Bryn headed for the window at the end of the hall, which opened onto a terrace. "Let's fly to Dragon's Bluff."

"It's such a pretty day, I wanted to drive," Valmont said.

"Oh, okay." Bryn tried not to let the disappointment show in her voice.

"What kind of car do you have?" Rhianna asked.

"It's a cherry red convertible," Valmont said. "You're going to love it."

They checked out at the guard post at the back gate. By the time they arrived at Suzette's Bryn's good mood was restored because Valmont radiated joy as he drove with the top down. She'd still rather fly, but she understood why he enjoyed driving his car in this beautiful spring weather. And watching him be happy made her happy. Maybe that was part of love, enjoying someone else's happiness more than your own.

The hostess at the restaurant grinned at Bryn. "I see you brought your knight with you again." Valmont had been allowed special permission to accompany Bryn into the restaurant, revealing its speakeasy nature on the condition he never reveal the secret.

"I'm sure I can count on you to keep your promise," the hostess said.

Valmont's hand went to his heart. "On my honor I will never reveal the secret of Suzette's."

"Good. Now, will the three of you be eating up front, or did you want to use one of our new private rooms?"

"Oh, let's try one of the new rooms," Rhianna said. "I've heard they're lovely."

"We are quite proud of them." The hostess led them toward an area where individual booths were enclosed and set behind French doors, which opened and closed to give them privacy. And the glass kept the view open, which made the space seem less claustrophobic.

"What a great idea." Bryn scooted into one side of the booth, followed by Valmont.

Rhianna sat across from them. Once they placed their orders, the waitress shut the doors.

"What did you want to talk to me about?" Bryn asked.

"I had planned on enlisting your aid in convincing Jaxon that I should have a knight, but that isn't necessary anymore. Maybe we could talk about how I should choose a knight."

"You should wait to meet the volunteers and find someone you have something in common with," Valmont said.

That was an interesting approach.

"Why do you say that?" Rhianna asked.

"Even if this person isn't your knight for an extended period of time," Valmont said. "You'll still be bonded. I think it's important to have some common ground."

Rhianna tilted her head like she was considering what he'd said. "If what Jaxon told me is true, they're going to pair me up with a female who has suffered a great loss. Even though I lost my status as Jaxon's intended, I still have him. Despite being injured, I can fly. What happened with Zane, well it was awful, and traumatic to see him die in front of me, but we'd just met. It would be nothing compared to the agony of seeing a family member die."

And this fun lunch had just bottomed out. "Maybe meet the candidates and find someone you feel comfortable with," Bryn suggested.

"I wonder who Jaxon will pick? Since he doesn't seem to like anyone but you." Valmont pointed at Rhianna.

"It might be ridiculous," Rhianna said, "but I am glad

the Directorate mandated he be paired with a male rather than a female, considering the way things have developed romantically between both of you, due to the bond."

"I don't think it's due to the bond." Bryn knew her statement sounded more defensive than it should have.

"Of course not." Rhianna blushed. "I'm sure it just helped move things along." Rhianna gestured toward Valmont. "After all, he *is* incredibly handsome."

"I knew I liked her," Valmont said.

Chapter Two

When lunch ended, Rhianna said her good-byes and left to do some shopping in Dragon's Bluff.

"Do you want to visit your family?" Bryn asked. Part of her hoped he'd say no. The rest of her knew that was immature and ridiculous. Just because his evil grandmother hated her, didn't mean the rest of his family should be cut off.

"I hoped we'd have time to stop by for a quick visit." They paid the bill and left, walking to Fonzoli's rather than driving his car, which was parked in a lot down the street.

It had been months since the attack on Dragon's Bluff, but there were still reminders of the night when fire had rained down on the town. Bryn, her grandmother, and the other Blues had done their best to beat back the fire with ice and sleet, but buildings still had been lost, and most of the decorative landscaping and trees had been burned to ash.

Valmont pointed to an empty area where new sod had been laid. "There was a huge old oak tree there which generations of kids loved to climb. I fell out of it when I was seven and broke my arm." He stared at the blank space as they walked past. "Strange that it's not there anymore."

"Maybe they could transplant some trees from the forest," Bryn said. "Not that I want any little boys to fall and break their arms, but the area looks so empty."

"You should ask your grandmother if the women's league would sponsor transplanting some trees."

"I'll call her when we're back on campus. She'll think it's a great idea."

The line at the front door of Fonzoli's Italian restaurant extended down the sidewalk.

"We should go in through the back." Valmont led her toward the back of the restaurant where the wooden shutters were thrown wide to let the heat out of the kitchen. The scent of garlic and oregano filled the air.

Bryn inhaled deeply. "That smells amazing."

Valmont smiled. "It smells like home."

When they reached the back porch, he bounded up the steps into the kitchen. She hung back, wanting to let him have his moment before his family members zeroed in on her. His grandmother may be the only one who'd stated out loud, and with much venom, that she didn't approve of her involvement with Valmont, but Bryn could tell the rest of his family resented her for taking him away. How could they not? After all, he'd given up his entire life to stay by her side twenty-four hours a day, as her personal bodyguard. Not that she needed a bodyguard anymore, but it was comforting to have him around.

She stood to the side of the open door and listened as exclamations of love and happiness were traded throughout the kitchen. The fact that he had so many people who loved him made her happy for him and slightly jealous. What she wouldn't give to be able to walk into any room and see her parents standing there, alive and well. The loss of them was like a physical ache which never went away.

Valmont poked his head out the doorway. "What are you doing? Get in here."

She entered and accepted all the greetings and kind words his relatives offered, but it was hard to keep a fake smile plastered on her face. She sat and drank lemonade in a corner of the kitchen while he caught up with everyone. Someone gave her a plate of breadsticks and red sauce, so she passed the time by eating.

"You look like you could use these." A young woman dressed in a wait staff uniform dropped a stack of napkins next to Bryn's plate.

"Thank you." Bryn wiped her face for whatever sauce she'd obviously dribbled and then met the waitress's gaze. She didn't look familiar. Bryn wiped her hand off before extending it in greeting. "I don't think we've met yet. I'm Bryn."

The girl laughed, and it reminded Bryn of Lillith, Jaxon's mother, whose laugh sounded like silver bells. There was no malice it. Nor was there any malice in her bright blue eyes and the genuine smile she directed at Bryn.

"Sorry. I knew who you were before I started working here. You're sort of famous. I'm Megan. It's nice to meet you."

"Nice to meet you, too."

Valmont strolled over to the table and put his hand on Bryn's shoulder. "I see you've met the new recruit."

The look of adoration Megan gave Valmont had Bryn reconsidering how she felt about her. "I did. She must have started working since you came to stay with me."

Megan beamed. "I've eaten here for years, of course, but I just started working three weeks ago. I'm still learning the ropes."

"Have you dropped anyone's food in his lap yet?" Valmont asked.

"No."

"Then you're doing all right. Although if someone is

being particularly snotty, it is acceptable to spill their drink, accidentally on purpose."

Bryn laughed. "Seriously?"

Valmont glanced around and then leaned in closer to Bryn. He gestured that Megan should do the same. "You didn't hear this from me, but you are allowed to spill one drink every six months. Any more than that and it will draw attention."

"I'll keep that in mind." Megan gave a conspiratorial glance around the room. "I better get back to work. It was nice meeting both of you."

"You, too," Bryn said, mostly meaning it.

"She seems nice." Valmont pointed at Bryn's empty plate. "And since you're done, and everyone is busy, I think it's time for us to go."

"We can stay longer if you want."

Valmont shoved his hands in the front pockets of his jeans. "No. It's hard for me to just stand here. I feel like I should be working. So let's bail before I start serving appetizers."

• • •

Sunday afternoon Bryn and Valmont hung out with Clint and Ivy at one of the covered picnic tables on campus. The weather made it too nice to stay inside.

Ivy inhaled and sighed. "I love the smell of spring."

"That's because you're the plant whisperer." Clint teased.

Ivy was skilled at transferring Quintessence from one plant to another in order to make it grow.

"Seems like plant vampirism to me," Valmont commented.

"That's a terrible way to look at it," Ivy said.

"Think of it as one plant being fused with another," Clint said. "For the greater good."

"Speaking of things fusing and combining, or whatever,

have either of you decided if you want to have a knight?" Bryn asked.

"Part of me wants to do it just to piss Ferrin off after that chemical lobotomy crap he pulled on me," Clint said.

Bryn clutched at her heart. "I knew there was a reason we were friends."

Rather than responding with a joke, Ivy picked at her cuticles. "I want to help and annoying Ferrin is a bonus, but does the Directorate know what it's doing? What effect will it have on the knight and the dragon if they are bonded and then un-bonded when the search is over? And if they don't break the bond, what will that mean for the dragon and the knight?" Ivy glanced up at Bryn. "You and Valmont were meant to be, but the rest of us would be faking our way through it. I'm not sure it's right, messing around with ancient magic."

Bryn hadn't thought about that angle. "I'm sure the Directorate sees this temporary bonding as a means to an end. Concern over the effect it might have on the dragon or the knight probably isn't even on their radar."

"Ferrin asked his own son to participate, so don't you think he would have investigated any downside?" Valmont asked.

"Good point." But she wasn't sure. "I'd appreciate one or both of you volunteering, if you're comfortable with it, because I'm supposed to recruit dragons I trust. And you're both in the top slot on that list."

"Thank you," Clint said. "Have you thought about asking anyone else?"

"I'm going to ask Garret, but he's busy working on his prosthetic wing, so I'm not sure he'll want to participate."

• • •

Clint, Ivy, Rhianna, and Jaxon were among the group sitting in a conference room in the science building. Garret had agreed to attend the meeting out of scientific interest, but as Bryn had predicted, he wasn't interested in signing up for a knight.

Mr. Stanton, the head of the Green clan and the Elemental Science teacher, entered the room followed by an older man and a young woman.

"I'd like to start by letting our volunteers introduce themselves. And to alleviate any concerns, you should know that showing up here today doesn't mean you have to go through with the bonding. We'd like to give all of you time to acquaint yourselves and figure out what you're comfortable with. We understand this process isn't to be taken lightly."

The man with sad brown eyes and silver hair cleared his throat. "I'm George. I lost my daughter when Dragon's Bluff was attacked. Now my grandchildren have to grow up without their mother." He coughed and looked down at his wrinkled hands. "I'm old. If we were going into battle, I wouldn't volunteer because I probably wouldn't be much use in a fight, but I can help you find doors and information."

Well, hell. Bryn had known the citizens of Dragon's Bluff had suffered losses, but the abstract idea of loss didn't do justice to the grief radiating off this man. Bryn sniffled and blinked her eyes trying to keep tears at bay. Valmont put his arm around her shoulders. She noticed he was blinking a lot, too.

"Thank you for sharing your story, George." Mr. Stanton pointed at the young red-haired woman.

"Mary is my name." Arms wrapped around her rib cage, her tone was clipped and tightly controlled. "I lost my brother. My baby brother. That's why I'm here."

"The tragedies these two and many other families in Dragon's Bluff have faced, is why we are here to try and ensure something like this cannot happen again," Mr. Stanton said. "If we can recover artifacts and keep the enemy from obtaining weapons, we might be able to prevent future attacks."

Jaxon stood and adjusted his shirt cuffs. Maybe that was the Westgate version of nervous fidgeting. He approached George and held out his hand. "My name is Jaxon. I'm sorry for your loss."

George shook his hand. "Thank you. You're the Speaker's son, aren't you?

Jaxon nodded. "I am. If you're interested, I'd like to work with you."

"That's why I'm here," George said. "So how do we do this?"

Mr. Stanton joined them. He pulled two syringes from his pocket. "The clear syringe contains the venom of a spider. It's not immediately lethal, but left untreated the victim would sicken and die. This blue vial contains anti-venom which if given immediately after the venom should curb the symptoms to a mild headache."

"Should cure the symptoms. What if you calculated the dosage wrong? Couldn't someone throw a knife at him instead?" Bryn asked. "George could step in front of him holding a shield. No weird venom necessary."

"Your concern for my well-being is touching, but I'm sure the Greens figured out the exact dosage." Jaxon scowled at the syringes with suspicion. "Still, the simplest solution is often the best, so let's try Bryn's idea first."

"Give me a moment." Mr. Stanton left the room and returned with a scalpel and a metal tray.

Valmont raised his hand. "Can I volunteer to throw the scalpel at Jaxon? For purely scientific reasons, of course."

Jaxon muttered something under his breath, which Bryn didn't catch.

Mr. Stanton held the blade out to Valmont. "I know you're used to a sword, but this is rather sharp."

"Got it." Valmont held up the slim instrument. "George, whenever you're ready."

George stood next to Jaxon and held the tray like a shield. "Count down from three."

"Okay." Valmont said. "Three, two, one." Valmont flung the scalpel. George thrust the tray in front of Jaxon. The scalpel made a ringing sound as metal hit metal, and then it ricocheted to the floor.

Jaxon stood there like he was waiting for something to happen. George tilted his head to the side. "I don't feel any different, so I don't think that worked."

"Maybe the magic knew Valmont couldn't really kill Jaxon with a scalpel," Bryn suggested.

"I do have my sword," Valmont indicated the blade strapped to his thigh.

"I think it's time for spider venom," Jaxon said like he hadn't heard Valmont's comment. He unbuttoned his right shirt cuff and rolled up his sleeve. He tapped the vein so it stood out.

"I think we'll shoot this into your shoulder." Mr. Stanton said, "and then George can administer the anti-venom into your blood-stream."

"Fine." Jaxon unbuttoned his shirt, pushing it back far enough so Mr. Stanton could access his deltoid. After the shot, he calmly buttoned his shirt and then held his arm out to George.

With steady hands, George tapped the vein in Jaxon's forearm and administered the medication. "That should fix everything," he said. They all stared and waited.

Sweat beaded on Jaxon's forehead. Rhianna moved forward to join him. "Are you all right?"

"I feel feverish," Jaxon said. "Nothing to worry about."

Rhianna pointed at George. "How do you feel?"

"Nothing so fa—" He stopped speaking, and his eyes,

which had been full of sorrow, now seemed full of purpose. He stood taller, straightening his shoulders. "I think it worked. It feels like I drank a pot of coffee, and I have the strangest sensation that I should be wearing my sword."

Valmont chuckled. "It will feel like it's a part of you now."

"I brought mine as instructed and turned it over to Mr. Stanton."

"Allow me." Mr. Stanton walked over to a box on the side table and retrieved a sword in a brown leather scabbard. "I believe this is yours."

"Yes." George wrapped the belt around his waist and unsheathed the sword, which gleamed in the conference room light. "I polished it before I came." He turned the sword back and forth so the light reflected off the fine edge.

Jaxon pushed to his feet. "I think it's time for a trip to the library."

"I'd appreciate it if you'd wait for the rest of our group." Mr. Stanton moved over to Mary.

Ivy stepped forward. "I'd be happy to work with you."

"Fine by me."

They repeated the steps with the venom and anti-venom.

Mary stood straighter after the latent spell in her blood was activated. She took a deep breath and let it out slowly. "It feels like a weight has been lifted off my chest and I can breathe again."

"I believe this is yours." Mr. Stanton passed her a sword in a cream-colored scabbard, and she strapped it around her waist.

"Didn't anyone else volunteer?" Rhianna asked.

"Since this is uncharted territory, I thought it best to start off small."

"That makes sense." Rhianna leaned over and whispered to Bryn. "Plus, it will annoy Ferrin that I didn't follow his orders, so it's a win-win."

"I'm oddly proud of you for that last thought," Bryn whispered back.

Mr. Stanton clapped his hands to gain everyone's attention. "Now, if you'll follow me, we're going to adjourn to the library where Bryn and Valmont will demonstrate how this magic works. Please do not be alarmed. They have undergone this procedure many times and, as you can see, they are both quite well."

Springing this level of weirdness on them didn't feel right. "Why don't Valmont and I explain before we go? That way, if you have questions, we can answer them here."

"Since the magic of the bond between a dragon and his knight is in their blood, literally," Valmont said, "there are certain spells that can be performed using Blood Magic."

Bryn stepped in, since she was the one who actually bled during the ceremony. "I give myself what amounts to the mother-of-all-papercuts on Valmont's sword. The drops of blood roll down the blade, touch the wall, and reveal a door."

"How'd you figure that out?" Mary asked.

"There was a clue above the door," Bryn said. "Only those who have given their all may enter. Those who have taken everything must give to see."

"Doesn't paint us in a very flattering light, does it?" Jaxon said.

"I think it refers to the fact that knights give up the life they had before to defend their dragon, if necessary," Valmont said. "And the dragons do take over the knight's life."

"As opposed to rejecting them?" Jaxon asked.

"If someone was willing to give their life to defend a dragon," Clint said, "and the dragon blew them off... awkward."

"Just like this situation has become," Bryn said. "So, what's next?"

"I faint at the sight of blood," Mary admitted, breaking

the tension.

Ivy made a noise like she was thinking. "*Hmmmm*…you could close your eyes and I'll tell you when it's okay to look."

"And I go everywhere she goes," Clint said, "So I'll catch you, if you faint."

"Problem solved." Mary rolled her eyes.

Ivy laughed. "You're going to fit right in."

They trekked across campus to the library where Miss Enid waited for them in the supplies room behind the front desk. The trap door, which led down to the vaults, was already open. Red dragons stood guard in the room, which was mildly disturbing, but after everything that had happened at the Valentine's Day Dance, having security around was probably a good idea.

"I'll stay here while you go down," Miss Enid said. "Come get me if you find anything interesting."

Bryn and Valmont went down the winding stone staircase first. The stairs were so narrow they had to walk single file. Valmont explained the stairs were more than likely built that way so any battles fought would have to be one on one, which would make the entrance to the vaults easier to defend. Hopefully, they'd never have to test that theory.

Once they had all made it down the steps and assembled in the archive room with the giant and totally unhelpful card catalog, Valmont pressed his sword to the wall where they had discovered the hidden room. Bryn ran her pointer finger down the blade of his sword, being careful not to flinch even though the cut stung. The drops of blood rolled down the blade to the wall, and the door appeared. Anyone who had not yet witnessed this, gasped.

Since Rhianna and Jaxon had been here before, they stood to the side. Rhianna chewed her bottom lip while Jaxon watched her every move. It was the first time they'd revisited this area since the night of the attack…since Zane's death.

Jaxon was probably concerned for Rhianna's mental state.

"Now that you've seen how the door was discovered, you have a more thorough and disturbing understanding of what we ask of you," Mr. Stanton clasped his hands behind his back. "The only way to find the hidden doors is to repeat the blood magic ritual. It's up to you to decide how many times you feel like trying this. If it's only once, that is acceptable."

Jaxon pointed into the room. "We know there is a Blue door back here."

"You're correct. We should probably start there. Two guards will investigate the tunnel once you open it," Mr. Stanton said, "so please do not enter. We don't know if our enemies are guarding it from their side."

That put a new twist on the situation. Bryn hated to think someone was waiting to ambush them.

George followed Jaxon into the room and over to the right hand wall.

Maybe it was Bryn's imagination, but she could swear there were still dark spots on the wall where blood had splattered during the battle. She shivered.

"Cold?" Valmont put his arm around her shoulders.

"No." She leaned into his solid warmth. "But this feels nice."

George put his sword to the wall where Jaxon indicated. Without betraying he felt anything, Jaxon slid his left pointer finger down the blade. As before, when the blood touched the wall, a door appeared. Jaxon studied the door, like he wanted to open it, but then he stepped aside to allow one of the Red guards to take his place. The second guard stood behind him like he was ready to take on any enemy who might try to come through the door. The first guard placed his hand on the door, hesitated a moment, and then pushed it open.

Bryn held her breath, listening for any telltale sounds of battle or discovery. All was quiet. The guard peered into the room beyond and then entered the hall. A moment later he stuck his head back into the doorway. "It appears to be empty. We're going to investigate. First, close the door to make sure we can open it from this side."

That's how the main room worked, but Bryn understood why they wouldn't want to assume all doors worked the same way. Being trapped in a tunnel underneath the library didn't seem like a fun way to spend the day.

The door closed, and the wall returned to being a wall. Then the door appeared again as the guard pushed it open from the inside. His face showed relief. "We're good."

"Mary and Ivy," Mr. Stanton said, "if you'd try next, please."

"Where?" Ivy asked looking around the room.

"Anywhere but there." Mr. Stanton pointed to where the Blue door had been.

"That's helpful." Mary pointed at the opposite wall. "Let's start over there and work our way around."

"No." Clint pointed at the back wall between two display cases housing daggers and decorative boxes. "If there's a door, it will be there."

"What makes you think that?" Ivy asked.

"The display cases have lightning bolts etched into the sides." Clint walked over and traced the tiny zigzag lines with his fingertips.

"Good eye." Ivy moved closer and checked out the carving. "I think Clint's right. We should start here."

"Sounds good to me." Mary placed the tip of her sword on the wall. Ivy slid her pointer finger down the blade, hissing against the pain "Wow. That stung more than I expected. Like a paper-cut times ten."

The red droplets hit the wall, and the outline of a door shimmered and became solid.

"I have the smartest boyfriend ever." Ivy grinned.

Clint reached for the door.

"Or not." Mary smacked his hand away from the door. "We're supposed to let the guards go first. Remember?"

"Thank you, Mary." Mr. Stanton gestured that they should move aside. A Red guard reached for the door handle.

"Stop," Bryn shouted.

Everyone turned to her. "Sorry, but did anyone tell the guards not to touch or move any objects they might find in display cases?"

Thank you for your concern," Mr. Stanton said. "But they were fully briefed."

"Maybe you should fill the rest of us in," Mary said.

"The cases are protected by clan magic," Mr. Stanton said. "If a dragon or knight of a different clan tries to touch or move an object not meant for them, they are shot with darts dosed with lethal poison."

"Okay, then." Mary stuck both her hands in her pockets. "No touching the shiny objects."

"Just when you think things can't get any stranger around here," Clint said. "They always do."

The guard opened the door. When nothing jumped out at him, he entered the Black dragon doorway and lit braziers on the wall. Rather than accessing a tunnel like the Blue door, this one seemed to open up into a room similar to the one they stood in.

Shelves lining the back wall were stacked two deep with boxes and books. A display case covered with a tarp took up most of the left wall. A small rectangular library table sat pushed against the right wall. Every surface in the room was liberally coated with dust.

Bryn edged toward the doorway. "Can we investigate, since it's a room, not a tunnel?"

"Why don't we let Miss Enid clean it up first?" Mr. Stanton suggested. "She'll best know how to preserve any items or books for the library."

"Would you like me to go find her?" Bryn knew the librarian would be thrilled to have more books to search through. Plus, the faster Miss Enid worked, the sooner Bryn could investigate.

"Take your knight with you," Mr. Stanton said.

"As if I'd let her go anywhere without me." Valmont had been assigned as her personal bodyguard after the last attempt on her life. While she didn't need a babysitter, it had ended up being a good thing. They'd grown closer and fallen in love. A fact they had to keep hidden from all but a select few friends.

"I have a question," Clint said. "I know the door to this room was clan specific, only a Black dragon could open it, but what about the door that leads into this main room? Could a dragon of any color open it, or is it hybrid specific?"

"Interesting question." Mr. Stanton tapped his chin like he was in deep thought. "Bryn, while you and Valmont retrieve Miss Enid, we'll see if Jaxon and George are capable of opening the main door."

"I want to stay and see that," Bryn said. "We'll get Miss Enid afterwards."

"Why do you want to stay?" Valmont asked.

"I never thought about the door being meant for hybrids only," Bryn said. "That would put an interesting spin on things."

Clint pointed at himself. "Who's the smartest person in the room now?"

Ivy laughed and grabbed his hand, tugging him toward the door. "Come on. Let's see what happens."

They exited the main room so they were back in the room with the card catalog. Jaxon seemed irritated that all eyes were on him, which was odd, since he normally didn't mind being the center of attention. When he slid his finger down

George's sword and the door appeared, he sighed in relief. "If the door was hybrid specific, it would've meant a much bigger conspiracy than we already knew we were facing."

Chapter Three

After collecting Miss Enid, Bryn bounced on the balls of her feet, waiting while the librarian investigated the new room. Miss Enid used her air magic to blow dust and mouse droppings into the far corner. Then she started in with her restoration kit, using brushes and cloths to further clean the books and boxes.

Something sparkly caught Bryn's attention. "What was that?"

"What was what?" Ivy asked.

Bryn pointed to the back wall. "Something sparkled at me…back there."

"Do you think it's something attuned to your key?" Valmont asked.

They had found the bracelet, which housed her elemental sword, inside a box in the front room. It had been meant for a dragon of Red and Blue descent. It melded her powers of fire and ice into one badass sword.

"I don't know."

"No fair," Ivy said. "You already have a cool toy."

She stared at the back wall and then sucked in a breath. "Something sparkled at me."

"Show me where," Miss Enid said.

Ivy led the librarian to a small wooden box coated in dust on the back shelf. Miss Enid used one of her brushes to clean the dust away. "Unlike the one Bryn found, there's no keyhole on this one."

"Can I touch it?" Ivy asked.

"Be careful." Clint moved closer to watch over his girlfriend's shoulder.

Ivy ran her fingers over the edges of the box. "It feels like a solid piece of wood. I can't find the opening."

"Do you need to bleed on it?" Mary asked.

"Maybe." Ivy frowned. "Whoever thought up this Blood Magic stuff was seriously disturbed."

Mary placed the tip of her blade on the top of the box. Ivy ran her finger down the edge. When the droplets of blood came into contact with the wood, the box shimmered and there was an audible click.

"Was that a good click or a this-box-is-going-to-blow-up type of click?" Clint asked.

"Since it wasn't Bryn, it's probably safe," Jaxon answered from the sidelines.

Bryn turned to glare at him.

He raised a single eyebrow. "Do you have a valid argument against my logic?"

"No, but it's not like I ask weird crap to happen around me."

"Yet, it seems to be your fate."

The sound of Ivy sucking in a breath made Bryn whip back around. "What is it?"

Ivy held up a black pearl and silver link bracelet. "I never considered myself the type to wear pearls, but these are awesome."

"It could be an actual bracelet," Miss Enid said, "or it could contain a spell and a challenge."

"What does that mean?" Mary asked.

"When I found this bracelet." Bryn revealed the platinum and sapphire cuff she wore, "It released a spell, which checked to see if I was of the proper descent to wear it." She'd never forget the creepy disembodied voice saying *Prove your worth or burn.*

"I remember the story," Ivy said. "We know this is for a Black dragon, so I think I'm good."

"Allow me." Clint took the bracelet and undid the clasp. "If anyone asks, I gave this to you as a token of my love and adoration." He fastened it on her wrist.

Ivy stared off into space for a moment.

"You might want to give her some room," Bryn said.

Everyone backed up a step, except for Clint. He moved to stand on the side opposite the bracelet. Ivy sucked in a breath, and what looked like a bolt of lightning, which was the Black dragon's Element, shot from her hand and formed into a sword.

"Holy crap." Ivy held up her hand, staring at the elemental sword. "This is amazing."

Mary's head snapped up like a dog listening for a sound. "Where's that music coming from?"

"There is no music," Miss Enid said.

"It's probably the sword mate to Ivy's bracelet." Valmont unsheathed his sword. "That's where this came from."

Mary crossed the room to the tapestry covered case. Together, she and Miss Enid removed the dust covered cloth. Inside the glass display lay several daggers with patterns etched onto the blades.

"There should be a button on the outside of the case which will open it," Valmont said.

Mary found a button on the top right hand corner of

the case which made the door pop open. She reached in and touched a blade with an ebony handle etched with lightning. "It's not a sword, but I like it."

"I think it's one of a matched set." Miss Enid pointed at a second blade of the same design.

"Cool." Mary picked up the blades and held them in front of her.

"I'm not sure the Directorate will allow you to keep what you've found," Mr. Stanton said in an apologetic tone.

"Why not?" Ivy asked.

"They will probably want to study them before giving them back to you," Bryn said. "That's what happened with mine."

Mary pouted. "We're the ones bleeding for these, or rather Ivy is. Why should we give them up?"

"They don't belong to any of us," Jaxon said. "They belong to the Institute. As Bryn said, after they're studied and made safe, they will more than likely be returned to you, since we are all on the same side."

"They did have to put a safety on my bracelet so it didn't activate accidentally." Since there was an odd tension in the room, Bryn tried to make a joke about it. "Skewering people when I reached for a pencil in the middle of class would have been a little unsettling for all of us."

Valmont stepped forward. "Actually, I was allowed to keep mine after clearing it with Bryn's grandfather. Maybe we could ask to meet with him, if he's here in his office."

Mary traced the lightning pattern etched into the handle. "I like that idea."

"Why don't I go upstairs and make a call to see if he's available," Miss Enid said.

They all nodded in agreement, and the librarian exited the room.

"Excuse me, but I think we've found something of

interest," one of the Red guards called from the main room.

Mr. Stanton went to see what the guard wanted, and they all followed.

"Sir, I believe it's safe to enter the Blue hall now if you wish to do so."

Jaxon moved forward. "Where does it lead? Is there another room like this one?"

"There are several rooms like this one," the guard said, "but the doors will not open for us." The guard held out his left hand. Red blisters covered his palm. "The lesson I learned today is just because you can see a door doesn't mean you should try to open it."

"I can heal you." Bryn stepped forward.

"It's not necessary," the guard replied, like it didn't even bother him.

"We need you in top form," Mr. Stanton said. "Why don't you let Bryn heal you?"

The guard frowned like he didn't agree with this decision, but he held his hand out to Bryn. She focused and held her pointer finger above his hand. She visualized Quintessence, her life force, in the form of light flowing from her fingertip to heal the blisters. Being as gentle as she could, she ran her finger along his wrist and on the outline of his palm. As she worked, the blisters on the edge flattened out and disappeared. When the skin on his hand was smooth and pink all the way across she stopped. "There you go."

He nodded at her. "Thank you. Now, I believe only someone of Blue descent should try opening these doors."

"Where does the hallway end?" Rhianna spoke from the corner where she'd been quietly observing everyone. "Does it lead outside? Is the exit being watched?"

"It lets out in a storm grate, and the entrance is guarded."

"So you wouldn't want to hang out in the hallway if it was raining," Clint said.

"Probably not." Mr. Stanton gestured that the guard should go first. Jaxon and George followed him, and the rest of them tagged along.

The stone passage they entered felt a bit damp. Bryn inhaled. Yuck. It smelled like mildew. She wrinkled her nose. "I hope the artifacts aren't damaged from the wetness in the air."

"I bet the rooms are airtight," Valmont said.

They all stopped at the first set of doors they found. Jaxon craned his neck, staring farther down the passage. "How many sets of doors are there?"

"Three in total," the guard said.

"It will be interesting to see if the doors lead to one large chamber or three smaller ones." Valmont said.

Bryn bet on the large-room theory because Blues never did anything small.

Jaxon approached the door and studied it before placing his hand on the tarnished silver handle. A quick turn of the knob and the door opened. He entered and they all followed.

"Bryn, can you light the braziers?" Jaxon asked.

She approached the candle on the right wall and sent flames through her fingertips to light the wick. The mirror behind the candle bounced light across the room to another brazier. After Bryn lit three more candles, they could see what was inside the dust-free room. An armory made up of swords and knives of all descriptions sat in racks upon the walls. Unlike the weapons Valmont and Mary had found, these were not works of art etched with different elements in fancy scabbards.

Bryn took a step closer to study them. These were utilitarian weapons meant to viciously wound and kill the enemy in battle. Maces with razor sharp points glistened in the light of the braziers. Battles axes hung on the wall next to broadswords with pommels as thick as her forearm.

"These are not meant for dragons." Valmont ran his hand along the pommel of a broadsword. "These weapons are meant for a legion of knights."

Jaxon headed out the door and stalked down the hall to the next room which revealed shelves full of saddles and lances. Bryn could almost taste Jaxon's frustration. She knew he wanted to find a weapon similar to hers. Instead, he was getting weapons for a legion of knights they did not have, which made the relics useless.

The third door revealed what appeared to be an office. There was an antique desk littered with paper. The only other object in the room was a chest, which didn't seem like a good use for this much space.

Jaxon approached the chest and tugged on the lid, but it didn't budge. He performed the Blood Magic ritual with George. Putting all his effort into it, Jaxon shoved the lid up and open. It creaked with age.

George stared into the chest. Jaxon didn't utter a word. He knelt down and retrieved a dull silver band about two inches high and a dozen inches across.

"Is it a necklace?" George asked.

"There's no clasp," Jaxon said.

And that's when Bryn understood, and she laughed. Of all the things for Jaxon to find. "It's not a necklace. It's a crown."

Jaxon turned the metal band over in his hands looking at it from every angle.

"Don't pretend this isn't your dream come true," Bryn teased.

Frost shot from his nostrils. "What in the hell am I supposed to do with this?"

Rhianna moved forward. "I used to pretend I was a princess when I was a little girl."

Jaxon placed the circle of metal on her head.

Nothing happened.

"Maybe it's just a—" Rhianna froze mid-sentence staring at nothing. The crown shimmered and then drops of silver rolled down her face, like wax dripping from a candle.

"I'm taking it off." Jaxon reached for it.

"Don't," Mr. Stanton warned. "If you try to remove it mid-spell, it could injure her."

"What's it doing to her right now?" Jaxon snarled.

"She's still breathing, and her color is good," Mr. Stanton said. "Have patience."

The silver wax-like drips continued trailing down Rhianna's neck and then stopped in a circlet at the hollow of her throat. She blinked and reached to touch her face. "It feels like I'm wearing a mask or a helmet."

"I don't like it," Jaxon said.

"Truthfully, I'm okay," Rhianna said. "But it is a strange sensation." She reached up to remove it, but it wouldn't budge. "We might have a problem."

Jaxon placed his hands on the metal band and pulled upward. Nothing happened. Panic showed on his face for a split second before he regained control of his features. "Mr. Stanton, could you solve this problem for us?"

Mr. Stanton cleared his throat. "I'm sure there's nothing to be worried about. It's probably a safety feature of some sort."

"Safe is not what I'm feeling right now." Rhianna's voice came out more high pitched than normal.

Mr. Stanton tried to remove the crown. It didn't budge.

"Let me try." Bryn approached Rhianna and touched the circle of metal. Instead of pulling up, she tried to turn it like the lid on a jar. "Nope."

Rhianna's golden skin paled.

"Maybe a knight has to remove it," Valmont suggested. He approached her, placed his hands on either side of the crown, and tugged. No luck.

"Blood magic would be the next logical step," Mr. Stanton said.

Valmont drew his sword and placed the tip on the metal band. Bryn ran her finger down the blade. When her blood came into contact with the crown, the silver droplets appeared to crawl up Rhianna's face. Once they'd retreated back into the band, Valmont pulled up and the crown came off.

Rhianna gasped as tiny cuts dotted her forehead. "It felt like that evil thing dug hooks into my skin and didn't want to let go."

Jaxon wrapped his arms around his girlfriend. "Are you all right?"

"Yes."

"What the hell is that thing?" Bryn asked.

"I don't know," Mr. Stanton said. "But I will figure it out."

George turned to the chest. "Something is singing to me." He reached down and lifted an oilcloth, and then he retrieved two boxes. One was small and covered in silver scales, and the other was long and thin and covered in chain mail. He passed the scaled box to Jaxon. "This one is yours."

"How do you know?" Jaxon asked.

"It's humming to me, but this one is singing an opera." George opened the box and removed a blade, too long to be a dagger, but too short to be a sword. Frozen flames were etched along the handle.

Jaxon opened his box and rolled his eyes. "Cuff links?"

Bryn laughed as the tension from the strange crown seemed to be broken.

"I don't think cuff links can be evil. Let me help you with those," Rhianna took one and slid it through the buttonhole on his shirt cuff. "See, it still works even if you have buttons."

Once the cuff links were in place. Jaxon tapped his foot, waiting not so patiently for something to happen, and then he closed his eyes and smiled.

Twin blades of ice shot from his hands. He opened his eyes and studied the weapons. "I don't understand why I'd need two, but I like them."

"Try releasing one," Valmont said, "like you're setting a sword down."

Jaxon did as Valmont suggested and the blade in his left hand disappeared.

"It does give you the element of surprise," Bryn said. "Your enemy wouldn't know you had two weapons."

"You have had a productive morning," Bryn's grandfather said from the doorway, where he stood next to Miss Enid.

Bryn started to say something, and then she noticed an area of the floor had parallel scratches like something heavy had been dragged from the room. "Something has been taken from here recently."

Everyone turned to look at where she pointed. "See the drag marks?"

"I would guess a rather large chest was removed from this room not too long ago," Mr. Stanton said. "That must be what the rebels came for."

"What was in it?" Valmont asked.

Mr. Stanton went to the desk and opened the drawers. He removed a leather ledger.

"Miss Enid, I believe this is your area of expertise."

The librarian put on a pair of white cotton gloves before gently opening the leather cover. Inside, handwritten on parchment paper, was a long list of items. "This appears to be the inventory. If we catalog all the items and cross reference it with this list, we'll know what's missing."

Ivy tapped Bryn on the shoulder and then pointed at her black pearl bracelet. "Let's go talk to your grandfather."

Bryn explained about the bracelet, and Ivy demonstrated how it worked. Mary reluctantly displayed her daggers.

"I don't believe the daggers are spelled. After we examine

them they'll be returned to you. The bracelet will require a few safety modifications."

George and Jaxon showed her grandfather what they'd found. "Cuff links?" her grandfather seemed amused. "I'd never consider them a weapon, which is why they are a brilliant choice."

"Better than the crown," Jaxon grabbed it and held it out to him. "I'd rather not demonstrate." He described what it did.

"That is bizarre," her grandfather said. "I'm not sure what purpose it would serve for a dragon. Unless it's spelled to shift with us like our clothes."

"I'll let someone else test that theory," Rhianna said. "If it didn't work, it would be like shifting with a metal noose around your neck."

"Maybe that's what it's for," Valmont said. "To keep a dragon from shifting."

All eyes turned to him. "Growing up, I heard a fairy tale about a dragon who kidnapped another dragon and used a metal collar to keep his captive from shifting. I'm not saying it's a great idea, but your comment brought back the memory."

"That's a disturbing thought." Rhianna sidled closer to Jaxon who put his arm around her shoulders.

"From now on, maybe we should let someone else play with the magical artifacts first," Jaxon said.

"Just a reminder, this is sensitive information you cannot share with anyone outside of our group. We don't want rebels or the curious trying to break in here to discover new treasures."

They all nodded in agreement.

As they exited the room and walked past the armory, Valmont stopped. "Is there a record of the Institute keeping weapons on hand to arm a legion of knights?"

Her grandfather gazed at all the weaponry. "None that I've read, but I'd wager your instincts are correct."

The sight of all the stockpiled instruments of death gave Bryn chills.

"Why keep all this hidden?" Clint asked. "The Institute has always had guards, either human knights or Red dragons, so why hide it with magic?"

"As with any society, there has always been a certain amount of unrest in our world," Miss Enid said. "Most of what I found in the outer room consisted of historical ledgers someone must have wanted preserved. Artifacts like the swords have been displayed throughout the library in times past. But this." She pointed at the armory. "This is something different. I think it's something someone wanted forgotten."

"Something a Blue wanted forgotten, since only a Blue could access it?" Bryn asked.

Mr. Stanton sighed. "We can conjecture all we want, but we have no proof. Maybe the different clans preserved items which were important to them. Blues always want to be prepared to defend the Institute, so it makes sense they would stockpile weapons. After some study, I'd be willing to bet we'll discover the items in the Black dragon's vault are of an artistic nature."

"I think we should allow Miss Enid and Mr. Stanton to work through the ledger," her grandfather said. "I'll post guards at every door and inside every room with express instructions not to touch anything."

"I would fail at that job," Clint said to Bryn.

"Me, too."

After leaving the library, Bryn, Clint, Ivy, and Valmont convened in her room.

Bryn leaned back on the couch. "Today, we found the Blues' weapon stash and a Black dragon's art closet. Makes me wonder what the Green, Orange, and Red dragons have stashed away."

"The Greens probably have scientific equipment," Clint

said.

Ivy nodded. "I bet the Oranges have mining records or files on some plant magic we no longer know about."

"What would the Reds have?" Valmont asked.

All eyes turned to Bryn. And she drew a blank, which made her feel strangely disloyal to her father. "I'm not sure. They are the middle class. They run all the everyday businesses. Maybe records of who owns what and how they kept their businesses prosperous."

"That doesn't sound worth hiding away," Clint said. "But I see what you mean. What would a Red treasure besides everyday life?"

"Maybe they kept photo albums and family trees," Ivy said.

"Since I'm a hybrid, I doubt I could open a Red clan door. We need to find a Red willing to take on a knight so we can figure it out," Bryn said, "because now it's going to bug me."

"You'd think your grandfather would ask one of the guards to take on a knight." Valmont said.

"They want to stick with students," Bryn said. "Maybe we could ask Keegan."

Valmont made a throat-clearing type noise. "Why does that name sound familiar?"

"He's in elemental science with us, and I went on one date with him a long time ago. And we decided we were better off as friends." That might be stretching the truth a bit, but Valmont didn't need to know she'd kissed Keegan.

"Am I better looking than him?" Valmont asked, shifting around so it looked like he was posing for a picture.

"Of course you are." Bryn laughed.

"Then I guess I don't mind."

The phone rang. "Okay. You're both here, so who is calling me?"

"Jaxon?" Clint said.

"I hope not." Bryn cautiously picked up the phone. "Hello?"

"Hello, Bryn." She recognized her grandmother's voice. "Your grandfather tells me you had an interesting day."

"I did. How was your day?"

"My day was spent handing Kleenexes to Lillith."

Uh-oh. Jaxon's pregnant mother was prone to tears. "Is everything okay?"

"I think Ferrin has been in a mood."

"Imagine that."

Her grandmother's silence sounded like disapproval. Time to backtrack. "Sorry, I've had my own run-ins with him lately."

"Yes, well he is the Speaker for the Directorate, and he does have a lot of responsibility."

Was this Blue party rhetoric or did her grandmother really believe what she was saying? "You're right, but Lillith shouldn't have to deal with it."

"I agree, which is why I wanted to invite you to have dinner with us tonight."

"That sounds great. I assume you realize Valmont will be coming with me," Bryn said.

"He'd be derelict in his duty if he didn't," her grandmother said. "I'll come to your room in an hour. Wear something nice."

"So jeans and tennis shoes?" Bryn teased.

"I believe you know the answer to that question." Her grandmother laughed. "I'll see you soon."

Bryn gave Valmont the good news. "We're going to dinner with my grandmother and Lillith."

"Is Jaxon coming?" Valmont asked.

Crap. "His name wasn't mentioned."

"I don't find that reassuring," Valmont said.

Bryn's grandmother arrived exactly sixty minutes later, and Jaxon was nowhere in sight, thank goodness.

"Are you ready?" her grandmother asked.

Bryn glanced down at her black sheath dress and heels. Was her outfit not up to her grandmother's standards? "Is that a trick question?"

"You need jewelry."

Okay. "Give me a minute." She went back to her bedroom and grabbed the sapphire earrings, which Lillith had given to her as a thank you for saving her and Jaxon's life, and the bracelet her grandfather had given her for Christmas. She didn't normally wear either because she wasn't comfortable walking around in expensive jewelry. It wasn't something she had done before coming to school, and not like it was a hardship, but she almost felt the need to apologize, like she was flaunting her wealth. Well, not *her* wealth but the Blue's wealth, her grandparent's wealth. Thinking about all that money made her want to redistribute some of it, like a modern day Robin Hood. Although, God help anyone who tried to steal from her grandfather.

She shook her head, trying to clear such random thoughts. Back in the living room, she struck a fashion model pose for her grandmother. "Better?"

"Much."

Valmont who'd been standing off to the side, said, "Wouldn't your elemental sword bracelet be a better choice, from a protection standpoint?"

She hadn't thought about that. "Could I wear both?" she asked her grandmother.

"Probably not." Her grandmother checked the time on her watch. "And since Valmont will be escorting us, I don't think you need another sword. We should go."

"Where are we meeting Lillith?" Bryn asked.

"Didn't I tell you? We're having dinner at the Westgate estate."

She so did not like where this was going. "Wouldn't Lillith rather get out of the house and socialize?"

"I presented that option, but I think this is also an excuse to show off the new nursery."

"That makes sense." And if this really was about baby stuff, Jaxon probably wouldn't be involved.

When the driver pulled up to Westgate Estates, Bryn had to bite her tongue to keep the snarky comments under control. The black wrought iron gate in front of the drive which lead to the house had three-foot-tall scrolling W's worked into the metal. The front door had a giant W engraved into the wood.

Bryn pointed at the front door. "That's unusual."

Her grandmother cleared her throat. "That is one way to phrase it."

Maniacal egomaniac was another.

"The theme carries on throughout the estate," her grandmother said.

"In case you forget whose home you're in," Valmont muttered.

"Even the silverware is monogrammed," said her grandmother. "And you'll probably receive a replica of that set as a wedding present."

Whack! Every time she managed to forget about the nightmare of an arranged marriage to Jaxon something popped up and smacked her in the back of the head.

Her grandmother hadn't been kidding about the inside of the house. The marble floor of the foyer showcased a gold W in the center, as in shiny looked-like-it-was-made-of-real-gold type of gold.

Valmont pointed at the ostentatious display of wealth and bad taste. "Do you think it's fourteen carat?"

"I'm hoping it's paint," Bryn said.

The staff member who met them wore a crisp white shirt with W embroidered on the front pocket.

"If you'll follow me, Mrs. Westgate is waiting for you in the arbor-arium."

What in the heck was an arbor-arium? Didn't arbor mean tree? Bryn had visions of a forest encased in glass like a giant terrarium. It wasn't far from that image.

Rather than containing plants, like her grandmother's indoor green house, this glassed-in area contained trees. Bryn stood, stunned for a moment at the impossibility of what lay before her. "This is amazing,"

"It is an agricultural feat," her grandmother said. "Ferrin hired Orange dragons to create an indoor park, and this is the result."

Lillith came toward them on a slate path between the trees with a rather large baby bump under her pale blue silk dress. There was a genuine smile on her face. She was practically beaming happiness. "Welcome to Westgate Estates. What do you think of our forest?"

"It's lovely," Bryn said.

"You have to come see the baby swing we installed for Asher," Lillith said. "It's this way."

Bryn, Valmont, and her grandmother followed Lillith down a side path to a huge oak tree. Hanging from the lowest branch, which was easily a foot thick, was a tiny basket swing.

"It's so cute," Bryn said.

"Isn't it?" Lillith's hand went to her stomach.

How could anyone married to Ferrin be this happy? Then again, he wasn't here at the moment, so that probably had a lot to do with it.

"Would you think me rude if we visited the nursery before dinner?" Lillith asked.

"Of course not," said Bryn. "I'm excited to see how your

snowflake theme turned out."

"I can't tell you how much I appreciate showing it to someone who actually wants to see it. Ferrin avoids talking about the nursery and Jaxon pretends to care, but men don't seem to understand." Lillith pointed back the way they came. "We'll take the main stairs."

The main stairs led to another landing complete with the requisite W in the center of the floor. Although this W appeared to be made of silver.

"How many W's are in this house?" Bryn asked.

Lillith sighed. "Ferrin is very proud of his lineage and rightfully so, but don't worry, Bryn, after you've lived here awhile you won't even notice them anymore."

Oh, hell no was the first response that came to Bryn's mind, but what she said, was, "Here? Why would I live here?"

Lillith tilted her head. "I assumed you and Jaxon would want to live here while your estate is under construction." She sniffled like she was about to cry. "Unless you've made other arrangements with your grandparents."

"No," Bryn jumped in to stem the tide of hormonal tears. "It's not that. It's just… Jaxon and I haven't talked about it. At all. So, no need to cry." And it's not like her marriage contract had actually been approved, yet. She held out hope Ferrin would use his evil influence to squash the plan like a bug. As long as his plan didn't involve squashing her, too.

"The nursery?" Her grandmother prompted.

"Right this way." Lillith turned down a hallway and went up a half set of stairs and then down another hallway which lead to ornate, double cherry wood doors with the dreaded W carved into them. "Valmont, would you open the doors, please?"

"Of course." Valmont seemed to understand she wanted a theatric flourish, so he opened both doors at once and then stepped to the side so he wasn't blocking their view.

"It's a winter wonderland." Bryn didn't know where to look first. The walls were painted the blue gray color of twilight. Artistic renderings of snowflakes in silver and white decorated the walls at random intervals. The bassinet was a dark wood with light blue bedding edged in snowflakes. A mural of a Blue dragon blasting frozen flames decorated the right hand wall. The dragon managed to look maternal and fierce at the same time.

"Isn't it lovely?" Lillith clasped her hands together like she was trying not to clap with excitement.

"The dragon mural is a work of art," Valmont said.

"Thank you," Bryn's grandmother said.

"You painted the mural?" Bryn knew her grandmother had decorating talent but hadn't known she could paint.

"I did, but no one outside of this room is aware of that fact, so let's keep it quiet. Your grandfather would not approve."

"That's ridiculous. You should be proud of your talents."

"Our world doesn't work that way," said her grandmother.

"I'm happy you broke tradition and painted it for me," Lillith said.

"It was my pleasure."

"Come see the clothes I ordered for Asher." Lillith practically skipped over to the dresser to show off the tiny articles of clothing. She held up a blue onesie covered in snowmen.

"It's so tiny." Bryn touched the soft fabric.

"And look at these socks." Lillith pulled out socks edged in white lace snowflakes.

"Do you have a picture of Jaxon in frilly socks?" Bryn asked. "Because I'd love to see it."

Lillith laughed. "I have photo albums somewhere with his baby pictures, but I'm not sure he'd appreciate me sharing."

"Which is precisely why you should share them with me," Bryn said. "Just one picture? A small one?"

"I don't think that would be fair," Lillith said. "But I may keep them on hand to encourage him to help with his baby brother."

"Have you chosen a nanny yet?" Bryn's grandmother asked.

"Not yet. I'd prefer to take care of Asher myself. I know I'll need help, but the nanny Ferrin hired when Jaxon was born tried to take over everything. She practically kicked me out of the nursery a month after he was born."

"And what did you do?" Bryn hoped Lillith had stood her ground.

"I told her Jaxon was my son and she was here to help me take care of him. And I may have threatened to blast her out the nursery window." Lillith shrugged.

Bryn laughed. "I should have known living with Ferrin would have prepared you to stand your ground."

"It's taught me to choose my battles wisely."

Bryn's stomach growled. "Sorry."

"That's okay." Lillith wrapped her arms around her stomach. "Asher agrees it's time for dinner."

When they reached the small dining room, the table, which seated a dozen, only held three place settings. And Bryn had a terrible feeling she knew why. Valmont was being treated as an employee rather than a guest. And that was not going to work for her.

"Are we short one place setting?" Bryn asked, like she hadn't already figured the situation out.

Lillith appeared confused, but then her gaze wandered to Valmont. "I didn't think to include your knight on the guest list. I'll ring the kitchen."

"That's not necessary," Valmont said.

Like hell it wasn't. "I'd feel better if you ate with us," Bryn said.

"It's no trouble." Lillith walked over to the buffet and

picked up the phone. After a short conversation, she returned to the table. "It's all taken care of."

One of the Westgate staff bustled into the room bearing a tray loaded with food. The savory scent of roast chicken made Bryn's mouth water. The young man placed four plates on the table, adding silverware and a napkin for Valmont. Then he smiled at Lillith with adoration in his eyes.

"Is there anything else you need, ma'am?"

"No, Gerald. Thank you."

Gerald nodded and left the room. It was no surprise some of the staff would be enamored with Lillith. She was beautiful and kind, and her personality must be a ray of sunshine compared to Ferrin's dictator mentality.

Valmont joined them at the table, but he seemed content to blend into the background rather than add to the conversation. Was he trying to play the role of an employee or did he not have much of an opinion on all the baby-related topics?

Bryn picked up her knife to cut through the thicker part of the chicken breast, and there was the W on the handle of the knife. She'd forgotten what her grandmother had said about the silverware. She looked at her fork and found the W engraved on the handle. Was Ferrin trying to compensate for Bryn's mom running out on him, or had he always been this proud of his family heritage?

When the topic of conversation rolled around to politics, Valmont seemed to sit up and take interest.

"Ferrin told me about the vaults you found beneath the library," Lillith said. "It's amazing to think generations of dragons concealed weapons and artifacts, but it makes me wonder who they were hiding the information from."

"Good question," Bryn said. "Now we're trying to find everything we can to keep it out of the hands of anyone who'd use it against us."

"You mean the Rebels?" Her grandmother's tone held a note of warning.

"Yes, of course that's who I meant, but I wish we knew who we were fighting. I've seen Rebel dragons who appeared to be hybrids, but there's no telling if they were using hair dye or wearing colored contacts to throw us off. I wish dragons who were discontented with the status quo would address the Directorate or lobby. There's no need to start a war."

"I'm afraid you're wrong," her grandmother said. "Challenging the Directorate means trying to change the fabric of our lives. And that is unacceptable."

Any type of response she made would be controversial, so Bryn nodded and took a drink of her water. She wanted to say that blind obedience was never a good thing and people should be allowed to ask questions, but neither of those comments would end in a pleasant conversation, and this dinner was for Lillith and her baby.

"Do you need to do any more shopping for Asher?" she asked, instead. "I'd be happy to meet you in Dragon's Bluff one afternoon to look at more baby things."

Lillith lit up like Bryn had offered her the world. "I'd love that. Maybe we could meet for lunch one day this weekend."

"And, of course, that invitation was meant for you, too," Bryn wanted her grandmother to know she was invited but didn't want her to feel obligated since she already spent so much time with Lillith.

"That sounds lovely, but Asher isn't the only person who needs new clothes. I'm sure we could all use a few summer outfits to round out our wardrobes."

Sadness clutched at Bryn's chest. Summers used to mean grilling hot dogs and wearing jean shorts and staying up late to watch the truly ridiculous monster movies her father had loved. All of that was gone. No more snow cones from the park. No more late-night card games betting pretzel sticks.

No more simple anything, ever again. Bryn closed her eyes and tried to breathe through the pain, pushing back the tears. Once she had herself under control, she opened her eyes and pretended everything was fine because her parents were gone and there wasn't a damn thing she could do about it except live her new life as best she could.

"What's your stance on wearing shorts?" Bryn asked her grandmother. "Just so I know what kind of battle I'm going to face when we go shopping."

"I tend to think of shorts as something for toddlers," her grandmother said. "But capri pants can be fashionable."

Bryn had another question, "What do dragons do over the summer while they are wearing their fashionable capris?"

"Normally, we travel, but this summer I have the feeling your grandfather and all the Directorate members will want to stick close to home."

"We can still have picnics and dances," said Lillith.

"Picnics sound like fun." If she never went to another dance again, it would be too soon.

Chapter Four

After dinner, on the ride back to the Institute for Excellence, Bryn's grandmother said, "It's strange, I never would have spent much time with Lillith due to our family history with Ferrin, but I find I enjoy her company."

"She feels like the big sister I never had," Bryn said.

"I want you to be aware, and I haven't discussed this with your grandfather yet, so please don't repeat it, but she's asked me to be Asher's godmother."

"Oh, that's wonderful." Bryn felt a surge of warmth for her grandmother.

"I think so, too." Her grandmother gave a sad smile. "It's funny how fate brings people into your life."

As far as she was concerned, fate owed her and her grandmother a little happiness. "I wouldn't mind babysitting for Asher."

"Have you ever cared for a baby?" her grandmother asked.

"In my former life, I helped a few friends babysit their little brothers or sisters."

"While I'm in no hurry for you to make me a great-grandmother, it's good that you enjoy children, and I'm sure Lillith would appreciate the help."

After reaching campus and saying their good-byes, Bryn and Valmont headed up to her dorm room. He had been uncharacteristically quiet this evening. Which could he be more upset over, the awkward employee/employer relationship issue or the constant in-his-face reminders that she might have to marry Jaxon?

As they headed up the stairs in the Blue dorm, two females Bryn didn't know came down the stairs toward her. "Hello," Bryn said, smiling at them.

The girls froze for a moment, like they didn't know how to respond, then they both gave polite nods and continued down the stairs.

Once they were out of range, Bryn said, "That was almost funny."

"Are you enacting the I'm-not-going-anywhere-so-you-might-as-well-suck-it-up-and-deal-with-it plan?"

"Yes. Do you like it?"

"I'm not sure it's going to work." Valmont's tone bordered on irritated and disinterested.

Something was definitely not right. "Pajamas and then couch time?" Bryn asked as she unlocked the door to her room.

"I'd like that."

Bryn retreated to her room and carefully took off the bracelet and earrings. Strangely enough, she'd forgotten she was wearing them, which was weird. The jewelry probably cost more than what a normal person would pay for a car. Changing into black yoga pants and a red tank top made her feel less like an entitled Blue and more like her normal self.

Valmont waited on the couch, wearing gray sweatpants and a white T-shirt. There was a furrow between his brows and a straight set to his mouth, which meant he needed to talk.

"Feel free to vent or gripe about anything that happened this evening."

"It's not a gripe really…more of a rant." He reached up and rubbed his forehead. "The Westgate's have a freaking forest inside their house. A forest. What the hell? Who lives like that? And why? Why do they think they need—or deserve—to live like that? It's ridiculous. I mean, I knew the Blues were wealthy, but the idea that someone is rich, versus the reality of a freaking forest inside a house… It's just… I don't have the words for how absurd the whole situation is."

This was about the trees? Okay. What could she say? "I agree. It's an insane amount of wealth. I'd love to redistribute it Robin Hood style, but I don't think my grandfather would allow that."

"What really bothers me is, they act like it's normal. Like they have every right to own all these ridiculous things. And in my life, or what used to be my life, I saw other dragons count out nickels and dimes to pay for lunch at Fonzoli's. And my family…every year we wait to turn on the air conditioning in the house until it's necessary because of the expense. I mean, don't get me wrong, we're comfortable. No one is suffering. No one goes without food, but…" He seemed at a loss for words. Throwing his hands up he said. "They have a freaking *forest* in their house."

"I get it. My parents weren't rich. They worked to pay the bills, and we ate a lot of mac-n-cheese…and sometimes it was generic mac-n-cheese. I never thought we went without. I was happy. And now…now my grandmother wants to take me shopping and spend obscene amounts of money on *fashion*. It's hard to integrate the two worlds."

"I know one thing for sure. If Ferrin had been there, I would not have been invited to eat dinner with you. And in the grand scheme of things, it shouldn't bother me, but it does."

"I wouldn't have eaten dinner if they hadn't added a place setting for you," said Bryn.

"Yes, you would have…for your grandmother's sake, and I understand that, but I really don't like it." He stood. "Being around such a ridiculous amount of entitlement made my head hurt. And the idea that you're going to be a part of that world makes my head want to explode."

"No matter what happens, I promise I will never act like a Westgate," Bryn said.

"No, but you'll become one eventually," Valmont said. "And maybe that's what's really bothering me."

Well, hell. What can I say? "Just so you know, the idea that I might have to become a Westgate one day is the stuff my nightmares are made of. It's terrifying. Like some sort of Devil's Bargain. I can have a life as a shape-shifting dragon, but only if I marry someone who I don't love—who is obnoxious 80 percent of the time."

"There is no good answer to this problem," Valmont said. "I'd say we should run away together, but I'd never leave my family and I'd never ask you to leave yours."

"We have a plan, remember?" Bryn reminded him. "You and me living in one wing while Rhianna and Jaxon shack up in the other."

"And while this multi-winged estate is being built, which takes who-knows-how-much time, you'll be living with Jaxon's parents. So how will that work? Will you hide me in the closet? Sneak me in through the butler's pantry?"

That did add a new and not-so-fun variable to the equation. "I don't know. My life is basically one of those choose-your-own-ending adventure books. Fate keeps throwing new and strange plot twists at me, and all I can do is pick the path that seems to make the most sense."

"That's an interesting interpretation." Valmont yawned. "I can't think any more big thoughts tonight."

"I'm going to bed." He leaned in and kissed her on the cheek. "Good night."

Rather than stretching out on the couch with her, he headed for his room. Maybe he needed some time alone. Not that she could blame him. It had been a strange day. Still, she felt oddly abandoned.

Maybe she should focus on what she could change. They still needed a Red dragon and knight to help search through the vaults under the library.

• • •

The next day in Elemental Science, Bryn pulled Keegan aside. "This is going to be a weird conversation, but my grandfather asked me to find a Red dragon I trusted who is willing to take on a knight to help in the investigation against the Rebels."

"Why would I need a knight to help you?" Keegan asked.

"This is where the weirdness kicks in." Bryn gave him an abbreviated rundown of Blood Magic and how the Institute would assign him a male knight.

"Seriously?" Keegan glanced back and forth between Valmont and Bryn like this might be some sort of joke.

They both nodded.

He rubbed his chin. "If you need my help, I'm in, but this is really messed up."

"Welcome to my life," Bryn said. "It's odd, but it's never boring. We'll let you know when they have a knight lined up for you."

After class, Bryn let Mr. Stanton know Keegan had agreed to help before she and Valmont headed for the library, since she'd been banned from history class for arguing with her teacher on her first day of school.

Valmont seemed back to his normal self this morning, so she didn't mention their conversation from the night before. All she wanted today was something close to normal.

"We talked to Keegan. What's next on the agenda?" he asked.

"I need to work on my term paper for Mr. Stanton." As they walked across campus to the library the spring breeze stirred up the scent of grass and new leaves. Bryn inhaled. "I love that smell."

"Me, too." Valmont stopped walking. "I wonder if we could work outside. There's no rule that says you have to write in the library, is there?"

"Not exactly, but someone who didn't know I'd been granted special permission to work in the library might think I was skipping class. If that were to get back to my grandfather, there would be hell to pay."

"Right, I forgot. With the Blues, it's all about appearances." Valmont's tone sounded a little bitter.

Apparently, last night's mood was still with him. Not that she could blame him. "Yes. Appearances are important, and it's best not to give my grandfather a reason to be upset." Especially since she'd started to like him lately. "I have to admit. He's not the ice king I thought he was."

"Ice king?" Valmont asked.

"Everyone uses ice queen to describe a cold standoffish woman, so I think ice king works for a man."

"I have no valid argument against that," Valmont said. "But it doesn't sound right."

"Fine. Then you can come up with a masculine form of ice queen."

Valmont tapped his chin, and then he grinned. "I've got it. You could say, 'He's not quite the *Jaxon* I thought he was.'"

Bryn laughed. She was glad to see him joking around again. "Uhm…you're not wrong but no, for the obvious reasons."

"I'll keep working on it." Valmont opened the door of the library for her. They entered and were stopped by two Red guards.

"Sign in if you wish to access the library." The guard thrust a clipboard at Bryn.

This was new. "Why?" Bryn asked as she signed her name.

"Tighter security measures are being taken," the guard held the clip board out to Valmont who scribbled his name without making a single comment, which showed a great amount of restraint.

After they'd passed the guards, Bryn said, "I'm surprised you didn't feel the need to comment."

"After our 'everything is about appearances' discussion, I decided to rein in my normal troublemaking instincts."

"I'm impressed." She headed for the stairwell they normally took up to the third floor. Valmont grabbed her elbow and steered her toward the front desk. "We're taking a detour. Miss Enid is holding a book for me."

"What kind of book?"

"A book for troublemakers."

When they reached the desk, the librarian was absent. "Maybe she's downstairs in the vaults."

Miss Enid emerged from behind a shelf of books. "Hello, Valmont. Your special request came in." She pulled a slim volume with the familiar title *Days of Knights* from underneath the desk.

"There are more of these books?" Bryn asked. They'd already read through five or six of them, which featured fairy tales involving knights and dragons from a time before the Directorate, when there hadn't been so many rules and restrictions.

"This is a smaller set of tales," Miss Enid said. "I think it has the story Valmont referred to about the strange crown that helped one dragon hold another prisoner."

That would be a cheery and highly controversial read.

"It might help us figure a few things out, and it gives me something to occupy my time while you do your homework."

"I've offered to let you do some of my homework," Bryn said, like she had tried to share something fun with him.

"Sorry," Valmont said, "My duties as your knight only go so far."

Once they were seated at their normal table on the third floor, Bryn found she couldn't concentrate on her essay. "It's like my brain is on strike." She shut the notebook and tossed it back into her book bag.

Valmont didn't acknowledge her comment. Eyebrows furrowed, he seemed completely absorbed in his book. "It's that good?" she asked.

He nodded and turned the page. "Let me finish this tale and then you can read it."

Five minutes later, he closed his eyes and sighed. "I'm not sure we should show this to anyone, least of all your grandfather."

"It's that bad?" Bryn asked.

"See for yourself." He flipped back a dozen pages and then handed it to her. "Each tale stands on its own."

Once upon a time, there was a world where certain dragons thought they knew what was best for everyone. The arrogance of this Clan was beyond measure. Dire steps had to be taken so the other Clans could prosper.

"I don't see this making my grandfather's top ten reading list."

"Keep going," Valmont said. "It gets worse."

"Great."

The smartest dragons joined forces with the most creative dragons. Together they designed a weapon that would render a dragon unable to shift. It was called a Tyrant's Crown. When placed upon a dragon's head, the crown would activate, creating a containment spell around the wearer's head and neck, which rendered them incapable of shifting. Stuck in human form, these dragons were less powerful. The crown could only be removed by a knight and a dragon working together using Blood Magic.

Bryn closed the book. "Even reading this makes me nervous, like if someone found out we had it, we'd be accused of conspiring with the enemy." She turned the book over in her hands. "I think we should return it to Miss Enid and let her decide what to do with it."

"I disagree." Valmont plucked the book from her hands.

Okay. That didn't happen very often. "Why? What do you think we should do?"

"I think we should search the book for clues which might lead us to more artifacts. Better we find them than they end up in enemy hands."

"I see your point, but the Directorate isn't one to give second chances. We should give it to Miss Enid or my grandfather."

Valmont flipped through the pages. "I suppose, but since it's checked out in my name, I'm going to finish reading it first. There might be valuable information we can use."

She didn't love his plan, but he had mentioned the tale to her grandfather already so it wasn't like he was hiding information. "Fine. We'll do it your way."

"I'll probably finish it this evening. You can turn it into someone tomorrow."

"Okay." She tried to keep the annoyance in her voice to a minimum. Valmont might be her knight, but he was still his own person, capable of making decisions for himself. Still, it rankled. How could he not see the risk he was taking by keeping this to himself?

In the locker room before Basic Movement, Bryn shared the situation with Ivy. "What do you think?"

"He's allowed to have his own opinion, but I'm not sure he's right."

Now she didn't feel so narrow minded. "Do you think I should call my grandfather and let him know we have the book?"

"That would cut down the opportunity for anyone to rat you out." Ivy said. "So it might be a safer way to play it."

As long as no one freaked out about the book before she had time to call her grandfather, it would be okay.

When they entered the gym, Mrs. Anderson was separating students into groups. Bryn, Ivy, Rhianna, Keegan, and Valmont were grouped together.

"Class, today we're going to try something new. Within your groups are several different Clans. We are going to run obstacle courses where you are encouraged to use your breath weapons to the best of your ability. Figure out how to use fire, ice, lightning, wind, and sonic waves to overcome the obstacles set before you. The team that finishes the fastest wins."

"Sounds like fun," Bryn said.

Ivy peered across the gym to where Clint was gesturing wildly as he talked to his teammates. "I hope they have medics on call. Without me to tone Clint down, he might do something crazy."

"The Clint we know is toned down?" Valmont asked.

Ivy nodded.

"Then this should be interesting," Valmont said.

Mrs. Anderson led them from the main gym to the stadium. Obstacles which had been stored in the rafters several stories above were now on the ground.

The way the course was set up reminded Bryn of the American Ninja Warrior races she'd seen on television. There were some walls you had to climb and some that you had to go under. There were bridges you had to cross and ropes you had to climb.

"Are we doing this in human or dragon form?" Bryn asked.

"Whatever works best," Keegan said. "When you have to squeeze through a tunnel, you're better off in human form. If you have to reach a flag at the top of a pole, you fly."

"Deciding which form to use is part of the game?" Bryn asked.

"Exactly," Keegan said. "And you play to your Clan's strengths."

Valmont pointed at Keegan. "Reds are the strongest, and besides Bryn, the Blues are the fastest fliers. Black dragons are creative, though I'm not sure how that will help, and I have a sword. I'm not seeing a game plan based on these attributes."

Rhianna sighed. "Blues are also supposed to be the most graceful and have the best balance, but due to my limp I no longer fit that description."

"You're still smart, and despite your outwardly proper appearance, I know you're competitive, so we'll figure this out," Bryn said.

Mrs. Anderson passed out colored belts, which they could wear to identify their team members. Bryn fastened the purple cloth strap that resembled a seat belt around her waist.

"Okay Purple team, let's see what we can do." Keegan led them toward the starting line. When a whistle sounded, they shifted and flew toward the first obstacle: a wall thirty feet high. There was a gap near the top big enough to stand on in human form.

"Should we fly up and then shift once we can grab the ledge?" Bryn asked.

"Sounds good," Ivy said. "But we don't know what's on the other side, so be careful."

Bryn shifted. Valmont climbed onto her back and settled between her wings. A rush of power flowed through her body from the dragon-knight bond. Pushing off, she flapped her wings and held steady when she reached the gap.

"Move closer so I can see what's on the other side," Valmont said.

Bryn hovered mid-air while Valmont grabbed the lip of the ledge and leaned through. "There's a wall on the other side, so you have to shimmy down between the two."

"That sounds slightly claustrophobic," Bryn said.

Valmont jumped off her back onto the ledge.

"How am I supposed to shift and join you?" Bryn asked.

"Good question." He pointed at Ivy. "Let's see how she does it."

Ivy tucked her wings against her body and came in for a landing sideways. She managed to wedge herself into the opening and then shifted so she was kneeling on the wall in human form. She wobbled a bit but was able to steady herself.

Bryn followed Ivy's example. Keegan and Rhianna performed their own awkward maneuvers.

"That was fun. What now?" Bryn asked.

Ivy leaned through the opening. "It's a sheer drop. Rhianna, why don't you use ice to make steps so we aren't falling blindly."

"I can do that," Rhianna held her palms out and blasted ice in intervals down the wall.

"I'll go first," Bryn said.

"I'll be one step behind you, literally," Valmont said.

Bryn placed her weight on the top step. It held. Slowly, she descended. The two walls were sandwiched together and stopped just two feet above the ground. When she reached the ground, Bryn lay down flat and rolled into the open space so she could stand.

Valmont and the others followed behind her. The next obstacle was a set of stairs encased in ice.

"Keegan, should we melt the ice so we can climb the steps?"

"Sounds like a plan."

Bryn inhaled, let heat build inside of her for a moment, and then blasted a fireball at the bottom step. Keegan blasted a steady stream of flames at the top step and worked his way down. Once the stairs were clear, they climbed up to the top where there were several flags suspended on poles.

"Is this a retrieve-the-flag moment, or a destroy-the-target moment?" Ivy asked.

"I don't want to carry them," Keegan said.

"Destruction it is." Ivy held her palm up and zapped each flag with bolts of lightning until the fabric burst into flame. When she finished the last flag, the pole fell over, landing on the top of a small concrete pyramid.

"We cross over there, and then what?" Valmont asked.

"Only one way to find out." Rhianna shifted and flew over to the pyramid.

"I would have walked," Bryn said, "and that would have been slower."

They all shifted and flew over to a platform on the pyramid. A few hundred feet away, targets were set up on the ground. Each one was a different color.

"Red for me," Keegan said, pointing at the targets. "Blue for Rhianna and black for Ivy. I guess that leaves the white one for Bryn and Valmont."

"They could have done purple," Bryn said.

Rhianna blasted the blue target with shards of ice until it fell over. "Remember, we are on the clock."

Ivy zapped her target with lightning while Keegan and Bryn took out their targets with fire. A whistle sounded, signaling they'd completed the course. Mrs. Anderson wrote their time down on a whiteboard.

"Eleven minutes and seventeen seconds," Valmont said. "Is that good or bad?"

"Anything less than fifteen minutes is respectable," Ivy said. "So I think we did pretty good."

They flew over to the sidelines while the course was reset for the next group. Keegan headed for a group of Reds. Jaxon came over to join Rhianna, and Ivy left to find Clint.

Bryn joined Valmont on the floor, sitting with her back against the wall. She scooted close so her shoulder rested against his. There were times when she just wanted to touch him or lean over and give him a quick kiss because she was happy, but she couldn't do that. Not being able to act like boyfriend and girlfriend in public sucked.

Valmont appeared contemplative.

"What's up?" she asked.

"You didn't really need my help out there, so I'm feeling a bit obsolete."

Males and their need for ego boosts no matter what their species, human or dragon, was something she'd never understand. "The course was designed for dragons, so they didn't include any knight-specific challenges. And I will always need you because without you I would face a future alone with Jaxon. And that is enough to give any girl nightmares."

• • •

That evening after dinner, Bryn remembered to call her grandfather about the strange book Valmont had checked out from the library. Since Valmont sat reading on the couch, he heard every word of her conversation, which was how she wanted it. She didn't want to keep secrets from him. As she suspected, her grandfather was less than pleased about the book.

"It wouldn't do for you to be seen reading anti-Directorate rhetoric in public."

"That's what I thought." Bryn didn't want to sound like a suck up, but she did want her grandfather to recognize she understood Blue Clan logic. And now it was time to show Valmont she wasn't throwing him under the bus. "Valmont is reading the book to search for anything that might lead us to more artifacts. As soon as he's done, we'll turn it in to Miss Enid with the message that it should be passed on to you. Does that work?"

"Yes. It does. Good night."

Bryn hung up the phone and sighed. She hated that she was finally beginning to understand how to play this stupid political game.

"Nicely done," Valmont commented from the couch where he was stretched out. "Not too suckup-ish but with just the right amount of recognition of authority."

"Thank you." Bryn pantomimed walking a tight rope. "I think I'm beginning to catch my balance in this strange world."

"Speaking of strange." Valmont flipped back several pages in the book. "The vaults under the library are mentioned in this tale. They don't come right out and name them, but the description matches what we've seen of the secret rooms so far. And, it makes it sound like there are doors in other places besides the vaults."

Bryn sat next to him on the couch and let that information sink in. "Okay. So there may be secret rooms all over campus?"

"Maybe. The author could have thrown in extra rooms to make the story seem like fiction or to make it harder for people to find the actual rooms."

"I understand some dragons would have wanted to hide magical artifacts like my elemental sword, or Ivy's bracelet, but I can't imagine there were tons of magical items that needed to be hidden, or my grandfather would have been more aware that at some point these types of things existed."

"So far, Miss Enid is the only dragon who'd heard of magic on this level, and she'd thought it was part of a legend, which makes me think it's not common."

"True, but these Days of Knights tales can't be the only source of information about a time before the Directorate. There have to be other factual accounts of dragon history from back in the day. If for no other reason than the Green dragons' compulsion to document, study, and understand everything."

"Maybe we should speak to Garret and convince him to take on a knight," Valmont said. "If there is a secret room created by a Green, it could be full of information and data which other Clan members might have wanted to destroy."

"That would be a good pitch to sell the idea to him," Bryn said. "I don't think a Green can resist the idea of a treasure trove of information."

"Did you ever figure out what a Red dragon might hide away?"

"No," Bryn said. "And it's making me feel disloyal to my father's memory."

"What does the Red Clan value above all other things?"

"Reds are like normal, middle class people. They have a good work ethic. They take pride in their accomplishments but they aren't egomaniacs. Family is important to them."

"With Keegan's help," Valmont said, "maybe we can find the answer to this mystery."

Bryn snatched the book from his hands and tossed it on the coffee table. "Serious time is over."

"It is?" Valmont asked. "Then what time is it?"

"I'll give you a hint." Bryn leaned close like she was going to whisper something in his ear but kissed him on the neck instead.

"I like the way you think." He turned so his lips lined up with hers and gave her a look that made her heart beat faster. "And I have a few thoughts of my own."

"I'd love to hear them."

He closed the distance between them, pressing his mouth against hers in a slow, languid kiss that started a low burn inside of her. When he moved his mouth to a spot on her neck right above her collarbone, she growled deep in her chest.

Valmont chuckled.

"What?"

"That's how I know I hit the right spot, but it still catches me off guard every time."

She grinned. "Think of it as a helpful road map."

"I don't need a map." He nipped at her earlobe and then did something to her ear that made her melt in his arms.

• • •

The next day, in Elemental Science, Keegan sat in a desk next to Bryn. "Any news on the whole knight-experiment thing?" he asked.

This probably wasn't the best place to have this conversation. "Not yet. Why?"

"There's something about it that doesn't feel right."

"You don't have to do it," Bryn said. "But Valmont and I could answer any questions you have, if that would make you feel better."

"I do have some concerns." Keegan said. "Can the three of us meet at the library tonight around six near the second floor study cubicles?"

"Sure."

Before meeting with Keegan, Bryn had a stop to make. She needed to deliver the book with the stories about the tyrant crowns to Miss Enid.

"Done with the book already?" Miss Enid asked, as Bryn set it on the front desk of the library.

"Yes, and it's a bit controversial," Bryn said. "So, rather than reshelving it, my grandfather would prefer you send it to him."

Miss Enid opened the book and ran her finger down the page of contents. "Maybe I'll make a copy before I send it to him, in case the book goes missing."

"Does that happen a lot?" Valmont asked.

"More than I'd like."

"I'm going to pretend I didn't hear that. Now we're going to meet a friend," Bryn said. "And as my grandmother would say, we don't want to be late."

Keegan was waiting for them when they arrived at the study cubicles. "I put my bag on a table over there."

They followed him to an isolated table in the back corner. Once they were seated, he leaned forward and spoke in a quiet voice. "Have you ever heard the term throwback?"

"Is that a sports thing?" Bryn asked.

"No," Keegan said. "It's what we call something from previous generations that shows up in families today."

"Like a family of blonds having one kid with black hair?" Valmont asked.

"Yes. Or like a family of Reds having a kid with two different colored eyes." He reached into his book bag and pulled out a package holding green disposable contact lenses. "My left eye is green like it's supposed to be, but my right eye is brown."

He said this like he was sharing an important secret with them. "That's unusual, but is it a problem for your family?" Bryn asked.

"It's not something we advertise, because it means a long time ago there was a hybrid in our family tree."

"Before the Directorate decreed all dragons had to marry within their Clans, didn't everyone have hybrids in their gene pool somewhere?" Valmont asked.

"Yeah, but by now it should have been bred out. Everything I've read claims it only takes a couple of generations for the throwback traits to disappear. In my family, in every other generation there seems to be someone who needs to wear one green contact. I'm telling you this because I don't know if it would affect the knight I bonded with. If we found something a Red should be able to open, and my knight and I couldn't do it, that would raise some questions."

"You're right." And she didn't want to land him in trouble, but there wasn't another Red she trusted as much as him. "Have you talked to Mr. Stanton about this?"

"No."

"I trust him. If you want, we can tell him your concerns."

"I'd rather not," Keegan said. "For my family's sake, it's best if we forget the whole thing."

Crap. She understood his decision, but that didn't mean she had to like it. "Thanks for considering it. And don't worry, I won't tell anyone."

Keegan grinned at her. "I know you won't." And then he picked up his bag and walked back the way they had come.

"I like him," Valmont said. "He's a good guy."

"He is," Bryn said.

"Who is number two on your most trusted Red Dragon list?"

"I don't have a number two. Since I've been at school, I've only hung out with Clint and Ivy, Garret, Rhianna, and Jaxon. My circle of friends isn't large."

Valmont tapped his fingers on the table. "There's something I don't understand. If every Clan started out with hybrid ancestors until it became monochromatic, for lack of a better term, then why would there still be throwbacks?"

"I'm not an expert on genetics," Bryn said. "But it does make you think a hybrid might have to be more recent in the family tree."

"If the Directorate really does test everyone's blood to see who is compatible for arranged marriages, wouldn't they see the throwback hybrid's DNA?"

"I don't think the process is that detailed. They have a spell that checks to see if the combination of genes would produce a dragon with undesirable traits, like overwhelming greed, or evil genius smarts with the desire to rule and conquer everyone, but I doubt the spell can tell the actual genetic makeup of the dragons being tested."

Valmont looked all around them like he was making sure no one was about to overhear what he was going to say. Leaning in he whispered, "Shouldn't Ferrin's parents have failed that test?"

Bryn laughed. "Maybe there are degrees of power hungry egomaniacs, and they barely made the cut."

Chapter Five

The next day, when Keegan wasn't in Elemental Science, Bryn had a bad feeling. When Mr. Stanton waved her up to his desk, her danger sensor went on high alert.

"I'll need you to stay after class today," Mr. Stanton said.

"Where's Keegan?" Bryn asked.

"He's resting," Mr. Stanton said. "Now take your seat."

What did that mean? He couldn't give her a cryptic answer and then expect her to go on with her day as usual. "Is he in trouble because of what I asked him to do?"

"He will be if you don't sit down and pretend everything is normal." Mr. Stanton pointed to her seat. "Go."

Bryn ground her teeth together as she walked back to her chair. Why was Mr. Stanton acting so strange? How hard was it for him to tell her what was going on? Just a sentence or two, like *Keegan isn't being interrogated* or *Keegan won't have a temporary chemical lobotomy like Ferrin gave Clint a few months ago* or *Keegan hasn't been eaten by piranhas.* Something to let her know he was all right.

She took notes throughout class, without really paying

attention to what she wrote. If they had a quiz on this tomorrow, she was screwed. But she couldn't concentrate. What did *He's resting* mean? Time seemed to stretch out and move more slowly. When class finally ended, it took effort to stay in her seat, rather than run up to Mr. Stanton's desk and demand answers.

After the last student left, Mr. Stanton said, "Valmont, close the door."

He did as requested while Bryn's fear for Keegan doubled.

"You met with Keegan in the library last night to talk about why he didn't want to have a knight." Mr. Stanton stated this like he already knew this for a fact, but he was waiting for her to confirm the information.

"Yes. What's going on?"

"The surveillance in the library has been tripled since the Directorate decided to keep offices on the top floor. The table where Keegan revealed his family secret was right below a camera. Your entire conversation was recorded and then observed by Ferrin and your grandfather."

Anger surged through Bryn's body, and fire crawled up the back of her throat. She focused on cold so sleet shot from her nostrils rather than flames. Keegan had revealed his family secret to her, and someone was watching and listening the entire time. "I'll skip the violation-of-our-right-to-privacy speech since the Directorate doesn't believe in that concept. What happened to Keegan?"

"A guard escorted him to the Directorate's office where they questioned him about everyone in his family. They took samples of his blood. Rather large samples, I'm afraid, and now he's resting in the medical bay under guard."

"Why is he under guard?"

"When Keegan mentioned he was a throwback, did you wonder where the term came from?" Mr. Stanton asked.

"No." And there wasn't a chance in hell she was going to

like what he was about to tell her.

"In animals, if a dog doesn't breed true and produce the desired traits, it's called a throwback. Sometimes the breeders keep the animals as pets or give them away. Sometimes they don't want to waste resources, so they eliminate them."

"Eliminate, as in kill?" Valmont asked. "Seriously?"

"Unfortunately, yes."

"That's so many types of wrong, but no one is going to eliminate Keegan, right?" Fire crawled up the back of Bryn's throat. She could taste smoke and knew she was on the verge of losing control. But if she did, Mr. Stanton would have to report it. Or maybe he wouldn't have to, because apparently they were all being observed twenty-four hours a day now.

"Keegan's life is not in danger, but I believe your comment about Ferrin's personality is the reason they collected blood until Keegan passed out."

Bryn roared in outrage but managed to keep the flames contained.

"So what happens now?" Valmont asked.

"Now, tests will be run on Keegan's blood and the blood of his family members to see if there are any DNA markers to discriminate the average Red dragon from a throwback Red. If there is, then my guess would be everyone on campus will be asked to donate blood for testing."

"Oh my God… They're going to assume anyone with throwback blood is siding with the Rebels, aren't they?"

"I believe they will investigate anyone who is hiding their true identity. I'm sure there are other students whose traits may not have bred true."

"Everyone knows I'm a hybrid," Bryn said. "But what if there are other hybrids on campus who are trying to blend in and live a normal life?" *Like Adam and Eve and their friends.*

Mr. Stanton frowned. "If there are other hybrids, it might be best for them to volunteer information before they are discovered."

Right. "Would you volunteer, if you were in their position?"

"I can't possibly answer that question. Now, instead of going to the library, I suggest you visit Keegan. And remember, security has been heightened all over campus. Don't say or do anything that would paint a target on your back or cause trouble for your friends."

"So, don't speak my opinions out loud, unless they align with the latest Directorate decree."

"That is one way to look at it." Mr. Stanton turned and went up to the chalkboard where he erased the day's notes.

"Wait a minute. I've been injured enough that the med lab has multiple samples of my blood. Did they run tests on it?"

"Of course they did," Mr. Stanton said, "and your blood shows markers from the Red and Blue clans."

"Which means they'll be able to identify a hybrid with ease," Valmont said.

"On a first generation hybrid like Bryn, the genetic markers are split almost down the middle. If she were to marry a Blue and have children, the second generation markers would more than likely go down 25 percent. In theory, Bryn's grandchildren would be 80 to 90 percent Blue. That's why it's rare now to have throwbacks, because genetically speaking, it's like drawing a wild card."

"So the further back the blending of the Clans, the less likely traits are to show?" Bryn asked.

Mr. Stanton nodded.

Something wasn't adding up. "The hybrids who attacked us the night of the Valentine's Day dance showed clear combinations of Clans. Does that mean they were first generation?"

"I don't see how they could be," Mr. Stanton said. "Unless

there are communities of dragons hiding from the Directorate. If a Blue-Red hybrid married another Blue-Red hybrid, then the hybrid traits would still occur. The more likely explanation is that the rebels you saw could manipulate Quintessence, and they did so to mask their true appearance."

"I guess that does make more sense." *Not.* But she didn't want to give away that she knew about hybrid communities.

"Let's go check on Keegan." Valmont put his hand on Bryn's shoulder and steered her toward the door. Once they were out of the building and walking across campus, he leaned close and whispered, "With all this talk of blood purity I'm not sure if Ferrin is trying to be Hitler or Voldemort."

Bryn laughed at the absurd comparison. "The sad part is you're not wrong. And I don't know if it would be better for hybrids to disappear from school or if that would make them look suspicious."

"Best-case scenario would be Keegan's blood doesn't have anything in it to differentiate him from the rest of his family."

Keegan was sitting up drinking orange juice when they found him in the medical lab.

"I'm so sorry," Bryn blurted out.

He gave a half smile. "Wasn't your fault. I picked the stupid table, and I'm the one who decided to tell you my secret."

"But Valmont and I were the ones who stuck around after you left. We joked about some things we shouldn't have, and that's why Ferrin took so much of your blood."

Keegan wrinkled his brow. "I wondered about that. I've given blood before, and I never passed out."

"Did the Medics tell you why they wanted it?"

"To run some genetic tests. I think everyone has heard rumors about throwbacks, but the families work so hard to hide it, that the medics don't have any data."

Apparently, he wasn't seeing the big, evil picture. "If your blood has some genetic marker that's different from your family's, they're going to make everyone give blood to figure out who's a throwback or some sort of hybrid."

Keegan's normal happy expression slipped. "That's absurd. It's not like I'm in league with the Rebels because my eyes aren't the same color."

"The last thing we need is a witch hunt," Bryn said. There were several choice names she'd like to call Ferrin, starting with egomaniacal asshat, but who knew if there were spy-cams pointed at her right now? This was all so frustrating. "Maybe I can use my student liaison title to intervene somehow."

A medic entered the room carrying an envelope. She smiled at Bryn and Valmont and then gave the letter to Keegan. "This is for you."

"Let's see if my day is going to get better or worse." Keegan opened the envelope and pulled out a piece of paper. As he read, his eyebrows came together like he was confused.

Bryn waited, not so patiently tapping her foot.

"Better or worse?" Valmont asked.

"I'm not sure." Keegan reached up and scratched the back of his head. "I've been summoned to the library this evening at seven where I'll be matched up with a knight. And I'm supposed to tell you to come, too. Is it me, or is it creepy that they delivered this at the exact time you stopped by to visit?"

"Definitely creepy," Bryn said. "And sort of ironic that you revealed your secret because you thought taking on a knight might out you—"

"And now that I've been outed, I'm getting a knight," Keegan finished her sentence.

The medic returned. "I'm going to scan you to make sure you're all right, and then you'll be released."

Bryn watched as the medic placed her hand on Keegan's

forehead and closed her eyes. She knew the woman was sending her Quintessence into Keegan's body, making sure he was healthy enough to leave. Every time she saw a medic working with a patient, it reaffirmed this was how she wanted to spend her adult life — healing and treating other dragons.

"You're good to go." The medic pulled a folded-up piece of paper from her pocket. "These are your discharge papers."

"That's new," Bryn said.

The medic nodded. "Apparently, part of the heightened level of security is knowing where everyone is at all times. You check in and out at the medical center now like you would at the back gate. I understand their reasoning, but the paperwork is a nightmare." The medic turned back to Keegan. "Your teachers have been informed that you're excused from classes today but will return tomorrow. Take it easy and be sure to eat plenty of food."

"Thanks." Keegan took the paper from her and shoved it in his pocket. "Bryn, you guys want to walk me back to my dorm? I have some questions about this whole knight process."

"Sure." The three of them exited the medical building.

Once they were out in the early afternoon sun Keegan said, "I know some of the other throwbacks. There are probably less than a dozen on campus. Should I warn them?"

"We have to assume everything we say is being monitored, and that you, especially, are under observation to see if you're part of some Rebel alliance. I wouldn't talk to anyone you don't normally talk to or do anything different from your daily routine."

"In other words, don't give Ferrin anything to use against me." Keegan shook his head. "When I'm back to my usual self, I'm going to beat the hell out of one of those Slam Mans in the gym."

Bryn had taken her own aggression out on one of those

man-shaped punching bags on more than one occasion. And she'd often pictured Jaxon's face on the dummy. From now on, she'd probably picture Ferrin.

At lunch she filled Clint and Ivy in on the Keegan situation without giving away his secret, which left the story disjointed and awkward.

"There's something you're not telling us, isn't there?" Ivy said.

"Yes, but it's not my information to tell," Bryn said. "I'd be betraying someone else."

"I get it," Ivy said. "I don't like it, but I get it."

"So everything we're saying could be monitored, at all times?" Clint asked.

Bryn nodded.

"That's messed up." Ivy glanced around. "Do you think we should let other people know they're under a microscope?"

"No, because what if some of the students *are* working with the Rebels? We'd be tipping them off."

"So, it's okay to spy on the bad guys, but not on the good guys," Valmont said, like he didn't approve of her statement.

"No. It's not okay for them to spy on us, but if we can't stop them then we shouldn't sabotage them, either. They *might* find out something that could stop the Rebels from hurting anyone else."

"I have no valid argument against that statement, but it still feels wrong," Valmont said.

"A lot of things seem off-kilter around here lately," Clint said. "It's like everyone is bracing themselves for a sneak attack. It's been peaceful since Valentine's Day."

"You know there's only a month and a half of school left," Ivy said.

Wow. "With all the trying-not-to-be-killed stuff that's been going on lately, I haven't thought about our junior year ending."

"It's a pretty big life event to miss," Clint said. "I think we should have a party to celebrate surviving our first year at the Institute."

"What will you two do over the summer?" Bryn asked.

"Well," Ivy said, "Clint and I will go home and hang out. We'll invite you to come over. Then maybe we can stay the night at your grandparent's monstrous estate."

"I'm not really looking forward to summer break." Bryn laughed. "I never thought I'd utter those words, but I almost went crazy over Christmas vacation being alone at my grandparent's house." Sure she was on better terms with them now, but three months was a long time to be away from everyone.

"But you won't be alone," Valmont said. "I'll be with you."

And now she felt like she'd said something completely thoughtless. "Your visits were the highlight of my Christmas break, but it felt like I was locked away from the outside world. I don't want to lose touch again."

Ivy held up her hand like she was pledging an oath. "I solemnly swear I will call you and visit."

"And you know I go where she goes," Clint said. "It might be fun to go exploring in that old mansion. I bet there are rooms no one has been in for ages."

"I explored when I first got there. I found my mom's old rooms. They'd been wiped clean, repainted, and all the furniture removed. It was sad." She'd also found the secret crawlway in the back of the closet which led to an attic where she'd found a picture of her mom and dad together in one of her mom's journals. Those had been the only items left of her mom in the entire house. "Knowing my grandparents as I do now, I wonder if they'd forgive my mother if she was still alive."

"They took you in," Valmont said. "So I think they would have made peace with her, eventually."

"I'd like to think so." A wave of tiredness hit Bryn. "I swear, I'm emotionally exhausted." Maybe summer being around the corner was a good thing.

A seven o'clock that night, Bryn found herself in Ferrin's office, standing off to the side, while Keegan was introduced to a man named David who'd lost his home in the attack on Dragon's Bluff. Keegan was injected with the spider venom like they'd done to Jaxon and Ivy. Then David injected him with the antidote, saving Keegan's life and activating the latent spell in his own blood.

David blinked and looked around. "Wow, it feels like I drank two Red Bulls."

"That means it worked," Valmont said.

"Now what?" Keegan asked.

"Before we go down to the vaults, I want to perform a few tests," Ferrin stated.

This could be bad. Ferrin could be tormenting Keegan just to flaunt his power.

"Tests you couldn't run on the gallon of blood you took from me yesterday?" Keegan asked.

"No." Ferrin pointed at what looked like a small treasure chest with flames engraved on the hinges. "Try Blood Magic on this."

"You only need to give a drop," Bryn said, in case Ferrin was going to be a jerk.

David placed his sword point on top of the box. "Just like this?" he asked.

"Yes," Valmont answered. "Your job is the easier of the two."

Keegan ran his pointer finger along the edge of David's sword. Several crimson drops ran down the blade and landed on the box. They waited for the box to pop open. Nothing happened.

"That is disappointing." Ferrin pointed at a book with a red binding which had flames stamped into the leather. "Try this one."

Keegan repeated the ritual. This time the cover of the book popped open. "Hey, I did it. So I guess my blood is as good as any Red's, right?"

There was silence as Ferrin stared at Keegan for a moment before responding, "That remains to be seen. Now that we know your blood is adequate, we'll visit the vaults. Follow me."

Ferrin swept by them like a king parading in front of his lowly subjects. Keegan fell into step beside Bryn. "We're going to try and open a vault?"

"No," Bryn said. "We are going to the basement of the library where they store artifacts."

"Then why don't they call it a basement?"

"They're Blues. Basement probably sounds too middle class."

Keegan laughed. "You better hope the stairwells aren't full of spy-cams."

"Since it wasn't a Ferrin-specific insult, I don't think the people listening in will care." At least, she hoped not.

They followed Ferrin to the front desk of the library where Miss Enid was typing on her computer.

"I need you to open the vaults," Ferrin said.

"Can't do that, I'm afraid," Miss Enid said, without looking up from her keyboard.

That was not the answer any of them expected her to give. Least of all, Ferrin. His eyes narrowed. "You will open the vaults. Immediately."

Miss Enid stopped typing and met Ferrin's furious gaze. "If I could open the vaults for you, I would, but Mr. Sinclair took back my key."

Why would her grandfather do that? Was he trying to keep Ferrin from searching for information without him? If so, his plan seemed to be working.

Ferrin whipped out his phone and stalked back into the storage room where the door to the vaults was hidden.

Bryn leaned in and whispered, "Did my grandfather really take your key?"

"Of course," Miss Enid said. "I'd never lie to a Directorate member."

Ferrin stalked back out of the room to join them. "I'm needed at a meeting. We'll continue this another time."

Once he was out of earshot, Keegan said, "Convenient how a meeting came up when he hit a roadblock."

"What do we do now?" David asked.

Keegan shrugged. "I'm hungry. You can come to the dining hall with me, if you want."

David checked the clock hanging on the back wall above the desk. "I should probably go home. My daughter will be going to bed soon. I don't want to miss saying good night. Ever since the attack, I don't take things like that for granted."

"I can call a car for you," Miss Enid said.

"No, thanks. I drove myself. My car is parked out back."

"Keegan, why don't you walk David to his car, in case anyone questions why he's on campus."

"Sure." Keegan and David headed for the door.

"Bryn, I found a book I thought you'd enjoy. I bet Ivy would like it, too." Miss Enid reached under her desk and pulled out a book with the title *Jewelry Through the Ages*.

Okay. Why does Miss Enid think I want to read a book about antique jewelry? Sure, I like sparkly things as much as the next girl, but not enough to read an encyclopedia about it. She picked up the book and faked a smile. "Thanks."

"I think Ivy will love the black pearl bracelet in the back

of the book," Miss Enid said. "It would suit her perfectly."

Oh. Now I get it. "I'll make sure to tell her about it."

"A little slow on the uptake," Valmont teased as they exited the building.

"Apparently. Do you think we have time to drop this off at Ivy's before curfew?"

The Directorate-mandated curfew was strictly enforced. Her grandfather would have a cow if she was ever caught breaking it. Not to mention, Ferrin would use it as an attempt to humiliate her and tarnish the Sinclair name. Still, Ivy would want the bracelet.

Valmont increased his pace. "We'll be fine, if we hurry."

Just to be on the safe side, Bryn broke into a slow jog. When they reached the Black dorm, Clint and Ivy were opening the front door to come outside.

Before she could say anything, Ivy snatched the book from Bryn's hands. "I'm so excited."

"How'd you know?" Bryn asked.

"Miss Enid called. Do you guys want to come up?"

"We better not," Bryn said. "Curfew."

"Right." Clint rolled his eyes.

Chapter Six

Once they were back in her room, Bryn changed into yoga pants and a T-shirt before joining Valmont on the couch. "I wonder if my grandfather took the key because he didn't want Ferrin poking around in the vaults without him."

"I'm sure that's why he did it. Since we discovered the vaults and handed the information over to your grandfather, Ferrin has never been in the lead on anything in this situation, and I bet it's driving him crazy."

Couldn't happen to a nicer person. "The man deserves some grief," Bryn said. "I can't believe Miss Enid kept such a straight face when she played her part."

"She's probably been waiting for a chance to get back at him after all the holier-than-thou comments he's made over the years."

"Probably true. You know—" Bryn almost said she was surprised someone hadn't murdered Ferrin, but then she stopped because her room could be bugged. And she hated that thought.

"What?" Valmont said.

"I was going to make a snarky comment about Ferrin, but I didn't because someone could be listening in on our conversation. I hate that it could be the new status quo, like I'm supposed to accept everything is bugged and as long as you don't speak your mind, and stick to the party line, it's no big deal."

"I can't imagine they'd take the time and effort to bug all the student rooms," Valmont said.

"Me, neither. But they might take the time to bug mine."

"I have no valid argument against that statement," Valmont said, "and I hate that I agree with you." He peered around the room. "Do you think we could spot a microphone if we saw one?"

Bryn yawned so big her eyes watered. "It's been a long day. I'm not sure I care right now. I think I'm going to go to bed."

"You better hope you don't talk in your sleep," Valmont said.

"That's not funny."

• • •

Ivy was practically bouncing out of her seat with excitement when Bryn showed up at breakfast the next morning. She held out her right arm. "Check out the amazing bracelet my wonderful boyfriend gave me."

The black pearl and silver link bracelet shone in the cafeteria lights.

"It's beautiful," Bryn said, playing her role in this lie meant to convince people the bracelet was nothing more than a normal piece of jewelry, rather than a device which channeled Ivy's lightning into an elemental sword.

"Nice job, Clint," Valmont said.

Clint nodded in acknowledgment as he crunched his way

through a strip of bacon.

Bryn frowned at her cheese omelet. "How'd I miss the bacon?"

Valmont slid two pieces of his bacon onto her plate. "I think you were still sleepwalking."

Bryn stifled a yawn. "I had the weirdest dreams last night starring a certain Directorate member. He locked us in the vaults and told us the only way we'd get out was if we found a secret tunnel or door. By the end of the dream I'd cut myself so many times I'd stopped bleeding, like I'd bled out. I collapsed on the floor, and it was like I'd given up. "

"I would never let you bleed until you collapsed," Valmont said. "So I find your dream insulting, both as a knight and as your boyfriend."

Bryn rolled her eyes. "I know you wouldn't, but my subconscious was throwing stress-bombs at me last night. In the real world, I trust you to have my back more than any other person on the planet. But in the dream, Ferrin had done something to you so you couldn't see me anymore. You thought you were locked down there alone." The cold horror of it settled in Bryn's stomach. Her voice caught in her throat. "You thought I'd abandoned you. That was the worst part."

"Sounds like a grade-A stress-induced nightmare," Clint said.

Bryn didn't want to visit the vaults in the near future. "I have no desire to go below ground level any time soon. And I'd prefer all the rooms I visit today to have large windows and multiple exits."

Fate seemed to be mocking her, because she received a note in Elemental Science telling her to report to the entrance to the vaults to meet with Keegan and Ferrin after her last class. She read the note and passed it to Valmont. "I don't suppose kicking and screaming like a toddler will get me out of this request."

"Probably not, but if you want to try, I'm game."

"Bryn." Keegan waved from a few desks over. "I'm guessing we're hanging out at the library this evening?" He held up the note, which looked exactly like the official piece of stationary she'd received.

"Looks like it," she said. "At least my grandfather's name is on here, too. So he should be there."

Jaxon peered over at Bryn and then came to stand at her desk. He snatched the note without asking for permission and read it. "What's this about?"

"You have no idea how badly I want to mock you by saying, 'It's official Directorate business.'"

He dropped the note back on her desk. "That's not mocking me, because it is official Directorate business."

"Maybe that's why it feels like the joke is on me," she muttered.

After her last class, Bryn trudged across campus toward her dorm. "I don't care what the note says, I'm dropping off my book bag, grabbing a snack, and a cup of coffee before we go to the library."

"Are you tired, or has Ferrin's fabulous demeanor dampened your sense of adventure?"

"Yes and yes." Bryn yawned until her eyes watered. "What I really want is a nap."

They entered the Blue dorm. Instead of heading for the stairs, Valmont put his hand on Bryn's lower back and directed her toward the restaurant in the back. "I know you. If we go up to your room, you will sit on the couch and then you won't want to get up. To head off any unpleasantness, we are going to have coffee and a snack down here and then go to the library."

"That's probably a smarter plan." They found an empty table, and a waiter came to take their order.

"Coffee," Bryn said. "I need a vat of coffee."

The young man smiled at Valmont like he was in on the joke. "I'm sorry, a carafe will have to do."

"What's the fastest snack you can bring us?" Valmont asked.

"A fruit and cheese tray, or bread and butter."

"Both," Bryn said, "and I want my own carafe."

The waiter looked to Valmont. "She's not joking?"

Valmont shook his head no. "She never jokes about coffee or food."

It took the waiter less than five minutes to bring their order. It took Bryn less than ten minutes to make the food and the coffee disappear. So she didn't know why Ferrin was so ticked off when she showed up in the library a few minutes after that.

"I said you were to come here after your last class," Ferrin said. "Where have you been?"

"I stopped off at my dorm for a minute. You didn't give an exact time. The note just said after…and this is after."

"No harm done," her grandfather said. "Let's proceed down to the vaults."

Keegan and David stood off to the side, like they weren't sure what their role was.

"Follow us," Bryn said as they headed into the storage room with the trap door that lead to the vaults. Ferrin and her grandfather took the lead. Bryn and Valmont followed along behind them while Keegan and David came down the stairs last.

"Good thing I'm not claustrophobic," Keegan said.

Bryn glanced back and saw his broad shoulders were brushing the walls. "Valmont said it's narrow for defense purposes."

"I feel like a cork in a bottle," Keegan muttered.

When they reached the room with the giant card catalog, two Red guards waited for them. Bryn and Valmont used

Blood Magic to make the door appear.

"That's amazing," Keegan said.

"Much cooler than the book we opened," David agreed.

"That is why we are here." Her grandfather gestured they should enter the room. "We're hoping you can find a door designated for a Red knight and dragon." He pointed at the right hand wall. "There was a Blue door there." He pointed at the back wall. "And a Black door here."

"So I should bleed on the wall over there?" Keegan pointed to the left-hand wall.

"Seems logical," Bryn followed along behind him.

"Any particular spot?" David asked.

Keegan scratched his chin and studied the wall. "There, between those two bookcases."

"Why there?" Bryn asked.

"That's where I'd put a door if I wanted one." After David put his sword point onto the wall, Keegan ran his finger down the blade. When the blood hit the wall, nothing happened.

"Disappointing," Keegan said. He walked around to the other side of the bookcase where a patch of wall two feet wide was exposed. "Let's try here."

Again he performed the ritual, and again, nothing happened.

"Huh." David moved to the next blank spot on the wall, which was only six inches wide. They repeated the process, and again, nothing happened.

"What am I missing?" Keegan checked the wall and then he looked down at the floor. There was a four-square-foot area marked off by three bookshelves like a square that was missing its fourth side. He pointed at the floor. "Let's try there."

"I doubt there will be a door in the floor," Ferrin said.

"The entrance to the vault is in the floor," Bryn shot back.

Keegan bled on the floor, and the flagstones shimmered,

revealing what looked like a manhole cover, except it was four feet across and there were hinges on one side and a handle on the other.

"Before I bleed on it, let's try opening it the normal way." Keegan pulled on the door, and the handle elongated like the telescopic handgrip of a suitcase. "This was definitely designed by a Red." He squatted down like he was going to do a deadlift, grabbed the handle, and pulled up. It clicked up two more times before the door opened a fraction of an inch. Keegan stepped back and rolled his shoulders. "That felt like a three hundred fifty pound deadlift." He opened the hatch with ease and peered down. "There's a ladder."

"The guards should go down first to make sure it's safe," Bryn's grandfather said.

Once the guards had descended into the opening, Bryn edged closer, trying to see what was below.

"Don't get too close," her grandfather said.

"Waiting patiently isn't my strong suit."

Five minutes later, Bryn was tapping her foot and staring at the hole in the floor, willing one of the guards to come back up. Lights flared on, illuminating the opening.

"Sir, there isn't anything down here," one of the guards called out. "It looks like it was a bunker."

Without waiting for anyone to give him permission, Keegan climbed down the ladder. David followed.

If they could go, Bryn reasoned, she could go, too. She moved toward the opening.

"No." Bryn's grandfather held a hand out to stop her. "Not yet."

Keegan climbed back up a moment later. "It's literally a concrete room with a desk and bed and what looks like some sort of plumbing system I'd rather not know about."

David climbed out of the bunker. "Nothing fun or exciting."

"No books?" Bryn asked.

"There's a crate of books next to the bed and some candles," Keegan said.

"What about the desk?" Bryn asked.

"It's dusty and covered in old paper and those feather pens," David said. "What do you call those… quills."

"So no treasures?" Valmont said.

The crate came up through the opening. Keegan grabbed it and walked over to set it on the library table. "Not unless there are some rare books in here."

"Are any of those books sparkling at you?" Bryn asked.

Keegan looked at her like she was crazy. "As a general rule, books don't sparkle at me."

"True, but enchantments that point the way to magical items would sparkle at you," Bryn said.

"And sometimes they sing," Valmont added.

"No offense," David said to Keegan, "but you have strange friends."

"Trust me," Bryn said. "The better you know us, the weirder we seem."

"Think of this as your grace period," Valmont said. "We are actually trying to appear normal."

"We'll ask Miss Enid to examine the books," her grandfather said. "For now, I think you four are free to go."

"But there has to be a reason that room exists." Bryn did not want to leave the vaults without some sort of payoff. "There must be something that makes it special to Reds."

One of the guards spoke from below. "It would be a good place to lay low. Most people don't look for doors in the floor—plus the walls of the bunker seem to be reinforced with metal bars."

"Bars meant to keep people in or keep people out?" David asked.

Everyone turned to look at him.

"What? I work at the bank in Dragon's Bluff. When a room is reinforced with bars or thicker concrete it's either meant to keep things in, like money, or meant to keep people out who might want to steal the money. Not that there's ever been much crime in Dragon's Bluff, but historically, it was a problem."

"So how could we tell what the room was designed for?" Bryn asked.

Keegan grabbed a brown leather novel from the box. "Start here." He flipped the cover open, and it separated from the book binding. "Sorry." He started to pick up the cover to replace it but stopped. "I should let Miss Enid take care of this."

"Why don't Valmont and I go find her? She can sort through the crate and share the information with us." She avoided eye contact with Ferrin and directed her words toward her grandfather. "I don't want to leave without knowing if we found something useful."

"Go find Miss Enid," her grandfather said. "We'll try not to discover anything exciting while you're gone."

"Thank you." Bryn exited the room with Valmont following behind her. When she hit the winding staircase, she was up it in a flash.

"How much coffee did you drink?" Valmont called out as he kept pace with her.

Bryn located Miss Enid and explained what they'd found so far and why they wanted her help. "There must be something in the crate which will give us information."

Down in the vaults, Miss Enid put on white cotton gloves and unpacked the books with great care. The titles ranged from Economics to Architecture. The last book she removed from the crate was slimmer than the rest. She set it on the table and opened the first page. "It's a journal."

Miss Enid read a few pages. "It seems the room you

discovered was a safe house, a place for dragons to lay low when there was trouble."

"What sort of trouble?" Bryn asked. It's not like the room was full of weapons.

Miss Enid pursed her lips. "He's not going into detail. I mean, he is giving details of his day and of businesses he was involved in, but it isn't telling me why he might need to hide there."

"Maybe it was a place for guards to rest when they weren't guarding what was in the other secret rooms," Valmont said. "It looked like only the strongest dragons could open the door, so it could only be accessed by other Reds."

Miss Enid pursed her lips and continued turning pages. "Here we go." She tapped the page. "He reports that dragons attempted to access the vaults through the trap door in the storeroom."

"The same storeroom where the trap door to the vaults is now?" Keegan asked.

"I would guess so. According to this entry, he was ordered to return to his bunker and observe the intruders rather than stop them. And he wasn't happy about it."

"How could he see any of that from down there?" Bryn asked.

"Good question." Valmont gestured toward the opening. "After you."

Bryn avoided eye contact with both her grandfather and Ferrin in case they meant to tell her no. She made it down the ladder into the dusty room. Keegan hadn't been lying. The room was a ten-by-ten gray concrete cell with a bed, a desk, and pipes attached to a metal box she did not want to know about.

Valmont ran his hands along the walls. "Maybe there is a secret panel that slides open."

Bryn tried to get her bearings. She pointed to the ceiling

on the right of the ladder. "The entrance is that direction?"

"I believe so." Valmont approached the metal box attached to the pipes. "My first guess is this is some sort of waste disposal, but maybe it's more like a periscope."

"If you're brave enough to test that theory, go ahead."

"Bravery and common sense are not the same thing. Common sense tells me Miss Enid should probably check this out so I don't break it."

"Right." Bryn nodded. "*That's* why you don't want to touch it."

"Miss Enid," Valmont called out, not acknowledging Bryn's comment.

When the librarian climbed down, she headed for the desk. "We might find something interesting in these drawers."

"Solve a puzzle for us," Bryn said. "Do you think that is antique plumbing, or a spy-scope."

Still wearing her gloves, Miss Enid approached the metal box. "I've no idea. Let's investigate." She touched the edge of the lid and gently pushed up. Rather than the lid moving, the side dropped down like the loading ramp for a truck. "There's a glass lens here but it's blank."

"Someone should go back up to the entrance," Valmont said. "Maybe we could see them."

"Let me figure out how this works first." Miss Enid fiddled with the box until it made a metallic clicking noise. The two shorter sides folded down, and the lens looked more like a screen.

"Amazing," Miss Enid said. "If I look straight down, I can see the entire store room and the trap door in the floor. It's like I have a bird's eye view. The guards would be able to keep watch over the entrance without physically guarding the room. Kind of an old fashioned version of the surveillance equipment we use today."

"So it's an antique spy-cam?" Valmont asked.

"That's one way to put it," Miss Enid said.

Bryn's grandfather descended the ladder. "Show me what you found."

He joined Miss Enid at the box. Four people in the room was a bit claustrophobic. "Let's go up so the others can come down." Bryn grabbed the ladder and headed up. Valmont followed. When she emerged in the room, Keegan and David were heading out the door.

"Bryn, you and your knight should leave as well," Ferrin stated.

For once in her life, she didn't feel like arguing, but just to annoy him, she went over to the ladder and hollered down. "We're going to dinner. See you later."

"Good night," her grandfather called back up.

Ferrin sneered.

"I'm too hungry to comment on that display," Bryn muttered to Valmont and then headed for the exit. When they reached the dining hall, Clint and Ivy were halfway done with dinner.

"I was starting to worry," Ivy said. "You never willingly miss a meal."

"True," Bryn said. "We were in the vaults."

"Keegan came in late with a guy we didn't recognize. Is that his knight?" Clint asked.

"Well done, Sherlock." She didn't think her grandfather would mind if she shared details with Clint and Ivy since they'd already been in the vaults and knew all about Blood Magic. "Keegan found a safe room where a Red could hole up and keep watch on the entrance to the vaults through some weird periscope thing."

"No multi-talented bracelets or cuff links?" Ivy asked.

"Nope, but I bet there are still some cool weapons down there for Reds. We just haven't found them yet."

"I don't think Keegan could get away with cuff links,"

Valmont said, "Which makes me wonder what type of jewelry a Red dragon could wear without drawing attention."

"A ring maybe?" Bryn said.

"Or a watch," Clint said. "That's about it. Anything else would stand out."

"Why did you and Valmont have to go with them?" Ivy asked.

"I don't know, maybe since I vouched for Keegan, they wanted me there."

"Or," Clint said, "maybe your grandfather wanted Keegan to feel comfortable, since Ferrin tried to bleed him dry."

She wasn't sure her grandfather had been concerned with Keegan's feelings, but he had probably wanted her there to rub it in Ferrin's face that it hadn't been his son who'd started the whole discovery process. And at this point, she didn't mind if that was his reason. Ferrin deserved all the grief he could get. He put nothing but bad karma out into the universe, so he shouldn't be surprised when it came back to bite him.

Chapter Seven

After finding the hidden spy-scope room in the vaults, the rest of Bryn's school week seemed oddly normal. On the walk back to her room Wednesday night after dinner, she kept turning around at every noise expecting something to jump out at her.

"What is your problem?" Ivy asked when they stopped in front of the Blue dorm.

It was hard to put into words without sounding like she was a paranoid pessimist. "I don't know. It's like the calm before the storm. I know the bad guys are out there watching and waiting to make their next move. I'm afraid if I let my guard down, something bad will happen."

"Maybe the Rebels have backed off since the Directorate increased security," Clint said.

"Maybe." She didn't trust that analysis. The Rebels didn't seem like the type to give up.

Valmont opened the front door to the Blue dorm. "It's almost curfew. We should go."

"Right," Clint said. "See you tomorrow. If the world isn't

overrun with brain-eating aliens while we sleep."

"Smart ass," Bryn said.

Ivy laughed. "What's that saying…just because I'm paranoid doesn't mean people aren't out to get me."

"Better yet, if I know I'm being irrational that means I'm sane, right?" Bryn said.

"We'll go with that for now," Valmont said.

"Good night." Ivy gave a half wave and then walked off hand in hand with her boyfriend.

"I understand how you're feeling," Valmont said as they entered the dorm and climbed the marble staircase to her room.

"It's like I expect things to go wrong all the time now, and I hate it. I don't want to be the person who is always waiting for the next disaster."

"It *is* better to be on guard than to be caught by surprise," Valmont said.

They reached the second floor where Bryn's room was located. As she stuck her key in the lock, she heard her phone ringing. That was weird, since Clint and Ivy were the only people who called her, and there was no way they'd made it back to their rooms in the Black dorm yet.

Pushing the door open, she crossed the room in four strides and picked up the receiver. "Hello?"

"Meet me in Rhianna's room," Jaxon ordered and then he hung up.

Bryn stared at the phone in her hand. *Okay, then.*

"Something wrong?" Valmont asked.

"That storm we were waiting for might have hit." She told him about Jaxon's odd command and then went into her bedroom to retrieve her Elemental sword bracelet. She slid the platinum and sapphire cuff onto her wrist and then squeezed the bracelet with her left hand to turn off the safety. When she pantomimed holding a sword, the blade of fire and ice shot from her hand. No matter how many times she did that it always gave her a rush to see her elements formed into such a cool weapon. And now she felt prepared to do battle.

Since she couldn't walk down the hall to Jaxon's room wielding a fire and ice sword, she pantomimed releasing it so the blade disappeared. She pressed the top of the bracelet to turn on the safety feature so she couldn't accidentally stab one of her friends. "All ready."

"Okay," Valmont said. "Let's go see what Mr. Sweetness-and-Light wants."

They exited Bryn's room and headed down the hall to Rhianna's. Bryn knocked quietly, not wanting other Blues to think anything was amiss.

Jaxon yanked the door open and waved them in. Rhianna sat on the couch with her arms crossed over her chest and her lips set in a thin line.

"What's going on?" Bryn asked.

"It's George, my knight," Jaxon said. "Someone's taken him."

"Taken him?" Bryn crossed the room to sit beside Rhianna. "As in kidnapped?"

"Yes." Jaxon paced back and forth in front of the coffee table.

Valmont came to stand next to Bryn like he was on guard. "And you know this how?"

"My father called half an hour ago. He received a photograph of George tied to a chair and bleeding from a gash on his forehead."

Anger stirred in Bryn's gut, igniting the flames inside of her. "What do the kidnappers want?" Smoke drifted from her lips as she spoke.

"That's just it." Jaxon continued pacing. "They've made no demands. It's like they want us to know they have him. Until they make a demand, there is nothing we can do." Frost shot from Jaxon's nostrils. "George is an honorable man. Just sitting here while I know he is injured is wrong." Jaxon growled. "I want to blast someone."

"I wish they'd call and tell us what they want," Rhianna said, "because waiting is only making the situation worse."

"Wait a minute. It's like that stupid uncomfortable couch," Valmont said. "Whoever took George is letting you stew in your anger so you won't be at your best when it's time to make a decision."

That is an interesting and, more than likely, accurate interpretation. "Okay," Bryn said. "Let's assume Valmont is right. Does that mean we have to sit here and wait for someone to make a demand?"

"There isn't much else we can do," Rhianna said.

"True," Bryn said. "But that doesn't mean we have to fall into their trap."

Jaxon stopped pacing and turned to glare at her. "Knowing they are attempting to manipulate me doesn't make me immune."

"It didn't make the God-awful couch any more comfortable, either," Bryn said. "But you're a Westgate and a Blue. Pull up that snooty facade you live behind and take a deep breath. Calm down. Think rationally."

"How dare you—"

"She's not wrong," Rhianna interrupted him. "If the kidnappers called and demanded we meet them somewhere, are we ready? Is there anything we should take with us?"

Bryn held up her arm and pointed at the Elemental bracelet she wore on her wrist, but she refrained from speaking, because Jaxon looked like he was two seconds from losing it. She didn't want to add to his stress at this moment. Although, she did reserve the right to antagonize him about it later.

"Fine." Jaxon stalked into his bedroom and came back

out a few moments later wearing his Elemental sword cuff links. The blank expression on his face made it appear he had his emotions under control. They'd put out that fire. Now, what should their next move be?

And then a terrible thought occurred to Bryn. "Did anyone check on Ivy's or Keegan's knights?"

"Keegan has a knight?" Rhianna said.

Jaxon nodded. "My father told me this morning they enlisted him to help find information that may have been hidden by Reds."

"Should we call Ivy and Keegan to make sure their knights are okay?" Bryn asked.

Jaxon grabbed the phone and called his father. The conversation he had was swift and to the point. He hung up and then held the phone out to Bryn. "The Directorate will send guards to Mary and David's houses. You should call Ivy and Keegan and let them know what's going on, just in case they're in danger, too."

Well, hell. She hadn't thought about that. Bryn dialed Keegan and explained the situation to him.

"What can I do to help?" Keegan asked.

"Right now it's a waiting game," Bryn said. "There isn't anything we can do until they make some sort of demand."

"As long as the Directorate sends someone to look after David, I can take care of myself. Let me know if you need anything."

"Thanks, I'll get back to you when I have something to share."

Next, she called Ivy. Her heart pounded as the phone rang and rang. On the sixth ring Ivy picked up.

"Thank God you're okay."

"Hello to you, too," Ivy said.

Bryn filled her in on the situation with George and their fear about Mary.

"We're coming over," Ivy said.

"Don't. It's after curfew," Bryn reminded her. "Plus, leaving your dorm could put you at risk."

"Who gives a crap about curfew?" Ivy said. "I need more information."

"I understand. When I have some, I'll call again."

Bryn could hear Clint talking in the background.

"Clint said you should have your grandfather send some guards to escort us to your room."

Her grandfather would never go for that idea. "I'll ask him. Stay put until you hear from me again. Okay?"

"Fine."

Bryn hung up.

"What's wrong?" Valmont asked.

Why did that particular question seem to be the theme of the evening? "Ivy wants me to ask my grandfather to send guards to escort her over here since it's after curfew. I'm not sure I should."

"You absolutely shouldn't," Jaxon said. "The Directorate members are working to solve this problem. Taking time out to babysit your friends won't help rescue George."

"You have to call your grandfather," Valmont said, "because you told Ivy you would."

The fact that she could see both points of view made Bryn's head pound. "You're both right." Where did that leave her?

"Call your grandmother," Rhianna said. "She could ask someone to escort Ivy and Clint without distracting the Directorate."

"You're brilliant." Bryn called Sinclair Estates. Rindy, the phone operator, placed the call through to her grandmother.

"I appreciate that your friends are concerned for Mary's safety," her grandmother said, "but sending guards to their rooms will only draw attention to them. Right now, this is a power play between the Directorate and the Rebels. Two Black dragons and a Black knight probably aren't even on the Rebels radar."

"I don't love your answer," Bryn said, "but I'll respect your decision."

Bryn called Ivy back with the not-so-good news.

"This totally sucks," Ivy said.

"I'm sorry. When I have any information, I'll let you know." She hung up and recapped what her grandmother had said.

"At least this way you asked," Valmont said. "You kept your word, and you did what you could."

Somehow, that didn't seem like enough, though all four of them sat and stared at the phone, willing it to ring. A stray thought occurred to Bryn. "Jaxon, why are you taking phone calls in Rhianna's room instead of yours?"

"These bastards took my knight, which means they want leverage over me or my father," Jaxon said. "I wasn't about to give them the chance to take Rhianna, too. She's been through enough already."

Jaxon did really love Rhianna. These glimpses of him being kind to his girlfriend were what made Bryn think that deep down, he was a much better person than his father.

"Is that why you asked Bryn to come here?" Valmont said. "Do you think she's in danger because of her association with you?"

Double hell. That's another thing I haven't thought of.

"It's not like she needs my help to be a target for murder or kidnapping," Jaxon said.

Valmont opened his mouth like he was going to argue, but then he sighed. "I have no valid argument against that statement."

"Sad but true." Bryn reached up to rub her temples in an effort to stave off the headache she could feel coming on. "So if you weren't worried about being the cause of my abduction, why am I here?"

"You two started this whole knight-Blood Magic situation, so I thought your perspective could help."

The phone rang.

Jaxon grabbed it and nodded along to whatever the person on the other end of the line was saying. "I understand." He slammed the phone down. "I'm leaving. Bryn, you and Valmont need to stay here with Rhianna."

"There's not a chance in hell that's going to happen," Bryn said.

"I know." Jaxon sighed. "But this way I can say I followed orders. Now, because I don't want to leave Rhianna alone, all four of us are going to meet the kidnappers and see what they want."

"Where are we meeting them?" Bryn asked.

"There's an envelope waiting for us at the back gate. It will tell us where to go."

"Seriously?" Bryn threw her arms up. "We're supposed to trust them and do what they say?"

Jaxon growled and frost shot from his nostrils. "I'm not happy about this, either. Right now they are in control. We'll bide our time, and then we will take them down."

Together, they exited the Blue dorm and headed for the back gate. Since it was after curfew, the only people roaming the campus were guards.

As she walked down the path, Bryn said, "I keep waiting for one of the guards to stop us."

"I'm sure they are aware of the situation," Valmont said.

At the back gate, a guard stood next to an SUV. He held a white envelope.

Jaxon marched forward. "Is that for me?"

The guard nodded and placed it in Jaxon's hand. From the envelope, Jaxon retrieved a set of keys and a note. He read it and then passed it to Bryn.

Drive toward Dragon's Bluff and take a right at the sign. Continue until the road dead-ends at a cabin.

"So we're doing this?" Bryn asked.

"The SUV should have everything you need." The guard gestured toward the black vehicle. "There's a special new tracking system so you can't get lost."

Did he mean like a GPS guidance system or something that would let the Directorate keep an eye on where they were going?

Jaxon climbed into the driver's seat while Rhianna rode shotgun.

"I don't like this." Valmont opened the back door for Bryn and then climbed in beside her. The vehicle smelled of hot plastic, like something in the interior had been drilled through or melted.

Valmont sniffed. "Not the new car smell I expected."

"More like new wiring smell," Bryn said. "Hopefully, that's a good thing."

Jaxon started the SUV. Its engine roared to life. He turned on the headlights, checking to see where the high beams were. "I hope we can see the sign the Rebels mentioned."

"What sign do you think they are talking about?" Bryn asked.

"I guess we'll know it when we see it," Rhianna said as Jaxon put the SUV in drive and headed down the road to Dragon's Bluff.

Bryn peered into the darkness as gravel crunched under the SUV's tires. Streetlights would have been helpful. She'd never realized how dark it was outside of campus at night. The scenery out the window was an ever-shifting mass of shadows and trees.

They'd driven for ten minutes when Rhianna shouted, "Stop." She pointed out the passenger side window. "See the sign over there? It says, Ice."

"There's no reason for anyone to be selling ice out here," Valmont said. "Maybe that's the Rebels idea of a joke since you're a Blue."

"It's a stupid joke." Jaxon leaned over and peered out the passenger side window. "This makes no sense. Do they really expect me to drive into the forest?"

"There must be a road," Bryn said. "Turn on your high beams."

Jaxon clicked on the brighter lights, and the faint outline of a well-packed dirt trail appeared. Would the SUV even fit on the path?

"One of the old roads was turned into jogging trail," Valmont said. "And the cabin it leads to was converted to a rest station. I bet that's where they have George."

"Describe the building." Jaxon turned onto the path, which was barely wide enough for the vehicle, and proceeded at a slow pace.

"I think there are restrooms, water fountains, and vending machines, plus a covered picnic area with benches and tables. It's not very big. Most of it's open, so they'll be able to see us coming before we can see them."

"We could get out here and fly in from above," Bryn said.

"I'm sure they've had eyes on us since we left campus. If they see us stop, they might hurt George," Jaxon said. "So we'll keep going."

"Do we have anything resembling a plan?" Bryn asked. "Because letting them call the shots is making me twitchy."

"Here's the plan. All four of us will go into the building. I'll release George from being my knight and then we imprison the Rebels."

Jaxon wasn't thinking clearly. "If you release him from your bond before the Rebels get what they want, they won't need him anymore. They might kill him," Bryn said.

"Fine." Jaxon tapped his fingers on the steering wheel. "Rescuing George is the most important order of business. Once he's safe, we'll capture the Rebels and question them."

Sure. Like it would be that easy.

When the headlights lit up the rest station, Jaxon slowed his speed to a crawl. "Keep your eyes open and follow my lead." He parked and hit the automatic unlock. "I'm leaving the keys in the cup holder in case we're separated and someone else needs to drive."

"I'd rather fly out of here," Bryn told Valmont.

"We'll keep that option open." Valmont climbed out of the car, and she followed him. Rhianna and Jaxon exited the vehicle, too.

"We're here," Jaxon called out. "Where's my knight?"

"Come inside," a male voice answered. "We prefer to do our business indoors."

Jaxon stalked toward the open doorway, which lead into the facility. Rhianna, Bryn, and Valmont followed. The light from the vending machines lining the right hand wall created an eerie multicolored glow that didn't quite reach into the depths of the cabin, which appeared to be one big room.

"Over here," a male voice said.

A bright light came on. Black dots danced in front of Bryn's eyes as she adjusted to the glow of the camping lantern set on a bench against the left-hand wall. When she could see clearly, she didn't like what she saw. George's hands were bound, and there was dried blood on his right temple and a goose egg like someone had hit him, hard.

"Are you all right?" Jaxon asked, completely ignoring the two Rebels who stood on either side of his knight. One had the golden tan skin of a Blue with the dark hair of a Black dragon. The other larger man had the dark skin of a Green dragon with the auburn hair of a Red. Both were dressed in jeans and plain T-shirts. If they hid their eyes with colored contacts or wore sunglasses and a hat, neither of them would have drawn attention in a crowd, which was kind of scary. Not knowing who the enemy was when they were in plain sight was disturbing.

"I'm angry as hell." George shrugged away from the men. "Other than that, I'm fine."

"You were supposed to come alone." The Red-Green dragon put his hand on George's shoulder and dragged him back a step.

"I didn't like those odds." Jaxon moved to stand in front of the men and held his hands up. "As you can see, I came unarmed."

"We didn't." The Blue-Black dragon pulled a knife from his belt and held it to George's throat. "Do as you're told and you and your friends might walk out of here alive."

Jaxon took a step closer to the Rebels. "Give me your word no one will be injured, and we'll do what you ask."

"You're in no position to negotiate." The Blue-Black dragon slid the knife on George's throat an inch to the left, creating a cut, which oozed blood.

Jaxon growled. "Fine. We'll do it your way." He lowered his arms slowly, and then lunged forward. Twin swords of ice shot from his hands stabbing both Rebels in the chest.

Both dragons roared in surprise and pain.

Bryn moved closer to add her sword as backup if Jaxon needed her.

"Now. We're going to play this game my way." Jaxon shoved the sword deeper into the Blue-Black dragon's chest. "Drop your knife and release my knight."

The knife clattered to the floor. George ducked low and climbed under Jaxon's swords to get away from the rebels.

"Valmont, since I'm otherwise engaged, would you cut George's bonds?"

"Of course." Using his sword, Valmont cut through the ropes. Angry red marks circled George's wrists. "How's your neck?"

George wiped at his spot where blood still trickled. "It's not deep."

"I only need to keep one of you alive. Who feels like talking?" Jaxon tilted his head and stared into the eyes of the men in front of him—first one and then the other.

"You can go to hell," the Blue-Black dragon roared.

Jaxon jerked upward and to the right on the sword of frozen flames buried in the man's chest, creating a gaping wound, which spouted blood. Then he pulled the sword from the body and watched as the man crumpled to the floor.

Blood poured from his chest in a rhythmic pattern matching his heartbeat. Bile rose in Bryn's throat as the copper scent of blood filled the air. This was so wrong. Why did everything have to end in violence?

"I guess you're the lucky winner," Jaxon said to the other hybrid. "Start talking. You're bleeding on my shoes."

"He was the nicer of the two." George pointed at the remaining hybrid. "He gave me water. I don't think you should kill him."

Frost shot from Jaxon's nostrils. "I won't kill him if he tells me what this was all about."

The Rebel spoke through gritted teeth. "We needed a Blue dragon and a knight."

"Why?"

The hybrid grimaced. "There's a book. It's protected by Blood Magic. Only a Blue can open it." He gasped.

"Where is it?" Jaxon asked.

"Not here," the Rebel said.

"He's lying," George said. "It's in his coat pocket."

"Doesn't matter if you take it," the man said. "You won't stop the revolution."

"Slowly reach into your pocket and retrieve the book." Jaxon twisted his sword. "Don't try anything stupid."

The hybrid grimaced. "Fine." With his right arm, he reached under the sword planted in his chest and into his interior left coat pocket. "If you removed your sword, this would be easier."

"Give me a reason to trust you," Jaxon said, "and I'll remove it."

The hybrid pulled out something that flashed in the light. "Jaxon," Bryn yelled in warning, but it was too late.

The rebel's knife slashed across Jaxon's stomach. Growling in surprise and pain, Jaxon brought his other sword up through the man's rib cage, slicing almost to his heart. Blood gushed.

"Idiot." Jaxon snarled. "You could've traded information for your life."

"Life under Directorate rule as a prisoner?" The man laughed, but it came out as a strange, wet gurgling sound. "That's no life at all." And then he toppled to the floor.

Blood flowed across the floor between the flagstones, creating an eerie checked pattern. Bryn backed up as the ribbon of red came toward her shoes.

Jaxon released his Elemental swords, making them disappear. He stared down at the two bodies on the floor and then he met Bryn's gaze. "I had to do it. They gave me no choice."

He wasn't wrong. "I know." The stain of blood on his shirt grew larger. Crap. How badly was he hurt? "Take your shirt off. Let me heal you."

"It's just a scratch." He grunted as he knelt down and searched through the rebel's pockets. "Here it is." He pulled out a book.

"I'll take that." Rhianna grabbed the book. "Now let Bryn heal you."

"She can heal him in the car," Valmont said looking over his shoulder. "I'll drive. We need to get out of here before the Rebels realize something went wrong."

George squatted down next to the larger hybrid and rifled through his jacket, retrieving the long knife that matched Jaxon's cuff links and then headed for the exit. They all followed.

Shadows danced in the trees, making Bryn's heart jump around in her chest. Would the Rebels ambush them? She picked up her pace. A cloud drifted over the silver white moon, momentarily blocking out the light. Now would be the perfect time to attack.

A twig snapped and Bryn spun around. The cloud passed so it was no longer blocking the moonlight.

"We're here to help." A Red guard stepped out from the shadows.

"No offense," Bryn said, "but you can help by staying right where you are." She didn't know this guard, and trusting a stranger wasn't in the cards right now.

He nodded. "We'll make sure no one follows you."

Which meant he wasn't alone. Maybe that should have made her feel better, but it didn't.

When they reached the SUV, Valmont climbed behind the wheel and George rode shotgun. Bryn and Rhianna sat on either side of Jaxon in the back seat.

As soon as the SUV started moving, Bryn reached for Jaxon's shirt. It was sticky with blood. "We need some light so I can see what we're dealing with."

"George check the glove box for a flashlight," Valmont said.

After rooting around in the compartment, George found a small flashlight and passed it back to them. Rhianna held it above Jaxon's abdomen so Bryn could see the extent of the injury.

Being careful, she peeled back the blood-soaked material. The knife had sliced into Jaxon's stomach right below his navel.

"It can wait until we get back to campus." Jaxon tugged at his shirt. His muscles were tense, like he was trying to hold still. The bouncing of the SUV down the old road had to hurt.

"No," Rhianna said, "it can't."

He knew she could heal him. She'd done it before. What was his problem? And then she realized it was probably more to do with the placement of the wound, because all of a sudden it did seem a little awkward that she'd be sort of groping him in the back seat of an SUV while his girlfriend watched. She clamped down on the urge to giggle. That was a stupid, immature thought. Eventually, she'd be a professional medic who'd heal all sorts of injuries on males and females. Still, this was Jaxon, which made everything a bit more awkward. Maybe she could place her hand on Jaxon's side. That seemed less grope-y.

"This isn't a big deal," she said in what she hoped was a professional voice. Placing her hand above his left hipbone, she focused on gathering her Quintessence as a ball of light in her chest. Then she imagined the light flowing down her arm, through her hand into Jaxon's abdomen. She stared at the cut, imagining the edges of the sliced skin coming back together and stopping the flow of blood. The SUV jerked around, which made the flashlight bounce around, which made it difficult for her to tell if the blood had stopped.

"Rhianna, is that better?" Bryn didn't think Jaxon would appreciate her inspecting his injury any closer than she already had been.

Rhianna used her sleeve to wipe away the blood. "I think it's stopped."

"Thank you." Jaxon's muscles unclenched, and he closed his eyes.

"You're welcome." Now, why did it feel like she was being watched? Maybe because she was. George had twisted around in his seat to see what they were doing. "Your healing magic doesn't work on humans, does it?"

"I don't honestly know," Bryn said. "I can heal cuts on dragons, but I've never tried to help with a goose egg like yours. The medics at the Institute will know what to do."

"I'd be happy with some ibuprofen and a bag of ice," George said. "But that was something to see."

They made it back to the campus gate without any further incidents.

Medics waited inside the fence. As soon as they parked and climbed out, Medic Williams approached Jaxon and lifted his shirt. "Let me check Bryn's work." She examined him with a flashlight and palpated his abdomen.

"How did you know I was injured and Bryn healed me?" he asked.

"Nice work, Bryn. And to answer your question, there are cameras on the interior and exterior of the SUV, as well as microphones. The Directorate and the guards were tracking your every move."

"That should be reassuring, but it's kind of creepy," Bryn said to no one in particular.

A medic held an icepack to George's head and gave him pills and a bottle of water. "I'm afraid this is all I can do for you right now. After you talk to the Directorate, we'll have a car take you to your physician in Dragon's Bluff."

Bryn glanced around at the medics who'd been waiting for them with the campus guards. No Directorate members were present. "Where to now?"

"We'll escort you to your Grandfather's office in the library," a guard said.

"Shouldn't we speak to my father first?" Jaxon said.

"He's in Bryn's grandfather's office because that is where the surveillance equipment is set up," the guard explained.

Bryn almost commented on Jaxon's my-father-is-the-speaker moment, but since he'd recently taken a knife to the gut, she refrained.

Valmont snorted but didn't make a comment. Bryn elbowed him. He rolled his eyes as they fell into step behind Jaxon, George, and Rhianna. "What? Don't bother denying it. You were thinking the same thing."

Ten minutes later, they sat in the aforementioned offices. Ferrin and Bryn's grandfather listened as George explained how he'd been abducted, and then Jaxon filled them in on what had happened at the rest station. The dispassionate, cold tone of Jaxon's voice as he described the hybrids bleeding out gave Bryn chills.

"Using your Elemental swords was quick thinking on your part," Ferrin said. "You represented your Clan well."

"You did a fine job," Bryn's grandfather said. "Although I am not pleased you brought Bryn and Valmont with you."

Jaxon gave a dry laugh. "Have you ever tried to stop Bryn from going somewhere she wanted to go?"

"She's much like her grandmother in that manner."

Funny how Jaxon wasn't admitting he'd asked for her help. Maybe he thought it would make him appear weak in front of his father. Blue males and their egos were so strange.

"I want to know what all this fuss was about. Can we get to the part where Jaxon bleeds on the journal?" Bryn gestured toward the book sitting on the table.

Rather than waiting for his father's approval, Jaxon pulled the book toward him. "George, if you'd do the honors."

George removed the knife from his belt that was etched with frozen flames and placed the tip on the binding of the book. "I don't have my sword, but I'm sure this will work."

Jaxon slid his index finger down the blade. When the blood came into contact with the book, the leather cover popped up a quarter of an inch like an invisible lock had been sprung.

"I think that did it." Jaxon flipped the book open and methodically turned the pages, scanning each one for something that might be important.

Both Ferrin and her grandfather watched him like hawks. Were they judging his ability to make decisions in a crisis or watching for him to prove himself in some manner?

"These are mostly entries about the sales of land." Jaxon flipped pages. "There must be something more. A-ha." Jaxon tapped a page covered in what looked like a treasure map and then turned it toward his father. "I imagine the Rebels wanted these maps that seem to show underground tunnels which run from Dragon's Bluff onto campus. I'm sure the Directorate will want to dispatch guards to investigate if these tunnels are still accessible."

Ferrin stood taller. "That is exactly what I plan to do."

"We'll have a car take George home," said Bryn's grandfather and then he pointed at her. "Why don't you, Valmont, and Rhianna walk him out."

Apparently, they were being dismissed. It's not like she wanted to hang around, and Jaxon would fill her in on anything she missed, but it rankled that she wouldn't hear the information first hand.

"Of course."

"Wait, George," Jaxon said. "I should release you, so this can't happen again."

George narrowed his eyes. "My grandkids need me, so I think you're probably right."

"Then I release you." Jaxon sucked in breath and then shook his head like he was clearing his thoughts.

George's shoulders slumped, and he seemed to shrink

back in his chair. "I'm going to miss that energy. Guess I'll have to drink more coffee."

"Are you both okay?" Bryn asked.

They nodded, but Bryn still found it unsettling.

Chapter Eight

After making sure George had a ride to Dragon's Bluff and Rhianna was home safe, Bryn called Keegan and Ivy to tell them everything was okay. She also told them about Jaxon releasing George from the dragon-knight bond. They could do what they wanted with that information. Then she and Valmont changed into pajamas and collapsed on the couch in her dorm room.

"So, that wasn't what I had planned for this evening." Valmont propped his feet up on the coffee table. "How about you?"

"Nope." There was a voice of doubt tapping away at her subconscious. She scooted closer to Valmont and leaned into him when he put his arm around her shoulders. She swore she could still smell blood. Whether it was psychological, or if she had blood from Jaxon or the Rebels under her fingernails, she didn't know. She'd washed her hands half a dozen times. "Logically, I know those hybrids probably wanted that book so they could sneak onto campus and convert us to their cause or kill us all, but it seems like there should have been a more peaceful solution."

"I'm not sure there was. And in a case of you-versus-them, I'm going to choose you every time. I believe that's what Jaxon was doing. He was protecting Rhianna and George and you the only way he knew how. Not that I need his help protecting you, but it's good to know he doesn't hesitate in a fight."

"Is that where the old saying, 'He who hesitates is lost.' comes from?"

"It definitely applies in this situation. If Jaxon had let one of those hybrids live and they'd been able to open the book and escape with it, then they could have taken over campus any time they wanted."

Logically, she knew that. Snuggling closer she laid her head on his chest and listened to his heartbeat. "I don't understand why everyone can't coexist peacefully."

"History is full of wars separated by stretches of peace. Hopefully, this war will end soon and lead to a time of peace. Until that happens, our best battle strategy is camping out on the couch this evening so neither of us has to be alone. Safety in numbers and all that." He kissed her on the cheek.

She turned her face so her lips lined up with his. "Who am I to argue with such a tried and true battle strategy?"

"Smart girlfriend." He pulled her closer and kissed her. Without breaking contact, he leaned backward taking her with him so they were lying down on the couch. For a moment, it felt like they were going to roll off onto the floor, but Valmont grabbed the arm of the couch and they didn't fall.

Bryn laughed. "Was that maneuver from the *How to be a Smooth Boyfriend Manual*? Cause I think it needs a little work."

"I guess we'll just have to practice."

"If we must." She threaded her fingers through the hair at the nape of his neck and pulled him into a kiss. She had a stray thought that they'd be less likely to roll out of her bed, since it was wider. Valmont kissed her neck, heat thrummed between them, and all rational thought disappeared.

• • •

At breakfast the next morning, Bryn and Valmont joined Ivy and Clint at their usual table in the dining hall.

"Is it true?" Clint asked before Bryn finished stirring sugar into her coffee.

She pointed at her cup. "Did you forget the no-talking-before-caffeine rule?"

"Then drink up," Clint said, "because I have questions."

Bryn sucked down half a cup of coffee and waited for the caffeine to reach life-supporting levels. "Okay. My brain is now engaged. Ask."

Clint leaned in. "Rumor has it Jaxon killed two rebels last night."

What the hell? Bryn hadn't shared that information with them when she'd called the night before because she didn't want to publicize the gory details, but she wasn't going to lie about it. "Unfortunately, that's true. I can't believe you heard about it already."

"That kind of information is hard to keep quiet. Jaxon probably told someone in his clan, and the information spread from there."

Ivy nodded toward where Jaxon sat. He wore a scowl worthy of his father as he ate his breakfast and ignored everyone around him. "I don't think Jaxon is the one who shared."

"Maybe you're right," Clint said.

"I bet his father bragged about it," Valmont said.

That sounded like something Ferrin would do. "I hope they're going to get him some counseling. It may have been the only option to keep us and everyone else safe, but that doesn't mean it won't mess with his head."

"And he's already screwed up enough," Valmont said.

Not that Valmont was wrong, but the desire to defend Jaxon reared up inside of Bryn. She drowned it out by drinking the rest of her coffee.

"There's another ridiculous rumor going around," Clint said.

Ivy whacked him. "Don't."

"But it's funny." Clint gave Bryn puppy-dog eyes.

"I know I'm going to regret this," Bryn said, "but go ahead and ask."

"Were you at any time in the back seat of a car with Jaxon and Rhianna?" He wiggled his eyebrows like she'd been involved in some weird tryst.

"For the love of… Where do you hear these things?" Bryn felt her face color.

Valmont set his coffee down. "The fact that you're blushing disturbs me."

"I'm blushing because idiots talk about things when they don't have all the facts. Jaxon was injured. I healed him. Rhianna held a light so I could see. End of story."

"And yet you're still blushing," Valmont tapped his fingers on the table.

She leaned toward Valmont. "If Rhianna had driven and you'd been the one back there holding the flashlight so I could heal Jaxon and people made stupid comments about that situation, how would you feel?"

Valmont flinched. "Point taken."

In Elemental science, Mr. Stanton rearranged the seating chart again. Bryn sat in a small group with Keegan, Ivy, and Garret.

"Just so you know," Ivy said. "I called Mary and released her. I didn't want to be the reason she was hurt."

Keegan nodded. "I did the same."

Bryn glanced at Valmont. "There seems to be a trend. Should I conform to peer pressure?"

"Nope." He poked her in the ribs. "You're stuck with me."

"Class, today, we are going to work on using your breath weapons to solve puzzles." Mr. Stanton passed out several books with old cracked bindings.

"Is it me, or does this look oddly familiar?" Valmont whispered.

The books did resemble the book Jaxon and George had opened the night before using Blood Magic. "Since you're the only knight in the room, I'm guessing I don't need to bleed on these."

Keegan backed his chair up a bit and then grinned at Bryn. "Just giving myself a little room in case you make something explode."

Garret scooted his desk back a bit. "He's not wrong. You do have a track record."

Bryn pointed at Ivy. "Want to give yourself room to duck and cover in case my life continues down its normal insane path?"

Ivy squinted like she was giving the idea serious consideration. "I'm good. Being your friend means I'm exposed to more chaos than usual, so I probably have faster instincts."

Bryn rolled her eyes. "You should ask Mr. Stanton for extra credit when you have to work with me." She opened the book they'd been assigned. Inside the cracked, faded red leather cover there was a title written in what appeared to be real ink. "It's blurry, but I think it says, Maps of the Forest."

Garret scooted closer so his desk was next to Bryn's. He flipped a few pages. "I'm not sure what we're looking for."

"Maps?" Keegan said like he was being helpful.

Garret snorted. "That part I understand, but maps of what? And don't even think about saying the forest."

"How are our breath weapons supposed to help us with this?" Ivy asked.

Garret turned another page, and then he pointed at something. "Look…there…and there." He tapped several places on the pages as he turned them. "Some of them have symbols of the elements in random places. This one has the symbol for wind. Let's see what happens." He exhaled a small twister of air onto his palm and then directed it onto the page so it touched down on the wind symbol. That portion of the map shimmered, and some of the lines darkened and shifted.

"What does that mean?" Bryn asked.

"I don't know," Garret said. "Use a pencil to trace the new lines while I maintain my twister."

She grabbed a pencil from her book bag and lightly shaded in the new lines. When Garret let his wind dissipate, they stared at the map.

"Is that a hidden road or a tunnel?" Ivy asked.

Keegan traced his finger along the original road. "It follows almost the same path as the first road, but it connects to a different road. Maybe it's a shortcut."

"Why would someone want to hide a shortcut?" Ivy asked. "If a dragon was flying, he could travel whatever path he wanted."

"Maybe it's a tunnel or something you can't see from above," Garret said.

Mr. Stanton stopped by their group. Garret explained what they'd done so far.

"I agree. It must be a tunnel or secret passage of some sort." Mr. Stanton picked up the book and studied the map more closely. "This may be one piece of a puzzle. Check out the other pages and see what you can discover."

By the end of class they'd used all of their Elements except fire to discover secret drawings added to the maps. Most of them appeared to connect existing roads, which didn't make a lot of sense.

"Why would someone add secret passages to all of these maps?" Bryn flipped through the pages. "Why not create one map showing all the secret routes?"

"Maybe we're looking at it backward," Valmont said. "Maybe the hidden parts are the original maps, and the other bits were added afterward to cover the information up."

Garret clapped Valmont on the shoulder. "That's brilliant. It's far more likely someone in the Directorate wanted information covered up rather than some Rebel going in afterward and adding new information."

"I won't argue with the brilliant part," Bryn said, "but why do you think one is more likely than the other?"

"The Directorate likes to preserve as much of our history as possible. They may alter the facts, but they like to keep things intact. Rebels have to move quickly and act without detection. Adding all these bits and pieces of magic to a book would take multiple dragons, adept in magic, weeks to complete. Rebels would probably have one map of secret places because that would be far more efficient."

"Now what?" Keegan asked. "Can we do something to remove the Directorate spells so we can see the whole book how it was meant to be?"

"We can't," Bryn said, "because that would probably break some sort of law, but Mr. Stanton could ask someone on the Directorate to do it." Bryn raised her hand. When Mr. Stanton came to check on them, he listened to Garret explain their theory.

"Well done. I believe your logic is sound. When you're done, I'll turn this book over to Miss Enid and see if she can attain the necessary permission to begin restoring the book to its original state or, at the very least, be allowed to copy the pages as they should be so we can compare the two."

"What made you decide we should look at these old books?" Keegan asked.

Mt. Stanton frowned. "It has come to the Directorate's attention that certain things have been concealed within the Institute. We are investigating anything from the era before the Directorate. We're asking students to help because you can examine these items with fresh eyes. Most adults see things as they always have been, and it's hard for us to look past what we expect to find."

"There's something profound about that statement," Ivy said.

"One question," Keegan said. "How am I supposed to apply fire to a flammable book without destroying it?"

"Interesting question," Mr. Stanton said. "Let me know when you've figured out the answer." And then he walked over to another group.

Something about this didn't feel right. "They can't be randomly picking books from a giant library for us to test," Bryn said. "Which makes me think there is something they aren't telling us."

"Maybe they're picking books by certain authors or publishers," Keegan said. "Or whatever they called the people who created these books way back when."

And then a lightbulb went off in Bryn's head. "I bet these are books from the vaults of the library."

"That would make perfect sense." Garret closed the book and turned it to look at the spine. "By the cracking of the leather, I'd bet this book is more than a hundred years old."

"Knowing where it comes from doesn't help us decode it," Keegan said. "Garret, turn to one of the pages with the symbol of fire. I want to try holding a fireball above the book."

"If it starts smoldering, extinguish your flame," Garret

said.

"I don't have to be a Green to figure that out." Keegan produced a fireball in his hand and held it a foot above the page. Nothing happened. He lowered the fireball in small increments until it was four inches from the paper. Parts of the map shimmered and most of the roads disappeared.

Bryn shaded in the remaining roads, and then Keegan extinguished his fireball.

Valmont pulled the book toward him. "I know that road. It runs in front of my cabin."

"Maybe a field trip is in order," Garret said.

"A Directorate-sanctioned field trip?" Bryn asked. "Or a sneak-out-and-hope-we-don't-get-caught field trip?"

"I'll speak to Mr. Stanton about it after class," Garret said.

Ivy opened her notebook. "And I'm going to make a copy of this map in case we need it."

After dinner, Clint and Ivy met Bryn and Valmont in her dorm room. They all sat at the library table in her living room and looked at the map Ivy had copied.

Valmont pointed to the road that branched off the main throughway and twisted through the forest. "This road leads back to my cabin."

"What else is back there?" Clint asked.

"Like I told Bryn before, there are cabins scattered throughout the forest. Long ago, the Directorate used them to house knights who protected those areas. This was pre-phone, so there are literally dozens of cabins or watch stations. In modern times, the Directorate allows citizens of Dragon's Bluff to buy the cabins for a nominal fee, as long as the new residents promise to keep up the structures."

Ivy traced the road with her finger. "If this represents the modern-day road, then what is this?" She pointed to a line that connected Valmont's cabin to another point in the woods.

"Maybe it's a foot path to another cabin," Valmont said.

"So you didn't notice any secret tunnels or underground lairs when you were renovating?" Bryn asked.

"I'm pretty sure I would have picked up on that."

"Who lived there before you?" Ivy asked.

"The cabin was empty for years before I renovated it, because the previous resident didn't update the air and heat. He relied on a fireplace for heat and opening the windows for air circulation."

"That so wouldn't work for me," Bryn said. "What kind of shape was it in when you started renovating?" Bryn asked. "Did you have to evict squirrels and fight through layers of dirt?"

"No. The Directorate pays a housecleaning service to keep the cabins functional. I think they drop by once a month to clean and make sure no creatures have taken up residence."

"If that's true," Clint said, "then the cleaning service must have a map of where all these cabins are located. Maybe we could compare their map to the hidden roads in the books."

"It only makes sense that the cabins would be connected in some manner," Bryn said. "Before there were phones, one guard would need to warn a guard farther down the road that trouble was coming."

"If that were true, then the Directorate would know the tunnels existed," Ivy said.

Valmont leaned back in his chair, like he was pondering something. "There was a root cellar behind the house. I didn't touch it. Growing up in a family that owns a restaurant, I couldn't see storing my food in what amounted to a hole in the ground."

"I bet that's it." Bryn stood and went to the phone. "I'm going to call Garret and see if he had time to talk to Mr.

Stanton about all of this."

"Or," Clint said, "Valmont could choose to go pick up a few items from his cabin. We, being the wonderful friends we are, could decide to accompany him so he wouldn't be lonely."

"I am rather sensitive," Valmont spoke in a mock-serious tone.

Bryn frowned as she considered her options. "Honestly, before I saw two people bleed out at my feet I wouldn't have hesitated to hop in Valmont's car to go on an adventure, but now…"

Clint sighed. "Fine. Be mature. Call Garret. Then maybe we can set up an officially sanctioned trip, but that does take some of the fun out of it."

Bryn made the call. Garret didn't answer. "That's weird. Maybe he's studying in a friend's room." Who else could she call?

"Try Mr. Stanton's office," Clint suggested.

Bryn dialed and was relieved when Mr. Stanton picked up on the first ring. She explained their theory about the cabins being connected and about Valmont's root cellar.

"I'll speak to Miss Enid. She'll know how to find a map with the information we need. I'm sure the Directorate would be aware of any official tunnels between the cabins, but there could be some they don't know about. Tomorrow before dinner, we'll take a trip out to Valmont's. Don't tell anyone about this."

"Did I mention Clint and Ivy are here right now and they'll want to come with us?"

"I am not surprised," Mr. Stanton said. "Fine. We should all fit in one of the Directorate's SUVs."

The next morning in Elemental Science, Bryn could barely keep from questioning Mr. Stanton about the map of the cabins, and what he thought they might find. But he seemed content to stick to his lesson plans where he had the students grouped the same as the day before, combing through old books. The book her group had been assigned today didn't have any markings that represented the Elements or anything else about it that signaled magic had ever been used to alter it.

"This book is boring," Ivy complained.

"Agreed." Keegan picked it up and flipped it open to the middle page before turning it face down so they could see the front and back cover and the spine. "The most interesting thing about it is the cover."

The green leather was stamped with golden ink, letting everyone know it was a book about the medicinal use of plants.

"It's a pretty straightforward book," Garret said. "We still use plants to make some of these medicines. Some of them are fused with Quintessence to increase their healing properties. That's not a secret."

"I guess every book can't have a secret treasure hidden inside," Bryn said. "Although it would be cool if it did."

By the end of the school day, Bryn was bursting with curiosity about the unknown root cellar at Valmont's cabin. She and Valmont, along with Clint and Ivy, headed to the faculty parking lot. Miss Enid waited for them alongside Mr. Stanton, who leaned against a large black SUV. Large didn't even cover it. It was more like a trailer. There were two rows of back seats and a huge storage area, which held a green duffel bag, and something underneath a tarp.

"We could go camping in that thing," Valmont commented.

Bryn pointed at the storage area and its hidden contents. "Are we stocking up on provisions, in case we need to excavate a tunnel?"

"No," Miss Enid said. "We are taking supplies, in case we run into anything interesting. Better safe than sorry. Let's get in, and I'll show you what I've found."

Which meant she didn't want to talk out in the open where

anyone walking by could hear. Whatever she was about to say seemed far more interesting.

Once they were all seated inside the car, Miss Enid put on a pair of white cotton gloves and then unrolled a parchment, brown with age. "This map shows all the locations where cabins were built." She pointed at an outer ring of cabins. "Valmont, I believe this represents your home. As you can see, on this map, there are no tunnels connecting the structures." She rolled the parchment back up and stuck it in a protective case. Then she opened a large manila envelope and pulled out a modern map. "This schematic shows all the Directorate-sanctioned cabins still standing. There are tunnels under some of them. Valmont's cabin," she tapped the area on the map where his home was located, "isn't listed as having a tunnel, but it may have been added later, or the marking you discovered on your map could delineate a footpath or a shortcut."

"Which are you hoping for?" Bryn asked.

Miss Enid grinned like she was going on a grand adventure. "I'd prefer a tunnel because there's the possibility of finding an archive of information."

"Everyone buckle up." Mr. Stanton started the SUV and drove toward the back gate. After the guards verified their identities, they were allowed to exit the campus. They drove down the main road, which lead to Dragon's Bluff—the same road they'd driven to rescue George.

"Amazing how peaceful this drive seems compared to the one we took the other night," Bryn said.

"I guess your destination can change the mood of the journey." Valmont paused and then he grinned. "Maybe I should start writing poetry."

Bryn laughed. "Maybe."

They took the turn-off that led up into the forest. Light filtered through the greenery, giving it a magical appearance.

"It's beautiful here," Ivy said.

"It is." Valmont's tone sounded wistful, like he missed living out here, which, of course, he probably did. "There's something about living among the trees that's so peaceful."

"Until rebels emerge from your root cellar and take over your house," Clint said.

Valmont snorted but didn't comment.

When they pulled into his driveway and got closer to the cabin, the lights in the living room came on.

"Is someone housesitting for you?" Clint asked.

"No. There's a motion detector in the driveway, so I never have to walk into a dark house."

Clint grabbed Ivy's hand. "Great idea. When we're married, we're going to have one of those installed in our driveway."

"It is a cool idea," Ivy agreed.

Clint and Ivy were so perfect together. Their parents were best friends and had petitioned for their children to be married. Clint had worked to win Ivy over, but in the end, it had all come together. Bryn envied the simplicity of their life and the happily ever after, which was their future. Her own future, featuring a nightmare of a marriage to Jaxon, probably wouldn't hold as much happiness.

Valmont leaned in close and whispered, "Why are you scowling?"

"Just contemplating the odds of finding anything good hiding in your root cellar," she lied, because it was easier than discussing the truth. And it wasn't like talking about it would change anything.

Mr. Stanton put the SUV in park and turned off the ignition. "Let the adventure begin."

"The root cellar is around back." Valmont climbed out of the vehicle and led them around the side of the house. The cabin had been a part of the forest for so long it seemed to have grown up from the surroundings. The wood was pale with age, and vines climbing up the side seemed to be one with the structure.

They kept walking until they reached what appeared to be a large patch of dirt about a dozen feet behind Valmont's back door.

"This is anti-climactic," Clint said.

"Did we bring shovels?" Bryn asked.

"Let's try a little wind first," Mr. Stanton said. He breathed a twister onto his hand and then let it grow until it was about a foot tall. He directed it to the center of the dirt patch and then moved it back and forth. Where the twister touched down, the dirt was sucked up into the funnel. The funnel grew in size and darkened as it ate more dirt. After five minutes, Mr. Stanton directed the twister out beyond the tree line and then let it dissipate, releasing the dirt in a circular spray.

"I bet that startled some birds," Valmont said.

Bryn pointed at the faint outline of a square made up of planks embedded in the ground. "Is that the door?"

"Where's the handle?" Clint squatted down and knocked on the exposed wood. It made a metallic ringing sound. That wasn't right.

"Knock again," Bryn said.

Clint repeated the action, and once again it gave off the sound like he was knocking on metal.

Weird. "Why would the door be made of metal but disguised to look like wood?" Didn't most root cellars have doors made of wood? Her experience with root cellars stemmed from old television shows. Who knew how accurate those were?

"Most doors would have been made of wood given the materials available to the home owners at the time," Miss Enid said. "Metal would have been reserved for swords and tools."

Valmont knelt down and knocked on the disguised metal

door. "Definitely not wood." He stood and turned for the house. "Let me see if I can find something to use as a crow bar to pry this thing open."

"Not necessary," Miss Enid said. "I have one in the SUV."

"In case you needed to pry open a treasure chest of books?" Ivy asked.

"Exactly." Miss Enid retrieved the crowbar and then ran it along the edges of the door, making the outline more distinct. "Better to clear more of the debris away. I'd hate to miss a latch because it was hidden by dirt and leaves."

When no latch appeared, Miss Enid worked the crowbar into the seam created by the edge of the metal. "On to option two." She put all her weight behind the crow bar. Miss Enid was as strong as any dragon, but the door didn't budge.

"There must be some sort of locking mechanism." Mr. Stanton paced around the door looking at it from different angles.

"Good thing you didn't want to use it," Bryn told Valmont.

He rubbed his chin. "When I bought the place, the bill of sale mentioned the root cellar, but I never bothered to investigate it. If it's locked, maybe there's a way to release it from inside the cabin."

"Like an automatic garage door opener?" Clint asked sounding skeptical.

"Something like that." Valmont strode toward the back door and opened it with his key. "You're welcome to come inside. My grandfather has been taking care of the place for me, so it shouldn't be too dusty."

How long had it been since Valmont had stayed in his own house? Four months? That old guilty feeling rolled over Bryn. No matter how much he claimed he didn't mind putting his entire life on hold to be her bodyguard, she didn't one hundred percent believe him.

Chapter Nine

Not much had changed since she'd last visited his house. The back door led into a small kitchen with a table and chairs he'd "borrowed" from Fonzoli's. The front living room held a couch and a coffee table. The one small hallway led toward a minuscule bathroom and a single bedroom.

"As you can see," Valmont gestured from the open concept kitchen to the living room, "there aren't a lot of places for a builder to hide a switch or a key. Feel free to poke around. Help yourself to a glass of water if you want one. I'm not sure what else there is to drink at the moment." He walked over to the refrigerator, opened the door, and laughed. "My grandfather has stocked up on ginger ale."

"It's a universal truth that all grandparents drink ginger ale," Clint said.

Bryn wasn't so sure that applied to Blues. Maybe their refrigerators were always stocked with fine wine.

"Where is the electrical box?" Mr. Stanton asked.

"In the hall closet." Valmont waved his hand indicating they should follow.

Mr. Stanton and Bryn were the only takers. Maybe because everyone realized there wouldn't be much room to investigate. Across from the bathroom there was a set of wooden louver doors, which ran on a track. Valmont opened the doors and pulled the string for the bare light bulb, which hung from the ceiling. An apartment-size heating system and a tankless water heater took up most of the space with the breaker box squeezed between them on the back wall.

"Was this closet original to the house?" Mr. Stanton asked.

"Yes. I widened it and took out the shelf that used to be here in order to update the water and heat."

"Did the house come with any mystery switches?" Bryn asked.

Valmont's eyebrows came together. "I don't understand the question."

"Our apartment had a mystery switch in the hallway that did nothing. Either it wasn't connected to anything or the connection had been broken accidentally, or on purpose, when the previous owner remodeled." The memory of her dad flipping the switch and making up stories about what it did, like letting Santa know she was about to go to sleep so it was okay to bring in her presents, or signaling the tooth fairy that she needed to come collect the tooth from underneath Bryn's pillow that night, made Bryn smile even though her eyes filled with tears. She blinked rapidly and sniffled.

Valmont took one look at her face and wrapped his arms around her. "Memory ambush?"

She nodded and focused on not crying. His warm sunshine-and-leather scent helped calm her. After a few deep breaths, she was okay. "Thanks." She stepped away from him.

Mr. Stanton was in the closet peering into the electrical box. "Mind if I play with the breakers?" he asked.

"Just don't knock out the power all together. I'm sure my

grandfather has the freezer loaded with lasagna."

"We'll try one at a time. Why don't you two go look out the back door and holler if the root cellar opens?"

"Okay." Valmont grabbed Bryn's hand, and they headed back into the living room where Clint, Ivy, and Miss Enid sat on the couch.

"We investigated all the cabinets and under the sink," Miss Enid said. "But we didn't find anything."

Bryn filled them in about Mr. Stanton playing with the breakers, and then she went to watch out the kitchen window. Valmont came up behind her and wrapped his arms around her waist. Pulling her back against his chest he said, "Sometimes I think about us running away from the Institute to come and live here at my cabin. We could be a normal couple, doing normal things, living a normal life."

"I'd love that." And she really would. It would be her fantasy life. "But I'm afraid normal isn't in my future."

"Maybe we could sneak away for a weekend," Valmont said.

"Maybe." She doubted it. But rather that burst his bubble, she kept watch out the window.

Nothing much happened except for random squirrels scurrying across the lawn. One squirrel darted onto the closed door of the root cellar, and in the exact center of the door, it started to dig.

"What's that squirrel doing?" Valmont asked.

"Maybe he's confused." Dirt flew from the spot where the squirrel dug. He unearthed an acorn and then scurried off with his prize.

"Either that's a Wolverine-type squirrel who can slash through metal, or there must be a recessed handle we didn't notice." Valmont headed out the door. Bryn followed. They both examined the door, which appeared as flat and smooth as it had before.

"Where did he find the acorn?" Bryn walked around the door. It appeared to be solid and flat.

Valmont got down on his hands and knees and felt his way across the surface. In the center, he stopped moving his right arm mid-swipe. "I can feel a depression here, even though we can't see it. It must be concealed by magic, like the maps in the books."

"Is it a handle?" Bryn asked.

"No. It feels more like a small metal steering wheel." His brow wrinkled in confusion. "I bet it's like one of those hatch doors on a submarine where you have to turn the metal wheel to open the hatch."

"Maybe you shouldn't have all your weight on the door while you're messing around with the handle," Bryn said. "Just a thought."

"Afraid I'll fall into a deep dark tunnel and never be heard from again?" Valmont asked.

"Yes. Let me try fire and ice on the door to see if the handle will reveal itself so we can see what we're doing, instead of going in blind."

Mr. Stanton came out the back door. "I'm guessing nothing I did with the electrical box had any influence. Did you discover something?"

"A squirrel dug an acorn out of the middle of the door." Bryn pointed at where Valmont had his hand.

"I can feel a depression and a way to open the hatch even though I can't see it." Valmont stood and wiped his hands off on his jeans. "Maybe one of Bryn's breath weapons will reveal what's really there."

"The same way it worked with the books?" Mr. Stanton nodded. "It's worth a try."

Once Valmont was out of the way, Bryn let the heat build in her chest and then huffed out a small fireball, which landed on the metal door and faded away. Nothing changed. Time to try ice. She inhaled and thought about cold and snow and winter, and then she exhaled sleet onto the door. Nothing happened.

"Clint or Ivy, it's your turn," Bryn called out.

Her friends and Miss Enid came out the back door. "Our turn for what?" Ivy asked.

"Zap the door to see if it reveals a handle, because right now we can feel it but we can't see it."

"I've got this." Clint held his hand palm out and sent a blast of lightning at the door. The entire door crackled like it was absorbing the electrical charge. When the glow faded, hinges were visible on one side and there was a recessed circular handle in the middle of what now looked like a hatch for a submarine, if submarine hatches were square.

"I win." Clint moved closer to the door and knelt down. "Does that mean I get first crack at opening it? It could be a giant safe full of abandoned treasure."

Mr. Stanton chuckled. "I'm not sure what we'll find. You should all take a few steps back, and I'll open it."

"It was meant for a Black dragon," Miss Enid said. "I think you should let Clint open it. Not that I think it's rigged with poisonous darts like the cases in the vaults, but it doesn't hurt to be cautious."

"I have no valid argument against your logic," Mr. Stanton said. "Clint, go ahead, but be careful."

Clint cracked his knuckles and squatted down by the door on the side with the hinges. He grasped the wheel handle and turned it to the right. It didn't budge.

Valmont cleared his throat. "I think righty tighty, lefty loosey is the standard."

"Forgot about that." Clint grasped the wheel again and turned left. It gave slowly, metal screeching against metal like it hadn't been moved in years. After turning the wheel one full revolution, something clicked and the hatch popped up half an inch. Clint tugged on the handle, pulling it open like a trap door.

Unconsciously, Bryn and the others moved closer to the opening.

And then the stench hit them. It was like nothing Bryn had ever experienced before. A rotten foulness, like spoiled meat that had been left to putrefy in the hot sun. The foulness crawled up Bryn's nasal passages and down her throat. Gagging, she doubled over, clasping her hand over her mouth to keep from vomiting. Dry heaving, Valmont grabbed Bryn around the waist and dragged her backward toward the house smacking his hand over his own nose and mouth.

Ivy turned away and vomited. Clint stumbled over to her, gasping for air. He shifted, grabbed her in his right talon, and launched himself straight up into the sky. When Ivy stopped retching, she shifted and glided down near the far side of the house.

Miss Enid used her wind to blow the smell away from them out into the forest. Once he stopped dry heaving, Mr. Stanton created a twister and directed it at the metal door, sliding it underneath and lifting it up until it slammed shut.

Clint and Ivy shifted back. He wrapped his arms around his girlfriend. "Worst treasure hunt, ever," he shouted.

Bryn laughed and then gagged. The foul smell was still in her nasal passages. She closed her eyes and focused on heat, igniting the fire inside of her. The welcome taste of smoke crawled up the back of her throat, neutralizing the vile smell. She exhaled smoke from her nostrils to kill off any lingering stench.

Valmont leaned in and inhaled the smoke. He must have understood what she was doing.

Once she felt better, Bryn let the fire die down and made eye contact with Valmont.

He looked stricken. "Something terrible happened down

there. It happened on my land. Behind my house."

"From the smell, whatever is down there is beyond our help." Mr. Stanton approached them. "We don't have the proper equipment to investigate. I'm going to make a few calls to see who can help us."

"Whatever happened down there wasn't your fault," Bryn said. "If your root cellar is part of a series of tunnels, they could have opened the door from the inside. There wasn't much dirt on top of it...not more than an inch. Or, they could have turned back around the way they came."

Without discussing it, they all went inside and sat at the table or on the couch. Miss Enid came in last. She went to the refrigerator and grabbed cans of ginger ale, passing them out to everyone.

Bryn sipped her drink. Valmont turned his can around and around on the table, like he was trying to figure something out. Even if he'd been here, rather than guarding her at the Institute, there was no way he would have known what was going on under his backyard. Saying that to him wouldn't make the situation better. Maybe they could talk about it later.

Mr. Stanton spoke to someone on Valmont's house phone. When he was finished, he hung up. "I've alerted the Directorate, and they are sending people who are trained to deal with...this type of situation."

There were people who investigated rotting bodies for a living? That would be one horrifically sucky job. Thank goodness someone could do it. She'd barely managed to keep from throwing up. Speaking of throwing up. "Ivy, are you okay?" Bryn asked.

"Yes." Ivy's voice sounded rough. "That smell, it just hit me...I...I'm not sure I want to know what's down there."

Clint put his arm around her shoulders. "I want to know why Black dragon magic was used to keep someone from finding the handle to the door."

Valmont stood and walked over to the kitchen sink, looking out the window above it. "Is there some way to determine when the spell to hide the handle was placed on the hatch?"

"I don't believe so," Miss Enid said.

Fifteen minutes later, the sound of a car pulling up the gravel drive had them all on their feet. Someone knocked on the front door. *Strange*. Why would the Directorate knock? They normally barged in and did what they wanted.

Valmont answered the door. A Red guard Bryn didn't recognize held a clipboard out to Valmont.

"You are the registered owner of this parcel of land. I'll need your signature before I can proceed."

Valmont accepted the pen and studied it like he wasn't sure what he was supposed to do with it. "What am I signing?"

"This gives the Directorate permission to investigate any and all leads necessary on your property."

Should he argue? Bryn didn't want the Directorate bulldozing Valmont's cabin for no good reason. And Ferrin was just the type of vindictive asshat who might do something like that.

"Whatever it takes." Valmont scribbled his name on the document.

"You can leave and go to another location or you can stay inside the cabin," the Red said. "You may not enter the backyard while we're working. Does everyone understand?"

They all nodded. Bryn nodded, too. It wasn't like she wanted to go near the hatch again, but why couldn't she go out there if she wanted to?

"Then we'll get to work." The Red headed back to his car.

Valmont closed the door.

"Do they not want us to see what they find?" Bryn asked.

"I'm quite sure you won't want to see what they find, but

given the level of decomposition, there may be biohazards," Mr. Stanton said. "That's why they're being so strict."

That answered her question. Morbid curiosity drove her to watch out the back window as men in hazmat suits opened the hatch, set up a pulley system, and descended into the root-cellar-from-hell.

Bryn couldn't stop formulating theories about what grisly remains the men in might find. Maybe an animal had wandered into one of the tunnels and been unable to find its way out. That thought was horrifying enough, much less the idea of dragons or humans being trapped, underground, unable to escape.

Approaching footsteps sounded. Bryn glanced over her shoulder, knowing who it would probably be. *Yep.* Valmont approached and stood behind her. He put his arm around her waist and pulled her back a bit so she leaned against him. "See anything yet?"

"No. They haven't come back up."

"I keep trying to come up with a best-case scenario for this situation," he said, "and I've got nothing."

A man in a hazmat suit lowered what looked like several long coffin-shaped white Styrofoam coolers down to the other men below ground. "They must have found something," Bryn said.

Valmont's arm tightened around her waist when the containers came back up. "I don't want to see what's in those boxes," he said. "But I need to know what or who it was."

Anything decomposed enough to create that horrific gut-twisting smell would be horrible to witness, but she also needed to know what they were dealing with. A tank with a sprayer hose was lowered through the open hatch. "Maybe they're cleaning up the tunnel so they can investigate." Or erase any trace of whatever had happened so they could create their own story. That seemed more the Directorate's style.

"Once it's cleaned out and safe, I want to go down there," Valmont said.

There probably wasn't a snowball's chance in hell they'd be allowed to explore, but Bryn didn't mention that because it wouldn't do any good to dash Valmont's hopes. He seemed to feel responsible since this happened in his backyard.

After the men climbed out of the hatch and started packing their equipment, one of them took off his hazmat suit and came to the back door. He had the dark complexion of a Green dragon. Before he could knock, Valmont whipped the door open. "What happened down there?"

The man's mouth set in a thin line. "It appears a family was hiding out, using the dead-end of the tunnel as their home. They had real beds and a crib."

Holy hell. "There was a baby?" That made everything seem much more tragic. Flames roared in Bryn's gut. Smoke drifted from her nostrils. She concentrated and pushed the flames back down. She needed to focus on being here for Valmont right now, not indulging in her own freak-out.

The man nodded and swallowed before he continued speaking, like he was trying to keep his emotions in check. "I think they'd lived there for months. They had food and toys. They must've been attacked during the night. The bodies... they were still in their beds—like they never heard their attacker coming."

"Dying in their sleep is probably the best case scenario for this God-awful situation," Bryn said.

"Could they have escaped...gotten out...if they had wanted to?" Valmont asked. "Through the hatch?"

"I don't know. There is a well-worn path leading away from their beds, which makes me believe they often traveled through the tunnels and exited in another location."

"Can we investigate and see where the tunnels go?"

Valmont asked.

"The Directorate will have to answer that question. For now, we will close and seal the hatch so the curious don't get into trouble." The man made direct eye contact with Bryn like she was plotting to race down there the second he turned his back.

"Don't worry about me. Nothing puts a damper on curiosity like finding dead bodies." One question bounced around in Bryn's brain. "The family...could you tell which Clan they were from?"

"Based on the remnants of a tattoo visible on the man's arms, I suspect they were hybrids, but we'll know more after we conduct an autopsy. If you'll excuse me, I have work to do."

Bryn shut the door and reached for Valmont's hand. "Do you feel better now, knowing those people, whoever they were, weren't trapped and they didn't suffer?"

Valmont stared at the door like he was trying to decipher something she couldn't see. The moment of silence stretched out until it became uncomfortable. She'd meant to comfort him. Had she done the opposite and made the situation worse? Now what? He seemed lost in his own world, so she let him be, waiting for him to come back to her.

He cleared his throat. "Actually, the only thing that would make me feel better is if they weren't dead."

"Agreed," she said. "And yet, the casualties seem to be piling up." She squeezed his hand to offer moral support. "This did not turn out to be the fun adventure any of us hoped for."

Mr. Stanton walked over to stand beside Valmont. "I think we should head back to the Institute."

Valmont's eyebrows came together, like he was mulling something over. "This will sound strange, but I don't want to remember my cabin as a place that smells of death. There should be lasagna in the freezer. Maybe we could all stay here for dinner and talk about happier topics, just to wipe the emotional slate clean."

As if on cue, Bryn's stomach growled. "Works for me."

"I'm sorry, but I'm certain the Directorate wouldn't approve. We need to return to school before dark," Mr. Stanton said, "but you could bring lasagna back with us."

Valmont's shoulders stiffened. "Not to be rude, but I'm not a student. This is my home where my family visits regularly. I don't believe we're in danger while we're in my kitchen." His voice grew louder as he spoke. "If the Directorate believed the people of Dragon's Bluff were in danger, they'd warn us. Wouldn't they?"

Miss Enid came over to join in the conversation. "I understand how you feel. But no one can predict where or when an attack will occur. As faculty, it's our job to make sure the students return to campus where there are armed guards who will do their best to protect us and them. And Bryn is the granddaughter of one of the most powerful Directorate members, which is why you are guarding her. She is a target, no matter where she is."

Valmont's shoulders slumped. "Fine." He stalked over to the refrigerator and pulled out a frost coated metal pan covered in foil. "Let's go."

On the car ride back to campus, Valmont was silent. What could she say to make him feel better? Not much. *Sorry you're stuck with me. Sorry the people camping in your abandoned root cellar were murdered in their sleep.* Giving up on finding the right words, she placed her hand on his forearm. "I want to say something comforting, but I can't come up with anything. So I'm sorry about all of this."

"As you said before, welcome to your world. It sucks but you get used to it."

• • •

Mr. Stanton arranged for the cafeteria to heat the lasagna and deliver it to one of the small dining rooms where meetings were often held. Bryn didn't expect her grandfather and Ferrin to join them, but *surprise*…they did. So much for a relaxing dinner.

"We need to hear every detail of what happened today," Bryn's grandfather said. "And why you decided to investigate Valmont's property in the first place."

Mr. Stanton explained about the maps with the altered roads and how Valmont recognized the road leading to his cabin but not the structure on the map. "I did send in a detailed report to the Directorate with copies of the book, detailing what the students found," Mr. Stanton reminded them.

"We are well aware of that," Ferrin snapped. "Tell us what happened after you left campus."

"Valmont, why don't you start," Bryn's grandfather said.

"Okay." Her knight launched into the story of how they found the handle even though they couldn't see it and how Clint opened it with his lightning.

"You found the handle due to a squirrel?" Ferrin stated like he thought they were making up the entire story.

"You know those small furry creatures who like nuts and live in the trees." Bryn added a silent *Asshat* at the end of her sentence.

Ferrin sent her a scathing glance. "I'm aware of what it is. I find it hard to believe this animal led you to a secret tunnel that had been under your nose for how long? More than a year?"

"I'm sure your estate is old enough to have root cellars," Valmont said. "Do you use them? Don't bother answering that question because we both know the answer is no. I never used the root cellar. And yes, I did know there was one in the backyard under the dirt, but I never went looking for it, since it's not the 1900s anymore, and I happen to own a working refrigerator. There could have been a million dollars in diamonds in that cellar and I never would have known."

"That would have been way more fun to find," Clint said before shoving a giant bite of lasagna in his mouth.

The spicy scent of Italian seasoning made Bryn's mouth water.

"We should eat before the food gets cold," Valmont said. "Feel free to ask questions. I can't promise I won't talk with my mouth full."

Bryn's grandfather shook out his napkin and placed it on his lap. "I think food would be good for all of us. We can talk afterward when we're having coffee and pie."

Thank goodness her grandfather wasn't being a jerk. "Food first is always a good idea," Bryn said. "And pie is a bonus."

Ferrin ignored the food. He sat silently seething on his side of the table while glaring at Bryn in the same manner Jaxon had done when they'd first met. After fifteen minutes, Bryn cracked. "You do realize we're all on the same side and we aren't trying to keep anything from you, right?"

"We," Ferrin emphasized the word, "are not on the same side. You are students with questionable common sense, in league with a knight who has no place on this campus, and you were supervised by faculty who do not have voting rights within the Directorate. There is no, 'We.'"

Everyone froze. Outrage burned in Bryn's gut and flames crawled up the back of her throat. She took a moment to control her fire, but smoke drifted from her lips as she spoke. "That is the most ridiculous statement I've ever heard. You are not the only person who wants to keep dragons safe. Everyone in this room wants what is best for the Institute and Dragon's Bluff. None of us are trying to hide anything from you. We called the Directorate to come and investigate the situation today. We are here to share information with you.

So when we tell you we found the door handle because we watched a freaking squirrel root around for an acorn in what appeared to be a solid piece of metal until Clint zapped it with lightning, then that is the truth."

"Then you are fools with nothing to offer." Ferrin stood and left the room.

"Feel better?" Bryn's grandfather asked her in an amused tone.

"Shooting a fireball at him would have been way more fun, but I figured you wouldn't approve."

"That probably would have been more entertaining." He grinned. "But I'm glad you refrained."

"Why is he like that?" Clint asked. "And I'm speaking to you as the grandfather of a friend, not a member of the Directorate."

"I'm not sure you can separate one from the other, and in either role, I don't have an answer for you. That is the way Ferrin has always been."

"It's often a self-fulfilling prophecy," Miss Enid said, "when an individual thinks the world is against him."

"That's kind of profound," Valmont said. "One of my favorite sayings is, 'Do what you know until you know better, and then do better.' It applies to cooking and a lot of situations in life. Although some people never seem to learn it."

After they finished the lasagna, one of the kitchen staff came in and passed out pieces of apple pie and coffee.

"Is this decaf?" Bryn's grandfather asked.

"No, sir, but I can make a pot if you like."

"No. Thank you. I never touch decaf." He sipped his coffee and sighed in satisfaction. "I never saw the point."

Talking with her grandfather like this was a treat. Even though he was one of the most influential men in dragon society, he didn't act like a diva-jackass as Ferrin did. After they finished telling the story of their strange day, and all of her friends except Valmont had said their good-byes, Bryn had one more question to ask her grandfather. "How much trouble would I get into if I ordered a pet squirrel online and had it delivered to Ferrin's estate?"

Her grandfather smiled. "I applaud your ingenuity, but it would be best if you didn't antagonize Ferrin any further."

Where was the fun in that?

Chapter Ten

Bryn was dead tired when they made it back to her dorm room, but she wanted to talk to Valmont about Ferrin and his "There is no We" speech. Where could they talk freely without fear of bugs?

"Do you want to sit out on the terrace?" she asked him. In reality, the terraces off the dorm rooms were places where students could shift into dragon form and take flight. Every terrace also came with a small umbrella table and two wrought iron chairs, but they weren't comfortable. They were probably only there for plausible deniability, like *nope, we aren't shape-shifting dragons who like to fly from our terraces. We're normal people who like to sit out on the patio and enjoy the fresh air in these completely uncomfortable chairs.*

"I was thinking more along the lines of the comfy couch." Valmont gave her an odd look.

She rolled her eyes. "I don't know, unlike the *library*," she emphasized the word, "I thought it might be a nice place to talk."

"Oh." He gestured down the hall toward the window,

which opened onto the terrace. "After you."

Once they were seated on the hard chairs, Bryn remembered why they didn't come out here very often. "First off, it sucks that I have to second guess where we can speak without worrying about bugs. Second, what is going on with Ferrin? He's acting like more of a control-freak dictator than normal."

Valmont glanced around the terrace. "It's been a hell of a day, so I'm not in the mood to think big thoughts, but Ferrin is probably going crazy because you're in the forefront of all these discoveries rather than Jaxon."

"Maybe, but he seems to be drawing a line between the Blues on the Directorate and everyone else. I know he's an elitist snob, but he relies on the Green dragons to figure things out, so I'm not sure why he'd risk alienating them. Did you see the look on Miss Enid's face when he categorized her and Mr. Stanton as lesser dragons?"

"No."

"It looked like she was literally biting her tongue to keep from lashing out at him. I'm not sure what kind of vengeance she can get at the library, but I don't think Ferrin will be checking out books or receiving helpful information from her any time soon."

"I remember Clint saying that each Clan has a role to play." He ticked items off on his fingers. "The Reds are the middle class worker bees. The Oranges are the miners and farmers. The Blacks are the artists and performers. The Green dragons are the problem solvers. The Blues are like the one percenters in the human world. They act like they earned their station in life when they were just born into a family. It's not an accomplishment to be born rich. It's luck, but it's not a skill. And I know ruling a government is probably complicated, but to act like he's above everyone else isn't smart. His holier-than-thou attitude is the reason Rebels exist."

"Agreed." Bryn yawned. "And maybe it's family bias, but I think my grandfather is more reasonable."

"He is far more approachable," Valmont said. "Ferrin never would have agreed to fund Garret's prosthetic wing project."

"You're right." Bryn stood and stretched. "And now it's time for sleep."

"On the comfy couch," Valmont added.

"Really?" Bryn played dumb. "I thought we might sleep out here."

"Smart ass," Valmont grabbed her hand and pulled her toward the window. He didn't let go of her when they climbed inside and he locked the window. He didn't let go of her when he pulled her to the couch. He didn't let go of her once he sat next to her and kissed her. No matter what weirdness happened in her life, as long as he never let go of her, she'd be fine.

How perfect would her life be if the Directorate did away with the arranged-marriage scenario? She'd be free to date who she wanted and wouldn't have to think about marriage for another ten years. The odds of that happening were slim to none, but a girl could dream.

• • •

In the middle of the night, Bryn woke up alone on the couch. She sat up and rubbed her eyes. "Valmont?"

No answer. Weird. Maybe he'd woken up and gone to the bathroom. She checked his room and found him stretched out on the bed. What the heck was that about? She leaned against his doorframe and wrapped her arms around her ribcage. Should she "accidentally" wake him and ask what was going on? That wouldn't be nice. He'd had a rough day and he looked so peaceful in his bed. Where did that leave her? Joining him didn't seem right. While they cozied up on the couch, and he'd joined her in her bed when she'd been sick, crawling into his bed seemed wrong. Well not wrong, but certainly not right.

She yawned. Time to pick an option before she fell asleep standing up. Should she head back to the couch or go collapse on her own bed? Since the couch without Valmont was way less comfortable than her bed, she went into her room and crawled under the cool sheets.

The sound of the alarm had her groaning and pulling the covers over her head. How could it be morning already? It had taken forever for her to fall back asleep and now she felt like crap. The sound of the piano shifted to the evil discordant melody meant to cause stress. She sat up and threw her pillow at the dresser.

The alarm played on, mocking her.

"Damn it." She climbed out of bed and whacked the top of the foul device.

Hopefully, a shower would make her feel more alive. Twenty minutes later, she joined Valmont in the living room.

He pointed at her feet. "Did you know you're wearing two different color shoes?"

She looked down. Sure enough, she had on one black shoe and one red. "Maybe I'm trying to start a new fashion trend."

He yawned. "I don't care if you don't. I just want coffee."

"Give me a minute." She went back into her room, kicked off the red shoe, and shoved her foot into the matching black pump. She gave herself a quick once over in the mirror to make sure she hadn't screwed anything else up. Nope. She was good to go, but something was bothering her. She wanted to ask Valmont his reason for leaving her to wake up alone on the couch. Not that it meant anything, but he should bring it up at breakfast to make sure she wasn't upset, right?

"Ready?" Valmont asked when she rejoined him in the living room.

Now would be the time to ask him about his defection, but he had dark circles under his eyes which matched her own. Without a word, she walked over and threw her arms around him in a hug. With no hesitation, he hugged her back. Being in his arms made her feel safe. She enjoyed the warmth for a moment, and then stepped away from him so she could see his face. "Why'd you jump ship last night?"

"I woke up at two, and then I couldn't go back to sleep. I didn't want to wake you, so I went into my bedroom and read for a while until I finally fell back asleep."

"Good. I thought maybe I snored and drove you away."

"Now that you mention it," Valmont teased.

Good mood restored, she smiled and headed for the door. "Come on. My coffee needs me."

She'd barely sat down with her breakfast when Garret approached her table. Before he could say anything, she held up her coffee cup. "Fair warning, I'm only on my first cup of coffee."

"So I should speak slowly and use small words?" Garret asked.

"Yes," Valmont, Bryn, Clint, and Ivy all chimed in at the same time.

"Okay then. I want to test my prosthetic wing this evening before dinner. Can you help me?"

"Yes. Where do you want to meet?"

"The stadium should give us plenty of room to maneuver."

"I'll be there."

There was a much smaller crowd in the stadium that evening than there had been when Garret had timed Bryn's flight at the beginning of the school year, which had turned into the race where she'd beaten Jaxon. Now, there were less than a dozen people. Most of them were Greens. Rhianna sat off to the side with some of the other "walking-wounded" as Garret referred to students who had been injured in the attacks. While there were several representatives from the Black, Green, and Red clans, Rhianna was the only Blue.

Garret waved Bryn over to where the prosthetic wing lay on the ground. "Let me show you how this will work." He pointed at the fabric panels. "I'll slide my wing between the panels. Once it's strapped in place, the buckle will form a handle which you can grab from above if something goes wrong."

"I can do that," Bryn said. "Where will you take off from?"

"I have dual ideas on how it might work. One, I could climb up to the top of the bleachers and jump from there, or you could lift me up and then let me glide away."

"Let's try the bleachers first," Bryn said.

"My only concern is I'm not sure how the landing will go," Garret said. "And since landings aren't your strong suit, I'm not sure how much help you'll be."

"I have no valid argument against that statement," Bryn said. "So why don't I swoop in and grab the handle to help you stay upright when you land. I can tread air above you."

"That should work." Garret shifted into his dragon form.

Bryn barely suppressed a gasp. She knew hailstones had ripped through his wing, causing irreparable damage, but the sight of his mangled wing was worse than she'd imagined. Ragged holes had developed scar tissue causing strange lumps in the membrane. She forced herself to blink and look away. Freaking out in front of Garret would be beyond rude, so she plastered on an interested expression and focused on the prosthetic device.

Two Greens in human form slid Garret's wing between

the twin fabric panels and then they wrapped the wide leather strap around his abdomen and buckled it in place. It was now or never. She jogged up to the top of the bleachers with Valmont by her side and then shifted. Once she was in dragon form, Valmont climbed onto her back, and she felt the familiar rush of warmth and power through their bond.

Garret awkwardly made his way up the bleachers with his good wing extended to balance out the other wing. When he reached the top, he closed his eyes and took a deep breath. Was he afraid the wing wouldn't work? She prayed to any higher power who might be listening that the prosthetic would give back Garret's ability to fly.

"Ready?" he asked.

"Yes."

Garret bent his legs and burst off the ground about five feet above the seats. He hung suspended for a few seconds before gliding a dozen feet. Bryn took to the air, hanging back to give him room. Something wasn't working right. He dropped to the seats too quickly. She swooped in and grabbed the handle with her talons, lifting his weight until he was twenty feet above the seats.

"Thank you. It's on to plan B. Let's try again from here," Garret said.

She released him and this time he managed to glide, tilting his body. He flew in a circle, maintaining his height. She followed along behind him looking for any sign of trouble, but once he had the hang of maneuvering, he stayed aloft. After every maneuver, he drifted lower and lower. When he was within a few feet of the ground, Bryn swooped in and grabbed the handle slowing her flight until she was flying in place, and then she released him, allowing him to drop the last few feet to the ground. She slowed her wings, dropping to the ground in the same manner, and then she moved around so she could see Garret's face. Tears rolled down his snout.

"Those are happy tears, right?"

Garret nodded yes.

"Want to do it again?" Bryn asked.

"Yes."

After three more flights, each a little better than the last, Garret suggested they stop for dinner.

Valmont and Bryn unbuckled the wing and removed it so Garret could shift to human form. There was a light to Garret's eyes she hadn't seen since his injury. "It feels like I got part of my soul back."

Bryn hugged him. "I'm so happy for you."

He froze for a second and then hugged her back with his good arm. "Thank you."

She released him, and her stomach growled. "On that note, I think it's time for dinner. Let me know when you want to fly again."

"I'm going to make a few modifications," Garret said, "and then we'll set up more trials."

When they were far enough away so no one would overhear, Bryn said, "I'm so glad that worked."

"Me, too. He didn't deserve what happened to him," Valmont said. "Nobody deserves that, but he was an innocent bystander."

"I know, and his wing…after seeing it…I really want to find the Rebels and shut them down."

"I've been wanting to ask something but couldn't ever think of a polite way to do it… Why is it that Rhianna's wing injury affected her leg while Garret's affected his arm?"

"When I first flew here with Garret and then shifted to human form, I complained my legs were tired. It felt like I'd run a marathon. He said the brain interprets fatigue from the dragon form and assigns it to the human body and most dragons interpret wing fatigue as soreness in the lower extremities. For about ten percent of the population, it's the upper extremities. They don't know why it varies."

"I guess he's lucky he's one of the ten percent, otherwise he wouldn't be able to walk."

At dinner, in between bites of her cheeseburger, Bryn told Clint and Ivy about Garret's progress with the wing.

"Thank goodness," Ivy said. "Not being able to fly is the stuff my nightmares are made of."

Clint snagged a French fry off of Ivy's plate. "I still don't know what the Rebels hoped to accomplish by attacking students."

"Me, neither," Bryn said. "Now it seems their attacks are more specific. It's almost like they're looking for something."

"I never thought about it that way," Clint said. "Big picture, I guess it's good they moved from random terrorism to specifically looking for artifacts."

"I think you're right," Valmont said, "But it makes me wonder what they are hoping to find. Are there weapons of mass destruction hidden somewhere on campus?"

"That's a disturbing thought," said Bryn.

"And with all the hidden rooms in the vaults under the library, you never know what you're going to find," Clint said.

"I wonder if Miss Enid was able to decipher the ledger she found in the Blue room and figure out what was taken," Ivy said.

"Good question. Maybe we should visit the library tonight after dinner."

• • •

"What are you four up to?" Miss Enid asked from her usual spot at the front desk of the library.

"We were wondering if you'd found anything interesting in those ledgers," Bryn said.

"So far, we've used the ledger from the Blue hall to check

the inventory of the armory. Most of the weapons seem to be in their assigned spaces."

"Most?" Valmont asked. "What's missing?"

"Half a dozen broadswords and a few battle axes," Miss Enid said. "But we have no way of knowing if they were taken recently, or if they've been missing for decades. Since the rooms are airtight and dust free there's no physical evidence to give us a clue."

"What about the chest that was dragged from the other room?" Bryn asked.

"There isn't much information about what was stored in it although there are some references to crowns which doesn't make much sense."

This could be bad. "Tyrant's crowns?" Bryn asked.

Miss Enid sucked in a breath. "I didn't make that connection, but you could be right."

"What's a tyrant's crown?" Ivy asked.

"Do you remember what Rhianna tried on?" Bryn asked not wanting to go into too much detail.

"The anti-shifting device?" Clint asked.

Bryn nodded. "And a chest full of those could cause all sorts of trouble."

"Which is why I will be contacting your grandfather immediately about this," Miss Enid said.

• • •

The rest of the school week flew by without any traumatizing events. Friday after their last class, Bryn, Valmont, Clint, and Ivy sat on the grass in the quad next to one of the few trees that had survived the Rebel attacks last semester.

Bryn inhaled and sighed in satisfaction. The fresh green new-growth smell was like a soothing balm. "I don't care what we do tonight as long as it's outside."

Valmont leaned back on his elbows and looked up at the leaves in the tree. "I think we should build a tree house."

"I'm game," Clint said. "But I'm not sure the Directorate will approve."

"And I'm not sure where the nearest hardware store is," Bryn said.

"I didn't say it was a practical idea." Valmont pointed up into the tree. "See where the branches fork right there? That's the perfect spot for a tree house."

"I had a tree house when I was little," Ivy said. "Until someone set it on fire." She looked pointedly at Clint.

Bryn laughed. "I sense there's a story that goes along with this disaster."

"A tale of love gone wrong," Clint said. "I was seven, and even back then I was trying to win Ivy's heart. So, I set up a candlelit lunch for two, complete with Little Debbie snack cakes and fruit roll ups. And I lit the candle before I went to knock on her door because I wanted everything to be perfect. Only she wasn't home, so I decided to go ride my bike, forgetting about the candle."

"By the time I came home from the zoo," Ivy continued, "the firemen were at my house. You should have seen Clint being brave and confessing what he'd done."

"Honesty is always the best policy," Valmont said. "So did you forgive him?"

"I was mad for about a week, but I got over it." Ivy reached over and ruffled Clint's Mohawk.

"I never had a tree house," Bryn said, "because we never had a yard." She eyed the branches above her. "We could build a platform of ice up there and pretend it's a tree house."

"That might hurt the tree," Ivy said. "Tell you what. After Clint and I are married, you and Valmont can come help us build a tree house in our backyard."

And there it was again, the easy certainty of Clint and

Ivy's future. They'd marry and live in a three-bedroom house near their families. After awhile, they'd have children who'd grow up and attend the Institute and the cycle would continue. Nothing about her own future seemed certain or easy.

If her grandparents had their way, she'd marry Jaxon. It wouldn't be a real marriage. Any children they might have would be created through artificial means, no nakedness involved. Still…she had always assumed that one day she'd fall in love with a guy like Valmont, move into a middle class subdivision and have a typical life. Instead, she'd live a lie in a ginormous mansion where she probably wouldn't be allowed to build a tree house, even if she wanted one.

"Do you think Blues build mini-mansions in trees for their kids?" Bryn asked.

"Probably not," Ivy said. "But you can come play in ours."

Bryn lay back in the grass. "I'm having one of those, who-kidnapped-my-life? moments. So excuse me, while I have a small pity party."

"I'll be there for you," Valmont said. "No matter what. Remember that."

What would she do without Valmont? He was her link to a normal life. "You're the best knight ever."

"Why are you laying in the grass?" Jaxon's voice preceded him as he walked toward her.

Bryn sat up. "We're making plans for a tree house. What's up?"

"Why would anyone want a tiny house in a tree?" Jaxon asked. "It makes no sense."

"Then you aren't invited to play in mine when I finally have the chance to build one."

"Imagine my devastation," Jaxon shot back.

She stuck her tongue out at him because it seemed like the thing to do. Surprisingly, he laughed which made her smile. "I know you didn't drop by to make small talk, so what's going on?"

"I have it on good authority that we'll be called to my father's office at six thirty tomorrow morning unless we go speak with him now."

Bryn turned to Valmont. "You choose. Do it now or get up early and go tomorrow."

"Is there a third choice?" Valmont asked. "Because I don't like either of those options."

Bryn pushed to her feet and held her hand out to him. "Come on. If we get this over with now, we can have the rest of the weekend to do what we want."

Valmont let Bryn pull him to his feet.

Clint and Ivy stood, dusting off their clothes. "We're coming with you," Clint said.

"Are you sure?" Bryn asked. "Have you forgotten how delightful Ferrin is?"

"Nope," Clint said. "But they're liable to say you can't share whatever information they tell you, but if I'm there and hear it firsthand, then I'll already know."

Jaxon opened his mouth like he was going to comment on Clint's convoluted logic, but then he shook his head, turned, and walked toward the library.

"I think you rendered a Westgate speechless," Valmont said. "Nicely done."

Bryn was surprised to find Keegan waiting in Ferrin's office and disappointed that her grandfather wasn't there. Ferrin left to his own egomaniacal devices could result in nothing good.

"Why are you here?" Ferrin asked Clint.

"Because we were with Bryn when Jaxon came to find her, and I like to know what's going on."

"What did you need to tell us?" Bryn asked, trying to redirect Ferrin so he'd get to the point and they could all get out of his office as quickly as possible.

"The blood work came back on your friend, Keegan, and there are no genetic markers for Throwbacks."

"I know where you were trying to go with this," Keegan said, "and you're way off track. Throwbacks would never side with Rebels. Our goal is to blend in with Dragon Society, not sabotage it."

"Prove it," Ferrin said. "Help Jaxon and Bryn collect the names of all the Throwbacks on campus and the Directorate will interview them to make sure they aren't a threat."

"Seriously? You want to round up a minority group of dragons because they're different and try to blame everything on them?" Bryn said. "You do realize that sounds slightly Hitler-ish, right?" Ferrin growled at Bryn like he was going to shift and physically attack her. Valmont drew his sword, and Bryn considered shifting herself.

"I'm sure Bryn didn't mean that to be as insulting as it sounded, Father. She lacks tact," Jaxon said. "But as student liaisons we could put out a message among the students that it would be wise for Throwbacks to get in touch with us so they don't come under suspicion, given the tense political climate. We can meet with them and ascertain any possibility of a threat. Once we have the information, we'll pass it on to you. I'm sure Keegan will be happy to help us."

"Sure," Keegan said. "I'll help in whatever way I can, as long as it's Jaxon and Bryn who are talking to the students."

"And that way the Directorate can use their time to focus on more important matters," Jaxon said. "Does this meet with your approval, Father?"

Would this work? Bryn kept her eyes on Ferrin. She could see the wheels in his brain processing the information and figuring out what would benefit him most. If they were lucky, putting his son in a leadership role would outweigh the Directorate interrogating and possibly harassing the other Throwbacks on campus.

"I approve of your plan," Ferrin said. "Now if you'll excuse me, I have far more important matters to attend to."

Bryn bolted out of the office and down the stairs. Once they were outside the library, she stopped under a group of trees and waited for her friends to catch up with her. Jaxon was the last to join them and he did not look like a happy camper. He kept coming until they were almost toe to toe.

"Never disrespect my father like that again." Sleet shot from his nostrils. "You may not agree with his opinions, but he is the Speaker for the Directorate." Jaxon emphasized each word of his father's title. "And you will show him the respect he deserves."

It had taken guts for Jaxon to intervene on her behalf. "Thank you for smoothing things over. I swear I'll try to keep my opinions to myself." What she planned to say next would probably send Jaxon over the edge. "Now let me ask you a question. Do you agree with the tactics he's taking?"

"He's doing what he thinks is best for the greater good." Jaxon said, and then he stalked off.

"He didn't really answer your question, did he?" Valmont asked.

"No," Bryn said. "Which is an answer in itself."

Keegan shifted his weight from his right foot to his left and then back again. "I agreed to help, and I will. I'll pass the word around that Throwbacks need to contact you or Jaxon, but I won't give you anyone's name."

"I respect your decision," Bryn said. "And I am eternally grateful your Throwback blood doesn't show any genetic differences from normal shape-shifting dragon blood. That could have been a real disaster."

"Agreed." Keegan caught sight of some Reds walking across campus and waved at them. "See you guys later." He jogged over to meet his friends.

"Well that was entertaining," Ivy said.

"There was a moment where I thought Ferrin was going to lose it," Clint said. "And I can't believe I'm about to say this, but maybe you should curb your outspoken tendencies around him. Not because of his position in politics, or out of respect to Jaxon, but because I think Ferrin is kind of unstable and he really hates you."

"I got that feeling, too," Bryn said. "You know, it's kind of funny. Every time I wonder how my parents could have abandoned this life and given up flying and magic, I have an interaction with Ferrin and it all makes sense."

• • •

Saturday afternoon Bryn and Valmont joined Lillith and her grandmother at Fonzoli's, which meant Bryn ate lunch with Lillith and her grandmother in the dining room while Valmont hung out in the kitchen visiting his family. She'd expected him to eat with them but couldn't blame him for wanting to visit.

Megan, the cute young waitress, stopped by their table to refill their water glasses. "Is there anything else I can get for you?" she asked.

Bryn tried to suppress a yawn, but failed. "Sorry, I'd like a cup of coffee."

"Are we boring you?" her grandmother asked.

"No. I've been having the strangest dreams about Rebel attacks and the vaults, and I'm actually relieved when I wake up, but it feels like I haven't slept."

"I dreamt Asher was like a doll-size replica of Ferrin, and he refused to wear the cute onesies I bought for him." Lillith laughed. "It's funny now, but at the time I was so upset."

"The mind can play strange tricks on you," her grandmother said. "Sometimes when you have strange dreams it's best to wake up early and start your day. Going back to sleep never seems to help much."

"That's exactly why I need the coffee," Bryn said. "I dreamt about being locked in the vaults with no way out. I was so grateful when I woke up, I didn't care that it was six on a Saturday. I stayed awake."

Megan came back with the coffee and a far too perky smile. "Valmont is such a great guy. You're lucky you get to spend so much time with him."

"Yes, he is, and yes, I am," Bryn replied, stomping down on the jealousy which reared up inside of her. Megan was a sweet girl, who had a crush on Valmont, which was totally understandable. Totally normal. Not a problem at all. Just because she was a human girl who his evil grandmother would probably adore…that was no reason to set Megan's hair on fire. Bryn sipped her coffee and pushed down the flames igniting in her gut over the thought of Valmont with a girl like Megan. A normal girl who could give him a normal life, which he totally deserved.

"Bryn?" Her grandmother's tone sounded concerned.

"Sorry, I tuned out for a moment. What did I miss?"

"I said we should tell Valmont to wrap up his visit, because after you finish the coffee which you so obviously need, we are going to look at baby clothes and then check out what's new in the boutiques."

"Oh, okay." Bryn finished her coffee in one long gulp and then stood and headed for the kitchen. She tried to walk in quietly, without interrupting, but everyone stopped talking when she stepped foot through the doorway. *Wow. Talk about awkward. What's that about?*

She approached Valmont. "Sorry to interrupt, but we're leaving in a few minutes."

"No problem," Valmont said. "Give me a minute to say my good-byes and I'll meet you at the table."

"Sure." Bryn plastered a fake smile on her face like nothing was wrong, like Valmont's family didn't openly resent her, and wandered back to the table.

Valmont joined them a few minutes later, and his expression said it all. Regret. He regretted having to walk away from his family. He'd never openly say that, but it was clear. When he'd first come to stay with her twenty-four hours a day, he had claimed he didn't mind being away from his relatives, but here was proof positive he'd lied. Or maybe he hadn't been gone long enough at that time for it to make a difference, but now, now he definitely missed his family. Not like she could blame him.

"I'm sorry," Bryn said. "We should visit more often."

"I'd like that," Valmont said.

Megan would probably like that, too. Bryn managed to keep that snarky thought to herself, but she still felt guilty about it.

After picking out several bibs and blankets for Asher, Bryn's grandmother led them to a boutique Bryn had never visited before. Per custom, her grandmother rang a buzzer to alert the staff they had a customer. It was beyond ridiculous that you had to be buzzed into a store. Without customers, these high-end stores would be nothing more than closets. The elitism of this system made Bryn grind her teeth.

When the saleslady glanced up and saw Marie Sinclair and Lillith Westgate on her doorstep, she practically danced across the room to open the door.

"Please come in. Mrs. Sinclair, Mrs. Westgate, it's a pleasure to have you in our store."

That was a little over the top. Bryn couldn't blame the woman, but the suckup-ishness was annoying.

"This is my granddaughter, Bryn and her knight, Valmont."

"Nice to meet you," the saleslady said like it was a common occurrence to have hybrids and knights in the store.

"Nice to meet you, too," Bryn said and then felt awkward

because the woman hadn't mentioned her own name.

"What can I help you find?" the saleslady asked.

"We're looking to spruce up our summer wardrobe," Bryn's grandmother said.

"I know just the thing." The saleslady led them to a rack of linen blouses and capris. Unlike a normal store, there were only a few outfits hanging on each rack. Why did fewer outfits in the store always seem to mean they were more expensive?

Bryn followed along as her grandmother pointed at items, which the saleslady rounded up and carried to their dressing rooms.

"I think we should try a few things on now," Bryn's grandmother said. They adjourned to their assigned dressing rooms. Bryn tried on a cream-color top with the matching cream and blue striped capris. The outfit was flattering, but the light-color blouse probably wouldn't survive breakfast the first day she wore it. Any crumb or tiny drip of coffee would show up immediately. Still, it was pretty. She stepped out to show her grandmother and was surprised to see Valmont and Lillith deep in conversation.

"What are you two plotting?"

Lillith's cheeks colored.

Valmont wore a frown he normally reserved for Jaxon. Not good.

Neither of them gave her any type of explanation. "Is everything all right?"

Valmont nodded.

"Everything is fine," Lillith pointed at Bryn's capris. "Those are so cute." She looked down at her belly. "I wonder if they make those in maternity clothes."

"We can order anything you want in a maternity size," the saleslady volunteered from across the room.

Lillith stood. "Then I'm going to look around a little bit more."

Did Lillith really want to look at clothes, or was she fleeing the scene because she didn't want to answer questions?

Bryn's grandmother came out in a blue dress, which practically floated as she walked.

"That dress is amazing," said Bryn.

"Thank you. I had one in a similar fabric placed in your room." Her grandmother tilted her head and studied Bryn. "I like the pants, but we should find the blue top that matches the stripe. The cream is too boring."

"I do think the blue would be better." Not for the same reason, but her grandmother didn't need to know that. Bryn headed back to her dressing room to try on another round of clothes. Half an hour later, Valmont was carrying two bags to the car for Bryn. Thankfully, Lillith and her grandmother's clothes were being shipped to their estates. Otherwise, they would have needed to make several trips.

Back in her dorm room, Bryn hung up her new clothes and waited to see if Valmont would volunteer any information. Nope. Zero. Zip. He didn't say anything. He just went into his room and shut the door.

That was a pretty clear signal. He needed time to think… which she understood. But after fifteen minutes of pacing in the living room waiting for her boyfriend to come out, she caved and went to knock on his door.

"Valmont? Are you okay?"

He opened the door and leaned against the doorframe. "No. I'm not."

"Can we talk about it?" Bryn grabbed his hand and pulled him out into the living room toward the couch.

He sat on the couch and rubbed his chin. "I like Lillith, but today she crossed a line."

That so didn't sound like Jaxon's mom. "What did she do?"

"She told me I needed to plan for my life when I'm no

longer your knight."

"Why would she say that?"

"According to her, once your marriage contract to Jaxon is approved, you'll no longer need me, so I should ride off quietly into the sunset and date someone like Megan."

"What the hell?" Bryn was offended on so many levels. "Why does she think she can tell you or us how to live our lives?"

"Just wait. It gets better. As Jaxon's mother, she claims she's looking out for his best interests. She can tell there is more going on between us than there should be, and she believes we should terminate our knight-dragon bond as soon as possible."

"I have no words." And she didn't. Lilith was the last person she would have expected to launch a sneak attack on her and Valmont. "Do you think maybe she's being overly maternal because she's pregnant?"

"Maybe." Valmont leaned back on the couch and held up his arm so she could scoot closer and snuggle against him. "The whole thing came out of nowhere, and I didn't feel like I could argue with her."

He hadn't said a thing about Megan and that bothered her. She didn't want to play the jealous girlfriend and felt the need to confess. "I might not like Megan on the sole basis that your grandmother who hates me, would love her."

Valmont chuckled. "I understand. I might deeply dislike Jaxon not only because he can be a pretentious, elitist asshat, but also because you're going to live with him at the house of many W's while your own W infested estate is being built."

Bryn laughed. "Okay, you win. Listening to my grandmother and Lillith go on about me marrying Jaxon is way worse than me thinking about how much your family would love Megan."

"She is sweet," Valmont said, "and I think she has a crush

on me."

Bryn poked him in the ribs. "Don't tease the dragon. She might flash fry you." She leaned in to kiss him. The phone rang, stopping the kiss before it even started. "Bad timing," Bryn muttered as she pushed up off the couch and went to answer it.

"May I speak to Valmont?" a woman asked.

Was it wrong that she wanted to ask who it was? It could be his mom. It's not like Bryn knew Valmont's family's voices. "Sure. Hold on."

"It's for you." Bryn held out the phone.

"Who is it?"

And she'd walked right into that one. She put the receiver back to her ear. "Who's calling, please?"

"It's Megan."

Her grip on the phone tightened. She held the phone toward Valmont. "It's Megan."

"Really?" he seemed amused.

Bryn produced a small fireball in her left hand.

"No need for that." He took the phone. "Hello, what's up?"

She wanted to sit and listen to his conversation, but he needed to know that fireballs aside, she did trust him. So she went to her room and picked out her clothes for the next day, and then she decided to paint her nails using Quintessence. She imagined her nails a deep shade of red. When she opened her eyes, her nails sparkled in the light. Now what? Maybe she'd add a black tip like a French manicure. She focused on her nails, and they turned completely black, which didn't look half bad, but she was pretty sure her grandmother would have a cow if she walked around with black fingernails. She changed them back to a shiny garnet color.

She heard Valmont saying his good-byes, so she walked back into the living room. The sappy smile on his face had her rethinking her stance on fireballs.

He sat down on the couch and patted the space beside him.

Bryn sat on his lap instead and put her arms around his neck. "Why did Megan call you?" It was her phone. He was her knight and her boyfriend. She had a right to know.

"My grandmother mentioned something she wanted for her birthday, and Megan called to tell me so I could buy it for her. I told her my grandmother used to tell me what she wanted so I'd pass the information on to my grandfather, which is what I asked her to do, since I'm not there to do it." He grinned. "Are you okay with that?"

"I guess, but as my knight and my boyfriend you should probably kiss me just to make sure I'm not too traumatized."

He leaned in and kissed the spot on her neck, right below her ear lobe. Heat shot through her body. She suppressed a growl, but when he scraped his teeth across the sensitive area, she gave up and let loose a low rumble that made him chuckle. Not that she minded. Half the reason she loved Valmont was because he always made her laugh.

"Feeling pretty manly, are you?" she teased.

"Knightly, would be a more appropriate term. Now hold on, we're going to try the lie-down-while-kissing-without-falling-off-the-couch maneuver."

She wrapped her arms around his neck. "All systems go."

He kissed her, and she held on to him as they shifted positions. As they over-rotated, she let go of him and grabbed the back of the couch.

He paused the kiss, opening his eyes. "So close."

"Practice makes perfect," she said. And then she pulled him down for another kiss.

Chapter Eleven

Putting out the word about Throwbacks had some unexpected consequences. People Bryn didn't know kept sneaking up on her and asking if they could meet someplace private.

"I feel like my life has turned into a spy movie," she complained at lunch. "And when I meet these people and tell them they have to meet with Jaxon to answer some questions, they freak out. So now I'm having to say nice things about him to convince people to come to the stupid meetings."

"It's like opposite day," Valmont said. "And it's disturbing to hear her sing Jaxon's praises—not to mention, annoying."

"And no one is going to him first. So I'm doing twice the work."

"How many Throwbacks have you met so far?" Ivy asked.

This was going to be awkward. "Not to leave you guys out, but I don't think I should say. We're trying to keep it quiet."

"Give us an estimate," Ivy said. "Twenty-something? Thirty-something?"

"We're not up to the twenties, yet." That didn't give too much away.

"Have you run across anyone whose genetics are more evenly split like yours?" Clint asked.

"So far, no. And I'm not sure if that's good or bad." She didn't want to out any hybrids who were living on campus trying to blend in, but if they were discovered, they'd look guilty. If her grandfather ever found out she knew about other hybrids, he'd think she was scheming against him.

• • •

"You are not going to make anyone sit on that couch while they wait to speak with us." Bryn pointed at the on-purpose uncomfortable couch outside of the conference room they'd been assigned to use on the top floor of the library.

"I didn't choose the room or pick out the furniture," Jaxon replied. "And they can stand, if they don't want to sit."

The first student was due in fifteen minutes. Bryn opened the door to the conference room and checked inside. There were a dozen chairs around an oval table. "We'll put some of these outside."

"Do whatever you like." Jaxon sat at the table. "I need to organize my questionnaires."

Without commenting, Valmont grabbed a chair and carried it out the door.

"Should we move the couch or put a warning label on it?" Bryn asked.

"Can I write the label?" Valmont asked.

"Knock yourself out."

They carried out two more chairs and then Valmont found a blank sheet of paper and wrote. "Beware of seriously uncomfortable couch. It will mock you." Then he taped the paper to the wall above the obnoxious piece of furniture.

Bryn nodded. "That works. We give them fair warning and a different place to sit."

The sound of approaching footsteps had Bryn turning around. Eve, the Red-Black hybrid who had approached Bryn last semester came toward her.

"You're Bryn, right? We worked together in stagecraft a while back."

She could play this I'm-not-sure-who-you-are game, especially if someone was spying on them. "I'm Bryn. I'm sorry. I don't remember your name."

"It's Eve." She looked around like she thought someone might be listening. "I heard you wanted Throwbacks to answer some questions."

"That's right." Bryn pointed toward the door. "If you'll come in here, Jaxon will ask you a few questions. It shouldn't take long."

Eve headed into the room and took a seat across the table from Jaxon.

Bryn sat off to the side with Valmont.

"Is this the part where we play twenty questions?" Eve gave an uncomfortable laugh.

"I do have some questions for you to answer. As long as you cooperate and answer truthfully this should be fairly painless. Let's do the obvious first, what's your name."

She folded her hands in her lap. "Eve Daniels."

Jaxon wrote her name down in elegant script. Good thing he wanted to fill out the paperwork, because Bryn's penmanship wasn't great.

"What is your Throwback trait?" Jaxon asked.

Bryn was curious to see what her answer would be.

"My hair is black. I use hair dye to make it auburn."

Jaxon sat back and stared at her. "Is this common in your family?"

"My great aunt had it. Black hair seems to show up every few generations."

"What is your opinion of the Directorate asking you to

come forward to register as a Throwback?"

"I've spent my whole life trying to blend in," Eve said. "I would never go against the Directorate or the Institute. I almost didn't come today because I was afraid I'd be labeled a Rebel sympathizer because of my hair, but if I didn't come and anyone ever found out about me, I'd be labeled a traitor or worse."

"Have you ever been contacted by Rebels hoping to sway you to their cause?"

Eve shook her head emphatically. "No."

"If anyone ever contacts you, would you be willing to speak to me or Bryn about it?" Jaxon asked.

"Yes. Like I said, I just want things to go back to normal."

"Thank you for your time," Jaxon said. "You're free to go."

That was probably a much nicer interrogation than Ferrin had in mind. As long as Jaxon gave his father a decent report, hopefully the Directorate wouldn't mind.

A Green male showed up a few minutes later. His answers mirrored the ones given by Eve. Once he left, Bryn stood. "Okay, our next meeting is on the second floor."

"We should have asked everyone to come here." Jaxon gathered up his papers.

"Some of them want to keep their Throwback status a secret. If we asked all of them to meet in a group, then that would blow their cover."

Jaxon headed out the door. Bryn and Valmont followed behind him. When they reached the second floor, a Black male was waiting for them at a table in the back corner. Bryn and Valmont kept watch while Jaxon asked questions. When he finished, Bryn checked the schedule she'd written out for the appointment times.

"Now we're going to the cafe in the Red dorm."

"Why would we meet someone in the Red dorm cafe?"

Jaxon checked his watch. "It's ten in the morning."

"We're meeting with Keegan and a Throwback named Lisa for coffee and hopefully, donuts."

Jaxon's eyes narrowed. "Did you schedule our appointments around food?"

"That's ridiculous. After meeting with Lisa we're coming back here, and then we're going to the dining hall where we'll have an early lunch with twin Greens who are both Throwbacks."

"Twins?" Jaxon asked.

"They are identical, so it makes sense they'd both have the same traits. We better go. Keegan and Lisa are expecting us."

Once they reached the Red dorm cafe, Bryn took out a notebook and scribbled in it pretending she was working on homework.

"Will people really believe we're doing school work?" Lisa glanced around like she was nervous.

"People meet to work in groups all the time," Keegan said. "Granted, the groups don't normally involve a Westgate and a knight, but Bryn tends to travel in interesting company, so it should be okay."

The waiter came and took their order for coffee and pastries. Bryn worked her way through two orange scones while Jaxon asked his questions. Before, she'd been annoyed that this was his show, but now she didn't care, since letting him ask all the questions gave her more time to eat.

After taking down Lisa's information, Bryn, Valmont, and Jaxon went back to the conference room on the top floor of the library.

"We're definitely going to get our exercise today," Bryn muttered as she trudged up the last three steps.

A female Red sat on a chair outside the conference room waiting for them. She smiled at Bryn. "You weren't kidding about the couch. That thing is awful."

"Yes, it is," Bryn agreed. "Have you been waiting long?"

"No."

"We can talk in the conference room." Jaxon entered the room, and they all followed.

Over the next three hours, Bryn made seven more trips up and down the library stairs to meet with Throwbacks at random tables or in study cubicles. They also visited the dining hall twice.

"How can you possibly be hungry?" Jaxon asked when he watched her eat a second lunch.

"Must be all the calories I burn being awesome," Bryn said.

Jaxon rolled his eyes. "Yes. That must be it."

They trudged across campus to the library.

"Is this the last one?" Valmont asked.

"Yes," Bryn said. "One final trek up the library stairs to the conference room."

After the last interview was complete Bryn slid down in her seat and sighed. "I declare it's officially nap time."

"Seconded," Valmont said.

Jaxon sorted through his stack of papers. Rather than appearing relieved, he seemed troubled.

"What's wrong?" Bryn asked.

"It's interesting… I never would've guessed any of the students we met with today were Throwbacks. They didn't have to contact you and come forward, but they did. It's the ones who didn't come forward that we might have to worry about."

"What will you tell your father?"

Jaxon sighed and slid the papers into a manila envelope. "I'll tell him I don't think we have anything to fear from Throwbacks. The one characteristic they all shared was the desire to fit in. If they wanted to change things, I think they'd flaunt their differences."

Bryn couldn't help but think about Eve. Her desire to fit in was true, but how much simpler would her life be if hybrids could admit who they were. "Do you think there will ever come a time where Throwbacks could walk around in their natural state?"

"Not in my father's time." Jaxon stood and exited the room.

Valmont, who'd been sitting in the corner said, "I can't believe I'm about to say this, but Jaxon isn't all bad."

"He's honorable," Bryn said. "Now, I guess we should move the chairs back in here, because I don't want anyone griping about the furniture."

"Okay, but I'm not taking down the sign."

Bryn laughed. "Fine we'll leave it up as a public service announcement."

Valmont checked his watch. "I think I'm going to call my grandfather, while you take a nap."

Bryn normally napped on the couch, but if Valmont planned on talking to his grandfather, the phone was in the living room. So it only made sense for her to sleep in her bed. As she drifted to sleep, she heard him laughing. It was a nice reassuring sound to fall asleep to. It made it seem like the world was still a good place.

After her nap, Bryn and Valmont met Clint and Ivy outside of the Black dorm. "Do we have a plan?" Bryn said.

"We're going to play cards," Clint held up a deck of playing cards. "Just for fun, of course. No cash involved."

"Okay, but it's nice, so let's stay outside." Plus, she wanted to talk about some things she didn't want to say indoors where Ferrin and friends might be listening.

"I don't want to sit on the ground," Ivy said. "Why don't we sit on the side steps of the library?"

"Sure." They walked over to the library and around the side where the yellow day lilies were still in bloom.

"It's pretty back here," Ivy said. "Maybe this should become our new outside hangout."

They sat on the steps. Bryn leaned back on her elbows and closed her eyes. The slight spring breeze was calming. The air smelled fresh and clean and wait…she inhaled again… what was that scent? It was sort of hot and metallic.

"Do you smell something strange?" Bryn asked.

Valmont inhaled. "No."

Clint and Ivy both sniffed and then stood and looked around.

"It smells like fire," Clint said, "and metal."

"Hot metal," Ivy said. "If that makes sense."

"Can you tell where it's coming from?" Valmont asked.

Bryn focused and inhaled. The scent seemed to be drifting from the left. She pointed toward the back of the library. "From back there."

"Do we investigate, or alert Miss Enid?" Valmont asked. "Because fire and the library are not a good combination."

"Maybe we should check it out first," Bryn said. "If it's a Green performing a science experiment or a Black dragon doing some sort of metal sculpture, I don't want to get them in trouble."

Clint stood and shoved the deck of cards into his back pocket. "Let's go."

With Clint and Ivy in the lead, they walked farther down the side of the building. The flower beds were immaculate until they reached the back corner of the building where several plants had been trampled down like someone had walked on them many times.

Something else about the space seemed off. Bryn pointed

at the stonework. "What's wrong with this picture?"

"Before we investigate, we should take precautions." Valmont crept forward and peered around the corner of the building. "There's no one here, but now I can smell what you were talking about."

"Do you think someone cut through a grate or a door lock or something to sneak into the library?" Ivy asked.

Clint pointed at the stonework Bryn had been staring at. "If you look at it long enough, the lines shift."

Bryn put her hands on the wall and ran them along the mortar lines between the stones. What she saw didn't match what she touched. "I think it's like the root cellar door. Something is cloaking the actual stone."

"Step back," Ivy said. "Let me use my lightning to see if it reveals the truth."

Ivy sucked in a breath and then exhaled a small streak of lighting, which hit the stones, crackled, and then disappeared.

"I guess it wasn't a Black dragon this time," Clint said.

"Let me try." Bryn exhaled a fireball. Nothing happened. Time for ice. She sucked in a breath and shot ice at the wall, but nothing changed.

"Let's go get Miss Enid," Valmont said. "We might need wind to solve this problem."

"Actually, you need a sonic wave," an unfamiliar voice said from behind them. Bryn whirled around and was slammed with an invisible wave. She stumbled backward into Valmont. He wrapped his arms around her waist and then they both fought to stay upright.

The pressure of the wave made Bryn's ears pop and her vision blur. Lightning arcing over her head toward the Orange showed that Clint and Ivy were putting up a good fight.

"Aim low," Valmont shouted.

Right. The sonic waves would be the strongest in the middle and weaker on the edges. She inhaled and blasted fire at the unknown Orange dragon's feet. Her flames broke apart into little sparks, which winked out. Damn it. What could she do against this guy?

Ivy screamed something Bryn didn't understand, and then a fresh round of sonic waves came from the side and slammed both her and Valmont into the stone wall of the building. Pain shot through her shoulder as the bone crunched against the wall.

They were outmatched. If they didn't get help soon, they were going to lose this battle. And this Orange seemed intent on crushing her against the wall. She needed to draw someone's attention. Aiming high, she shot a fountain of flames into the sky. Then she aimed for a tree, blasting it until it caught fire.

"Stop her," a male voice shouted.

Bryn blasted fireball after fireball high into the air. Someone would have to see one. Right?

Lightning arched up into the sky as Clint and Ivy must have realized what she was doing.

She couldn't take a full breath. The bombardment of sonic waves increased, and the pressure against her body doubled, smashing her against the unyielding stone wall and crushing her chest. Spots danced before her eyes, and then the world went dark.

Chapter Twelve

Bryn fought to breathe. The pressure was gone, thank goodness, but her head ached like someone had tried to crack her skull open like a walnut. Those sonic waves were crazy strong. She inhaled again and winced at the stabbing pain in her side. Had she broken a rib? She pushed to a seated position, ignoring the sharp pain in her shoulder.

Where was she? It was pitch black. And why did her face feel weird? She touched her head and felt cold metal. What the hell? She traced the metal band all the way around her head. And her face…it felt like she was wearing a mask… holy hell…a Tyrant's Crown… Instinctively she grabbed at the circle of metal and tried to pull it off, even though she knew it wouldn't budge. Panic flared in her gut. Her breath came faster. Flames shot from her nostrils as she lost control of her element.

Claustrophobia hit…she was trapped…trapped in human form. The urge to shift overwhelmed her.

Valmont. She needed Valmont and Blood Magic to get this foul thing off of her head.

"Valmont?" She wanted to scream his name but what if the dragons who'd captured her were nearby? Her heart raced as she tried to focus and fight the claustrophobia that was clawing at her chest. "Valmont?"

She heard a muffled sound. Producing a fireball, she crawled toward the noise. Boots, she saw black leather boots at the end of jean-clad legs. Needing more light, she made the fireball bigger.

Valmont lay on his side with his hands tied behind his back. He was gagged, but his eyes—his eyes were open, and he was staring at her with a mixture of fear and rage. She removed the gag.

"Are you all right?" he asked.

"For the most part." She untied his hands. "What about you?"

He sat up rubbing his wrists. "I'm furious, but I'll live."

"Tell me you still have your sword." It was hard to tell in the dim light of her fireball.

He reached down to his side. "I do."

"Thank goodness. Get this freaking Tyrant's Crown off my head."

"Make your flame bigger so I can see what I'm doing." Valmont unsheathed his sword and pressed it against the metal band. "I'm ready."

Bryn reached up and slid her finger down the blade. She knew when the blood hit the crown because it felt like worms were crawling up her face. It was creepy and it itched, and if she ever found who did this to her, she was going to rip their throats out.

"This might hurt." Valmont lifted up on the crown. It felt like the damn thing had tiny claws in her skin and was refusing to let go. When he finally pulled it free, blood trickled down her forehead.

"Are you all right?" Valmont put his arm around her

shoulders and wiped her forehead with his sleeve.

"Much better." She leaned her head against his chest and took a deep breath. The scent of dust and spices made her cough. "Where are we?" She produced a larger fireball in her left hand so they could check out their surroundings. "And where are Clint and Ivy?"

They were in a room lined with shelves and cabinets. It looked like someone had ransacked the place, grabbing everything they could carry and leaving broken wooden boxes and dried herbs in their wake. There was a library table and chairs in the corner.

"Are there any candles?" Valmont asked.

Bryn investigated and found a wall sconce with a short fat candle. She lit it and then wiped off the mirror behind it. The light reflected across the room to two more candles.

"This looks like one of the rooms from the vault. Do you think we're in a room no one has discovered yet?"

"That would be my guess." Valmont pointed at a large wooden armoire. "Why is that cabinet the only one still closed?"

"Good question." Bryn crossed the stone floor, threading her way through the mess. She yanked the door open. The inside was like an empty closet, but a seam of light ran down the back wall. That was weird. "I think this might be a door."

Valmont joined her and peered into the closet. "Allow me." He reached in and pushed on the back panel, which moved about an inch before catching on something.

"It must be latched from the other side," Bryn said.

"Bryn, Valmont, is that you?" Ivy's voice came through the opening.

"Yes," Bryn said. "Are you guys all right?"

"We're not the ones stuck in a closet," Clint said. "Give us a minute and we'll get you out."

"This is a door between our rooms, disguised as a cabinet,"

Bryn said. "Step back and I'll blast through the door."

"Go ahead." Clint's voice came from far away.

Bryn inhaled a measured amount of air and shot a small, controlled stream of fire at the back wall until she burned a hole through the center. Then she doused the fire with snow.

Clint and Ivy sat at a library table. Ivy was holding her elemental sword while Clint held a ball of lightning. They both wore Tyrant's Crowns.

"Besides wearing the crowns from hell, are you both okay?" Bryn asked.

"We're both emotionally traumatized from these evil creations." Clint pointed at Valmont. "Please tell me you can take them off."

"We removed Bryn's, so we should be able to take care of yours."

Bryn and Valmont performed the Blood Magic ritual for Ivy and then for Clint.

"Thank you," Ivy said. "I never realized I could feel claustrophobic in my own body."

Bryn noticed Ivy was cradling her arm to her chest. "Are you hurt?"

"Yes, but nothing is as bad as those crowns. I thought I'd hyperventilate before Clint talked me down."

"I know the feeling." Bryn pointed at Ivy's arm. "What's going on there?"

"I got slammed into the wall pretty good, but so did you." Ivy grimaced. "Sonic waves suck."

"Want me to see if I can fix it?" Bryn asked.

Valmont pointed at one of the chairs. "Why don't you sit and heal your own injuries before you heal Ivy's."

"If they were really bad, I would've taken care of them already," Bryn said. "Let me help her."

"Nope." Ivy shook her head. "You first."

"It's three against one, in case you were wondering." Clint

pointed at the chair.

"Fine." Bryn sat and closed her eyes. She imagined Quintessence flowing to her shoulder and taking the pain away. Once that was taken care of, she focused on her ribs. Fixing bone seemed to take more effort than healing cuts, but her pain faded. She opened her eyes and waved Ivy over. "Come here."

Ivy pointed to her forearm. "I'm afraid it might be fractured."

Crap. That was new territory. "I can heal myself easier than someone else because I can sense the injuries inside my body. With you, I'm going to focus Quintessence into your arm and hopefully, it will know where to go to fix the bone. If anything feels wrong, tell me and I'll stop."

"Got it."

Bryn laid her hand on Ivy's arm and imagined Quintessence flowing out her fingertips.

Five minutes later, Ivy said, "That's better. You can stop."

"Okay," Valmont said. "Let's figure out where we are."

"The books in this room are about mining and plants," Ivy said.

"This can't be an Orange room," said Bryn, "because there aren't any Orange knights."

"We don't know that," Valmont said. "The dragons who attacked us could have been hybrids or Oranges."

"Do you think there could be knights we don't know about?" Clint asked.

"After kidnapping George, and losing two men, the Rebels could have decided it would've been easier to make their own knights rather than steal someone else's." Valmont glanced around the room. "Since there aren't any more cabinet doorways, we need to figure out another exit."

"Let's try Blood Magic first, Bryn said.

Valmont drew his sword, and placed it against the wall

opposite the closet door. Bryn slid her pointer finger down the blade. When the blood hit the wall, nothing happened.

He moved the sword over a few feet and they tried again, methodically working their way around the room. When no doors appeared, they went back to the room they woke up in and tried there. Again, no luck.

A tickle started in Bryn's throat. She tried to clear it but ended up coughing. Must be the dust. She needed a glass of water. Or, she needed something to use as a cup. Seeing nothing that she'd want to drink out of, she exhaled snow into her hand and then took a bite, letting it melt in her mouth.

"Is that the same thing as drinking your own spit?" Clint asked.

Bryn laughed. "I don't know, but I'm willing to share if anyone else is thirsty."

"No thanks," Ivy said. "Blood Magic didn't work. What's our next step?"

"I think it's my turn," Clint said. "I'm going to try blasting through a wall."

"We'll stay out of your way." Bryn sat at the table with Valmont and Ivy.

Ka-boom-boom-boom.

The lightning blast echoed through the room and shook Bryn and the chair she sat in. Mortar dust drifted through the air.

"I'm not sure that did any good," Clint said. "But I bet someone upstairs heard the noise. Hopefully, they'll come investigate."

"Do it again," Bryn said.

Ka-boom-boom-boom.

Bryn's teeth rattled with the blast.

Valmont clapped his hands over his ears. When the noise stopped, he shook his head. "Someone had to hear it."

"How long should I wait between blasts?" Clint asked.

"Maybe we should stick to a pattern so they'll know when to expect the next round," Ivy said.

"Like a song?" Clint grinned. "See if you recognize this one."

Kaboom-boom Kaboom-boom Kaboom-boom Kaboom.
Kaboom-boom Kaboom-boom Kaboom-boom Kaboom.

It took Bryn a minute to catch on. "Is that *Twinkle Twinkle Little Star?*"

"Yes." Clint grinned. "I thought about going with *Jingle Bells*, but I think this one works better." He repeated the blasts in the same rhythm, and then they waited.

"That wall is looking a little worse for wear." Valmont walked over, placed his palms flat on the stone and shoved. The stone blocks under his right hand gave, moving in an inch.

Bryn joined him at the wall. "Maybe we won't need anyone to rescue us." She pushed against the stone blocks, and they gave a little more.

"Be careful," Ivy said. "You don't want the wall coming down on top of you."

"Good point." Bryn walked back over to the table. "Help me put this against the wall, so if it collapses, it won't land on us."

Valmont put the short end of the rectangle against the wall and stood at the other end. Bryn joined him. "On three. One. Two. Three."

On three they pushed, and the stone wall groaned. "Again," Bryn said. They counted down and pushed the wall four more times before one of the stones by the ceiling broke loose and crashed down on the table, breaking it in half.

"I'm glad that wasn't one of our heads," Valmont said.

Breathing heavy but trying not to show it, Bryn grabbed half of the table and pushed it out of the way. Valmont took care of the other half.

"Stand back and let me handle the rest of it," Clint said. "I can clear a path without worrying about the debris."

"Good idea." Bryn backed up.

"And I might as well stick with *Twinkle Twinkle* while I do it."

Kaboom-boom Kaboom-boom Kaboom-boom Kaboom.
Kaboom-boom Kaboom-boom Kaboom-boom Kaboom.

On the last blast, the wall gave way. Blocks of stone crumbled and tumbled outward creating a mini landslide. Mortar dust filled the air like smog. Bryn covered her mouth and nose with her sleeve in an attempt to block the dust. As the haze settled, she moved toward the new exit they'd created, with Valmont by her side.

He grabbed her arm. "I'm not letting you out of my sight."

"Good plan." She produced a fireball in her right hand and held it high, because the area beyond the wall was cloaked in darkness. Leaning out of the opening, she peered to the left and then to the right. "We need more light." She increased the size of the fireball.

"It's a hallway," Valmont said. "So, we have two choices, left or right. Which direction should we go?"

"We'll need to see where we're going. The candles don't give off much light. We should make some torches," Clint said.

Valmont walked back into the room and grabbed the broken table, breaking off one of the legs near the base. Then he picked up a tattered book. "I'd never encourage book burning, but in this case, it seems appropriate." He shoved the skinny end of the table leg through the binding of the book and then held it out to Bryn. "Your turn."

She touched the pages of the book and sent a blast of fire through her palm. The pages smoldered before catching fire. Clint and Ivy made their own torches in the same manner.

"Valmont and I will go first. You guys can guard us from sneak attacks."

"Because as we learned earlier," Clint said, "those really

suck."

"Yes, they do." Bryn held a fireball in her right hand and strained to see farther down the hallway as they moved forward. The hall ended in a T intersection. "Left or right?" Bryn asked.

"Let's go right," said Valmont.

They came to another T intersection a few minutes later.

"Left this time," Bryn said. "Just to keep us from accidentally walking in circles."

"Hold on a minute." Clint pulled the deck of cards from his back pocket shuffled them around. "I'm going to put them in order from ace to king. I'll leave an ace here. That way if we come back we'll know it's one of the first hallways we investigated." He took the ace and wedged it between two stones on the wall.

"Good idea."

They continued walking. Whenever they came to an intersection, Clint left a card. By the time they were on the nine of hearts, the air seemed less stale.

"Does it seem like we've been moving slightly uphill?" Ivy asked.

"I don't know." Valmont inhaled. "But the musty smell is gone."

Both of those were positives. Or they would be, if they could find a door out of this place.

"I'm starting to think we aren't under the library," Ivy said. "I just don't think there'd be this many hallways. And if we'd been placed in rooms guarded by magic, could we have broken out?"

"The magic keeps people from finding the rooms, but I don't know if it keeps people from leaving the rooms," Bryn said.

"We've been missing for what, about an hour now?" Ivy said.

Clint nodded. "That's what it feels like, but we were unconscious when they stuck us in there. Who knows how long we were out?"

"I never thought about that," Bryn said. "But setting that tree on fire and shooting fireballs and lightning into the air would have had to attract some attention. Someone *should* be looking for us."

"I hope it's your grandfather," Ivy said. "Because he won't stop until he finds you."

The hall they were walking down curved to the right.

"Did you hear that?" Clint asked.

They all froze. Bryn closed her eyes and listened. There was a pattern to the noise. The *thunk* of metal against stone, over and over again.

"It sounds like shoveling. Where is it coming from?" Bryn moved forward a few feet and listened again. It sounded fainter.

"Maybe I should make some noise," Clint said, "so they know where we are."

"Go for it," Valmont said.

Ka-boom-boom-boom. Ka-boom-boom-boom.

As the sound of thunder faded, Bryn listened. The shoveling sounded like it was closer.

Valmont moved to stand next to her. "Where's that coming from?"

Dust sifted down onto Bryn's head. She looked up. A crack appeared in the ceiling above her head. "Shift!" She shouted to warn her friends as she shifted and launched herself sideways, taking Valmont down to the floor and covering him protectively with her wings.

Debris rained down. Someone growled. Another person screamed. Heavy objects smacked into Bryn's back and bounced off her scales. She'd be bruised, but the stone couldn't penetrate her hide.

"Bryn?" her grandfather yelled.

"Over here."

"It safe to shift back," another voice yelled.

Valmont lay on his side curled in a ball. "Are you all right?" she asked.

He coughed and sat up. "I think so."

She shifted back to human form. Her eyes watered, and she coughed.

"Everyone close your eyes," a voice that sounded like Miss Enid called out.

Bryn did as instructed and a light wind blew past her carrying grit that scratched her skin. After a moment, the grit was gone. "Now we should be able to see," Miss Enid said.

The first thing Bryn saw was her grandfather stalking toward her. Before she could get out a word, he hugged her. She hugged him back hard. "Thank you for finding us."

He released her and stepped back, regaining his composure. "How in the world did you end up three stories under the library?"

"The quick version is we interrupted Orange dragons who were doing something on the back corner of the library. They knocked us out with their sonic waves, and we woke up in a room without doors. We blasted our way out, and we've been walking ever since."

"Did you intentionally set the tree on fire?" her grandfather asked.

"Yes. Once I realized we couldn't beat them, I tried to signal for help."

"Smart move," her grandfather said. "You can fill in the details once we're above ground."

"I don't suppose there's an elevator nearby," Valmont joked.

"We should be able to fly up one floor, and walk from there." Miss Enid said. "We'll have someone come reinforce the openings later and build proper stairs so we can investigate."

Bryn shifted back to dragon form and moved her tail around so Valmont could use it as a step. "One winged elevator at your service."

He grinned and climbed on, settling between her wings. She felt a rush of warmth as the power of the dragon-knight bond flared between them. Watching her step, she threaded her way between the broken stones and then pushed off, aiming for the opening in the ceiling. She used a little too much oomph and had to shoot her wings out wide to keep from smashing her head and her rider into the ceiling of the next room.

"You could use some work on that maneuver," Valmont teased.

"Sorry." She stood off to the side as Clint and Ivy hopped up through the opening. As the others came up, she checked out the room they stood in. It looked exactly like the hallway below. Weird.

"You can shift back." Her grandfather shifted and led them down the hall and up a forty-five degree incline to another hallway and up another ramp until they came to a set of stairs which led them to what Bryn recognized as the hallway leading into the main vault room with the card catalog.

"Please tell me we don't have to climb three flights of stairs to tell you our story," Bryn said.

Her grandfather stopped. "What if I promise you food in my office?"

"Bribery works," Bryn said.

"Good. Go ahead. I'm going to call Marie and assure her you are safe and sound."

She walked up the spiral staircase and through the trapdoor onto the main floor. And then she headed for the stairs that lead to her grandfather's offices. "There had better be a lot of food," she muttered as she trudged up the last flight of steps.

Clint sighed. "I hope your grandfather doesn't mind if I camp out in his office afterward, because I am not walking back down those stairs. I need food and a nap."

"I can show you a really uncomfortable couch, if you're desperate," Valmont said.

Inside her grandfather's office, Bryn didn't wait for anyone to offer her food or drink. She sat down and grabbed a bottle of juice and drank the whole thing in two swallows.

"I still feel like there's dust in my throat," she said.

Valmont coughed like he agreed with her and then he drank a bottle of water.

Bryn ate three granola bars and an apple before she finally felt like dealing with questions.

"Okay. I can think now."

"Why don't you start at the beginning and tell us every detail, no matter how small."

Bryn recited the strange and terrifying events of their day.

"That part about the Tyrant's Crowns is most disturbing," her grandfather said. "We didn't know they existed until a few days ago, but our enemies knew where they were, managed to steal them and now seem to have them on hand and ready to use."

"Disturbing doesn't even begin to describe those freaking things," Clint said.

"I'm sure. It was smart of you to leave a trail of playing cards so we can find the rooms where you woke up," her grandfather said. "It sounds like a maze down there."

"Did you know those rooms existed?" Valmont asked.

"The architectural drawings of the library indicate passageways that were used when the structure was built. I want to know who the Oranges are that attacked you and what they were doing down there."

"I think the room we woke up in contained a bunch of dried herbs," Bryn said, "because they were scattered all over the floor."

"Maybe they wanted herbs to make medicine," Miss Enid said.

"It wasn't the two Orange students on campus who attacked us," Valmont said. "These were adults."

"I could sketch them for you," Clint said. "Before the sonic waves blurred my vision I got a pretty good look at two of them."

Miss Enid handed Clint paper and pencil. The moment the pencil touched the page, it moved fluidly like paint instead of charcoal. Bryn knew Clint could draw, but she'd never seen him do it. "That's amazing."

"I'm not just a pretty face," Clint said.

Bryn caught sight of the clock on the wall. "It's two in the morning? No wonder I'm so tired."

"It's two in the afternoon," her grandfather said. "You've been missing for almost eighteen hours."

"What?" Ivy said. "But we just woke about an hour ago."

Medic Williams came into the office. "Good timing on my part. Now I don't have to tell you why I need to scan you."

"So it's Monday afternoon? We were unconscious for sixteen hours?"

Medic Williams placed her hand on Bryn's forehead. She felt the warm honey sensation of Quintessence as it flowed down her head toward her shoulders. It felt so relaxing. When the medic was done, she said, "You don't have any internal or cerebral injuries, but I should probably check your shoulder and your ribs when I'm done with your friends."

When the medic checked Ivy, she frowned. "What did you to do to your arm?"

Bryn sat forward. "Please tell me I didn't screw up her

arm."

"You did this?"

"It hurt, so she tried to fix it." Ivy moved her arm. "See, it works."

The medic held out her own hand so her palm was parallel to the ground. "Try moving your hand like you're telling someone to stop." The medic demonstrated by moving her hand from horizontal to vertical.

Ivy tried and her hand only went up to a forty-five degree angle.

And Bryn was going to throw up. "Oh my God."

Ivy paled. "What's wrong?"

"I think Bryn fused part of the distal radioulnar joint. I'll have to break it to repair it."

And now she really was going to throw up. "I'm so sorry."

"Can I be asleep while it happens?" Ivy asked.

"Yes. Why don't you come to the Medlab with me now, and we can take care of it. And Bryn, don't try to heal anything but flesh wounds until you're trained."

Bryn nodded. How had she been so stupid to think she could do that?

Clint shoved the picture of the Orange dragons he'd drawn toward Miss Enid. "Hope that helps." He held his hand out to Ivy. "Come on. This is no big deal." As he walked past Bryn, he patted her shoulder. "Don't worry. We've got this."

Bryn forced a smile, but her eyes filled with tears. She could have screwed Ivy's arm up for life.

Valmont put his arm around her shoulders. "You tried to help her, and you took her pain away. Those are both good things."

Sure. "And now she has to let someone break her wrist because I screwed up."

"Your heart was in the right place," Valmont said.

"Your friend will be fine," Bryn's grandfather said. "Now

show us on these blueprints where you encountered the Orange dragons.

"The back right-hand corner." Bryn pointed to the spot. "The flowers were trampled down, and it smelled like hot metal."

"That coincides with what we saw," her grandfather said. "Why don't you two get some rest."

Back in her room, Bryn stared at the ceiling, unable to sleep. Why did she think she could heal Ivy's arm? That old saying kept taunting her. A little knowledge is a dangerous thing. Just because she could heal scratches and stop bleeding didn't mean she could heal bones.

Valmont knocked on her door and stuck his head in. "I'm betting you can't sleep."

She sat up. "Not a wink."

"Let's go get something from the cafe downstairs. Maybe that will help."

That sounded as good as any plan she could come up with. "I'll be out in a minute." While her grandfather was happy to have her back, she doubted he'd want to hear that she went to dinner in her pajamas.

After changing into jeans and a T-shirt, because there was only so much bending to societal pressure she was willing to do right now, they headed to the cafe.

On the way down the stairs, something strange happened. Blues made eye contact with her. Some of them nodded. A few smiled. So she nodded and smiled back. Maybe they'd heard she and her friends had disappeared and they were glad she was okay.

Once they were seated at the restaurant, Valmont said, "Did we wake up in some alternate universe where Blues are…I won't say nice, but civil?"

"Either that, or they're glad we aren't dead, on general principal."

Valmont snorted. "So it's not personal."

"Who knows?"

The waiter who'd brought Bryn a carafe of coffee a few days ago appeared at the table with bread and butter. "I figured you'd be hungry."

"Thank you." Maybe this guy could fill her in. She'd need to be vague because who knew how much he already knew or if her grandfather wanted everyone to know. Still, she'd give it a shot. "What are people saying about the incident on campus?"

"They're saying that you and your friends helped stop an attack by the Rebels." He leaned in. "Is it true they were Orange dragons?"

"We think so," Bryn said.

"Glad you guys are okay. Now what can I get you for dinner?"

They ordered steaks and baked potatoes. Once the waiter left, Bryn said. "Did we stop an attack?"

"I think we interrupted them while they were gathering supplies. Maybe you should call your grandfather and ask him what happened or what the Directorate is claiming happened so we can keep our facts straight."

True. The Directorate was good at spinning stories to suit their needs. She was probably lucky Ferrin hadn't taken control and accused her of siding with the Rebels.

Chapter Thirteen

Missing Monday classes meant all three of them had homework to make up. and Valmont got to listen to them gripe about it for most of Tuesday.

"You'd think they'd give us a break and not expect us to make up the work," Clint said as they sat down at their usual table in the dining hall for lunch.

"Maybe the homework is balanced out by the fact you're being credited with foiling a Rebel attack," Valmont said.

"According to Miss Enid and the Directorate, we interrupted them in the middle of some sort of espionage, but I wish they'd give us more details." Bryn ripped open her bag of chips. "Right now, I feel like a fraud."

"Well, they obviously weren't here to throw a surprise party," Ivy said. "They slammed us into the wall, rendered us unconscious, and put those evil crowns on our heads, so they must've been doing something they didn't want anyone to find out about."

Bryn cringed. "How's your wrist?"

Ivy waved her hand up and down and all around. "See,

it moves in all directions like it's supposed to, so please stop apologizing."

"I'll try to keep the 'sorrys' to a minimum, but you'd be doing the same thing, if the situation were reversed." Something else was bothering her. "Why won't Medic Williams tell us how the Rebels knocked us out?"

"Either she doesn't know," Clint said, "or she thinks we won't want to hear that the sonic waves damaged our brains."

"I don't want to hear that," Valmont said. "But I do want to know why the Rebels knocked us out and shoved us in a secret sub-basement, rather than killing us."

"I'd like to think that murdering us wasn't an option," Clint said. "Because that is all sorts of disturbing, but I wonder if they knew we would wake up and escape. They did shove us in doorless rooms several floors underground without food or water, not counting drinking Bryn's spit-snow."

"Don't forget about the Tyrant Crowns," Bryn said.

"I've tried," Clint said. "Believe me."

"If they wanted us dead, there are many more efficient ways to kill us." Valmont pointed at his sword. "I realize the Tyrant Crowns were disturbing, but they could have slit our throats. And they didn't steal my sword for which I am hugely thankful, so I think they meant for us to survive."

"Even if they did mean for us to wake up and find our way out, why were they messing around with the library in the first place?" Clint asked.

"The herbs they took from that room could be rare," Ivy said.

"Would they really risk being captured for dried plants?" Valmont asked.

"Some herbs grow for years before they can be harvested," Ivy said. "So maybe."

"All this guessing is getting us nowhere. Let's visit Miss Enid after dinner tonight and see if she has any news to share," Bryn said.

Miss Enid was sorting books when they found her that evening. She took one look at them and said, "If you've come to me for answers about the attack, I don't have any because no one is answering my questions. The Directorate sealed off the lower levels of the libraries, and they are not asking for my help in their investigation."

"And that is super annoying," Bryn said.

"Yes, it is." Miss Enid adjusted a stack of books. "Guards have been placed around the library at all known entrance points, so there is that."

"Do you know anything about sonic waves and how they are used as weapons?" Valmont asked. "Because we want to know if the Rebels knocked us unconscious using their element."

"Prolonged exposure to sonic waves can result in death," Miss Enid said. "But we have no way of knowing if that's why all four of you passed out. It's more likely they knocked you out with their sonic waves and then drugged you before dumping you in the sub-basement."

"They'd need Orange knights to access those rooms, right?" Bryn said.

"Unless they were really good at knocking down and repairing stone walls in a short span of time, then I'd say yes."

"So why isn't my grandfather giving an Orange dragon a knight so we can investigate those rooms?"

"I asked the very same question," Miss Enid said. "And I was not given the courtesy of an answer."

"So basically, you're as much in the dark as we are," Ivy said.

Miss Enid sighed. "I know they must have their reasons for this behavior, but I still find it highly irritating. I was hoping your grandfather had shared something more with you."

"Not yet." Bryn pointed toward the stairwell that led up

to the Directorate offices. "What are the odds that walking up several flights of stairs will result in us getting any answers?"

"You won't know until you try," Miss Enid said.

"Then I guess we're hitting the steps."

Halfway up the last flight of stairs, Bryn stopped. "Forget it. I changed my mind."

"You've been awfully tired today," Valmont said. "Even more than I would have expected."

"Valmont's right," Ivy said. "I think this may have hit you harder for some reason."

Way to make her feel like a wuss. "Maybe it's because I ran all over creation with Jaxon the same day this happened. I was tired going into the situation."

"Could be." Valmont moved ahead of her and held the door open. "Just a little farther."

Ugh. I am so done with stairs. If I ever have a chance to update the campus, I am adding elevators to every single building.

No one prevented Bryn from knocking on her grandfather's office door.

"Come in," her grandfather called out.

She opened the door to see him studying blueprints of the library. She almost started the conversation by saying she was sorry to bother him, but that wasn't true. "Hey, we were wondering if there was any news on what the Rebels were actually doing here on campus."

Her grandfather set the drawings of the buildings down. "We found charges underneath two of the other corners of the library and part of a detonator."

"Detonator as in they were going to blow up the library?" Bryn asked.

"No. The charges were too small," her grandfather said. "We think they were trying to excavate something from one of the lower levels."

"They already have the chest of Tyrant's Crowns, which we know about firsthand," Bryn said. "And they cleaned out the herb storage. What else were they looking for?"

"More weapons would be my guess."

"What do the rest of the students think happened?" Clint asked. "Because people are being unusually nice to us."

"I think news of the detonator leaked, so you are probably being credited with stopping a possible bomb threat. And that is not a bad thing."

"No. It's not. But we have another question. Why haven't you given an Orange dragon a knight to help find Orange doorways?"

He shuffled some papers together on his desk. "At the moment there are no Orange dragons on campus."

Okay. "What happened to Octavius and Vivian? The two Orange dragons in our year?"

"They have been sent home as a precaution."

Bryn was about to have a hissy fit. She opened her mouth to object, but her grandfather held up his hand to silence her. "It was for their own good. Other Directorate members wanted them thrown in jail. Sending them home on a precautionary probation was the lesser of two evils."

Her grandfather really was one of the good guys. "Thank you for doing what you could to take care of them."

He nodded. "Political games are afoot. Ferrin is preaching a more radical approach which will turn into a witch hunt, if we aren't careful."

"I don't suppose we could send him home on some sort of probation," Bryn said.

Her grandfather smiled. "Unfortunately no. And you shouldn't make jokes like that while you're on campus."

She hadn't been joking. "Understood. I guess we'll go do our homework now. Unless you wanted to give us a pass on Monday's work since we helped thwart a Rebel plan?"

"Nice try." He opened a folder and picked up a piece of paper. "But you foiled a Rebel attack so your homework should be a breeze by comparison."

"Bryn, you've been outsmarted," Clint said. "Or outsmart-assed. I'm not sure which."

Her grandfather chuckled. "That was highly inappropriate. Now go."

Bryn and her friends left and pulled the office door closed behind them. "Want to hang out in my room?" she asked.

"Sure." They descended the stairs, and by the time they reached her room, Bryn was out of breath. "Something isn't right."

Valmont frowned. "That's what I thought. I'm going to call a medic."

Bryn sat on the couch and closed her eyes. The sound around her faded as she drifted but didn't quite sleep. Sometime later she felt the warm honey sensation starting at the top of her head, which meant Medic Williams had arrived and was scanning her. That was good. She opened her eyes and did a double take. The last thing she remembered was closing her eyes on the couch, and now she was in a bed in the Medical Center.

"How'd I get here?" she asked.

Her grandmother, who sat in a chair on the left side of the bed, moved in closer and held her hand. "Thank goodness you're awake. How do you feel?"

"Okay, I guess. What's going on?"

"We're trying to figure that out," Medic Williams said.

"Where's Valmont?"

"Right here," he said from the doorway. "You would wake up the moment I left to run to the restroom." He crossed the room and stood to her right. Reaching for her hand, he gave it a tight squeeze.

Everyone seemed so serious. "I feel normal. Why are you

all looking at me like I've been in a coma for six months?"

Bryn's grandmother made eye contact with the medic but didn't say anything. Valmont looked away.

Okay, then. "I'm about ten seconds from a panic attack." And she wasn't joking. Flames were igniting in her gut and the taste of smoke crawled up the back of her throat. "Someone needs to start talking."

"What's the last thing you remember?" Medic Williams asked.

"Falling asleep on the couch in my room while we waited for you."

"That was more than twenty-four hours ago," Medic Williams said. "And you've woken up about every four hours since then. Do you remember waking up here before?"

"No." Bryn turned to her grandmother. "Is she serious?"

Her grandmother nodded. "We've had this conversation quite a few times, but you never seem to remember it."

And the panic attack hit. Flames crawled up the back of Bryn's throat. She focused on turning them to snow and exhaled sleet across the bedding. What did they mean she'd been awake before now? *How's that possible? Wouldn't I remember?*

"Calm down," Medic Williams said. "Whatever it is, it doesn't appear to be life threatening. We think a drug was introduced into your system which could cause repetitive temporary black outs."

"Why?" Bryn managed to choke out the single word before ice blasted out of her mouth, hung suspended in the air a moment, and then crashed to the floor splintering into a million pieces.

"Bryn." Her grandmother's tone was like the crack of a whip. "You must maintain control."

Right. Control. Control is important. Except control over her own life had been slipping away bit by bit over the past year. This was the final straw. She was done. And she was damned if she was going to apologize. Focusing on fire, she let the heat build inside of her, fanning the flames of her frustration and anger. Smoke poured from her nostrils with every exhalation.

Valmont stood and went over to a window. Yanking it open, he said. "I know you're scared and mad. Come here."

She stood on shaky legs and concentrated on putting one foot in front of the other. When she reached the window, she sat on the ledge and stared outside. The window faced a green space with flowers and trees. She didn't want to take her anger out on them. Aiming up and away she took a deep breath and then blasted flames into the air, venting all the despair and confusion about the mess her life had become recently. When she was done, a lethargy overtook her. She reached for Valmont's hand. He pulled her over so she sat on his lap and kissed the top of her head.

"It's okay. We'll figure this out."

She could hear her grandmother talking on the phone, alerting the school that they were performing a test on Bryn's element, and she'd passed with flying colors. Nothing to be worried about. If only that were true.

"Can we talk now?" Medic Williams asked.

"Yes," Bryn said. "I don't foresee another mental breakdown until the next time you wake me up and give me this terrifying news."

"I understand you're stressed, but we need to work on this while you're awake. From what I've been able to determine, the drug is meant to cause serial blackouts. It seems as if someone is holding you hostage, without holding you hostage, and they should be contacting your grandfather and the Directorate with their demands soon."

"That's freaking wonderful," Bryn said.

"Better than actually being held hostage," Valmont said.

"I guess. But it's still not how I want to spend my free time." Bryn sighed. "What if I drink a ton of coffee, would that keep me from blacking out?"

"It couldn't hurt," Medic Williams said.

"I'll go order coffee and food." Bryn's grandmother stood and left the room.

"You should know," Valmont said. "Your grandmother is barely holding it together. The first time you were awake and then fell back asleep in front of her, she didn't understand what we were trying to tell her. Bryn...she thought you had died. It was terrible. She fell apart.

Way to make her feel guilty. Not that it was her fault she was sick or poisoned or whatever, but doing that to her grandmother made her feel awful.

"Let's concentrate, people," Medic Williams said. "We're trying to figure out what you might have done or been exposed to that the others weren't."

"When we woke up, we used Blood Magic to remove the Tyrant's Crown. We found the door to Clint and Ivy's room and removed their crowns. Then, Valmont and I searched for doorways out, so I cut myself about ten times on his sword."

Valmont sucked in a breath. "My sword. I was surprised they let me keep it because common sense would tell you to disarm the enemy, but maybe they coated the blade in something knowing we'd need to use Blood Magic to remove the crowns and search for doors."

"That's brilliant and terribly disturbing," said Bryn.

"Give it to me." Medic Williams held out her hand.

Valmont unstrapped his sword belt and passed it to her in the leather scabbard. "I'd warn you it's sharp, but you probably already know that."

"Keep Bryn talking, while I take some swabs from the blade and run some tests." Medic Williams exited the room.

Bryn's grandmother came back in the door followed by a

Red pushing a cart loaded with coffee, sandwiches, and candy bars.

"Come here." Bryn threw her arms wide, indicating she wanted a hug.

Her grandmother didn't hesitate. She crossed the room and wrapped Bryn in her arms.

"I'm so sorry about all of this," Bryn said.

"Why are you apologizing to me? It's your grandfather's fault this is happening."

That's new. But best not to ask now. "If this is freaking me out, I know it's freaking you out, too." Seemed like the simplest explanation.

Giving one more squeeze before releasing her, her grandmother said, "You have no idea. Now, it's time for coffee." She poured a cup and handed it to Bryn. "Let's see if we can't keep you awake for awhile."

Bryn downed the cup of coffee without adding sugar, which proved how desperate the situation was. "We may have figured something out." She explained about the sword.

"If they can isolate whatever drug is doing this, then maybe they can counteract it."

Her grandmother's cell phone rang. "Excuse me." She answered and nodded along to whatever the person on the other end of the phone was saying. "I understand." She ended the call. "Your grandfather received a phone call from someone claiming to be responsible for your condition. They want Jaxon to escort you to a location they'll pick. They claim they'll give you the antidote if Jaxon brings the ransom.

"Why involve him?" Wasn't what she was going through torture enough without adding Jaxon to the equation?

"Probably because the two of you represent the most wealthy and powerful dragon families."

"What do they want as ransom?" Valmont asked.

"They want the deed to a large area of land where there

used to be a mining community. They claim they'll leave us alone, if we leave them alone."

"Why does that sound too good to be true?" Bryn asked.

"Because it is," her grandmother said. "We'll never trust them to keep their word, and they'll never trust us. It makes me think there must be something else on the land they want."

"Or under it," Valmont said. "Did anyone ever investigate where the root cellar behind my cabin lead to?"

"I don't have access to that information. Let me make a call." She dialed her phone and mentioned Valmont's question about the land.

Raised voices could be heard coming through the phone. Her grandmother's eyes narrowed as she hit the button to hang up. "Your grandfather didn't have time to talk. Ferrin was shouting in the background. He doesn't want to go along with the ransom plan."

Bryn laughed. "Of course he doesn't. He'd be happier if I disappeared. Jaxon could marry a proper Blue and keep the pure Westgate lineage he's so proud of."

Medic Williams came back into the room carrying Valmont's sword and a computer printout. "You were right. The sword was coated in a combination of herbs I've never seen used together before. I'm assuming you don't polish your sword with any strange herb-filled mixture."

"Nope."

"That's what I thought. Now we should be able to manufacture an antidote. It will take time. Several Greens are working on it as we speak."

A wave of tiredness hit Bryn. "Damn it. It's happening again."

"Can't you give her something to keep her awake?" Valmont asked.

The medic pulled a vial and a syringe from her pocket. "We could try a shot of epinephrine."

"Good idea," Bryn said. "Because I'd rather not relive this fun conversation."

Medic Williams plunged the syringe into the vial and drew out half an inch of liquid.

"Are you sure it's safe?" Bryn's grandmother asked.

"Seventy percent sure." The medic held the needle up to the light and flicked it for air bubbles.

"I don't like those odds," said Valmont.

"Shouldn't this be my decision?" Bryn griped.

"No," Valmont and her grandmother said in unison.

"It won't hurt you to go back to sleep for a little while," Valmont said. "We'll be here when you wake up."

"We could have the antidote by then," her grandmother said.

"I want the shot." *How can they not understand how terrifying this is?*

The medic moved closer and held out the syringe. "It's a small dose."

"If I were in your situation, I'd insist on the shot, too." Bryn's grandmother sighed. "Go ahead."

"Thank you."

"This goes in your thigh." The medic moved the sheet covering Bryn. "And you're going to feel it."

Valmont grabbed Bryn's hand and squeezed. "Do it."

The jab of he needle wasn't as bad as the plunger being depressed. The pain seemed to jolt her awake, or maybe that was the drug. The tiredness faded as Bryn's heart rate sped up.

"I think it worked."

"We've bought you some time," Medic Williams said.

There was a knock on the door.

Bryn adjusted her sheets. "Come in."

Jaxon entered the room slowly, like he wasn't sure what he might find. When he saw she was awake, he smiled. "Have you considered asking them to name a room after you? You seem to spend a lot of time here."

She rolled her eyes. "Hello to you, too."

Jaxon nodded toward Bryn's grandmother. "My father doesn't know I'm here, so if he contacts you, you might not want to mention it."

"Thank you for coming," her grandmother said.

He nodded in acknowledgment. "Catch me up on what's going on."

Bryn told him about the sword and their hopes to make an antidote.

"So we may not need to meet with the Rebels, after all."

"We don't know how long it will take to produce the antidote," said Medic Williams.

"Where does that leave us?" Jaxon asked.

"I guess we wait and see," Bryn said.

Her grandmother's phone rang again.

Was this it? Were the Rebels about to make their demands? Marching off to meet the Rebels with Jaxon by her side didn't sound like a wonderful idea. And if they thought she was going anywhere without Valmont, they were going to be quite disappointed.

Why couldn't the Rebels move someplace and set up their own way of living? The Directorate was strict and their ways of thinking were outdated, but not all of them were as power-crazy as Ferrin. Her grandfather had turned out to be reasonable about most things.

"Bryn, are you all right?" her grandmother asked.

"What? Sorry. Just lost in thought."

"Your grandfather suggested a compromise where Valmont would escort you along with a few trusted guards. Jaxon wouldn't need to be involved."

"Did the Rebels go for it?" Valmont asked.

"No. As a compromise, they suggested a meeting at your cabin in the tunnels behind your house but they're still insisting Jaxon go with you."

"Why meet in the tunnels?" Bryn asked.

"It's a defensible position," Valmont said. "We'd be at their mercy as we climbed down to meet them. I don't like it."

"We'll make them come to us," Jaxon said.

"How?"

"We tell them we figured out how they poisoned you and we're not sure we even need their antidote, but to speed up the healing process we'll meet with them in Valmont's cabin. If they want the deed to the land, they have to send two men with the antidote in to talk with us. We can have our people in the forest waiting for any sign of trouble. They can have their own people doing the same thing, so they should accept the compromise. And that way we don't have to go down into an unknown tunnel where they could be waiting to ambush us."

"That might work." Bryn's grandmother made the call. After explaining the idea she hung up and said, "Now we wait for the Rebels to contact us."

Ten minutes later, a knock sounded on the door.

"Come in," Bryn called out.

Eve entered the room. Her eyes were red rimmed, and she had her arms wrapped around her rib cage.

"What's wrong?" Bryn asked.

"Someone took Adam. They said if you don't follow their orders, they'll kill him."

"Who is Adam?" Jaxon asked.

"Her boyfriend," Bryn said.

"Why involve you?" Jaxon asked. "They already told us what they wanted."

"I think they're punishing me because I came forward as a Throwback." Eve sniffled.

"Again, why would that matter to them?" Jaxon asked.

Eve made eye contact with Bryn like she was asking a question.

"You can trust us," Bryn said. "We know you're a victim here, too." She wasn't going to out Eve.

"The truth is," Eve took a shaky breath, "I'm not a Throwback. I'm a hybrid."

Bryn prayed her expression of surprise was convincing.

Jaxon's eyes narrowed. "The Rebels, do you know them?"

"I'm not associated with them, I swear. What I told you in the interview was the truth. I just want to live my life and blend in. I want to be normal."

"Your boyfriend," Jaxon said. "Is he like you?"

Eve nodded. "Please. You have to help me."

"If you help us," Jaxon said, "we'll help you. Tell us everything you know about the hybrids who've attacked us."

"There are good hybrids out there, who want to live a normal life. Then there are radicals who want to overthrow the Directorate. They live in the forest in dragon form most of the time." Eve spoke to Bryn. "The guy who died of an aneurysm at your grandparent's estate? He was one of them."

"Alec was a hybrid?" Bryn gasped. "What about his sister Nola?" Her ex-boyfriend's chosen mate. "Is she a hybrid, too?"

"I don't know. I've never seen her anywhere but school." Eve bit her lip like she was trying to decide how much to say. "Mrs. Sinclair, can you give me your word, as a Blue, that nothing will happen to my family and my friends?"

Bryn's grandmother picked up her phone and then she put it down. "Yes. I believe I can give you my word as a Sinclair and Jaxon can give you his word as a Westgate that your family and friends will not be harmed."

Jaxon appeared surprised. "You're asking me to make a Directorate decision on my own, without consulting my father?"

"Your father isn't here right now. Neither is my husband, but we are both intelligent Blues. I believe we can and should speak for the Directorate, since time seems to be of the essence."

Jaxon stared off into space for a moment. "I suppose you're right. If my father disowns me, I could always marry Bryn for her money."

Bryn laughed. "We have the important matters taken care of. Eve tell us everything."

"I come from a small town with other families like mine. Everyone is a mix of Red and Black. About a year ago, some of the dragons who live in the forest came to a town meeting and talked about how they wanted to change things. They tried to recruit us, but we've been taught since birth that it's our job to fit in. So they didn't have many takers.

"How old is your town?" Bryn's grandmother asked.

"It's as old as the Institute. Our town lore claims dragons who were denied marriages, and Mistresses who became pregnant, snuck off together and created their own community. As the town's population grew, they knew they risked discovery, so everyone trained in Quintessence to hide their true coloring, like Bryn does with her hair. Any dragons skilled enough to blend in with the Clans attended the Institute. Anyone who couldn't, or didn't want to, was homeschooled."

Bryn's heart ached. If her parents had found a community of hybrids, they might still be alive.

"Are there other communities like yours?" Bryn's grandmother asked.

"I believe so, although I've never visited them."

"We need to know more about the Rebels," Jaxon said. "Can you give us names of dragons who you know for sure are involved?"

Eve sniffled. "I don't know them by name. I've seen a few of them on campus. When the merchants of Dragon's Bluff had the fair a few months back, the Rebels were the ones who flew in and startled the guards."

"We need more specific information," Jaxon said.

"If I tell you, do you swear you'll help me?" Eve asked. "If I tell you who he is, and he finds out—"

"We will do all within our power to keep you safe," Bryn's grandmother said.

"Onyx," Eve said. "He's the one who is always talking about how dragons should be free to make more choices. He's the one who gave speeches at our town meeting. Some of the Rebels were with him."

Bryn's grandmother gasped. "That traitor."

Valmont's stare was a tangible weight on Bryn's shoulder. She knew what he was going to say. "You're wrong." No matter what type of jerk her former love interest Zavien had turned out to be, he couldn't be involved with the Rebels.

"How do you know?" Jaxon asked.

"The same way I knew Onyx gave me the creeps from day one because he seemed like a sleazy television lawyer. The same way I'd bet Nola and her pretentious fake flowing dresses are involved, and she's probably the bitch who poisoned me and stole the snowflake bracelet my mother gave me. Alec said he had people on the inside. The Rebels who attacked on Valentine's Day said they had people everywhere."

"My driver, who tried to kill Bryn, did you know him?" her grandmother asked.

"No, but if he was a hybrid, they could have threatened to expose him or his family. And the general belief of my kind is that Ferrin Westgate will have any hybrid executed because he's still bitter over Bryn's mom running out on him. No offense, Jaxon, but it's what everyone believes."

Jaxon seemed to choose his words carefully. "My father is an honorable man, but Bryn's mother betrayed him and damaged his reputation. That would have affected his feelings toward hybrids in general."

"You are not your father," Bryn's grandmother said. "And

while I don't condone what my daughter did, innocent people shouldn't suffer for her transgressions. Do you agree?"

"Of course I do. But my father will never concede that point. We can't tell him we know of other hybrids, because I can't guarantee he'll believe they aren't behind the attacks. Which is why the information Eve gave us should probably never leave this room. But we now know that Onyx is a key player. That is information we can pass along to my father."

Bryn's grandmother's cell rang. She checked caller ID. "It's Ephram. Follow my lead." She pressed a button. "Ephram, I've put you on speaker so Bryn can hear, too."

"Fine. We have the deed the Rebels asked for and a contingency of guards ready to escort Bryn and Jaxon to the designated area."

"There's something you should know," Bryn's grandmother said. "We have it on good authority that Onyx is involved with the Rebels and he is in contact with the Revisionists who live in the forest."

"How did you learn this?"

"A Throwback named Eve came forward. The Rebels kidnapped her boyfriend Adam because they wanted her to lead Bryn and Jaxon into a trap. We think it would be better to tell the extortionists we're close to coming up with our own cure and we'll meet them in Valmont's cabin to discuss a truce. Tell them to meet us there in an hour with Adam, and we'll trade them their cure and Adam for the deed."

"That is unacceptable," Ferrin boomed in the background. "You will not endanger my son with some half-baked plan."

"It's a good plan, Father," Jaxon said. "I believe it will work, and I'm choosing to participate. Maybe if we give them some land where they feel safe from persecution, they'll leave us alone."

And the room went dead quiet. Ferrin couldn't undermine his son in front of witnesses. Jaxon was his key to controlling the Directorate after he retired. "If you believe this is a wise choice, I will trust you."

"Thank you, Father. Can you relay the message to your contact that we'll meet them in an hour? And about the guards—I don't want them attacking unless I give a signal."

"And what signal did you have in mind?" Ferrin asked.

"Valmont, it's your cabin," Jaxon said. "What do you suggest?"

"Not burning down my cabin," Valmont said.

Jaxon glared at him.

"Fine. Sorry. Trying to lighten the mood. If there is trouble, I can toss some oil on the fire and the smoke coming from the chimney will turn black."

"I'd rather not depend on your aim and the ability to see what color smoke is drifting from your chimney," Jaxon said.

"Can't you give us one of the bugs or cameras that are in the library so someone can hear us? If there's trouble, one of us could say a code word."

"That might work," Bryn's grandfather's voice came through the phone. "The code word should be something you won't accidentally say."

"Zen," Bryn said. "The code word should be Zen since we're hoping for peace."

"And we're not likely to accidentally say that," Valmont said.

"Fine. I'll send an SUV to pick you up at the medical center."

"If we're going to do this," Bryn said. "I need real clothes. I'm not facing the Rebels in a hospital gown."

Her grandmother pointed to an overnight bag against the wall. "I asked Valmont to pack a bag for you, so you'd have something to put on once you were well."

"Thank you." Bryn picked up her empty coffee mug and held it out for a refill. "One more cup, just to be safe."

Chapter Fourteen

Jaxon drove the SUV while Valmont rode shotgun, and Bryn sat in the backseat checking the connection on the listening device she'd inserted into the seam of her shirt. Thank goodness Valmont had been the one to pack her bag for the medical center. He'd included a dress her grandmother would approve of and a pair of jeans and a shirt Bryn liked to wear on the weekends when the dress code wasn't an issue.

The fact that he'd picked her Munch's The Scream shirt was amusing because screaming was pretty much what she felt like doing at the moment. The caffeine from the coffee and the boost from the adrenaline shot Medic Williams had given her were wearing off. The world was starting to grow hazy around the edges as she blinked to maintain focus.

"Valmont, we may have a problem," Bryn said.

He whipped around. "What's wrong?"

"I'm not sure how much longer I can stay awake."

"That is why I borrowed this when Medic Williams wasn't paying attention." Valmont pulled a syringe and a vial of epinephrine from his pocket.

"Doesn't it go against your knightly code to steal?" Jaxon asked.

"My dragon comes first," Valmont said, like it was the absolute truth. "Bryn, do you want me to give you a small dose? We could do half of what the medic did."

There was no way she was sleeping through the negotiations with the Rebels. "Do it."

"Pull over so I can get in the back seat with Bryn," Valmont said.

"What if someone is watching us?" Jaxon asked.

"They'll probably understand why I'm doing it because they know Bryn is still ill."

"Fine." Jaxon slowed down and pulled off onto the side of the road.

Valmont joined Bryn in the backseat. Before he could put on his seatbelt, Jaxon was back on the road.

"In a hurry?" Bryn asked.

"The longer we take to get there, the more opportunity there is for something to go wrong," Jaxon said. "I can assure you, the Directorate is looking for any excuse to attack the Rebels. We need to limit the time we're in the Rebels' company as much as possible. We do not want to be caught in the middle."

"Isn't that where we are right now?" Bryn said. "Caught between two forces who want different things?"

"Which is why we need to get in and get out," Jaxon said.

"You won't get any argument from me. Once Bryn has the antidote, I say we run for the proverbial hills." Valmont drew out a small dose of epinephrine and then held the syringe up to the light, tapping it for air bubbles. "I'm going to do this through your jeans. Ready?"

"Okay." Bryn looked out the window so she wouldn't see the needle jabbing into her thigh. That didn't stop her from wincing.

"Sorry," Valmont said. "There. It's over."

"Good." Her heart rate increased, and the fuzzy quality of her vision cleared up. "That stuff is a miracle drug."

"Too much of that miracle drug will make your heart explode," Jaxon said.

"Seriously?"

"Maybe not literally, but it can kill you, so no more shots unless they're from a medic," Jaxon said. "That's just common sense."

"Sure." It's not like she *wanted* any more shots, but desperate times called for desperate measures.

They turned up the winding road, which lead to Valmont's cabin. The epinephrine made Bryn hyper-aware of every bump the SUV hit. Why did people like to drive these things? She wanted a car that smoothed out the bumps. And it would be awesome if it came with its own coffee maker. *Wait. What? Where did that thought come from?* She shook her head.

"What's wrong?" Valmont asked.

She tried to explain. "My mind is wandering in weird directions, like my brain isn't up to full speed."

"You're probably exhausted." Valmont brushed hair back from her face. "It's been a rough couple of days."

"With all the sleeping I've done, you'd think I'd be rested." When they pulled into the drive, Bryn shivered. "Is it me, or do you feel like you're being watched?"

"I'm sure we are," said Jaxon. "Both inside this car and once we step outside of it. Keep that in mind." He drove to the top of Valmont's driveway and then stopped the SUV, putting it into park. "Bryn, Valmont should help you walk up to the cabin. Don't let them know your true strength and maybe they'll underestimate you, which could give us an advantage."

"I really hate it when he's right," Valmont muttered.

Bryn chuckled. "Okay then, let the fun begin."

Valmont helped her from the car, keeping his arm around

her lower back for support, and Jaxon walked ahead to open the door. Inside the front room Bryn was startled to find Adam and Onyx sitting on Valmont's couch. She stumble-stepped in response.

"Surprised to see me?" Onyx grinned like he'd played a huge joke on her.

She'd had a head's up, thanks to Eve, but she never imagined he'd be the one meeting them. And she hadn't thought he'd be by himself. "What are you doing here?"

"I'm here to negotiate a truce. There are many peaceful hybrids who'd like a place where they could feel safe."

"And you speak for them?" Jaxon asked.

"No," Onyx answered. "I speak for several factions of dragons. They don't all want peace, but they don't all want war, either."

"What?" Were the meds making her fuzzy headed or was Onyx making zero sense?

"We came, so let Adam go," Valmont said.

"You're free to leave," Onyx said to the hybrid dragon. "I suggest you exit by the front door and don't make any sudden movements."

Adam stood. "You saw Eve. She's all right?"

"Worried about you," Bryn said, "but she's fine."

Adam left by the front door.

"Did you bring the antidote?" Valmont asked.

"Did you bring the deed?" Onyx asked.

Jaxon held out an attaché case. "We have it right here. Let's trade and be done with this."

Onyx stood. "It's not that simple. I wasn't sure you'd hold up your end of the bargain, so I took certain precautions by leaving the antidote in the tunnels out back."

"What kind of crap are you trying to pull?" Bryn asked.

"Just trying to protect my interests." Onyx gestured toward the back door. "If you'll come with me—"

"No way," Valmont said. "You'd have the tactical advantage. Someone could be waiting at the bottom of the ladder to kidnap Bryn, or worse."

"My goal today is to secure a safe place for hybrids and Throwbacks. Killing Bryn wouldn't further that goal. If you want the antidote, follow me."

"No," Jaxon said. "If you want the deed, retrieve the antidote."

"Sorry." Onyx continued walking toward the back door. "It's not going to work that way."

"Now what?" Bryn asked, hoping someone would have an answer.

"I guess we follow him," Valmont said.

"Absolutely not." Jaxon turned toward the front door. "We can't trust him. We're leaving."

Bryn felt like she was caught in a political game of tug-of-war. "Wait. I'm the one who is poisoned and I know Onyx is annoying, but I don't think he wants me dead. Plus, if he kills me, there isn't a chance in hell he'll ever be able to set up a sanctuary for hybrids."

"I knew you were the smartest of the three," Onyx called out from where he stood in the back doorway.

"Let's go." Bryn took a few steps, and then remembered she wasn't supposed to let them know she was doing okay, thanks to the epinephrine shot. "Valmont, I might need your help."

"And that's why you shouldn't be making any important decisions," Jaxon muttered as he followed along beside her.

Did he not understand she was faking weakness? Then again who knew when the shot would wear off. "You don't have to go with us," Bryn said. "You could stay here."

"Have you ever heard of the divide-and-conquer strategy? That's exactly what we'd be allowing him to do."

"You're the only one left in the cabin," said Bryn.

"There's not a chance in hell Onyx doesn't have people hidden inside and outside this cabin, but since you seem to be leaving me no choice…" He gestured that she should go first.

What were the odds Onyx wasn't up to something? Slim to none. But she truly didn't believe he meant her harm. He wanted more rights for dragons, but she didn't think he was behind the attacks. They exited the house and walked over toward the root cellar. The square metal door stood open. When they were half a dozen feet from the door, she paused to sniff the air.

"At the moment, I don't think there are any rotting bodies in the tunnel," Valmont said. "Let's hope the same can be said after we go down there."

"Way to be positive," Bryn muttered to him.

"Before we go down there, have your men come out," Jaxon said. "And I don't mean the ones down in the tunnel."

"As you wish." Onyx cupped his hand to his mouth and hollered. "On the roof and behind the house, show yourself to our young friends."

Two dragons stood up on the roof and one appeared from behind a tree.

"I'm sure your father and Bryn's grandfather have taken similar precautions," Onyx said.

"And I'm sure you have more men stationed around this cabin than those three," Jaxon said.

Onyx pointed toward the ladder leading down into the root cellar. "After you."

"I really don't want to go down there," Bryn said. "Now that we're out here and you have us outnumbered, why don't you go get it while we wait here."

"Would it help if I told you there was someone down there who wanted to speak to you?" Onyx asked.

"Like who?"

Onyx leaned in and said. "Someone you thought you'd

never see again."

Was he trying to mess with her head? He couldn't mean… ugh…there was only one way to find out. She moved to the opening, sat down and then scooted over to the edge.

"Wait." Valmont joined her, positioning himself between her and the ladder. "Let me go first. I can catch you if you fall."

"Fine."

He swung down and descended the metal rungs. As soon as he was clear, she grabbed the ladder rail and placed her foot on a rung about two feet below the opening. The metal bar was skinny and felt awkward under her foot. She scrambled down as quickly as possible and landed in a dimly lit area, which smelled of disinfectant. Whatever the body recovery team had used to clean this place must have been strong.

"Hello?" Bryn called out. If Onyx had tricked her into coming down here, she was going to kill him.

"Move," Jaxon ordered, and then he dropped from halfway up the ladder to land in a crouch on the ground.

Bryn produced a small fireball and held it out, trying to see through the shadows.

Onyx descended the ladder and then straightened his suit. "Come this way."

What else could she do but follow? Valmont stayed by her side. Jaxon skulked along behind them like he expected someone to jump out at him. Not that she could blame him.

Onyx grabbed something from a hook on the wall. Bryn tensed until he fiddled with the object and it flared to light. A lantern. He'd grabbed a lantern. She doused her fireball.

The farther they went into the tunnel, the stuffier the air became. The floor was hard-packed dirt, which made her think this was a high-traffic area. "Where does this lead?"

"This tunnel and several others like it lead between the cabins and to different places in Dragon's Bluff. Just a little bit farther now." He rounded a corner.

Bryn braced herself, producing a fireball in both hands. Around the corner, she found a command post of sorts. Folding tables and chairs took up most of the space. There were cases of bottled water and what looked like canned goods stacked off to the side. The thing Bryn couldn't take her eyes off of was the blond woman sitting in the corner. Her jeans and T-shirt were streaked with dirt, and there was a scar on her right arm. She looked years older than Bryn remembered.

"Mom?" Bryn croaked.

"Oh, baby." Her mom ran to her and wrapped her in a hug.

"It's you?" Bryn clutched at her like she might disappear. "It's really you?"

Her mom laughed. "It's me." She stepped back but kept her hands on Bryn's shoulders. "I'm so sorry I couldn't contact you, couldn't let you know we were okay, but we barely escaped the bomb and—"

Tears rolled down Bryn's face. "We? Dad's alive?"

Her mom nodded and wiped at her own tears. "He wanted to come, but he can't fly anymore."

Her heart felt like it would burst with joy, or maybe that was the epinephrine. "What happened?"

"Onyx contacted us and told us he thought there would be an attempt on our lives. He'd heard rumors of a bomb. Your dad didn't take him seriously, but we took some precautions. He used a discovery spell on the Christmas presents and when his flame burned dark gray instead of white, we ran for the attic and made it up to the roof just before the bomb went off. I swear your father was only a few seconds behind me, but one of his wings…it's burned beyond repair. He can still walk with a cane, but he can't fly."

"As heart-warming as this is, Bryn, you should take your

antidote before you pass out again," Jaxon said.

Her mom peered at Jaxon for a moment, and then her eyebrows shot up. "You must be a Westgate."

"He is," Bryn said. "But he's not nearly the asshat his father is."

"And he's not wrong," Valmont said.

Onyx pointed to a small wooden-hinged box on the table. "It's in there."

Bryn flipped open the box. The top made a ringing sound as it smacked against the table. She picked up what looked like a small perfume bottle filled with orange liquid. The container felt oddly warm. She pulled out the stopper, which came loose with a pop, tilted the bottle to her lips, and sipped the contents. The bitter taste of orange rind filled her mouth, followed by something like aspirin. She grimaced and tilted the bottle, swallowing almost the entire dose in one gulp, and then she put the stopper back in and slipped the container in her pocket.

She waited to see what would happen. How would she know if it worked? Pain sliced through her hands. She gasped as the cuts, which had healed on her fingers split open like an invisible knife had reopened the wounds. "What the hell?" If felt like her hands were on fire.

"Your body is expelling the poison," Onyx explained. "From the original entry wounds."

"A little warning would have been nice." Bryn gritted her teeth and stared at her fingers in fascinated horror. Blood the color of oranges dripped from her fingers and splattered onto the dirt floor.

Her mom wrapped her arm around her lower back, supporting her weight. "Don't worry. I've got you."

A wave of dizziness hit. Cold sweat prickled her skin. Nausea rolled through her body followed by a flush of cold. She took shallow breaths, concentrating on not throwing up.

Slowly, the urge to vomit receded, but she needed to sit down, because her legs weren't cooperating with the whole standing-up thing. She didn't want to appear weak, but her body didn't seem to care about her agenda. Her mom helped her to a chair.

"Now the deed," Onyx held his hand out to Jaxon.

"That's all Bryn needed?" Jaxon said. "She's cured?"

"Yes," Onyx said. "I'm a man of my word."

"As am I." Jaxon tossed the attaché case so it landed by Onyx's feet.

Bryn's head cleared and strength flowed back into her body. "I think I'm okay now."

"Then this meeting is coming to a close," Onyx said.

"Wait. I don't understand. Besides reuniting Bryn with her mother which could have been done in a number of ways that did not involve poison, what was the purpose of all this?" Jaxon asked.

"None of this was planned," Onyx said. "Bryn stumbled into some of my friends when they were trying to retrieve a few items from the library. And without my consent, they took advantage of the situation. They used the Tyrant's Crowns to frighten you, knowing you weren't alone so you'd be able to remove them. The herbal mixture they used was non-lethal, and it's completely curable. Hopefully, this incident will teach the Directorate a lesson they need to know."

"What lesson would that be?" Jaxon asked.

"We are not unreasonable. We will keep our word. We, too, can be honorable." He pointed at Bryn's mother. "And kind, if given a chance."

"And you had to drag us down here to accomplish this?" Jaxon seemed baffled. "We could have done all of this in the cabin up above."

"True." Onyx pointed at Bryn's mother. "But some of this information needs to remain a secret."

Two terrible thoughts occurred to Bryn. One, she was wearing a wire, so everyone already knew her mom was alive, and two it didn't sound like her mom was coming with her.

"You're not coming with us?"

"I'm sorry. I can't. I have to get back to your father."

"Just bring him here," Bryn said. "If you're worried about your parents, they were going to let you come to Christmas. They both cried when they thought you were dead. And I'm wearing a wire anyway, as a safety precaution."

"That's why we met here, honey." Her mom reached out and touched Bryn's cheek. "The hybrids live here because bugs don't work this far down."

"Your grandmother is probably ready to storm my cabin," Valmont said. "We need to get back up there."

Bryn ripped the bug from the seam of her shirt. "Go. Tell them we're okay. We'll be coming up soon."

Valmont took the bug and ran back toward the ladder.

"Please come with me." Bryn hugged her mom. "I just got you back, I can't let you go again."

"I'll be around. Your father and I plan to build a home on the deeded land."

"Too many things could go wrong between now and then. You could live at Sinclair Estates."

Her mom laughed. "I'm not sure my parents would agree."

"You won't know until you ask them. And I'm not giving you a choice in this matter. I'm telling them whether you want me to or not. I won't keep this from them."

Her mom appeared stunned. "You've bonded with them? I never imagined that."

"They are set in their Blue dragon ways and some of their beliefs are bizarre, but they are good people."

"You can tell them, but you can't tell anyone else."

"Okay."

Her mom pointed at Jaxon. "Will he be a problem?"

"No." Bryn didn't even have to ask. She just knew.

"Your new life is full of surprises. I can't wait to hear all about it, but for now you have to go."

"I understand why she wants to remain hidden," Jaxon said to Onyx, "but why didn't you come forward with the antidote. There was no need for all this subterfuge."

"I wanted to talk to you specifically, without interruption, and your father never would have allowed that. I wanted to make you understand…to see our point of view. You grew up proud of who you were. My friends shouldn't be ashamed of who they are because they are different. Change is coming. My friends' numbers grow larger every year. Eventually, they might outnumber the traditional clans. Keep that in mind when you make your laws and pass your judgments."

"I'm flattered, but as far as the Directorate is concerned, you attacked Ephram Sinclair's granddaughter," Jaxon said. "Keep that in mind the next time you want to appear reasonable, because if you do something like this again, the Directorate's response will be swift and severe."

"Duly noted." Onyx turned to Bryn. "One other thing. You should know that those who died down here didn't die by our hands."

"The family…who were they?" Bryn asked.

"They were peaceful hybrids living out of sight, and someone had them hunted down," Onyx nodded toward Jaxon. "His father knows what I'm talking about."

"If you mean to be honorable and want our respect, then stop with the riddles," Bryn said.

"Ever since the attack at the Christmas ball, Ferrin has sent out guards with the express order to execute any hybrids they can find, which is why I placed the spell on the hatch to hide the handle and keep the entrance hidden. Not that it did much good."

Jaxon took a step forward. "My father would never kill unarmed dragons."

"He didn't do it with his own hands, of course, but he ordered it done," Onyx said. "Now, if you'll do me the favor of leaving out the hatch and taking all your hidden guards with you…" Onyx said.

This was all so crazy. "You didn't have to let me know my mother was alive or give me the antidote, so thank you. I'd like to think, if everyone acts reasonably, we can develop some sort of peace."

"That's a lovely thought." Onyx gave a sad smile. "But if your grandfather has his way, I probably won't live out the night."

"Then why do any of this?" Bryn asked.

"I wanted to show them who we were. There are Radical dragons in the forest, but the majority of my friends want to live their lives peacefully, and I wanted you to see the Directorate more clearly."

Was he acting again? "I know the Directorate is old-fashioned and some of their thinking is downright archaic, but you're the one I don't understand. When I first came here, you gave me a protection charm. Why?"

"Alec had become unstable, and I feared he'd make an attempt on your life. I was trying to do what I could to keep you safe without breaking any of my allegiances."

"What are your allegiances?" Jaxon asked. "Because it seems like you're playing on several sides."

"Perhaps I am. I don't want war, but I don't want things to continue on as they've always been. I think change is coming, and it is overdue. I'd prefer it happen in a peaceful manner, but I'm not sure that's possible. I'm hoping this safe haven I plan to create for hybrids and Throwbacks will alleviate some of the tension and bad blood between the Directorate and its citizens."

Damn it all, if she didn't believe him. "I think you're aiming for a worthy goal, but I'm not sure you're going about it in the right way. Clashing with the Directorate will never lead to peace."

"Believe me when I tell you I'd love to keep the casualty list at zero, but I'm not the only player on the field."

"Instead of all this sneaking around, why don't you meet with the Directorate and present your concerns," Jaxon said.

Onyx laughed. "I'd be dead as soon as I entered the room with them. They aren't the forgiving types."

"I'd like to give you my word that you won't be harmed," Bryn said. "But I'm not sure my word carries much weight."

"Mine does," Jaxon stated with absolute conviction. "I'll give you my word as a Westgate. No harm will come to you, if you agree to meet with the Directorate."

For the first time, it appeared Onyx was at a loss for words. "Why?"

"Because, it's clear to me now that Throwbacks and hybrids aren't all bad, but some are. It's the ones who attacked Dragon's Bluff and the Institute that we need to fight against, not the ones who are seeking access to campus and trying to blend in."

"I look forward to a time when you are running the Directorate, Jaxon Westgate, but for now, it's best if my friends and I disappear for awhile. Your father's temper might make it hard for you to keep your word."

"Follow me." Jaxon headed toward the ladder. They all followed. "Give me a minute." He climbed up the ladder. "Valmont, bring me that microphone."

Bryn heard a reply but couldn't make out the words.

"Because I asked nicely," Jaxon snapped. "And the faster you do this, the faster we can leave."

"To anyone who is listening," Jaxon said in a loud voice, "I have given my word as a Westgate that no harm will come to Onyx if he wishes to speak to the Directorate. Do not make the mistake of crossing me. You've all been witness to how long one of us can hold a grudge."

"Nicely done," Bryn shouted up to him.

"Time to go," Jaxon said.

With her arm around her mother's waist, Bryn headed for the ladder. Tears filled her eyes. "Please come with me. We can keep you safe. We can keep Dad safe, too."

Her mom wiped at the tears running down her own face. "I am so proud of you, and I'd love to come with you, but I can't. I'll be in contact with you soon."

Bryn indulged in one final hug.

"Go on," her mom said.

Walking away from her mother now was so much harder than it had been when she'd left for school. "Promise me you'll stay safe. I've already mourned you once. I can't do it again."

"I promise…and tell my parents I love them and I look forward to reuniting with them."

Bryn sniffled and climbed up the ladder. It felt like she was being torn in two. She had to keep moving. She had to get back to her grandparents.

"Shut the hatch when you leave," Onyx called out.

Jaxon and Valmont waited for her. Bryn stood and grabbed the hatch door, slamming it closed so Onyx could lock it from the inside.

"Talk so they know you're okay." Valmont handed her the microphone as they walked to the SUV.

"The antidote worked. I'm fine."

Once they reached the SUV, Jaxon said, "Bryn sit up front with me. We need to present a united front."

"Okay." She didn't necessarily understand his logic, but she climbed in when Valmont opened the door for her.

They took off like a rocket.

"In a hurry?" Bryn asked.

"You know they'll be waiting to talk to us."

"Of course they will," Bryn said. "And they better have food. That antidote drained my energy."

"Probably because it drained some of your blood," Valmont said.

"Yeah, and that was disturbing." Bryn looked at her hands. No cuts were visible. "And strange."

"Did you keep the bottle the antidote came in?" Valmont asked.

"I assumed Medic Williams would want to study a sample of it." Bryn pulled the bottle from her pocket and showed him the tiny bit left in the bottom.

They'd barely driven back onto campus and parked the SUV when Bryn's grandmother yanked the car door open. "Are you all right?"

"I'm a little weak, but I think I'm okay." Bryn leveraged herself out of the SUV and hugged her grandmother. She desperately wanted to tell her that her mom was alive but that would have to wait until they were alone.

"You really do need to stop scaring the life out of me," her grandmother whispered before releasing her.

"Gladly." Bryn glanced around and spotted Medic Williams. "I better hand this over before someone marches me off to a meeting."

"No one is marching you anywhere." Her grandmother placed a hand on Bryn's elbow as if to hold her in place. With her other hand she gestured for the medic to join them.

Bryn held out the bottle. "I'm not sure what's in it, but I saved you a sample."

"Good idea." Medic Williams placed her hand on Bryn's forehead. "Let me do a scan to make sure you're all right."

Bryn felt the familiar warm honey sensation flowing through her body.

"Everything appears to be in order. I'm going to channel

a little Quintessence into your body because you're weak from fatigue."

Bryn closed her eyes and another lovely warm sensation flowed through her muscles, giving her energy. "Thank you. That's much better."

Medic Williams pointed at Bryn like she was about to give her a lecture. "Take it easy for a while. We don't know the long-term effects of whatever this was."

Valmont moved a step closer and said, "Don't worry, between Mrs. Sinclair and myself, we'll make sure Bryn doesn't over exert herself."

"Now we're going for a short walk to one of the private rooms in the dining hall where you will eat and Jaxon can explain what happened." Keeping her hand on Bryn's arm, her grandmother headed down the walkway.

"How did you get Ferrin to agree to come down from his office on high?" Bryn asked. "He normally makes us trudge up there."

"I informed him where the debriefing would be and invited him to attend." Her grandmother gave a wicked smile. "You should have seen the expression on his face. Your grandfather wasn't pleased at first, but he came around."

Bryn loved that her grandmother was openly stepping up. She knew her grandmother had always contributed to her grandfather's business and political decisions, but previously, she'd stayed in the background.

"Your grandfather is probably being agreeable because he wants to make sure you have an influence in the Directorate after he retires," Valmont said.

Her grandmother nodded. "I think you're right. Now we need to get Jaxon on board."

"I think he's already on board," Bryn said. "If for no other reason, than he knows I'm not the type to keep my opinion to myself." She glanced around. "Speaking of Jaxon, where is he?"

"I believe he took off for the dining hall while the medic was examining you," Valmont said. "I imagine he has a few questions he wants to ask his father."

Poor Jaxon. If his father really had ordered the execution of innocent dragons, how would he deal with that?

Once they made it to the private room in the dining hall, Bryn saw that Jaxon sat beside his father, his expression unreadable, like an upper class Blue who thought a gathering was beneath him. It was the exact same expression Ferrin wore.

"That's not good," Valmont whispered to Bryn as he pulled out her chair.

Bryn's grandfather greeted her with a nod. "You look much better."

A door opened and the scent of pizza wafted into the room. "That smells fabulous." Bryn's mouth watered.

"I thought you'd approve," her grandfather said. "Don't bother waiting for the rest of us, you need to eat."

"Thank you." As soon as the waiter set the thick crust cheese pizza on the table, Bryn grabbed a slice and took a bite. It was spicy-cheese-and-tomato-sauce-covered-carbohydrate-bliss. She finished off two slices and felt more like herself. "There. That's much better."

"Perhaps now we can get down to business," Ferrin stated in his holier-than-thou tone.

"Good idea," Valmont said. "Did you order the execution of hybrid dragons like the ones living on my property?"

"You," Ferrin pointed at Valmont, "have no right to speak in this meeting, so I will ignore your absurd question."

"Then I'll repeat it," Bryn said. "No disrespect *okay, that is a big fat lie* but Onyx told us some disturbing things this evening. Did you order the execution of hybrids?"

"No," Ferrin stated and then sat back and crossed his

arms over his chest.

"How do we know you're telling the truth?" Bryn asked.

"I am the Speaker for the Directorate," Ferrin said, like maybe she'd forgotten that fun fact. "I'm trying to stop a war, not start one."

That was one of the most reasonable things she'd ever heard Ferrin say. Whether she believed him or not was another story. Not to mention that he hadn't really answered her question.

"Jaxon already gave us a report of what happened at Valmont's cabin and down in the root cellar," her grandfather said. "Bryn, we'd like you to retell the story, leaving nothing out."

"Okay." Bryn launched into the tale of the drive to the cabin, her conversation with Onyx, the disturbing effects of the antidote, and the part about Jaxon guaranteeing Onyx's safety. She said nothing about her mother. "Will you honor Jaxon's promise?" Honestly, she wasn't sure he would.

"I don't approve that he gave his word as a Westgate to keep a traitor safe, but I will honor his agreement for now. However, there was no time frame stipulated." Her grandfather smiled. It wasn't a happy smile. More like an I'll-get-my-way-in-the-end kind of smile.

Jaxon cleared his throat. "Will you meet with Throwbacks and hybrids who want to live peacefully?"

"It's not that simple," Ferrin said. "There's no real way to determine who is with us and who is against us."

There he went, sounding like a crazy dictator again. Bryn clamped her lips shut to keep from addressing him as He-Who-Must-Not-Be-Named.

"What if there was some sort of trial period where hybrids could come forward and apply to live on the deeded land," Jaxon suggested. "As long as they are peaceful, they'll be treated with respect."

That sounded like the American Indian Reservations where the natives were intentionally given smallpox. What were their other options? How would they know who to trust? "There is really no good way to do this, is there?" Bryn addressed her grandfather.

"As disillusioning as that realization is, I'm glad you've come to it," her grandfather said. "The Directorate has worked for centuries to keep the peace—by force and law."

"You can't tell a person is bad until they do something bad," Valmont said. "Can't you just up the security and keep a watch out for anything suspicious?"

"Why not open the Institute as a sanctuary?" Bryn said. "The Orange Dorm is almost empty. Anyone who wishes to live peacefully could move in."

"Brilliant idea." Ferrin leaned forward. "Invite the enemy to move in with our most valuable resource."

"Must you always be so combative?" Bryn asked.

"It's his way," Jaxon said. "And moving possible Rebels into the campus would give them access to way too much information. Besides, they have the deed to twenty acres and a small abandoned town on the other side of the forest. Anyone will be free to move there. They can set up their own schools and live their lives how they want."

And now they'd entered the Separate But Equal time period. Maybe humans and dragons weren't so different after all. "Giving them their own town is great, but you can't exclude them from other places like they aren't good enough to sit on the bus."

Jaxon wrinkled his brow at her. "What are you talking about?"

History wasn't her strong suit, but come on. "Rosa Parks… the black woman who refused to give up her seat on the bus to a white person…ring a bell?"

"Human history isn't emphasized in the curriculum," her

grandfather said. "Although I do recognize and appreciate the comparison, I'd be lying if I said I thought hybrids were on equal footing with the Clans. The Directorate actively works to keep certain traits from coming to light while the hybrid's genetics are random."

Had she just been insulted? "So I'm random?"

"Yes," her grandfather said. "But the combination of your genes didn't breed a problem."

Ferrin snorted and muttered something under his breath.

Asshat. Bryn leaned forward. "So you know, at this point, I'd marry Jaxon just to spite you."

Her grandmother chuckled. Neither Ferrin nor Jaxon seemed to think it was funny, and the irritation flowing off of Valmont was palpable like a fog.

Her grandfather cleared his throat. "Personal matters aside, we are treading in uncharted territory. The Directorate has assigned a contingent of guards to keep track of Onyx and his movements. We will take note of who moves onto the deeded land. If they appear to be preparing for a war or speaking against us, we will take action against them."

After all this talk, wait-and-see seemed to be the decree of the day. Bryn yawned, and then stressed about the fact that she yawned. "How do I know this is regular tired and not some weird go-to-sleep-and-forget-everything kind of tired?"

"I guess we'll know when you wake up," her grandmother said. "And don't worry about attending classes tomorrow. I think you need one more day of rest."

"That's the best news I've heard all day," Bryn said. "And I was hoping I could talk to both of you privately before I went to sleep. Maybe you could come back to my room for a few minutes?"

"I'll go with you," her grandmother said. "I'm sure your grandfather has a few things he needs to take care of."

"I do. Your grandmother can fill me in later if there is

anything I need to know."

Oh, he's going to want to know this. "Okay." Bryn headed to her dorm room with Valmont and her grandmother.

They'd barely shut the door, when Bryn said. "Mom's alive. I saw her tonight."

Her grandmother's expression froze. "What do you mean?"

That was not the response she expected.

"Onyx had warned mom the Rebels might come after her and dad. They figured out a package was a bomb, and they barely escaped. My dad was injured. He can't fly anymore, but Mom said Onyx has given them a place to stay."

"She's in league with Onyx?" her grandmother's tone was sharp enough to cut a diamond.

"No." That was not the takeaway from this information. She tried again. "Onyx speaks for the peaceful hybrids and Throwbacks. He didn't poison me. Some of his associates put the herbal stuff on Valmont's sword. Onyx helped us by giving me the cure and by telling me my mom's alive. He wants peace. It's the Rebels in the forest that are trying to hurt people."

Her grandmother sat at the library table. "Did your mother say anything else?"

"She's sorry about letting us think she was dead. She said to tell you she loves you."

Her grandmother sat there, staring off into space. "Did you ask her to come back with you?"

"I did."

"Why did she refuse?"

The way her grandmother phrased the question, Bryn knew this was a pivotal moment. The why had to be important, it had to show honor and loyalty. And the answer shouldn't be anything to do with her dad, so Bryn improvised. "If she's still a target, she'd be putting us in danger, and she didn't want that."

Her grandmother's stiff posture relaxed. "I can't believe…I almost don't want to believe it's true."

"Why not?"

"Because none of us are safe. And I've already grieved my daughter twice. I cannot do it again."

"Should I not have told you?" Bryn sat next to her grandmother at the table.

"No. You should have, but I'm not sure I should tell Ephram. He's furious at Onyx and associating your mother with him in any way would be a bad idea."

She sort of understood. "You can tell him when you think the time is right," Bryn said.

Chapter Fifteen

Valmont was quiet as she hugged her grandmother and said good-bye. It had been a craptastic day, but she thought she knew what was keeping him so silent. He was probably ticked off about what she'd said earlier about marrying Jaxon. The funny part was, she'd sort of meant it. At this point, she'd marry Jaxon, if for no other reason than to make Ferrin miserable. She could imagine explaining her marriage to someone. "Did you marry for love?" "Oh, no. I married for spite." God, her life was bizarre.

Time to hash this out. She pointed at the couch. "Sit with me for a minute so we can talk?"

"Sure." Valmont plopped down on the couch and crossed his arms over his chest.

"I wanted to make sure you realized when I talked about marrying Jaxon, I meant a business partnership, not an actual marriage."

Valmont pressed his lips together and nodded. "Got it. But I still hate it. And it worries me that you're acting like you're okay with it. Before, you were repulsed by the idea, and now you talk about it like you're planning a trip to the grocery store…like it's no big deal."

Why had she thought this conversation would be easy? "You're right. The idea of being betrothed to Jaxon used to make me want to run screaming from the room. Now it seems inevitable—like writing a term paper or taking a test. I'm not happy about it, but I realize it might be necessary."

Valmont didn't seem appeased, and she didn't have it in her to continue this conversation. "I think we've both been thoroughly traumatized by the events of the past couple of days. I don't remember everything that happened—"

"I do." Valmont said. "I remember every single detail. I watched you pass out and wake up six times. Six." He rammed his hand back through his hair. "Every time you blacked out, all I thought was *what if this was the time you didn't wake up? What if you died?* And every time you woke up, I was so grateful because I can't imagine living my life without you."

Oh, hell. "I'm so sorry. I didn't think about all those other times and how hard that must've been on you. Then I joked about marrying someone else right in front of you, which makes me a nominee for the most insensitive person of the year award."

Valmont opened his arms. "Come here."

She scooted over and sat on his lap, wrapping her arms around him. She leaned into him so her face was against the crook of his neck. "Did I mention that I'm sorry?"

He hugged her tight. "Since you've been the victim of an elaborate   being-held-hostage-without-actually-being-held-hostage scheme, and you've just discovered your parents are alive, I guess I can cut you some slack."

"Thank you." She moved so her mouth lined up with his and then she kissed him. As tired as she was right now, there was no place she'd rather be than in his arms. The rest of the world faded away as heat pulsed between them. Whether it was from the bond or the love she felt for him or both, she didn't care. What they had was good and right, and no stupid fake marriage could take that away.

• • •

The dreaded piano music worked its way into Bryn's dreams. The music became louder and more discordant as it continued, and for the first time she didn't mind because she remembered everything that happened the day before, which meant the cure Onyx had given her actually worked. And her parents were alive. She wanted to shout that from the rooftop.

She untangled herself from Valmont's arms and legs and went first to her room to smack off the alarm and then to Valmont's. By the time she made it back to the living room, he was sitting up rubbing his eyes.

"I don't even know what day it is," he muttered.

"You're asking the wrong girl," Bryn said. "I slept through several."

Valmont yawned. "Friday…I think it's Friday."

"Thank God I don't have to go to class." She rejoined him on the couch. "I say we sleep as long as possible."

"No argument there." He settled back onto the couch, and she curled up against him, using his chest as a pillow. For the moment, everything felt right in her world. She didn't expect it to stay that way for long, but she was learning to appreciate the little things while they lasted.

Too soon, Valmont was rubbing her shoulder. "Bryn, we should probably wake up. I think we missed lunch."

Fuzzy headed, Bryn sat up and tried to process that information. "I slept through lunch?"

"I think the pizza you had before bed last night counted as breakfast, but you probably need to be fed." Valmont stood. "I'm going to shower and then we'll talk about food."

"Okay." Her stomach growled. How had she slept through two meals? That evil herbal potion had kicked her butt.

After a quick shower, Bryn threw on jeans and a T-shirt. As far as she was concerned, if she was excused from classes, there was no reason to observe the stupid dress code.

Valmont pointed at her outfit. "Did you know your shirt is on inside out?"

Bryn looked down. Sure enough, he was right. "Crap. Hold on." She went into the bedroom and pulled her shirt off, flipped it right side out, and put it back on. Back in the living room, she said, "If anyone asks why we're not observing the dress code, we can say we thought it was Saturday."

"Works for me." He checked his watch. "The cafe downstairs should be empty since everyone will still be in class for two more hours."

"Good. Then no one will see how much I eat." Now that she was fully awake, her stomach was protesting the lack of regular meals.

The waiter in the restaurant seemed surprised when Bryn ordered three entrees, but he didn't comment.

Valmont sat back and watched her finish off her third helping of Chicken Cordon Bleu while he drank his second cup of coffee. "I'm hoping if I caffeinate myself I can stay awake and go to bed at a reasonable time."

Bryn yawned. "I know exactly what you mean. I swear I could go right back up to the room and fall asleep, but I don't want to. It feels like I've missed too much already."

"Clint and Ivy will make sure you're awake and don't miss out on dinner."

"I probably should have called them last night." Bryn took one last bite of food and then pushed her plate away. She wasn't hungry anymore, but she wasn't full of energy, either. "Would it be wrong if I went back to sleep?"

"You can go to bed," Valmont said. "I think I'm going to

call my family. The restaurant should be slow right now."

"Okay."

Bryn lay in bed, listening to Valmont's end of the conversation. It's not like she was eavesdropping on purpose. Not really. But he was sitting on the couch, which backed up to her bedroom wall. While she couldn't decipher all his words, he laughed often, which made her feel better about taking over his life.

Still she couldn't drift off to sleep. Lillith's words from a few days before wriggled around in her brain. Bryn never would have guessed Lillith would be the one to try and call them out on their relationship. And the fact that she'd suggested he start seeing Megan irritated the living hell out of her. Lillith put up with a loveless marriage to Ferrin. How could she want the same thing for her son? At this point, Bryn respected Jaxon and appreciated his intelligence and fierce determination, but that didn't mean she wanted to kiss him.

"Megan? Oh, hello, how are you?"

Bryn sat up. Why was Valmont talking to Megan on the phone? Weird.

And now he was laughing.

Why would Valmont's family put Megan on the phone when he called? She'd bet her grandparent's fortune that his grandmother was the one who suggested it. Evil, scheming, terrible-licorice-flavored-cookie-baking woman.

Fire stirred in Bryn's gut. There was no reason to be upset. Megan was just a cute girl with a crush on Valmont. One of many, Bryn assumed. The waitress wasn't anyone special to him. Not yet, at least.

The type of bond Bryn shared with Valmont, no other female could ever share with him. She was his dragon. Human females couldn't compete with their connection. Right?

"You know you'll have to break the bond when we're married," Jaxon said.

Bryn blinked. When had Jaxon come into her room? And why in the hell was he standing there wearing nothing but navy boxer shorts decorated with glittery silver W's that twinkled like a disco ball?

This could not be real. Nope. She had to be dreaming.

She slammed her eyelids closed and rubbed her eyes. Not real. Had to be a dream. She opened her eyes and Jaxon stood in front of her dresser staring into the mirror and flexing his biceps. "I've been thinking about growing my hair longer, so I could wear one of those man-buns. Do you think that would be a good look for me?"

Okay. She really needed to wake up now.

A knock on the door had her sitting upright with her heart beating like crazy. "Hello?"

The door opened and Ivy popped her head in. "Sorry to wake you, but it's time for dinner."

"I've never been so glad to be awake in my life. I just had the weirdest dream."

Ivy laughed and entered the room. Bryn did a double take. Ivy was wearing black pants and a white shirt with a W embroidered on the front pocket. And she was pushing a cart full of food.

"Women in your condition do have the strangest dreams, Mrs. Westgate."

"My condition?" Bryn threw off the covers and looked down at her legs, what she could see of them, the part that wasn't obscured by her very large, very pregnant belly which sported its own sparkling silver W. "Oh, hell no."

"Sorry," Ivy said. "I didn't mean to offend you, Ma'am."

"What? No, you aren't the problem. It's this stupid dream." She really needed to wake up. Closing her eyes, she focused on feeling the pillow underneath her head or the sensation of the sheet draped over her body. She was in bed, in her dorm room. And she was going to wake up. Now. Slowly, she opened her eyes. Valmont stood next to her bed, concern etched on his forehead. "Bryn, are you all right?"

"That depends, am I awake?"

"I hope so. You were tossing and turning when I came in. I had to shake you to wake you up."

"I was having the most bizarre dreams," Bryn sat up and touched her stomach, which was in its normal, not-possibly-knocked-up-with-Jaxon's-child state, thank goodness.

"Ivy called. They wanted to make sure you were coming down to dinner. I told them we'd meet them in half an hour."

"Good."

"What were you dreaming about?" Valmont asked.

No way would she tell him about Jaxon in his twinkling disco ball boxer briefs. "It was a bunch of weird stuff thrown together. I knew it was a dream, but I couldn't wake up. Jaxon asked me if he should grow his hair out and wear a man bun."

Valmont's eyes went wide and then he said, "Bizarre is an understatement."

Bryn yawned. "I've slept more than enough. Why do I still feel like crap?"

"Want me to ask Clint and Ivy to bring you carry-out?"

Yes, but she needed to show the world she was okay. Rumors about her condition had to be running rampant. She needed to show the Rebels that they hadn't beaten her. Because she was a Blue, and apparently that's what Blues did. Even if she did feel like death warmed over. "No. Give me a few minutes to get ready." She changed into a plain black skirt and a gray blouse hoping she'd blend in rather than stand out. She'd had enough attention lately, thank you very much.

Apparently, her bland clothing didn't do the trick. Dinner in the dining hall was proving to be a test of patience. Everyone was back to whispering and staring at her. "Seriously? Haven't I played this game enough?"

Ivy shrugged. "Everyone is curious about what happened.

You can't really blame them."

"I understand, but occasionally I'd like to pretend my life is normal. And all of this," she gestured at everyone in the vicinity, "is making that a little difficult."

Clint's eyes went wide. "Your life is about to get stranger. Jaxon is headed this way."

"What's he wearing?" Bryn asked, praying his ensemble was disco-sparkle-free and provided full coverage.

"Normal clothes," Ivy said. "Why?"

Thank goodness. "Long story. Strange dream. I'll explain later."

She turned to greet him but didn't get a word out.

"We've been summoned to the library tomorrow evening. We're supposed to report there at six."

"Why?"

"I don't know." He shoved his hand through his hair. "It doesn't matter. They asked us to go, so we're going."

"We who?" Bryn asked. "We, meaning me and Valmont, or everyone at the table?"

"Neither," Jaxon said. "We as in you and me, alone. Your knight can escort you, but he isn't invited into the conference room. He can stand guard in the hall."

Like hell. "Where I go, Valmont goes. And in case you feel like arguing with me, it was my grandmother who laid down that decree."

"I don't give a rat's ass if he comes or not. I'm just passing along a message." And with that friendly response, Jaxon turned and headed back toward his table.

"What was that about?" Ivy asked.

"Who knows?" Bryn took a drink of her iced tea. "But I don't like it."

"I'd like to point out that Jaxon used a Bryn-ism," Clint said. "And those are words I never expected to hear from a Blue, so it's worth noting."

"It didn't sound quite right coming from him, did it?" Bryn asked.

"No." Valmont checked his watch. "I do know one thing. I don't want to arrive early tomorrow evening and have to stand in the hall while everyone else arrives. That would be awkward."

"It they won't let you into the room, then I won't be going in, either," Bryn said.

"Yes, you will," Valmont said, "because we'll need to figure out what's going on."

"I'm not sure I want to know." Bryn glanced over at Jaxon. "He's acting like his normal snooty self, so I guess it's nothing too earth shattering."

"So what's the plan for tonight?" Ivy asked. "I know you're probably exhausted, but I thought maybe we could go back to your room and hang out."

Clint held up a small rectangular box. "I bought a new deck of cards. I almost feel like I have to carry a set with me everywhere I go in case we need to leave a trail to find our way home."

"A deck of cards should be added to everyone's survival gear," Valmont said. "You can stave off boredom or use them to mark where you've been."

"That's not a bad idea," Bryn said. "Maybe you should talk to your family about selling personalized decks of cards. The front of the cards could say Fonzoli's so they'd work as advertising, too."

"I like it," Valmont said. "When we go back to the room, I'm going to call my father and suggest it. He'll probably think I'm crazy, but it will be fun to hear his reaction."

Back in Bryn's room, she sat at the library table with Clint and Ivy playing Go Fish, while Valmont spoke on the phone. The sound of him laughing made Bryn smile.

"You're such a sap," Clint said.

"I am not. I grew up in a house with a lot of laughter. It's nice to hear it again."

"Do you have any fours?" Ivy asked.

"Go fish," Bryn said. She matched the pairs of cards in her hand and moved the unmatched ones to the side. "Do you have any sevens?"

Ivy handed over a seven. "We should talk about fun summer plans."

"Like what?" Bryn asked.

"What do you normally do during the summer, "Clint asked.

"At my house, summers always meant hanging out with friends, going to the dollar show, and staying up late to watch bad monster movies."

"If it's bad, why would you watch it?" Clint asked.

"I asked my dad the same question once. He said it was like the audience was in on the joke. The movie didn't take itself seriously, so it was fun to watch. Most of the time, if we stayed up late enough, we'd go to an IHOP down the street for pancakes."

"What's an IHOP?" Ivy asked.

"International House of Pancakes... Surely you've heard of them."

Clint and Ivy gave her blank looks.

"Where you do you go for pancakes?"

"The diner," Ivy said. "Every small town has a diner and a few nice restaurants."

"And you never venture out into the world to try anything else?"

"The Directorate doesn't encourage fraternizing with the rest of the population," Clint said. "Any time you venture into the human world, you put the entire dragon population at risk."

Wow. She'd never thought of it that way. "Then I guess

I'm glad I got to experience the outside world before I came here, but there isn't a chance I'd be able to resist sneaking out."

Ivy frowned. "Since we were toddlers, our parents have told us fairy tales about dragons who ventured into the human world and were discovered. The humans all wanted to study and dissect the dragons or use them to make a profit. Those stories still give me nightmares."

"Maybe that's why my parents kept their identities under wraps," Bryn said.

"And since you didn't know you were a dragon, they never told you those stories," Clint said.

"If those tales kept you from wanting to roam, they must have been really effective," Bryn said.

Clint nodded. "Dissection is a definite deterrent."

"Now that you've freaked me out, tell me what you like to do during the summer."

"We have an amazing park with a pool and water slide," Ivy said. "And there's a lake. Bonfires are always fun because it's a way to have s'mores without camping."

"S'mores work for me," Bryn said.

Valmont hung up the phone and came to join them. He was chuckling to himself. "My father is going to take the deck of cards idea and run with it. But he wants the cards to be round, so they're shaped like pizzas."

"Wouldn't those be hard to shuffle?" Bryn asked.

"I mentioned that, but he didn't think it would be an issue," Valmont said.

"And if round cards don't sell, you can use them as coasters," Ivy said. "So they wouldn't go to waste."

The next evening, the closer it came to six, the more nervous Bryn became. She changed her outfit three times.

"What do you think of this one?" she asked Valmont.

He glanced up from his book. "It looks good, just like the

last two outfits did. Why are you acting like this?"

"I don't know. The fact that you aren't supposed to come in with me makes me think it's some snooty Blue dragon event."

"And you're afraid your outfit isn't snooty enough?" Valmont teased.

"Yes." She stuck her tongue out at him. "I'd like to look as snooty as possible."

"As long as you're wearing those earrings and the bracelet your grandfather gave you for Christmas, you are top-tier snooty, so don't worry about it."

He was probably right. She smoothed her hands down the front of the navy and cream striped blouse she'd put on with her navy skirt. "Then I guess I'm ready to go."

They walked across campus with Valmont staying a step behind her, playing his role as her dutiful protector and employee. He stayed behind her as they entered the library and climbed the stairs to the top floor. She understood why he was doing it, but it still annoyed the crap out of her. Her grandmother waited for her in the foyer. That was a surprise.

"What are you doing here?" Bryn asked as she moved in for a hug.

Her grandmother beamed as she returned the gesture of affection and then held Bryn at arms length. "I'm here to celebrate the approval of your marriage contract to Jaxon."

Holy hell. The floor shifted under her feet. "Excuse me?"

"The Directorate approved your contract," her grandmother's smile was genuine.

Bryn opened her mouth and then paused because she had no idea what to say. "I…so the Directorate approved our marriage contract?" She was hoping maybe she'd misunderstood her grandmother.

"Yes. It passed by a slim margin, but that's all we needed."

No way. I'm not ready for this. "I thought this wouldn't

happen until later, like in the far away future. Can't we put it on hold for awhile?"

"No. This is happening tonight."

Nope. Not now. It can't happen now. There has to be a way to stop this. "But what about Ferrin? He despises me. I can't understand how he'd let this happen." She'd harbored hope he would somehow save her from this fate.

"Ferrin was resistant to the idea at first, but he came around after your grandfather discussed a new and very profitable business venture with him."

Seriously? "So you bribed him to accept me as his daughter-in-law. That must have been one hell of a business deal." Bryn laughed. Neither Valmont nor her grandmother joined in.

"Sorry, that was me using inappropriate humor as a coping mechanism." She took a deep breath and blew it out slowly.

This could not be happening. Fire sparked in her gut. The taste of smoke filled her mouth. She pushed the flames back down. A wisp of smoke drifted from her lips. "Do I really have to do this?" Bryn hoped against hope her grandmother would suggest some alternative. "There's no other way?"

Her grandmother gestured across the lobby toward the mahogany conference room door. "After you."

Okay. This was it. She either bent to her grandparents' will or she walked out of their life forever. Good-bye flying. Good-bye Clint and Ivy. Good-bye magic and fire and becoming a medic. Good-bye to life as she knew it. If she refused this marriage contract, her grandparents would disown her. She'd lose everything, and if she was lucky, she'd escape to the human world where she'd spend the rest of her life living a lie, afraid to fly, afraid to use magic, afraid to become too close to anyone because she'd risk exposing the shape-shifting dragon community.

All of these thoughts led to one terrifying conclusion. She really had to do this.

Her grandmother pointed down the hall. "Everyone is waiting for us. I knew you'd be surprised by this news, so I wanted to tell you ahead of time and give you a moment to compose yourself."

"That…that was a good idea." A moment? She'd need way more than a moment to deal with this, but she nodded and bit her lip while she tried to figure out how to handle this catastrophic event. At least her grandmother had thought to warn her in advance. Not that this was enough warning. Why was it happening now? It didn't make sense. And holy crap, what must Valmont be thinking? She turned to him, wanting to say something comforting or share a joke, but he was staring at the floor. "Valmont?"

"Go on," he said in a voice devoid of any warmth. "You wouldn't want to be late to your party."

"He's right," her grandmother said. "This is the start of your future."

"Can't I wait to start my future?"

"No," her grandmother's tone was kind but firm. "This is the only way."

Okay then…the only way to move forward in her life was to agree to this antiquated arrangement. And it wasn't really a marriage. It was a stupid agreement. That's all. She could do this. It's not like she had a choice. Okay. Deep breath. Put one foot in front of the other.

With every step her feet seemed to become heavier. A part of her brain screamed RUN! FLY! Another part of her brain ran through a list of facts. Marriage was a business partnership. Jaxon understood this. It's not like he'd try to kiss her. Dear God, she hoped that wasn't part of the ceremony. Since Blues were so formal, the odds of that happening were miniscule. She needed to find out before she entered the room of doom.

"How am I supposed to behave in there? I don't want to embarrass you because I don't know the rules." Her grandmother should believe that.

"You're overthinking it. Just smile and nod. If anyone asks, you reply, 'It's a good match.'"

Okay. Nothing physical seemed to be involved. That ramped her panic down from a ten to a seven. *Breathe in. Breathe out. Breathe in. Breathe out. I can handle this.* She could, but she so didn't want to. She looked at her grandmother. "Say something encouraging, please."

"You're forming a business partnership with Jaxon, and you two already seem to work well together."

"True." Bryn reached for the door handle. She could do this. She was a kick-ass shape-shifting dragon. This was no big deal. Nope. Not a big deal at all. If that was true, then why did she feel like lying on the floor and throwing a temper tantrum worthy of a toddler?

"Allow me." Valmont stepped around Bryn and pulled the door open for her. His face was a blank mask, which gave away no emotion, but his eyes…the look of anger and betrayal that shone from them made her heart hurt. This wasn't her fault. She wasn't doing it on purpose. This was being thrust upon her. He couldn't be mad at her for this. That wasn't fair.

"Bryn," her grandmother prompted, "it's time."

Valmont stood to the side, staring at her with accusation. Inside the room, Bryn saw her grandfather discussing something with Ferrin and a few other Directorate members. Lillith stood off to the side with her arms wrapped around her belly, exuding maternal joy. Jaxon stood by himself. His gaze met hers. He raised a brow and walked toward her like he was issuing a challenge. When he reached her, he said, "I suppose you've heard the joyous news."

She nodded and swallowed over the lump in her throat.

"I have."

"Then you have a choice to make," Jaxon said. "Are you coming in, or not?"

Every instinct in her body told her to run, but she couldn't do that to her grandmother. So, she stepped over the threshold and entered the room.

"Good choice," Jaxon said. "And now that you've chosen to make this commitment, my father asked me to give you a message."

This should be interesting. "Did he tell you to welcome me to the family?"

"Not exactly. He said, if you pull the same stunt your mother did, he will hunt you to the ends of the earth and slit your throat."

Bryn realized her mouth was hanging open. She snapped it shut. "Seriously?"

Jaxon shrugged. "He wanted to make sure you understood the stakes of the game before you agreed to play."

Oh, she would play their game all right, but she'd be making her own damn rules. If any of them expected her to sit quietly and accept the status quo, they were all in for a surprise. If they were going to force her to become a Westgate, she would use all the power behind that name and her grandparents' influence to change how society was governed. But, rather than explain any of that to Jaxon she went with a simple nod and an, "I do."

"Good. Now let's pretend we're happy about this." He placed his hand on her lower back and steered her toward his father and her grandfather.

She plastered a smile on her face and spoke through her teeth. "How are you not freaking out?"

"I'm freaking out on the inside," he said. "Play your part, and we'll be able to leave in an hour."

"An hour?"

"Bryn." Her grandfather toasted her with a glass of champagne. "I'm sure you're thrilled to learn your marriage contract was approved."

"Yes." Bryn nodded in agreement. What was that line her grandmother told her to use? "I think we're a good match."

"I believe you are," her grandfather said. "And I know you'll make your grandmother and me proud."

"I'm sure she will," her grandmother said from behind her.

Bryn glanced back. The door to the hallway was closed. Her escape route cut off. Was there any way she could get one of those glasses of champagne or maybe a Valium? Anything to quell the instinct to run screaming from the room.

"Did Jaxon deliver my message?" Ferrin asked in a tone like he'd sent her a have-a-good-day smiley-face cookie.

"He did. And I understood every word."

"Good." Ferrin leaned toward her. "Because I meant every…single…word."

Would it be wrong to start off her new life by kicking Ferrin in the balls? Probably. So she settled for nodding and biting her tongue.

"It's time for a toast," her grandfather said. A waiter passed out champagne. Bryn was surprised when he gave her a glass. Maybe it was meant to calm her nerves. Whatever. At this point she'd drink moonshine if they had any on hand.

Her grandfather cleared his throat and waited for everyone to quiet down. Then he raised his glass and said, "Tonight we are here to celebrate a new chapter in our lives. To Jaxon and Bryn. They are both fierce and loyal. Together they will make a formidable couple. Cheers."

"Cheers," everyone repeated and then sipped their champagne.

Bryn sipped hers and smiled and nodded at anyone who made eye contact with her.

Lillith joined them in the center of the room. "I can't tell you how happy this makes me." Her eyes went wide and then she laughed. "Apparently, Asher is happy, too. He's kicking up a storm. Ferrin, feel how strong your son is."

Bryn couldn't tell if Ferrin was intrigued or confused as he placed his hand on his wife's belly. Then he smiled, and it was a genuine smile, the likes of which Bryn had never seen from him. Still, it would take a lot more than one smile for her to believe he wasn't a psychotic asshat.

For the next hour, Bryn played her part. She must have said, "Yes, we are a good match," a dozen times to people she didn't know. They all nodded like they agreed with her. As every minute passed, the new reality crashed down on her. She really had to marry Jaxon. Her name would be Bryn Westgate. How had her life spun this far out of control?

"Squeeze your champagne glass any tighter and you'll break it," Jaxon said in a low voice as another couple approached them with well wishes.

She relaxed her grip. "Just trying to ward off a panic attack. How are you remaining so calm about this?"

"Mentally, I'm curled up in the fetal position and rocking in the corner," Jaxon said. "If that makes you feel any better."

She laughed. "It does, actually."

Finally by some unspoken agreement, people started exiting the room. Thank goodness. "Can we go now?" she asked Jaxon.

"If the party is in your honor, then you're the last to leave," Jaxon stated like it was the law.

"I'm going to have to learn all this social crap, aren't I?"

"Yes," Jaxon said, "because I don't want you tarnishing the Westgate name."

She snorted. "For your own safety, I'm going to assume that was a joke."

When it was just her grandparents and Jaxon's parents

left in the room, Bryn slouched. Holding perfect posture for the last hour had worn on her.

"In time, you'll see this was the right decision." Her grandmother gave her a hug. "The party is officially over, so you're free to leave. Jaxon will walk you back to your room."

"He doesn't need to do that," Bryn said.

"Yes, he does," her grandfather chimed in. "You need to show everyone a united front."

"It will save time if you don't argue," Jaxon said. "Besides, we're going to the same building, so it's a moot point."

"Good night, Bryn," her grandfather said.

That was a matter of opinion. "Night," Bryn replied.

Jaxon stayed by her side as they walked to the door, which he opened for her. The first thing Bryn saw in the hallway was Valmont standing against the wall staring off into space. "We're finished," she told him, because she couldn't think of anything else to say.

He fell into step behind her and Jaxon. As they walked back to the Blue dorm, Bryn felt like all eyes were on them. "I guess everyone has heard."

"So it would seem." Jaxon sped up his pace.

She matched his speed, wanting to get away from everyone…to have a moment by herself to process what all this meant. And time to smooth things over with Valmont. God, what was she going to say to him? There was one other party who'd be affected by this news.

"Have you told Rhianna yet?"

"I slipped out and called her as soon as I learned what was really going on," Jaxon said. "Because I didn't want her to hear it from someone else."

"How's she dealing with this?" Bryn asked.

"She's not happy," Jaxon said.

"That makes four of us," Bryn said, sort of joking.

"Agreed," Jaxon said. "Watch what you say in public or

anywhere someone might be listening."

"Which is pretty much everywhere on campus," Bryn said.

Jaxon didn't argue the point.

When they reached the dorm, Bryn braced herself for the scrutiny she was sure awaited her from the sea of Blues in the lobby. So it was strange when the students nodded at her and Jaxon and went about their business.

Climbing up the staircase, she said, "I've never had so many Blues be civil to me before."

"It's your new status," Jaxon said.

"Seriously? Because of my association with you I'm now on the approved list?"

"You're welcome." Jaxon smirked at her.

"Gee, thanks." They parted ways. She headed to her dorm room with Valmont hanging a step behind her. She was getting really sick of that maneuver. "Couch time?" she asked once they were safely behind closed doors.

"Not tonight." Valmont headed for his bedroom. "I need some time to think."

"You can't be mad at me," Bryn blurted out.

He turned back and gaped at her. "Yes, I can. I can be mad and angry and sad and any other emotion I want to be, because you made your choice. You chose to leave me in the hallway. You chose Jaxon over me."

She opened her mouth to argue. Tears filled her eyes. "I did what I had to do in order to stay in this world. And it's not like I had an alternative."

"You could have refused."

"And I would have been ostracized. I would have lost all the ground I'd gained with my grandparents." She almost said they were the only family she had left, but thank goodness that wasn't true anymore. Still she had to make him understand. "I wasn't ready for this, either. I thought we had more time."

Valmont shook his head. "In theory, I knew this would happen…one day. But not like this. Not now."

So the situation was not ideal. She understood that, but why was he acting like this? "I know this is horrific. I was blindsided by it, too, but it doesn't have to change anything between us."

"I wish that were true, but you're wrong." Valmont's voice broke. "This changes everything."

Chapter Sixteen

What the hell? "No, it doesn't."

"You can't be that naive. Everyone will be watching to see how we behave. It's a good thing I started walking a step behind you, because that's where I'll have to stay."

"You're being ridiculous."

"Am I? Do you think we can walk across campus holding hands now?"

"Why not?" He was really starting to piss her off. "I'm sure Jaxon and Rhianna will still act like normal, so why can't we?"

"Maybe because what we have isn't normal." Valmont scrubbed his hand down his face. "Did you notice in all those Tales of Knights we read, not once did they talk about romantic love between a knight and a dragon?"

She had noticed, but there wasn't a chance in hell she'd admit it. "So what? They did say the dragons and knights loved each other and were devoted to each other."

Valmont leaned against the wall and shoved his hands in his front pockets. He averted his gaze as he spoke. "That doesn't mean they shared anything more than familial love."

A base drum started beating in Bryn's head. "What about the stone dragon on the bluff that Dragon's Bluff is named after? Legends claim she fell in love with her knight, and when he died on the field of battle, she was so heartbroken she couldn't go on. She sat by his grave day and night, until the magic turned her to stone, allowing her to stay by his side and watch over him forever."

"I know the legend, and if that's true, then it just reinforces why dragons and knights shouldn't fall in love with each other," he said.

"It's a little late to avoid that fate, because I'm pretty sure you don't think of me as a sister or a friend."

"No." He turned his face and met her gaze. His eyes were filled with pain. "I don't, but maybe I should. What we've been to each other…I don't think we can be that anymore."

His words smacked into her chest like a physical blow, making it difficult to breathe and knocking her off balance. She stumbled backward.

He could not do this to her. Not now. Not after everything they'd been through. Not after everything that had happened tonight. It was absurd. "Valmont, what are you saying?"

"I will honor my vow to protect you. I will still be your knight, but I can't be anything more than that."

This could not be happening. Her eyes burned. Despite her best effort, the tears flowed. She took a shaky breath and tried to speak. Flames crawled up the back of her throat. If she opened her mouth, she'd set the room ablaze. But there were things she needed to say, damn it. She closed her eyes and focused on cold and snow. Once she was under control, she said. "So you're just going to turn off your feelings for me…stop loving me? How? How does that work?"

"I don't know, but I think it's the honorable thing to do. It's what I should have done all along, but you're so smart, and funny, and wonderful that I let my guard down and I made a mistake. Seeing you with Jaxon tonight reminded me of my place in your world. Or rather, that I don't have one." He gave her the saddest smile she'd ever seen. "My grandmother was right. I can see that now. You and I…we were never meant to be together as a couple."

The cold in her stomach spread through her body. It felt like shards of ice were stabbing through her heart. It hurt to breathe. "How can you say that?"

"I had an hour to think about this…about us… while you were on the other side of that door with Jaxon and your family. It's the right thing to do. You aren't going to change my mind."

She could not let him walk away from her. She had to make him see how wrong he was. "Why do you get to make this decision for both of us? Why can't we talk about it? I'm sure we can figure something out."

"There's nothing to figure out. It's done. I don't want to talk anymore. I'm exhausted. I just want to go to sleep."

And then he walked away from her.

No. No. No. No. No. This could not be happening. She needed him by her side. Without him how was she supposed to deal with the insanity of her life? "Valmont, wait."

He didn't respond. He just walked into his room and pulled the door closed. How could he declare their relationship over? Like what they'd had was nothing? Like he didn't love her anymore.

The phone rang, startling her. She stared at it for a moment, not sure if she wanted to answer it. She'd had about all she could take for one evening. But, it might be her grandmother, so she better pick up.

"Hello?"

"I heard what happened," Ivy said. "Do you need me to come over?"

"Yes," was the only word Bryn got out before her dam of self-control broke and she started sobbing.

"On my way," Ivy said.

Bryn stood at the window to the terrace watching for Ivy, hand over her mouth, trying to muffle the sound of her crying. When she arrived, Ivy pushed up the window, came inside, and pulled Bryn into a hug.

"I'm so sorry. This thing with Jaxon must be a terrible shock."

Bryn tried to control her tears. It took a minute, but she managed to slow her breathing. "That's not the worst part."

"Being betrothed to Jaxon isn't the worst part?" Ivy went into the living room and sat on the couch. She patted the cushion next to her. "What the hell else happened?"

"Valmont." Sleet shot from Bryn's mouth as she said his name. "He used this as an excuse to break up with me."

"What? Why would he do that?"

Bryn explained Valmont's theory about why they shouldn't be together anymore.

"Maybe he just can't deal with the thought of you and Jaxon." Ivy pointed toward Valmont's bedroom door. "Is he in there?"

Bryn nodded. "He insists he still wants to be my knight."

Ivy produced a ball of lightning in her hand. "Can I zap him?"

"No, but thanks for offering." Bryn wiped at the tears streaming down her face. "This is all so stupid. He has to realize he's wrong, right?"

Ivy allowed the ball of lightning to fade. "Maybe it's his pride that's wounded. Once he's come to terms with the whole marrying Jaxon thing, he might come around."

"This entire night has been so screwed up. Going along with the stupid marriage contract, which my grandfather basically had to bribe Ferrin to accept…it feels…it feels like

I sold my soul to the devil. Then we come back here and Valmont acts like an idiot, and now it feels like someone ripped my heart out and stomped on it." Bryn sniffled and then pointed at her face. "And apparently I can't stop crying. How am I supposed to deal with this?"

"I don't know," Ivy said. "I could ask Clint to speak with Valmont. Maybe another guy's perspective would help."

Bryn wiped her eyes on her sleeve. "This is ridiculous. The whole arranged marriage to Jaxon thing is stressful enough without Valmont dumping me."

"You know Valmont is a good person," Ivy said. "Maybe he just needs time, and since it's the weekend, you don't have to go out in public if you don't want to. We can hide out here, eat carry-out, and do girly things."

A new hairstyle was not going to make this go away, but Ivy was trying to help. "Thank you. That sounds good."

"Want me to run down to the restaurant and stock up on chocolate?" Ivy asked.

"Yes."

The next morning, Bryn woke up with a fork full of chocolate frosting stuck in her hair. Thank goodness she was in her bedroom where Valmont couldn't see the extent to which his stupid break-up had driven her. With Ivy's help, she'd moved from gut-wrenchingly sad, to sparks-flying-out-of-her-mouth angry. As long as she didn't set anything on fire, she'd be okay.

Ivy slept curled up like a cat at the foot of the bed. Bryn let her sleep and headed for the shower. Once she was clean and dressed and her hair was chocolate-free, she woke Ivy. "It's time for breakfast."

Ivy yawned. "Give me a minute." She took a shower and borrowed some of Bryn's clothes. "Okay, let's go tell Valmont it's time for food."

Bryn opened her door, and the scent of coffee made her mouth water. She walked out to find Valmont sitting at the library table with Clint, who must've brought breakfast for all of them.

"I thought you might not want to face the masses," Valmont said like everything between them was normal. "So I asked Clint to bring food."

Fine, she could play his nothing-is-wrong game. "Good idea." She sat and inhaled a stack of pancakes and half a dozen pieces of bacon while Clint and Ivy carried the conversation.

Once they'd finished off the food, Clint said. "Okay. Now let's get the awkward part out of the way. Valmont, Ivy told me that you think you need to be all noble and break up with Bryn since she's now officially promised to marry Jaxon."

Valmont nodded. "It's the right thing to do."

"In my opinion, the right thing isn't always the best thing," Clint said. "I prefer the live-for-the-moment-because-we-could-all-die-in-a-Rebel-attack-tomorrow type of life plan."

"What he said." Bryn crossed her arms over her chest and glared at Valmont.

"In the long run, you'll see I'm right," Valmont said. "Plus, you have to break the dragon-knight bond before you're married, so what's the point in continuing any sort of personal relationship?"

Where was this craptastic logic coming from? "A few weeks ago you said you'd still be interested in me without the bond. Do you remember that?"

"I do, but now that seems like a fairy tale." Valmont wadded up his paper napkin. "The reality is, I'm a waiter who was magically turned into your knight. And I'm not sorry that happened. But once you're with Jaxon, you won't need me anymore, and maybe I'd like to go back and be around my family and be a normal person again." He looked up from the crumpled napkin. "I miss my family, a lot. I gave up everything to be here with you. And now, maybe I see a chance to get it all back. It's not wrong for me to want that."

"Is that what this is about? Your family?" Why hadn't he told her? It would be so much less hurtful. "You're using this arranged marriage crap as an excuse to go back to your life? You don't need an excuse. You can tell me you miss your family."

"I do. I miss them and how simple and happy my life was before all of this, before you, before becoming your knight."

Oh, hell. A coldness settled deep into her bones. "You've already broken up with me. Are you planning on abandoning me as well?"

"No." Valmont seemed offended. "I'd never leave you, as your knight, I mean."

And there went her last bit of hope that everything might be okay. And none of it made sense. She wouldn't cry in front of him again. Focusing on anger, she said, "A month ago it was you and me against the world. Last night you accused me of choosing Jaxon over you and then you claimed dragons and knights shouldn't be involved in romantic love even though the dragon on the bluff proves otherwise. This morning, it's all about getting back to your family. So what the hell is going on here?"

"It's all of those things. It's like my life is one of those games of dominoes people set up. Once one falls, it knocks into the next one, and they all go down. Jaxon knocked down the first domino and started this chain reaction, and the others have been falling ever since."

"And did one of those dominoes erase your feelings for me?"

"No." Valmont leaned forward. "But maybe they made me see my feelings weren't natural."

*If this was going where she thought it was going…*Bryn

produced fireballs in both hands. "Choose your next words wisely."

"You asked for honesty," Clint said. "You aren't allowed to blast him with fireballs if he's being honest."

Bryn closed her eyes and concentrated on morphing the fire into snow. Once she could feel the wet coldness on her palms she opened her eyes. "Fine. But I will pelt him with non-lethal snowballs if he claims he only has feelings for me because of the bond."

"That seems fair." Ivy gave Clint a look, which told him he shouldn't argue.

"Carry on then." Clint gestured that they should continue.

"No," Valmont said. "I'm not continuing this conversation if you're going to threaten me. No matter how ridiculous the threat." He pointed at the snowballs.

"This isn't a conversation." Bryn dropped the snowballs on the carpet. "It's me wondering who stole my boyfriend and left this pod-person in his place."

"Look at it from my point of view. I have followed you around for months, devoted my every waking moment to you, and then you agree to spend your life with someone else."

"No, I didn't." How could he not see this? "I agreed to become business partners with someone else."

"Maybe as a human, it's hard for me to see the difference," Valmont said. "Maybe the bond allowed me to look past all the reasons we shouldn't be together. If you remember, in the beginning, I didn't want a relationship. You're the one who started us down this path."

"I call bullshit," Clint raised his hand. "Sorry, dude, but you flirted with her while she was with Zavien. And you continued to flirt with her once you were her knight."

"She's a beautiful girl, and Zavien was a jerk who needed to be taken down a notch."

And that painted Valmont in a lot less flattering light. "So, you flirted with me to annoy Zavien, and then you flirted with me because you thought I was pretty, not because you actually liked me or wanted to date me? Because I call bullshit on that."

"That's not what I meant. I did what I did because I liked you, but I don't think things would have become so serious if it weren't for the bond and for us being together twenty-four hours a day. If I were still in Dragon's Bluff and you stopped by to say hello on the weekends, we wouldn't be where we are now."

"Are you sure I can't blast him with a small fireball?" Bryn asked Clint.

"No," Clint said. "And he does make a good point. Lots of couples here at school get together because they are living in close proximity."

"You have just stepped in the mother of all piles of dog doo," Ivy said. "And I suggest you dig yourself out quickly."

"Please." Clint laughed. "I've been chasing you since we were toddlers. You know that. So this doesn't apply to us. Unless it's backward, and you finally caved because we're together all the time. And please notice, I'm not upset about that fact if it's true." Clint pushed his chair away from the table. "And on that note we are out of here. Sympathy anger can be a dangerous thing." He held his hand out to Ivy. "You can come back later if Bryn needs you."

Ivy stood. "Call me when you need me. I'll bring chocolate, or a body bag…whatever the occasion calls for."

Bryn nodded. "Thanks for helping."

Once her friends exited, Bryn leaned forward and covered her face with her hands. "No matter what I say, you're going to insist we're broken up, right?" She sat up and took a shuddering breath. "I don't understand your change of heart, literally. At the Valentine's dance, you told me you loved me, so what's changed?"

"Nothing has changed, Bryn. I still love you, and I probably always will."

And her head was going to explode. "If you love me, then why are you pushing me away?"

"You have no idea how painful it was, watching you walk into that room last night with Jaxon, walking away from me, choosing him, making it official… It was an ugly reality check, and it made me see that no matter what fantasy life we'd planned, you and I could never be together. Standing in the lobby by myself, I think I went through all the stages of grief: anger, denial, bargaining, depression, and acceptance. After I accepted that we weren't going to have our own happily ever after, I started to wonder if there was anyone else who could make me happy."

Bryn had a sneaking suspicion she knew where this was going. "Answer me one question, and I promise not to blast you, no matter how badly I want to, but does Megan have anything to do with this change of heart?"

He didn't respond, and that's when she knew. *Son of a bitch.* She imagined barbecuing him. But she couldn't do that, because, despite how bad his timing was, he wasn't wrong.

"Is it all due to her? Or is she the final piece in the puzzle?"

"I think she, or someone like her, is the final piece…just a normal girl I can live a normal life with."

"That's great for you," Bryn said. "And not to sound selfish, but what about my happily ever after? I had this scenario all planned out in my head about the giant mansion with two wings."

"After the party last night, do you still believe that could work?"

She wanted to lie and say *yes*, "I don't know. I was hoping to find a way. I still want you in my life. More to the point, I still want *you*." She couldn't put it any more simply than that soul-baring statement.

"And you're upset because you think I don't want you anymore," Valmont said. "The truth is I'm choosing not to want you because it's not healthy for either of us."

"Why can't we enjoy the time we have left? Why does it have to end now?"

"Because the longer it goes on, the harder it will be to end."

She wanted to stomp her feet like a toddler. "It's not like it's easy to end it right now. At least not for me."

"It's not easy for me, either, but I know it's right. And I know it's better than it would be if we wait to break up until your grandfather or someone else insists we do so. This way it's our choice."

"It's your choice," Bryn snapped. "I'm not choosing this."

"You're beginning to understand my argument, aren't you?"

"You have no idea how badly I want to blast you out of that chair," Bryn growled.

"Because you know I'm right?"

"No, because I understand your stupid logic, and I hate it."

"I'll always be here for you. And I'll always be your friend."

"Nope. Doesn't work for me. I can't have you around twenty-four hours a day like this. It will kill me faster than any Rebel plot." She tried to laugh, but it came out like a half sob. "You need to go."

"I won't leave you unprotected."

"I'm a kick-ass shape-shifting dragon, remember?" Bryn sniffled. "Despite all the attempts on my life, I am pretty good at taking care of myself. I don't need a babysitter. If you don't want to be my boyfriend anymore, then I don't need you in my life. "

"You're being ridiculous."

"Sucks to be the one arguing your case when the other person has made up their mind already, doesn't it?"

"Yes," he said.

"It might be immature, but if you can't be more than my knight, then I can't have you here. Besides, Lillith said I'd have to release you after my marriage contract was approved. Who knew she was psychic?"

"You can't break our bond over this," Valmont protested.

"A minute ago you wanted a simpler life. I can give you that with three words."

"Stop and think before you do this out of spite. I am still willing to lay down my life for you."

"I understand, but if we do this now, when I'm riding a wave of anger, it's like ripping off a Band-Aid. We don't have to draw it out. No one on campus needs to know the real reason you bailed on me. They'll all think it's because my marriage contract was approved." She chuckled. "Look at me, thinking like a Blue."

Valmont sat back in his chair and crossed his arms over his chest. "Ultimately, it's your choice, but you're forgetting one important fact. If I leave, who do you think your grandmother will insist stay by your side twenty-four hours a day?"

And just when she thought this situation couldn't get any worse. "She'd want Jaxon to spend every waking moment with me which is ridiculous, because I can take care of myself. I don't need anyone to protect me."

"Your grandmother thinks otherwise. So, you can calm down and let me do my assigned job as your knight, or you can kick me out and deal with Jaxon."

Her head started pounding. She was trapped. "I'm pretty sure I hate you right now."

"Bryn, I'm sor—"

She pushed her chair back from the table. "Oh no you don't. You don't get to say anything nice, or supportive, or sensitive. I need to stay angry or I'm going to fall apart. And you can keep up the, you're-only-my-employee-bullshit you started by keeping small talk to a minimum. We aren't going to hang out, and we aren't going to be friends. Because if we start laughing and having fun together, I'll miss us. Maybe we can be friends later, but not now. Got it?"

"You're serious? That's how you want to leave things?"

"None of this is how I want to leave things, but if you insist on staying and being my knight, then that's how it's going to be. Understand?"

"Yes, Ma'am."

The impersonal tone was exactly what she'd asked for, but it still hurt. "Fine. I'm going to call Ivy and I am going to bitch up a storm, so why don't you go hide in your room or on the terrace."

"Now I'm relegated to the servant's quarters?" he asked.

"Yes, as a matter of self-preservation. Check back with me in a month and maybe we can renegotiate our arrangement."

Valmont headed into his room and slammed the door.

And Bryn crumbled.

She pulled her knees up to her chest, curled into a ball, and let the tears flow. How had her life turned to such utter crap? Why did every guy she ever liked turn out to be such a complete moron? Was there something wrong with her? Sure, being officially promised to marry Jaxon made being with Valmont a little more difficult to manage, but they could have worked something out, if he thought their relationship was worth fighting for. And since he didn't, why wouldn't he just go away? Being around him every day was too painful to imagine.

She dabbed at her face with the napkins left on the table until they fell apart in her hands. What was she supposed to do now? This was all so damn frustrating. Since she was out of napkins but not out of tears, she went into her room and climbed into the shower. She could call Ivy later. Right now, crying in the shower would be therapeutic.

You'd think she'd be used to this, my-life-is-not-my-own scenario, but Valmont dumping her was a complete shock. Just when she needed emotional support, he decided to be all business. Then again, maybe he didn't want to watch the playacting she and Jaxon would have to do in public.

And what about Rhianna? How was she dealing with this? At least she'd still have Jaxon to lean on. No one would expect them to break things off. And it's not like Bryn wanted him. The strange thing was that out of all the males in her life, he was probably the only one, besides Clint, she could rely on right now. Since they were legally tied together, according to the Directorate, he couldn't leave her. How was that for irony?

When her fingers started to prune, she got out of the shower and dressed in her favorite yoga pants and T-shirt. A knock on her bedroom door made her heart jump. "Bryn, it's Rhianna. Can I come in?"

"Yes."

Rhianna peeked in the door. Her normally flawless complexion was blotchy and red.

"I see you've been doing the same thing I have," Rhianna sniffled. "I thought we could commiserate and maybe eat some chocolate." She held up a box of cookies.

"How'd you know I'd be crying?" Bryn asked.

"Ivy called to check on me, and she told me about Valmont. She figured I might need some girl time and that my Blue friends wouldn't be open to listening to me gripe, and she was right."

"That sucks for you."

"You have no idea," Rhianna said. "Since I've been relegated to Jaxon's mistress, I'm supposed to be happy and not care that his marriage contract was approved."

"Yours never should have been voided in the first place," Bryn said.

"Agreed, and your knight should realize nothing has to change between you two."

"I tried telling him that," Bryn bit into a chocolate cookie. The light brown chips were peanut butter. "Oh my God. These are awesome."

"I know. I ate two before I came over." Rhianna laughed.

And then it hit Bryn. The one good thing about being married to Jaxon might be spending time with Rhianna. "How do you think polite dragon-society would react to you and me hanging out together in public?"

"I'm sure they'll be shocked, but I don't care. There's something freeing about being off societal radar. I've developed an if-I'm-not-good-enough-for-them-then-I-don't-have-to-follow-their-rules attitude."

"I'm so jealous." Bryn took a giant bite of cookie. "I should probably ask how Jaxon is dealing with all this. I'm sure he's not thrilled, either."

"No. He's angry with his father for springing this on him. Ferrin should have given him and you advance notice, so you'd be prepared."

"It makes me wonder why they did it this way. Why now?" Bryn broke a cookie in half while she thought about it. "I bet it was more my grandparents than his parents." And then there was Lillith.

"From a strategic point of view, maybe they wanted to show the Rebels that the top two influential Blue families were united."

"If that's true, then Ferrin and my grandfather could have walked around campus hugging or something."

Rhianna laughed. "That would have been a sight."

And then another more logical explanation occurred to her. "I bet they wanted to show the Rebels that I'd aligned myself with the Blues…that even though I was a hybrid, I'd chosen to back the ruling Clan."

"That makes a lot of sense," Rhianna said. "And it also shows everyone else that you aren't in league with the Rebels."

Either way you thought about it, Bryn didn't love the logic. What's done was done. Next topic. "Did Jaxon tell you about the message his father gave him for me?"

"That was a bit harsh," Rhianna said. "Ferrin can be scary."

"And Lillith is so sweet. I don't know how she's put up with him." And now Bryn would have to put up with him at holidays and birthday parties. Not that she could gripe to Rhianna about that, so she decided to gripe about the current thorn in her side instead. "I still can't believe Valmont bailed on me. Our idea about the mansion with two wings where you and Jaxon could live on one side while we lived on the other could have worked. My wing is going to be a bit boring now."

"I'm sure you'll find someone else," Rhianna said.

"I don't know. First there was Zavien and now Valmont. Maybe I have sucky taste in men."

"I think maybe you're a victim of your unusual circumstances," Rhianna said. "And once all this war stuff is over and you release Valmont from his bond, you'll have a chance to find someone new."

She had her doubts. "What do you think is going to happen with the Rebels? Will the Directorate let them live off by themselves, or are they waiting for an excuse to squash the uprising?"

Rhianna reached around and touched her lower back. "My life was changed in more ways than one due to the attacks…and not for the better. I wish we could find the Rebels responsible and bring them to justice."

How had Bryn forgotten that? Okay it wasn't like she'd forgotten, but she'd been fantasizing about hybrids, Throwbacks, and the Directorate living in peace. "I'm sure the

Directorate has been hunting down the dragons responsible, but I don't know if they'd share with us that they found them."

"You'd think they'd want to let us know we're safe," Rhianna said.

"Or not." Bryn rolled the idea over in her mind. "This might sound ridiculous, but what if Ferrin has been executing the dragons responsible for the attacks and not telling everyone, so we think we still need to hide behind them."

"That's a little extreme, even for Ferrin." Rhianna said. "Plus, the Directorate would want to parade their victory in front of everyone to show us they were right all along."

"Right about what?" Bryn asked.

"Right about not approving certain marriages because they'd produce undesirable dragons."

"I'm mildly offended by that statement," Bryn said. And she wasn't joking.

Rhianna pointed at the box of baked goods. "First off, I'm sharing my cookies with you, so you don't get to be offended. Second, you have to admit any dragon who would try to hurt or kill students cannot be right in the head."

Bryn snagged another cookie. "Good point. Attacking innocent students and the people of Dragon's Bluff isn't the act of a sane, reasonable dragon. But neither was voiding your marriage contract due to a non-hereditary limp."

"True." Rhianna leaned back on her elbows. "There doesn't seem to be an answer to any of these problems, which is quite frustrating. It would drive Garret crazy." Rhianna sucked in a breath. "What if the Greens developed a test to see which hybrids and Throwbacks would have come from parents who would have failed the blood combining test? Could that tell us which ones were unstable?"

"I have no idea. It sounds like racial profiling. And who's to say nurture wouldn't overcome nature? Just because the child was at risk for developing a certain behavior doesn't mean they would definitely develop that trait."

"There's no good answer to this dilemma," Rhianna said. "Which might be why someone is hunting down the hybrids."

Bryn's stomach growled. "These cookies are good, but I think I need real food. Do you want to go to lunch?"

"Where at?"

"Just to be perverse I feel like telling Valmont we want to have lunch at Fonzoli's."

"That's not a bad idea," Rhianna said. "He'd get to visit his family which might make him feel better."

"It also seems like there are so many ways it could backfire." She told Rhianna about Megan. "I'm not sure I can maintain my cool around her. I'm sure she's perfectly nice, but right now I hate her and every girl like her who can give Valmont the life he wants. And I desperately want to incinerate his grandmother."

Rhianna nodded. "I see. Maybe we should go downstairs to the restaurant."

"That might be a lot easier." Bryn hopped off the bed. "Let me go ask…I mean tell Valmont what we want to do."

"Are you planning on being mean to him?" Rhianna asked.

"Maybe," Bryn said. "But I'm also practicing playing my role as a Blue. My grandmother would never ask an employee if they wanted to go somewhere. She'd just tell them what she wanted to do."

"Don't let the power go to your head," Rhianna said.

Chapter Seventeen

Bryn exited her room and knocked on Valmont's door. He opened it a few inches. "Yes."

"Rhianna and I want to go down to the restaurant for lunch."

"Give me five minutes, and I'll be ready to escort you." His tone was flat and unemotional.

"Fine," Bryn didn't let on that his response cut deep. She'd hoped maybe he'd had a change of heart. Apparently not.

The seating arrangement in the restaurant proved interesting. "Table for three?" the waiter had asked.

"I don't know." Bryn looked at Valmont. "Are you eating with us or do you plan to stand off to the side staring at nothing."

He pressed his lips together in a thin line but didn't respond.

"Why don't I set a table for three and you can figure it out as you go?" the waiter suggested.

"I insist he eat with us," Rhianna said. "It's more efficient that way."

"Okay." The waiter looked at Bryn and then at Valmont. Since neither of them argued, he followed Rhianna's instructions.

Bryn was halfway through her steak before she noticed what was happening. "Everyone is staring again, aren't they?"

Rhianna nodded. "Who wants to take bets on whether it's because you're eating lunch with your future husband's future mistress or because Valmont is being an asshat?"

Bryn almost choked on her food.

Rhianna giggled. "I've always wanted to say that, and it does seem to fit the occasion."

Valmont continued eating as though he hadn't heard her. Bryn wanted to poke him with her fork and ask if he was awake, but she didn't. "I wonder what Jaxon will have to say about all this staring?" Maybe he could play the alpha male and make them all back off.

"I'm sure he'll deal with it in his own way," Rhianna said.

Kah-boom! Bryn froze. "Is that thunder?"

Kah-boom!

"It could be a normal storm," Rhianna said.

Kah-boom-boom-boom!

The lights flickered.

Bryn stood and headed for the front door. Valmont caught her arm. "Don't."

"Back off," Bryn growled at him, literally. "You can follow my lead or you can go back to being a waiter."

He dropped her arm like it burned his hand. "Think, before you act. That's all I'm saying."

Too bad. If he didn't want to be a part of her life anymore, then he didn't get to have input on how she acted. She headed for the front door and peered out through the glass. Wind whipped the trees around. Lightning flashed through the sky. She didn't spot any dark shapes flying around, and the lightning didn't hit the ground.

Rhianna came up and stood by her side. "What's the verdict?"

"I'm not sure."

"What should we do?" Rhianna asked.

"Let's go back to my room and make a few calls." Bryn headed up the stairs. Valmont would either follow her or he wouldn't. She had more to worry about than his allegiance right now. She sprinted up the steps and down the hall to her dorm room. Jaxon pacing in front of her door didn't make her feel any better.

"Where's Rhianna?"

"She's right behind me," Bryn said. Should she feel bad that she ran when Rhianna couldn't move as fast? She opened her door and went inside to grab the phone. After punching in the number to Sinclair estates, she paced back and forth.

"Sinclair Estates, this is Rindy. How may I direct your call?"

"It's Bryn. Can you put me through to my grandmother?"

"Just one moment."

Bryn listened to the dead air on the line, hoping it wasn't some sort of foreshadowing for what might be happening.

"Bryn, what's wrong?"

"Is it storming where you are?"

"It's raining, but I haven't seen any lightning."

"There's lightning on campus. There's no evidence it's an attack, but it's making me nervous."

"Stay on this line. I'm going to call your grandfather on my cell."

Rhianna entered the room with Jaxon by her side. Where was Valmont? Bryn covered the receiver, "Valmont?"

"I'm keeping watch by the terrace window," he called out. "I'll alert you if I see anything suspicious."

"It could just be a storm, right?" Rhianna said.

Jaxon frowned. "Whenever Bryn is involved, the answer

is usually no."

And then there was a big blank space in the conversation where Valmont would have said, "I have no valid argument against that statement." And Bryn's eyes burned. She turned away so Jaxon wouldn't notice she was about to lose it. She blinked trying to hold back the tears. Damn it. She'd been feeling better staying angry and now it felt as if someone had ripped the emotional rug out from under her again.

"Bryn, your grandfather isn't concerned at this time, but I'm not sure I share his optimism. Are you in your room?"

A single word she could fake her way through. "Yes."

"Do you know where Jaxon is?"

"He and Rhianna are here with me now."

"I see." Her grandmother didn't sound like she approved of the situation. "In any case, he should escort you to the library. Your grandfather mentioned he wanted to speak with both of you, and the library was designed to withstand a siege."

"Okay. We'll go now."

"Wait a moment. There's something else wrong, isn't there?"

There was no point in lying. "Yes, but I can't talk about it."

"Is it Jaxon?"

"No. It's not him."

"Valmont?" her grandmother guessed.

"Yes, he's changed."

"I think I understand," Her grandmother said. "Your marriage contract made him withdraw his...friendship."

That was one way to phrase it. "Pretty much."

"Would you ask him to come to the phone, please?"

"You know I don't need a babysitter. And we should probably head over to the library."

"Bryn, you put him on the phone right now or I will fly there and speak to him personally."

Crap. Her grandmother was not one to make idle threats. "Valmont, my grandmother would like a word with you."

"Why?" Valmont came around the corner with a concerned look on his face.

Bryn held the phone out to him. "I don't know."

He accepted the phone like it was a snake that might bite him. "Mrs. Sinclair?"

He nodded along and said, "Yes, no…but…I see." And then he hung up. "We are all going to the library."

"Why?" Rhianna asked.

"Because Marie Sinclair has spoken." Valmont gestured toward the door. "After you."

"What did she say?" Rhianna asked.

Good question. Valmont didn't seem inclined to answer.

"Give me a moment," Bryn went into her room and put on her elemental sword bracelet. When she returned to the living room, she pointed at Jaxon. "Are you wearing your cuff links?"

Jaxon pointed at his shirt cuff. "As soon as I heard the thunder, I put them on."

"So I'm the only person who is unarmed?" Rhianna said. "That hardly seems fair."

"I could give you a cuff link," Jaxon said.

"No, you'd lose the element of surprise in a fight."

"I can offer you a dagger," Valmont said. "It isn't magical, but it is sharp."

"Thank you," Rhianna said. "I'll take it."

Valmont went into his room and retrieved a dagger in a leather pouch about ten inches long with a strap that buckled. "This is meant to go inside your boot." Valmont pointed at Rhianna's heels. "I'm not sure how you want to wear it."

She accepted the dagger. "I have boots. We'll stop on the way to the library so I can change outfits."

• • •

After Rhianna changed into very stylish, more than likely designer, black leather knife-hiding boots, they went out onto her balcony. It was raining, which put Bryn at ease. Maybe she'd been worried over nothing. Sometimes lightning could just be lightning.

"Maybe we should go down to the lobby and walk to the library," Valmont said.

"That's ridiculous," Jaxon said. "We can fly there in five minutes."

Valmont sighed. "I'm not sure Bryn and me flying together is a good idea."

"Why?" Bryn asked. "Are you afraid you might feel the power of the bond and realize you've made a huge mistake?"

Jaxon pointed at Valmont. "I don't care about your personal life. We're flying because it's faster. End of story." He shifted and launched himself into the sky, treading air above Rhianna who shifted and dove off the terrace toward the library while Jaxon shadowed her from above.

Damn it. This was going to totally suck. Flying with Valmont had always been one of her favorite things. The power of the bond flowed through them making her feel powerful and like she was part of something wonderful... something warm that had felt like love.

"If we're going to do this, we might as well get it over with," Valmont said.

Well, that put an end to the warm, fuzzy moment she'd been having. Jerk. It was his fault this was going to be emotionally traumatizing. At least she wouldn't be suffering alone.

Bryn shifted and whipped her tail around for him to use as a step. Valmont placed his hand on her flank. It was the first time he'd touched her since he'd broken up with her.

The familiar warmth of his hand made her breath catch. He climbed onto her back, sitting between her shoulder blades. Bryn braced herself for the familiar rush of power, but it was more like a flow of water. Not nearly as powerful as the crashing wave she'd experienced every other time they'd connected. Maybe their relationship had enhanced the bond rather than the bond enhancing the relationship. She didn't have time to think about that right now, so she dove for the library. The air was unpleasantly wet and cold. It felt like flying through fog.

They landed in front of the library doors without incident. Bryn stumble-stepped a little, but no worse than usual. Jaxon and Rhianna stood waiting for them. Valmont hopped off Bryn's back as quickly as possible. She shifted before his feet touched the ground. The sense of loss she normally felt after they flew together was absent, and that felt wrong.

Ferrin and her grandfather stood waiting for them inside. Ferrin didn't bother to hide his disdain for Rhianna. Jaxon either didn't see it or chose not to acknowledge it.

"Bryn, I believe this is a natural storm," her grandfather said, "But we could use Jaxon's and your help with a situation that's come up."

"That's nice and vague," Bryn said.

"Come with us, and we'll fill in the details." Her grandfather headed to the entrance of the vaults rather than up to his office. Ferrin followed.

"Any idea what this is about?" Bryn asked Jaxon.

"No." He took off after his father.

"Since the two crappiest things I can imagine have already happened, I guess I have nothing to be afraid of," Bryn said. She walked toward the entrance to the vaults with Valmont on her heels.

They descended through the hatch and down the stone steps to the landing where Red guards stood waiting for them.

"What you are about to see might disturb you," Bryn's grandfather said. "Be assured that we are treating them as humanely as possible."

"Maybe you should go back up to the library," Jaxon said to Rhianna.

"I'm staying." Rhianna crossed her arms over her chest.

"This way." Ferrin headed down one of the newly excavated hallways.

"Does this lead to where we woke up after the ambush?" Bryn asked.

"We won't be going that far down," her grandfather said.

"Not comforting," Bryn mumbled as she followed behind him.

They came to a door, which resembled the first door they'd uncovered in the main room. Ferrin produced a key from his pocket and unlocked it. Bryn entered the hallway. Ahead of her on either side she could see openings, like rooms without doors. As she came closer to the rooms, the acrid scent of sweat and fear grew stronger.

"What have you done?" Bryn asked her grandfather.

"We have done what was necessary," he replied.

When they came even with the first room on the right, Bryn saw the entrance was blocked with metal bars, like a prison cell. Inside the ten-by-ten room, four young men, probably no older than herself, sat on the bottom bunk of two bunk beds that had been crammed into the space. The remains of lunch or dinner sat on a tray in the corner.

"What's going on here?" Bryn asked.

"We found these cells when we excavated the lower level, and we put them to good use," her grandfather said. "Anyone found living in the forest was rounded up and brought here for questioning."

"How long have you had them here?" Valmont asked.

"We keep them until we are sure they are no longer a

threat," Ferrin said.

"How do you determine if they are a threat?" Jaxon asked.

"The medics have assisted us," Ferrin said. "We've given them the same potion we give students who are out after curfew which makes them answer our questions truthfully."

"And what have you learned?" Bryn asked.

"We learned the location of several Rebel camps," her grandfather said. "We were able to send Guards out to capture or kill them if necessary."

Bryn's stomach twisted. "So you've been rounding up anyone who lives in the forest? What about the people who moved onto the deeded land?"

"The deeded land is under strict supervision." Her grandfather continued walking down the hall.

The next cell they passed held one man, who sported a black eye and a swollen lip. "Why is he injured, and why hasn't he been healed?" Bryn asked.

"He was injured resisting arrest. Once here, he bragged about his participation in the attacks on campus and Dragon's Bluff."

"This entire campus will burn," the man stated.

Okay. Her sympathy level dropped.

Rhianna moved closer to the bars. "What did you hope to accomplish by injuring students and humans?"

The man smirked. "Our goal was to create chaos and to show the Directorate that they were no longer in control."

"Then you and your friends are the reason I was injured and my marriage contract voided."

He shrugged. "You have to break a few eggs to make an omelet."

Metal flashed and then the man looked down, his mouth open in an "O" of surprise at the dagger Rhianna had thrust into his chest, stabbing him in the heart. Blood spurted from the wound, spattering Rhianna's blouse. She didn't seem to notice. She just stared in apparent satisfaction as the man stumbled and then dropped to the floor.

No one spoke a word. Everyone in the hallway had gone silent. Rhianna turned to Valmont. "Sorry about your dagger. I'm sure Mr. Sinclair can have someone retrieve it for you."

"I have other daggers," Valmont said.

Bryn had no idea what to say. Rhianna deserved some sort of satisfaction or vengeance but Bryn never expected to see it in action.

"Good thing we were done interviewing him," Bryn's grandfather stated. "Let's keep moving. There's someone we want you to see."

He couldn't be talking about her parents, could he?

Two cells down, Onyx sat on a bunk bed, playing solitaire with a deck of cards. He didn't appear inconvenienced by his current situation. When he caught sight of Jaxon, he stood. "I was wondering when they'd bring you to see me."

"How long have you been here?" Jaxon asked.

"Around forty-eight hours," Onyx said. "I willingly drank their potion and answered all their questions, but they haven't answered any of mine."

"After thorough interrogation, we determined that he is aware of the Rebels, but he doesn't encourage them. Although he does encourage dragons to work toward changing the way the Directorate governs."

"If he's not a threat, why haven't you let him go?" Bryn asked.

"We plan to place him under house arrest once facilities are made ready," Bryn's grandfather said.

"What about all these other people?" Bryn asked. "Were they all involved in the attacks?"

"Most of the ones who admitted their guilt have been executed," Ferrin stated. "The rest will be released and confined to the deeded land after we are assured they aren't working against us."

"Why show us this?" Bryn asked.

"We wanted Jaxon to see that we honored his promise to keep Onyx safe if he wished to speak with us. We wanted both of you to be aware of what we're doing, in case students come to you with questions," her grandfather said.

"Why not share this with everyone so they realize what the Directorate is doing to keep them safe?" Valmont asked.

"Because we aren't done yet," Ferrin said, "and there could still be traitors among us."

"Did you find out anything about the Orange dragons who ambushed us?" Bryn asked.

"We have pieced together some details," her grandfather said. "They were retrieving herbs from storage and another box of Tyrant's crowns."

Bryn shivered, "We need to find those things and melt them down."

"That is the plan," her grandfather said. "Now, I'll escort you upstairs."

What about her parents? Had they learned that her mom and dad were still alive? If they were monitoring the deeded land as closely as they claimed, it would only be a matter of time until her parents were discovered.

By the time they emerged in the room that housed the trap door to the vault, Bryn's nerves were wound tight. "There's something I need to discuss with you, but I'm not sure how you're going to handle it. I'd like you to keep an open mind. I already told Grandmother, and she said she'd share it with you at the appropriate time—"

"I know about Sara and your father," he said. "Marie told me the same night you told her."

His tone gave nothing away. "And?"

"And they have been accounted for on the deeded land.

They are being watched like all the others. If they make no move against us, they will be allowed to live out their lives peacefully."

That was a non-answer if ever she heard one. "What does that mean? Have you talked to her? Will you go see her? Because when all this war crap is over, I'd like for them to visit us. For you all to start talking again."

"I'm glad she is alive and that you have your parents back, but my daughter, the Sara that I loved, died a long time ago." With those chilling words he exited the room.

"So much for a family reunion." Bryn sniffled and waited for Valmont to say something comforting. Seconds ticked by and nothing. Damn him. She needed her Valmont, the one who cared about her, not this pod-person. She needed couch time. She needed someone to tell her everything was going to be all right.

As they walked out into the damp evening air, a wave of sadness swamped her. Should they fly back to her dorm room? Flying with him and feeling the weakness of their bond would make her feel worse. "Let's walk back."

"I don't mind flying." Valmont reached up and rubbed the back of his neck.

"We probably won't be able to avoid flying together," she said, "so I guess we better adjust to the new sort-of-sucky-no-longer-enhanced-by-love bond."

He blinked and stepped back from her. "Forget it. We'll walk."

Now his feelings were hurt? He'd brought this on himself. "Bite me. You can walk. I'm going to fly." She didn't wait to hear his response; she shifted and launched herself into the night sky. Rather than aiming for her dorm room, she performed a barrel roll. Flying alone was so…freeing. See… she didn't need a knight. She was a kick-ass shape-shifting dragon. She dove toward the ground and then looped up into the sky, tucking her wings to her body and performing a free fall before spreading her wings again. And then she aimed for her dorm room terrace, where she knocked over a chair when she landed. Since there was no one there to witness it, she didn't need to apologize. Her flying high lasted until she tried to open the terrace window. It wouldn't budge, because it was latched from the inside. Damn it. She'd forgotten about that. Now what? She could break the glass and then pay someone to fix it, or she could knock and wait for Valmont to let her in.

He was still her knight, after all, and opening the window wasn't a hardship. She tapped on the glass and waited. Nothing happened. He should have made it inside by now, but maybe he'd decided not to head straight back to her room. She peered in and knocked louder.

"Just a minute," Valmont called out. He came out of his room and looked at her like he was confused. "Do you require my assistance?"

He knew perfectly well what she needed. "Unlock the damn window."

He flipped the latch and then turned around and headed into his room. He could have opened the window for her. She yanked it up and climbed inside, making sure to latch it behind her. She glared at his closed door, and before thinking about it, she banged on it.

"What?" Valmont called out.

"Can we talk?"

He opened the door a few inches. "About what?"

"About our delightful new situation."

"The one where you walk away from me, leaving me to worry about you?"

"Yes, the one where you know I'm emotionally upset and you offer no comfort."

"I should have said something after your grandfather walked away," Valmont conceded. "I'm sorry."

Better late than never. "Thank you. Do you think there's any hope he'll ever forgive her?"

"Honestly," he said, "I don't know."

Her stomach growled, breaking the emotional moment. "Uhm, I haven't checked a clock, but I'm pretty sure it's dinner time."

He leaned against the doorframe and crossed his arms over his chest. "I don't want to go to the dining hall. Why don't I run downstairs and pick something up for us."

The fact that he said us made her feel a little better. "I'd appreciate that."

• • •

Bryn tried to think of suppressing her feelings for Valmont as training for her new social status. But so far, the whole situation just sucked. How was she supposed to get over a guy who followed her around all day long? Not to mention the fact that everyone pretended not to notice the strained relationship between her and Valmont. And Jaxon went about his life as his normal irritable self. His relationship with Rhianna was unchanged, which seemed completely unfair.

The only place she could get away from Valmont was the girl's restroom, which was why she dragged Ivy into every bathroom they passed.

"There are only so many times you can pretend to use the restroom before someone is going to suggest you see a medic," Ivy complained Thursday afternoon. "You need a new tactic."

"I know." Bryn growled in frustration. "But if I can't get away from Valmont for a little bit, I'm going to go insane."

"Maybe you should release him from the dragon-knight bond," Ivy said. "And yes, I know Jaxon will become your new shadow, but at least then he'd be as miserable as you."

"I hadn't thought about it that way." Bryn washed her hands, to pretend she had a reason for being in the girl's room in case anyone else came in. "Maybe I should cut him loose."

Ivy checked her watch. "Come on. We don't want to be late for Proper Decorum."

"Can we skip class?"

"I'm sure Clint would be happy to skip with you, but I'm betting your grandparents would not approve."

They went back out into the hall where Clint leaned against the wall looking bored, and Valmont wore his game face. How would he react if she broke the bond right now? Should she do it? Just end it and let the chips fall where they may? Maybe tonight.

"There you are." Clint hooked his arm through Ivy's. "We don't want to miss today's epic class. We're discussing what type of caterers to hire for different occasions."

"Just hire Fonzoli's," Valmont muttered as they headed down the hall.

That brought a funny question to mind. In the future, when she was hosting some ridiculous event in a house, which would probably have way too many W's, would Valmont show up in his caterer's uniform and serve lemon ice? How weird would that be?

In class, the teacher divided them into small groups. And surprise…Jaxon was in her group.

Bryn rolled her eyes as she studied a seating chart for small dinner parties, which meant twenty or fewer couples. "Why does it matter where everyone sits? Shouldn't everyone be capable of choosing their own seats?"

"Only if you want bloodshed," Jaxon said. "We stand united as a Clan, but that doesn't mean our personalities always mesh. Since people tend to drink at parties, sometimes they say things they shouldn't. As the hostess, it's your job to know who to keep apart."

"If you know all this crap, why should I bother learning it?" Bryn asked.

Jaxon reached up to rub his forehead. "It's your job to know all of these things."

"Nope. It's not," Bryn said. "My grandmother can play party planner. She loves that stuff. Problem solved."

"That's not how it works," Jaxon muttered.

"Just so you know, in our marriage, we're going to switch things up a bit," Bryn responded. "So that's how it will work."

After class, Jaxon practically fled the room with Rhianna in tow.

"I love it when you give Jaxon hell," Clint said. "It restores my faith in the balance of the universe."

"Nothing about the world seems balanced right now," Bryn snuck a look at Valmont. He was staring off into space. She reached over and poked him in the shoulder. "What are you thinking?"

"All this talk of catering has me thinking about my family. If we're not on lockdown, I'd like to visit them."

"I don't see why you can't go visit. I could hang out with Clint and Ivy, and if my grandmother insists, Jaxon and Rhianna, while you're gone."

"I can't go unless you go with me," Valmont said. "I can't leave you behind."

Bryn laughed. "Hello, Irony."

"What?" Valmont asked.

"You not wanting to leave me behind...given the current state of our relationship...it's funny to me."

"It's not to me." He clammed up after that. It's like he was trying to freeze her out. For the rest of the week, he only spoke if she asked him a direct question. Thursday night, when it was time to go to sleep, she'd had enough.

"How much longer are you going to pout?" she asked him. "Because it's not very knight-like behavior."

"I'm not pouting. I'm doing my job, watching over you. Small talk isn't part of the deal, remember?"

That was it. She was swearing off men. She'd become a Westgate and live in an ostentatious mansion where she'd pay people obscene amounts of money to create ridiculous things. Maybe she'd have Ivy do her plant whisperer thing and grow a forest to rival Ferrin's. That might be more trouble than it was worth. What else could she do? She loved animals. Why not have an animal sanctuary in the house? She could dedicate different floors to different species. And when Ferrin came over she could accidentally lock him in a room with a man-eating polar bear. That thought made her smile.

Now…what to do about the other man in her life who she wanted to make disappear? Maybe she should call her grandmother and see if she wanted to meet for lunch in Dragon's Bluff tomorrow. Then she could explain that she didn't need a babysitter. And yes, it did make her feel like a bit of a loser that there wasn't a guy who wanted to spend Saturday afternoon with her, but apparently that was her life now. It sucked, and she didn't want to get used to it. If she bit the bullet and cut ties with Valmont, it's not like she'd be free to date. He could date Megan or some other human girl who could give him the simple life he wanted. And maybe one day she'd be happy for him, but for now she was stuck in resentment-land because it appeared everyone else was destined to have a happily ever after while she played this weird wife-of-a-Westgate role that left her not-really-married, yet not allowed to date.

But, dwelling on it would not make the situation better, so she called her grandmother.

"I think lunch this weekend sounds like a wonderful idea," her grandmother said.

"Good. I was hoping to make you see that I don't need a babysitter. Although I will probably eat large amounts of dessert to cope with my new life."

"We can discuss the situation," her grandmother said. "I think we should drop Valmont off at Fonzoli's and then you and I can go to Suzette's. I'll have two personal guards escort us, so you can speak without him standing behind you."

Bryn's throat grew thick. She tried to keep her voice on an even keel. "Sounds good. Although I can't imagine an outcome to this situation that doesn't suck."

"The right decision isn't always the easiest," her grandmother said, "but I think you'll feel better once you've made a choice. Now I'll meet you at your room on Saturday at one."

"Thanks." Bryn hung up and went to her room to stare into her armoire. If she picked her clothes out ahead of time, she'd feel better. What to wear? She needed an outfit that projected confidence. Something that showed people she was moving on and had accepted her new life. Something that showed she was ready to leave Valmont behind, even if that was the furthest thing from the truth. No one, including Valmont, needed to know that. And that gave her an idea.

Bryn did her best to act normal on Friday. She didn't drag Ivy into the bathroom even once. After their last class, Ivy grabbed Bryn's arm and dragged her into the bathroom. "What is going on with you today?"

Okay. Maybe she hadn't been as convincing as she'd thought. "Am I acting like a pod-person?"

"Pretty much."

"Sorry. Meeting with my grandmother tomorrow will give me the perfect opportunity to end things with Valmont, but I'm not sure I can go through with it."

"I'm not going to pretend I understand how much this

sucks for you, and I'm not sure I can say anything to make it better, but I'm here when you want to talk."

Bryn nodded. "Just promise me I won't be the odd man out. Having Valmont around meant I wasn't the third wheel, and now…"

"You're our friend. Both of ours, so you're never a third wheel."

"Thanks for lying to me," Bryn laughed.

"I'm not," Ivy objected.

Facts were facts. "Thanks. I plan to eat my weight in cherry pie. Do you want me to bring some back for you?"

"Sure. If you remember."

At quarter til one on Saturday, Bryn checked her reflection in the mirror. The navy cashmere sweater she'd put on felt like a hug, which she needed. The gray pants and black boots looked elegant but not snooty. She wore her elemental sword bracelet and her sapphire earrings since her grandmother had made it clear she deemed jewelry a necessary part of any outfit.

She emerged from her room to find Valmont sitting on the couch reading a book. He didn't look up from the page. While she'd love to believe he was caught up in whatever he was reading, odds were he was avoiding her. Should she suggest he pack his belongings? That would start a fight, and it's not like he had much here.

A knock on the door sounded. Bryn opened it and found her grandmother and Lillith. "I added one to our lunch date," her grandmother said, "I didn't think you'd mind."

While she was still annoyed at Lillith for telling Valmont they should break the bond, it's not like she was the one who made him break up with her. "Technically, I think you added two more people, and of course, I don't mind."

Lillith grinned and stroked her belly. "Asher and I appreciate it. We…or at least I am feeling antsy today."

Valmont followed behind her as they walked to the SUV, and he stared out the window on the drive to Dragon's Bluff. When they pulled up to the back door of Fonzoli's, Bryn said, "Your grandmother knows you're coming."

"What?" He seemed confused.

"You said you missed your family, so I called your grandmother and told her you were coming to lunch at her house, not the restaurant. The rest of us are going to Suzette's."

Valmont's eyebrows came together like he was conflicted. Then he glanced at Bryn's grandmother. "You're okay with this?"

"Yes. That's why we brought two guards. Go enjoy your family."

Valmont smiled at Bryn, and it was a smile she hadn't seen in a while. The one that made his dimple stand out. Her heart clenched, but she smiled back and said, "Go on."

"Thank you." He left the car and jogged up to the back door of his grandmother's house. It was flung open before he could knock, and his dad was hugging him and pulling him into the house.

That's when she knew it was time. Valmont deserved to be happy. And it's not like she'd be alone. She had her parents back, which seemed like a huge cosmic gift. Her grandparents had turned out to be very dependable. And heaven help her, Jaxon wasn't all bad. Loving Rhianna had worn off some of his sharper edges. And Lillith was like a big sister or an aunt and Asher would be fun to play with. Ferrin…well she just wouldn't think about him.

"Are you all right?" Lillith asked.

"I will be." Bryn sat back in her seat. "Bring on the pie."

"You have to eat a proper meal first," her grandmother said.

"Not a problem."

As soon as she entered Suzette's, Bryn realized something

strange was going on. Every single female in the place made eye contact with her and either smiled or nodded. Bryn returned the gesture. Would she have to do this all the time?

"Will this continue?" Bryn asked after they were seated, explaining the new development.

"What did people do before when you walked into a room?" Lillith asked.

"Half would say hello, but the other half avoided eye contact, pretended I was invisible, or insulted me," Bryn said.

Lillith frowned. "I had no idea."

"Apparently, making the marriage contract between Jaxon and me official has taken me off the social pariah list."

"I see you're adjusting to your new situation," her grandmother said.

"There are perks, I suppose," she leaned in. "But I'm drawing the line at a house full of W's."

Lilith giggled and her grandmother grinned. "You will learn to pick your battles."

"What battles did you pick?" Would her grandmother respond to the question?

"Ephram had a fondness for silk flowers because they required so little care. It took me a few months, but I managed to change out all the silk arrangements for real plants."

They made pleasant small talk while Bryn worked her way through a plate of beef medallions and two pieces of cherry pie. She could have eaten more, but for the first time she worried about what people would think of her, and she hated that.

"You want another piece of pie, don't you?" her grandmother said.

"I do, but I was trying to be polite," Bryn said.

"I'd like a cup of coffee," her grandmother said, "so why don't you order another piece."

"If you insist."

While they waited for the coffee and pie, Bryn wondered how much she should say in front of Lillith. "Can I trust the future daughter-in-law bond will keep you from repeating anything I say here?"

"Yes, but if you'd like to talk privately with your grandmother, I could go visit with another table."

Maybe she'd leave out the gory details. "I'm considering releasing Valmont from our bond. He's been missing his family a lot. Since my marriage contract was approved, he feels like I don't need him anymore."

Lillith blushed. "I have to confess, I suggested to Valmont that after your contract was approved he should bow out of the bond. I'm sorry. I think I was feeling fiercely maternal that day, and I felt the need to protect Jaxon's future interests."

As if Jaxon was interested in her in that manner. "Valmont mentioned that, but it's not the reason we're considering breaking the bond now. It seems like our relationship has run its course."

"And I could post a guard outside your room," her grandmother said. "You'd have a lot more privacy."

"I don't need a body guard. I can take care of myself."

"You're the only granddaughter I have. Security will be assigned to you whether you want it or not."

"Can it be security that I don't see and that others don't see? I don't want to appear weak." Holy hell. She really had turned into a Blue.

Her grandmother sipped her coffee. "When you put it that way...I see your point."

On the drive back to Fonzoli's, Bryn tried to bolster her courage. She could do this. She could set Valmont free to go back to his normal life. He deserved to be happy, though she resented the hell out of the fact that he didn't think he could be happy with her, and given the chance she'd blast a small non-lethal fireball at his grandmother. That might be immature, but she could only take the high road so far.

If she could make Ferrin disappear, life with Jaxon wouldn't be so awful, because it wouldn't really be life with Jaxon. It would be life with Rhianna and Lillith and Asher, too. Maybe Asher would calm Ferrin down, or at least distract him enough to keep his attention off of her.

And one thing she knew for sure. Her parents would be welcome in her stupidly large home whether Jaxon felt that way or not. She wished she could speak to her mom. Knowing her parents were out there brightened her depressing life, but that wasn't the same as having them where she could talk to them or ask for a hug.

When they pulled up to his grandparents' house, Bryn heard laughter and loud voices. It sounded like Valmont's lunch was ongoing. Should she go back to school and leave him here? A knot of unease grew inside of her. She wanted to say good-bye…not that she really wanted to do it, but she needed some sort of closure.

"Instead of releasing him, you could tell him you don't need a bodyguard anymore," Lillith suggested.

That sounded a lot less painful, but was it the right thing to do? "What do you think?" Bryn asked her grandmother.

"Well," her grandmother pursed her lips like she wasn't sure what to say. "You have two choices…you can sever ties completely, or you can keep him as your knight until you're married—with the understanding that he would not have to be your guard 24/7 and he could live in Dragon's Bluff."

Maybe if he was out of her personal space they could move toward being friends. "I guess I should go talk to him and ask him what he wants." And pray she could avoid crying or blasting him with a fireball while she did it.

When she knocked on the back door, Megan answered it. Bryn stomped down on her resentment and did her best to fake civility. "Hello, Megan. Can you ask Valmont to come outside for a moment?"

Disappointment was clear on the girl's face. "Does he have to leave?"

"No. I just need to speak with him for a moment."

Megan practically bounced with excitement. "Would it be wrong of me to tell you how wonderful I think he is?"

Bryn imagined shifting and biting the girl's head off. After a calming breath Bryn said, "No, I'm glad you like him." *LIAR!* Her subconscious screamed.

"I'll get him for you." Megan ran off.

This was totally going to suck, but it was the right thing to do. If he didn't want her, she didn't need him.

Valmont's smile faded as he came toward her. "Is it time to go?"

"No. Can you come outside with me for a minute? I think we need to talk."

His brow furrowed. "I'm not sure I want to hear what you have to say."

"Hear me out before you object." She walked over and sat on the porch steps and waited for him to join her. He hesitated, glancing back into the house before joining her.

"We have two choices. I can release you or you could remain my knight, but do it from a distance. You can stay here and live your life… Be happy with your family. If I need you, I'll call."

Valmont frowned.

"I am trying to be the bigger person. And like you said before, our relationship might not have turned in the direction it did if you weren't living with me. I'd like to think we can be friends, once I no longer want to set Megan's hair on fire."

Valmont grabbed her hand, sliding his warm fingers between hers. The familiar gesture shredded Bryn's resolve. Her chest ached. She closed her eyes to try and stem the tide of tears.

"I'm sorry about all of this," Valmont said. "I never meant to hurt you."

She couldn't talk without crying or setting something on fire, so she just nodded and exhaled smoke as the taste of ash filled her mouth.

"I can follow you back in my car and pack my things," he said.

Focusing on snow, she tamped down the fire inside of her. "Unless there's something you need immediately, I'd rather mail it to you."

"You could come visit me in a few days and bring my stuff," Valmont said.

"I might need more than a couple of days to get past this," Bryn said. "Right now I'm practicing my Blue dragon social skills, pretending to be fine with all of this, but I'm not. So a visit will have to wait."

"You can't avoid me forever," Valmont said. "You like Fonzoli's food too much."

She laughed, and it came out as a half sob. Why had she thought this was the right thing to do? And why did the right thing have to hurt so much?

"You'll always be my dragon," Valmont said.

She almost said, *You'll always be my knight.* But that was a big fat lie.

Some day in the not too far off future, she'd become a Westgate, and now that he was no longer required to be her bodyguard, he'd go back to being a waiter. He deserved to live his life with the family he loved…find a normal girl who could make him happy. All of these random thoughts led her to one sad conclusion. "Valmont, I release you from our bond."

He gasped like someone had stolen the air from his lungs. She clutched at his hand as her heart constricted and missed a beat. It felt like someone had piled weights on top of her chest. She fought to breathe, and then her body relaxed.

Dropping her hand he pushed away from her. "Why did you do that?"

"Better now than a few months from now." A strange icy calmness flowed over her. "What's done is done. Take care, Valmont."

"Wait." He undid the scabbard holding the sword etched with fire and ice and held it out to her. "You might have another knight one day, and he'll need this."

Was he trying to be honorable, or was he trying to hurt her? "Keep it as a parting gift. If I ever need it, I'll know where to find it."

Numb. She felt numb as she stood and headed for her grandmother's SUV. Whoever had come up with that ripping-something-off-like-a-Band-Aid-to-get-it-over-with idea had forgotten to mention that you shredded part of yourself in the process. That's what it felt like as she climbed into the SUV and the driver headed back to school…like some of her magic or Quintessence had been stripped away.

"Bryn?" Her grandmother sounded concerned. "Are you all right?"

"No." Why should she lie? "I feel like I lost part of myself."

Chapter Eighteen

Thankfully, both Lillith and her grandmother let her be on the ride back to school. She wasn't up for one of those, this-was-for-the-best speeches. After hugging her grandmother good-bye, she headed for her dorm.

Students were outside enjoying the cool crisp weather. Some were sitting in the grass, while others hung out beneath the protective shelters. She took her time walking across campus, putting off the inevitable. When she stood outside her door with the key in the lock, she hesitated. Waiting wouldn't rewind her life to a happier time, so she went inside and changed into jeans and then called Clint and Ivy and arranged for them to come over, all the while avoiding looking at the closed door to Valmont's former room.

Her friends showed up at her terrace window five minutes after she called. Clint carried a bag of candy bars and a box of tissues.

"I see you came prepared." Bryn accepted the bag of chocolate and headed for the couch. Not that she wanted to sit on the couch where she'd spent so much time with Valmont, but she needed to suck it up and deal with it.

"So how did you leave things?" Ivy asked.

Bryn told her what happened. "Do you think I made the right decision?"

"I think this was inevitable," Ivy said. "Maybe it was best to get it over with."

"Do you want me to go in his room and pack up his stuff?" Clint offered.

"Yes, please," Bryn said. "I was dreading that."

"I got this." Clint headed over to Valmont's room.

Bryn ripped the wrapper off a candy bar and ate it in three bites. "Releasing Valmont hurt, but the worst part is that I've come to the conclusion that I'm not meant to have a boyfriend."

"That's ridiculous. You'll find someone. Maybe there's a nice hybrid guy waiting for you at the new settlement."

Bryn laughed. "Right. I can see that conversation going really well. Hi, I'm married, but it's just a business partnership, and I was wondering if you'd like to go grab a cup of coffee."

"You never know," Ivy said. "Maybe things didn't work out with Valmont because you're meant to be with someone else."

Her friend was being far too optimistic, but she was trying to help, so Bryn said, "Maybe."

Clint emerged from Valmont's room carrying a leather-bound journal. "I found something, but I'm not sure if you'll want to see it."

"What is it?" Ivy stood and went over to look at the open pages of the book. "Oh…" was all she said.

Not good. "What is it? A love letter to Megan?"

"No," Ivy said. "It looks like Valmont was writing down the pros and cons of your relationship."

"Let me guess, his main issues were his family, the bond, us being different species, his honor, and my arranged marriage to Jaxon."

Ivy nodded. "Pretty much."

"So what's in the plus column?" There had better be a few pros or she was going to be pissed.

"There's just one thing," Ivy turned the book to face her.

In Valmont's neat script it said, *I love her.*

Bryn breathed through the tidal wave of pain that crashed over her, keeping her tear ducts under control. "And yet that wasn't enough."

Ivy handed her a candy bar. "At the moment, this is the only help I can give you."

Bryn leaned back in her seat and stared up at the ceiling. "I don't understand how a relationship that felt so right could go so wrong." Something dropped from the ceiling and landed on her bottom lip. Instinctively she spit and wiped at her mouth. "What the heck?" As if she needed this day to get any worse.

"What was that?" Ivy asked.

"Probably some rare spider that's going to make my lips swell up like balloons." She went to the bathroom and washed off her face. She even brushed her teeth for good measure. When she went back into the living room, she pointed at the shoulders of Clint's black shirt. "Either you've developed a case of dandruff in the last few minutes or something is shaking this building."

Raised voices could be heard in the dorm rooms and from the hallway. "What's going on?" Bryn opened her door and saw half a dozen students with the same clueless looks on their faces. They weren't going to be any help.

Ivy headed toward the terrace window. "My instincts say if a building is shaking, it's time to leave for more steady ground."

"Agreed." Bryn followed her friends out on the terrace, shifted, and launched herself into the sky. From this vantage point, she couldn't see anything unusual. Scratch that. There was a line of people at the back gate waiting to check in at the guard station. Maybe a bunch of students had gone to Dragon's Bluff for dinner.

"What are you doing?" A Blue flew toward her. Jaxon's face flashed across his dragon features. "You shouldn't be out in the open like this."

"But you're out here," Bryn said.

"I'm not sightseeing. Rhianna and I are on our way to the library to find out what's going on. Come with us."

It's not like she had a better plan, so she aimed for the library and dove. Her friends followed.

And that's when they heard the screaming and the roaring. Bryn whipped around and tried to make sense of what she saw. Dragons were bursting from the ground like water from a geyser. Multi-colored dragons emerged from the ripped-open green spaces. Dragons with both Black and Red scales flew next to dragons who had Orange and Green scales. There were more color combinations than Bryn had ever dreamed possible.

"They must have tunneled in," Jaxon said.

Any student in human form shifted. Enemy dragons attacked, dive bombing the students.

A Black dragon with Red scales flew at Bryn. Nola's features flashed across the dragon's face. "I've been waiting for this day," Nola sucked in a breath and blasted lightning at Bryn.

Bryn tucked her wings and dove, avoiding the lightning and blasting Nola's left wing with fire. Jaxon blasted her other wing with ice, and Nola dropped toward the ground, with her underbelly exposed.

"It's your kill," Jaxon said.

"No." Bryn flew away from Nola. "No one has to die."

"You're wrong," Nola roared, flexing her wing and

shaking off the ice. "It's past your time to die."

A Red guard swooped in and bit down on Nola's neck, ripping the flesh and sending copper scented blood spatter through the air. *Why is this happening?*

As Nola's body dropped, the Red turned to Bryn. "This is war. Fight, or get out of our way."

A siren sounded and reverberated off the walls of the buildings. A little late for a warning. Now what? Clint and Ivy were nowhere to be seen. Bryn panicked.

"Down here," Ivy shouted.

Bryn whipped around to see Ivy and Clint treading air, near the entrance to the library. Should they shift and go inside?

Red guards poured onto the field of battle. Where were they coming from? And that's when Bryn saw it. They were streaming out of the Orange dragon's dorm—a dorm where students no longer lived. Her grandfather must have snuck hundreds of Red dragons onto campus and housed them there, waiting for an attack. And here it was.

Something smacked into Bryn's back, sending her tumbling end over end toward the ground. A Green with Blue scales had blasted her with an icy wind. She righted herself and shot fire at the enemy.

"You chose the wrong side, Bryn." The dragon taunted her as he dodged her flames. "Today the Directorate's reign of oppression ends."

Jaxon roared and dove at the Rebel dragon, aiming for its neck. He bit down and tore at the hybrid's flesh, just like the guard had done. Another hybrid darted in, aiming for Jaxon. Bryn dove to intercept the enemy, but she was too late. Rhianna flew between the hybrid and Jaxon, blasting ice at the attacker.

Going too fast to slow down, the attacker twisted and came in talons first, digging into Rhianna's flank and slashing her side open. Blood gushed from Rhianna's wounds as she roared in pain and fell toward the ground. Time seemed to slow down as something that looked like red rope bulged from the wound and slid out, hitting the ground before the rest of her body followed with a sickening thump. Dead. Rhianna was dead. Sweet, innocent Rhianna was dead. And for that, someone would pay.

Bryn dove at the attacker, talons extended and blasting fire. She managed to grab a portion of his wing and ripped through it, shredding the membrane. He roared in pain and struggled to stay aloft as she bit down on the joint that attached his wing to his body. Jaxon slammed into his back, driving him to the ground. Bryn stared in fascinated horror at the piece of wing she still held.

Jaxon's roar of anger drowned out the hybrid's cries of pain as Jaxon eviscerated him. Bryn flew to Rhianna, hoping maybe she'd been wrong, but Rhianna lay still and unbreathing.

Pain blossomed in Bryn's chest, or maybe that was fire waiting to be released. She launched herself into the air and searched for someone to take out her rage on. Reds had overwhelmed most of the Rebels. There seemed to be a take-no-prisoners policy. The guards fought without mercy, leaving bloody limbs and corpses in their wake. How had it come to this?

Students had shifted back to human form and were gathered behind a protective line of Red guards in front of the library. Bryn spotted Clint and Ivy among them. *Should I shift and go join them?* A roar of agony made her spin around. Jaxon crouched next to Rhianna, covering her body with his wings like he could somehow protect her.

Taking care not to startle him, Bryn landed near to him, offering silent support because there was nothing else she could do.

A medic Bryn didn't recognize arrived in human form. "Shift back," she ordered.

Bryn did as she asked.

"Are you injured?" the medic asked.

"Nothing serious." She had a few deep gashes, but nothing life threatening. She placed her hand on Jaxon's flank, which was slick with blood. "Shift back so she can treat you."

"What about Rhianna?" Jaxon retracted his wings.

The medic looked down at Rhianna's body. "I can shift her, but I cannot bring her back."

The air around Jaxon shimmered as he changed to human form. His shirt was shredded and soaked with blood. Bryn couldn't tell crimson cloth from shredded skin. His breathing was labored.

The medic placed her hand on Jaxon's forehead and closed her eyes. The gashes on Jaxon's torso stopped oozing blood.

"You have several broken ribs," the medic said. "This will hurt."

Jaxon looked like he couldn't feel anything anymore. "Do it," he said. He sucked in a breath at one point, and then exhaled in relief. "Thank you."

"Now you." The medic placed her hand on Bryn's forehead. Quintessence flowed through Bryn's body, healing her wounds.

"Both of you should go sign in at the library so your families know you're okay."

Jaxon didn't budge.

"I will restore her so you may say good-bye," the medic said. "But you cannot be with her while I do it."

"I'm staying," Jaxon said.

"Your father will want to know that you're alive," the medic said.

"Your mother will be frantic," Bryn said. "Please come

with me and check in."

Jaxon met her gaze, and what she saw made her heart ache. Haunted. His eyes looked haunted and empty, like part of him was no longer there. She wanted to say she was sorry, but he knew that already, and it wouldn't make a difference. So what was the point? Rhianna would still be dead.

As they approached the library, people around them grew silent. Anyone in their path moved out of their way. Like they were important. Then again, it may have been because they were covered in blood and gore.

Bryn's grandfather waited for them at the sign-in table.

"You fought well," her grandfather said. "Both of you." He placed his hand on Jaxon's shoulder. "I am sorry for your loss."

Jaxon nodded, but he didn't respond.

"What happens now?" Bryn asked.

"We're doing a sweep of the campus to make sure no enemies are left behind. You may stay here or go to the dining hall until the all-clear is given."

Bryn swiped at the front of her blood-spattered shirt. Something skin-like and squishy fell to the ground. "I'd like to change clothes."

"That will have to wait," her grandfather said.

"My father?" Jaxon asked.

"He's waiting for you in the lobby where he is coordinating the guard's efforts."

Jaxon turned to Bryn. "Will you contact the medics and ask them when…when I can say good-bye?"

"Of course."

"Thank you." Jaxon left to go meet with his father.

"Go with your friends to the dining hall," her grandfather said. "I'd like to know exactly where you are."

· · ·

Bryn sat at their usual table, eating her food without tasting it. Because some things never changed, everyone was whispering and pointing at her again.

"What is that about?" Bryn asked.

"Well," Clint said, "you are covered in blood and gore."

"Thanks for pointing that out." She speared a carrot with her fork. "I'm not the only one who fought."

Ivy laughed and then blushed. "Sorry, that was inappropriate nervous laughter because other students may have fought, but you and Jaxon…you guys were badass."

She wanted to snap that watching your friend die in front of you had that effect on a person, but she knew Ivy didn't mean to be insensitive. This whole situation was surreal.

"What are dragon funerals like?" Bryn asked. She'd seen human funerals on television, but had never attended one.

"There will be a memorial for friends and family, and then the people closest to her will be present at her funeral pyre."

It took Bryn a moment to attach a meaning to the last word. "Like a Viking funeral?"

Clint nodded. "But without the water. Dragons don't bury their dead, because we can't take the risk of anyone discovering the bodies."

Bryn finished her food in silence. When the siren sounded again, she tensed, but one of the guards in the dining hall announced it was the all-clear signal.

And suddenly she didn't want to go back to her room by herself. "This will spoil my badass image, but would you guys mind walking me back to my room, just to make sure no one is waiting to get me…since I live alone now."

"Sure. I could stay the night if you want," Ivy said.

"No. That's not necessary. Just a quick check of any place big enough for someone to hide and jump out at me will be okay."

After her friends performed the room check, Bryn made

sure the door and window were locked before climbing in the shower. She washed her hair until the water no longer ran red, which took a disturbing amount of time. Once she was dressed in yoga pants and a T-shirt, she walked into the living room and stared at the phone with dread. How was she supposed to ask the medics about Rhianna without crying? But Jaxon needed her to do this, so she placed the call and spoke the minimum amount to acquire the information she needed. Hopefully, the medic wouldn't think she was rude. Next she called Jaxon. When he answered the phone, his voice sounded hoarse.

"It's Bryn. You can say good-bye this evening after eight."

There was silence on the line and then a quiet, "Thank you," followed by a dial tone.

Once that was done, she was exhausted. What she needed was to turn her brain off for a little bit so she'd stop thinking about everything. Maybe a nap would work.

She lay in her bed, trying to relax, but her mind wouldn't stop spinning. She tried to think through all the changes that had happened and what was yet to come. In the win column, her parents were alive and, hopefully, well. And that seemed to be the only good thing. The Rebels, who all appeared to be psychotic hybrids, were dead. Would the hybrids and Throwbacks at the new settlement be left in peace, or would the Directorate make an example of them? One thing for sure, the arranged marriage law wouldn't be overturned any time soon. Not that she'd ever admit it out loud, but maybe it was necessary. If the Directorate would agree to tell dragons why they were being denied, maybe that would make the situation better. If a couple knew they risked giving birth to a child who would be overly aggressive or sick with greed, maybe that could soften the blow of their contract being denied.

And that thought led her to the fun fact that she was legally obligated to marry Jaxon. A month ago they'd had a plan—he'd continue seeing Rhianna and she'd continue seeing Valmont. But now…what would they become? She considered him an ally and maybe one day he'd become her friend. That was the best she could hope for. No. That was wrong.

She could hope to be a good aunt to Asher and a friend to Lillith. Maybe between the two of them they could prevent Ferrin from passing his toxic personality traits to the baby. Maybe that would be her new goal. What else could she focus on? Garret would continue his work on the prosthetic wing. She could help him. Her parents would need help re-entering dragon society and making peace with her grandparents, and Bryn could help smooth the way for them. Funny, how even though she'd lost control of her life, she'd regained her family.

Her phone rang. It's not like she was sleeping anyway. She threw off the covers and trudged into the living room. "Hello?"

"Bryn," Valmont's voice came through the phone. "I heard about the attack. I needed to make sure you weren't hurt."

"I was," Bryn said, "but the medic healed me."

"Good."

An awkward silence stretched out between them.

"I saw your journal," she admitted.

"You saw what I wrote?"

"I did. And I have a question for you." Did she really *want* to know the answer to this question? She needed to know, but that wasn't the same thing. "Whatever your answer is, it won't change my mind about how we left things, but now that the bond is broken, do you still feel the same way about me?"

Valmont laughed, but there wasn't much humor in it. "The joke is on me, because yes, I do. The bond didn't make me love you. Loving you made the bond stronger."

Bryn's heart clenched. "You'd think I'd get some sort

of satisfaction from that admission, but I don't. Good-bye, Valmont." She hung up the phone and waited to see what life would throw at her next. Whatever it was, she was strong enough to handle it on her own, but grateful that she wouldn't have to. She had friends and family who would look out for her, and Jaxon, although she wasn't sure what category he belonged in. They'd just have to figure that out as they went along.

Acknowledgments

I'd like to thank Erin Molta and Stacy Abrams for their editing expertise. Thank you to Entangled Publishing for believing in my dragons.

About the Author

Chris Cannon is the award-winning author of the Going Down In Flames series and the Boyfriend Chronicles. She lives in Southern Illinois with her husband and several furry beasts.

She believes coffee is the Elixir of Life. Most evenings after work, you can find her sucking down caffeine and writing fire-breathing paranormal adventures or romantic comedies. You can find her online at www.chriscannonauthor.com.

Discover more Entangled Teen books...

GARDEN OF THORNS
a novel by Amber Mitchell

After years of captivity in the Garden—a burlesque troupe of slave girls—Rose finally finds a way to escape. She flees one captor only to find herself in the arms of another, this one as charming as he is dangerous. Rayce has a rebellion to lead, and Rose's connection to the Gardener, a known government accomplice, is just what he needs for leverage. But her pull on his heart has him questioning whether her freedom is worth more than his political gain.

IN TRUTH & ASHES
an *Otherselves* novel by Nicole Luiken

On the True World, Belinda Loring has known from childhood that she must Bond with the son of another noble First Family. So she pushes away her feelings for gorgeous, steadfast Demian, who isn't noble. When the Bonding magic goes disastrously wrong, Belinda becomes a national disgrace. She turns to Demian for help getting revenge on the man who ruined her: the radical Malachi. She's met Malachi before, but she cannot remember him. And Demian may hold the key to recovering all that she's lost…

The Lying Planet
a novel by Carol Riggs

Jay Lawton has been aiming for the colony of Promise City his entire life on the planet Liberty. All that stands in his way is The Machine, a mysterious device that will scan his brain and Test his deeds. But when, in one sleepless night, everything he thought he knew about the adults in his colony changes, it'll be up to Jay and the beautiful rebel, Peyton, to save the others before the ceremonies are over and the hunting begins.

Conspiracy Boy
an *Angel Academy* novel by Cecily White

Life is hell. Demons attacking. Cheerleaders screaming. Vampires and werewolves asking where the bathroom is. Just another day here at St. Michael's Guardian Training Academy. If I can survive Luc's deadly Sovereign Trials and keep my evil twin sister from starting a war, Jack and I might actually have a chance of saving the world. If not, at least I won't have to worry about what to wear to prom.

Discover the **Going Down in Flames** *series…*

GOING DOWN IN FLAMES

BRIDGES BURNED

TRIAL BY FIRE

Also by Chris Cannon

BLACKMAIL BOYFRIEND

THE BOYFRIEND BET